Miss Gazillion$

By Richard Weber
(writing as R. H. Weber)

Homeland: A Novel

Miss Gazillion$

Richard Weber

Thomas Dunne Books
St. Martin's Minotaur ♏ New York

THOMAS DUNNE BOOKS.
An imprint of St. Martin's Press.

www.minotaurbooks.com

Book design by Irene Vallye

ISBN 0-312-33140-1
EAN 978-0312-33140-5

First Edition: March 2005

10   9   8   7   6   5   4   3   2   1

To Elizabeth, Julia, and Emma

And to the memory of Irene Katherine Weber,
a.k.a. Mom

To get rich is glorious.

—Deng Xiaoping

Miss Gazillion$

Ten Years Ago

$ $ $

I

That last morning, I was piloting my motor yacht, the *Madonna Maris*, from St. John to Virgin Gorda, when a stiff northerly started kicking up, the opening blow of the Caribbean's Christmas winds.

The weather change roughed up my charter cruise that day; between some snorkeling and diving around a couple of reefs and a wreck, I was still hustling to keep the clients entertained for their money. When the winds got too strong for swimming, I stopped to give them a stroll on shore, leading them along sandy paths through Virgin Gorda's volcanic rocks, a sheltered tourist spot known as The Baths.

By late afternoon, as I was rounding St. John's north point, heading back toward my home port of Cruz Bay, the wind suddenly dropped, the skies cleared, the air warmed. The sea was shimmering in the golden sunset, the island's cliffs glowing a rich red hue.

My idea of heaven.

And I was enjoying this moment of paradise in peace as my passengers stayed aft, sipping the chilled chardonnay I always served at the end of a day's outing.

I could hear them congratulating each other on their exploits, and for the great luck of having found me, and the sixty-foot *Madonna Maris*, through the concierge at the Muscade Bay Hotel. That alert agent of our common good fortune was Lafayette Bramsen, a St. Johnian descendant of Creole slaves and Danish plantation owners: Laffs, to all. Laffs got an under-the-table ten percent, all cash, of whatever business he shilled for me.

After pulling into port, with my customers shunted back to Muscade for dinner and an evening of calypso, I was stowing the gear from the trip and hosing down the deck, when a car—rental, I could tell from the plate—drove onto the dock and pulled up alongside the *Madonna Maris*.

The setting sun shone into the car's windshield, highlighting two large men in the front seat. Both wore sunglasses, Panama hats, tan silk suits. I didn't recognize them, which was unusual, as I knew almost everyone in Cruz Bay. Their suits marked them as mainlanders, maybe Miami was my first guess.

They sat there for a couple of minutes watching me work. Their silent, motionless examination was unnerving. They looked out of place on St. John, a very open and friendly island.

I was about to ask them to move on, so I could unload the day's debris, when they climbed out of the car, stretching and yawning, rubbing their bellies with slow, almost reflexive motions, looking around the port as if they owned the place and didn't much care for the way it was being managed.

They certainly looked determined enough to be able to set it straight.

They sauntered over to dockside and peered down at me. I didn't think it likely they were looking for a charter.

"I seen better," said one, in a fading Latino accent. They both laughed. "Your boat—"

"You're asking?" I said.

"I'm asking." He reached inside his jacket and withdrew a thick envelope. I caught a glimpse of a gun butt in a holster on his hip, but he didn't seem to care if I noticed.

"O'Sullivan?" he said.

I nodded.

"Daniel O'Sullivan, Junior?"

"That's me."

"Got something for you."

Next, they were on the boat.

"Read all right?" The armed messenger handed me the envelope. "Make it fast."

The envelope was indeed addressed to me, from Hague, Gordon, Amsterdam & Ridder, a maritime law firm on Wall Street with offices in Florida.

It contained an order from Federal Court, Southern District New York, declaring my father bankrupt, and an order from the local court in Charlotte Amalie—the main town on our neighbor island of St. Thomas—dispossessing me from the *Madonna Maris*.

Also, a job offer was enclosed.

Both judicial decrees were issued at the request of the New York offices of Star Ace Corporation, headquarters Zug, Switzerland. The job offer—for a position in New York—came from them as well.

"Actually, it's my father's boat. He owns it, not me."

"Not no more."

"Look, I can't do anything now, not until I talk to my father." I held up the eviction order. "He know about this?"

"Doubt it." The tidings bearer eyed me coldly. Then he shrugged. "Died yesterday, up in New York."

A natural death, it developed, but no less a shock for that, even if the old boy had been in poor health for some time. We never got along, my father and I, but now I felt suddenly adrift and alone without him.

Even worse, without his boat to call my own.

This was not the kind of Christmas I'd planned on celebrating.

My evictors watched impassively as I collected my few belongings. They relieved me of the boat's keys and then got back in their car and drove off.

2

I'd just turned forty and had been living in the Caribbean for nearly twenty years.

So losing my boat came as no small shock to the system. I was devastated. My life had never been one of deprivation and, for all those years in the islands, boats made up most of that life, at least the part since getting kicked out of Yale a half-year short of my bachelor's degree in biology. Concentration: ichthyology.

Which is what brought me down to the islands in the first place: a research trip, from which I split to hunt girls rather than rare fish, had myself a field day, and that was that. My classmates all went back to New Haven.

The start of two glorious decades for me. Bum in the sun, by some lights, captaining boat charters: to my eyes, a swell existence and a living of sorts.

More than of sorts.

In my books, a feast, however narrow my subsistence may have been when measured by conventional standards, however self-indulgent, escapist, endlessly adolescent, and utterly lacking in ambition and goals. In spite of these deficiencies, or perhaps because of, this unhurried, unharried life was all I'd ever wanted.

And when I come to think about it now—especially after all that's happened to me since the day I lost the *Madonna Maris*—I'd be willing to bet it's just the kind of life a lot of people in this world would kill for, if they were ever offered the chance.

And so while forty is supposed to be a time in your life when you take stock, survey your emotional history, figure out where things might have gone wrong and how perhaps they can be righted—a time when your past is said to loom as large as your future, and dreams start getting tempered by regrets—in fact, I'd already been living my dream for twenty years.

And my only regret at this point was over losing it.

But the big loss—my beloved boat—had, in point of law, indeed been my father's, and never mine.

Dad would have been seventy-five, had he lived through the winter. But apart from a single trip, years before, down to the islands—*Got a helluva life down here, kid, don't you ever get bored?*—he'd never used the *Madonna Maris*, preferring to remain in New York. Which was fine by the both of us, I suppose.

Dad.

As I said, neither of us had cared much for the other, certainly not over the years since I'd been kicked out of college. Never forgave me that failing; always had his heart set on an Ivy League grad for a son, his only child.

And I was never a grad, anywhere.

As for the boat, my residence and sole source of income, it was just another one of Dad's tax dodges, a write-off for his construction business.

Plus a way to keep me busy, out of sight, and out of trouble.

It may have been ungrateful of me, but I'd always resented what I considered my father's dirty money from a dirty business, construction in New York.

And he'd always regarded me as not much more than a freeloader.

Perhaps we were both right.

In those twenty years, we saw each other just that once, when he came down to lecture me on what a fool I was, approaching forty and wasting my life away in the islands.

And I never went up to New York. Much more than that I can't say about our relationship, because it was never much of a relationship. My mother had died when I was nine.

Mom.

Our relations had been short, but never clouded. In my mind's eye, my mother's face is always smiling, forever sunny, perpetually patient with me and my father.

And while maybe it wasn't always that way, that's how I choose to remember her.

I can still remember her funeral.

My father at the cemetery . . . impatiently checking his watch, eyeing the nearby limousine where his latest awaited him. He introduced her to me—me, a nine-year-old kid—as his newest "secretary," and he had the driver take us to one of his favorite restaurants, Gargiulo's in Coney Island. Where the freshly minted widower buried his sorrow in a few dozen oysters before digging into a two-pound porterhouse. He was a large man, my father.

On the way back, we passed a seaside complex of apartment houses he was developing—with the Williamsburg Savings Bank, I believe—and he marveled for us at the number of kitchens he could pile up—kitchen on top of kitchen on top of kitchen. Dad loved his food all right.

"Oh sure, and bedrooms, too," he added, lest his latest secretary feel left out of his thoughts on this special family day. "Hundreds and hundreds of bedrooms, one on top of the other. . . ."

Apart from his mistresses, Dad's only life had been his construction business. *Daniel O'Sullivan, Contractors.*

He'd named me Dan O'Sullivan, Jr. But I dropped the Junior, his pet name for me, when he shipped me off to prep school, Pomfret, a socially first-class if academically second-tier institution in New England. Dad chose the school because it wasn't Catholic—as were all the schools he'd been subjected to—and it wasn't near him. If by that he wished to keep me from father worship of any kind, he certainly succeeded.

So I trust it doesn't shock anyone when I say that I wasn't entirely distraught to be packing my bags and heading up to New York for my father's farewell affair.

Only the thought of what I was leaving behind truly depressed me.

3

"Listen, Laffs, my whole life's down here, I got nothing else. Zip. *Nada*. . . ."

Bemoaning my sudden reversal of fortune, I was unburdening myself on poor Lafayette Bramsen. We were seated behind closed doors in his office at the Muscade Bay Hotel, that playground for the rich and famous.

My rich and famous clients, formerly.

Laffs brought in a shaker of sundowners for the occasion, and I was working my way through it.

"Who, Dani-*el*? Who got her, mon?"

"Star Ace Corporation . . . whoever the hell they are. Screw 'em, I know who they are. Some sleazy bastards my father did business with, before he—"

"Dan-*ny*, I'm so sorry."

"Not your fault. . . ."

"But you know . . ." Laffs smiled warmly, "'bout me, too, for sure." His dark shiny face wrinkled up and he shook his head. "My best boat. Losin' part of you, that's ten *per*-cent. We both sad."

Laffs was right. It was mainly the *Madonna Maris*, and surely not my father, that we were mourning.

I tapped my glass for another drink, my fourth in less than an hour.

"Hey, you rocking the boat kinda early." Laffs frowned disapprovingly. "You drunk?"

"Moderately. Getting kicked out of paradise, hell do you do?"

"You know, Dan-*ny* . . ." Laffs fiddled distractedly with a swizzle stick. "Maybe I get you a job here . . . maybe the front office . . ." His voice trailed off. He stared at the swizzle stick.

"Thanks," I said, "nice offer."

But I shook my head. If there was one thing both of us knew,

I couldn't hang around St. John any longer, like some beached rotting carcass of a whale. A skipper without a boat was simply too pathetic.

The look of pity on Laffs's face confirmed this, and made me even more uncomfortable.

On top of that, I was busted. Never saved a penny, blew it all away on good times and women. Not girls, women; I was forty, remember. I just eyed the girls, and sighed.

"Well, you think it over, mon."

"Don't have to," I said. "Got another job lined up."

"You fast, Dani-*el*." Laffs raised his eyebrows, questioningly. "Where?"

"Up there. New York."

His faced sagged like a Brooklyn tenement. "Gonna miss you."

"And me you," I said, and I told him about the job proposition presented by the gentlemen from Star Ace Corp. In what seemed like some final murky deal with my father, the details at that point still unclear to me, their company—owned by a Mister F. J. Starace—would provide me with a place to live and a job, of sorts.

And that was it, my old man's last legacy to me. The ticket up to New York cleaned me out of whatever money I could scrape together on my own.

4

Dad's funeral was a simple affair.

Few people attended the mercifully brief, nondenominational service in the chapel at Frank E. Campbell's funeral parlor, Madison Avenue.

The event was just a few blocks from the patriarchal duplex on Fifth, a penthouse overlooking the park—a view Dad took great pride in—and where I'd spent my childhood in the care of au pairs and nannies until Dad got tired of them or they quit because they couldn't run any faster than he could.

As I said, not many showed up at Campbell's for his departure.

But there was a slight flurry of excitement among the onlookers—*mourners* might be a bit of an overstatement—when a woman, a woman of a certain age, to whom I'd yet to be introduced, turned to me and, in a patrician voice straining at this trying moment to sound both kind and generous, said: "The coffin's all yours."

Well.

I was startled as much by what she said as by her demeanor. Straight honey-tinted hair hanging down over one eye, and the other eye, a vital violet, winking at me.

She had the angular face of a model, but a face so faceted that its proud prisms tossed off in that brief moment a flash of worldly intelligence and broad experience, which is to say, of wisdom. Such a face, however eccentric, is not accidental, but earned.

Neither do such eyes—so vital, so violet, so deeply set with alert animal lives all their own—fall into the possession of ordinary women.

Her voice was muted, not merely for the occasion, but naturally, as cello-contralto as a dove's.

"Ssshhh!" someone hissed.

And a clerical-looking gentleman from Campbell's staff emerged to intone a prayer over the coffin, custom-built to accommodate my father's almost spherical shape (all that eating). The box looked almost like a case for a bass fiddle, but handcarved of solid oak.

The prayer itself was inoffensive, I suppose. An all-purpose, generic enough piece for the occasion, although I'm sure Campbell's must have written it themselves as I've never heard it anywhere else, not that I make a habit of going to many funerals. Or to church. But I must say people generally do show off their better sides at these events: considerate and kindly, usually forgiving, and steadfastly upbeat regarding their own prospects for immortality.

During Campbell's house prayer, I began contemplating the woman's cryptic remark.

"The coffin's all yours."

The very first words I ever heard from my father's last mistress.

And then that wink.

Actually, I recognized Lydia Sands from some photographs Dad sent me: Handsome, aging couple dining in Manhattan club. Champagne toasts at the track. Begowned and black-tied theatergoers at a premiere.

I guess Lydia must have been about ten years Dad's junior, which would have put her somewhere within sniffing distance of sixty-five then.

But you'd never have known it.

She was still a knockout in her class, looking closer to a trophy fifty. Sort of a female Warren Beatty, I suppose.

She was still as fashionably thin and smartly dressed as any teenage model in *Vogue*. Which pages, it developed, she'd graced in her own salad days. Seeing her at the funeral, I could comprehend my father's attraction to the woman—and understand the profound changes she'd wrought in his existence.

For Lydia's presence in my father's life was unique, in a manner of speaking.

The service at Campbell's jarred my memory. With all that hanging around you have to do at such events, images from the past just came flooding back.

Like my father at my mother's funeral . . . *and this is Anna Marie, my latest secretary.* . . .

He rarely had fewer than a half-dozen Anna Maries whom he was seeing regularly, which for him meant at least once a week. And he liked to turn over the entire cast of players every few months. A very busy man, my father.

But in the autumn of his days, after he met Lydia Sands, Dad's furious racing from bed to bed slowed to a more monogamous trot. That's the unique part I was mentioning.

My father's funeral was over almost before it began. The flowers (weren't many) were gathered up at Lydia's command: "Send them to the apartment."

Suddenly, the coffin looked lonely out there on a bare stage.

The funeral's few attendees shuffled about. Unsure of what to do next, some just slipped out the rear exit.

A woman wandered in looking very upset and sank to her knees to start praying, but then stopped, looked around, and suddenly realized she'd wandered into the chapel too early, and was almost caught up in the wrong cremation.

Or was it a full-bodied burial?

I hadn't a clue. Would doors now open somewhere nearby and that grand box simply roll off the stage and out into the flames?

Or were we all expected to pile into waiting limos for the ride to a cemetery?

The coffin's all yours.

As my father's only offspring, maybe I, at this point, was supposed to make a decision. I shuddered at the thought. I hadn't considered this: I weighed the possibility that Lydia as his, well, his closest would take care of all the necessary arrangements.

"Thank you," she was saying, to several deserting onlookers. "Thank you all so much, he'd have been very pleased. Now do go and have a good lunch, that would please him even more."

Then, to me: "And you?" Her violet eyes were assessing. "You *are* Dan, aren't you?"

"Right." I felt foolish, at a loss for words appropriate to a woman of her particular anomaly. "And you're . . . Lydia?"

"Indeed." She smiled warmly. "He spoke of you, Dan—not constantly, but often enough I suppose . . . especially toward the end."

"Yes, I suppose it was time . . . for the end."

"*Time?*" Lydia glared.

Time, you understand, was clearly a touchy topic. True, Lydia Sands was still an extremely attractive woman, but she was inching her way up there.

"Your father had *tons* of time left, if they hadn't . . . Well, never mind. That," she said regally, in the direction of the coffin being wheeled offstage, "that can be delivered later. Let's go." Lydia gave a queenly toss of her head, careful not to lose its invisible crown. "I need some fresh air."

Delivered later . . .

My conclusion: Dad's mistress was bonkers. Out of her mind with grief.

5

Walking up Madison Avenue with Lydia Sands that cold December day, arctic blasts whipping round us, I was growing homesick for Caribbean sun and sea.

I was also beginning to realize why Dad had never introduced me to Lydia, but left her back in New York for that one trip he made to the islands to see his boat and lecture his son.

Which was understandable, for there was nothing at all ordinary about Lydia Sands.

Lydia was a bombshell, so I would learn, a live wire, as unpredictable as she was uncontrollable: Lydia on the loose—anywhere—was not to be imagined. But I'm getting ahead of myself.

Lydia could talk: Like many great old beauties, Lydia was sufficiently self-centered to enjoy herself immensely as the conversational subject of choice.

"Hear you know all about fish," she shouted, battling the Manhattan gales. The reference was to my long-ago foreshortened studies at Yale. "I hate fish. Got sick as hell once, eating fish in Greece, nearly expired right there on Hydra."

"Sorry to hear that," I shouted back.

"What do you see in them? No personality, fish. So I'll never understand why your father insisted . . . but don't *let* me get started. We'll get to that later. I'm hungry."

"Me, too."

"And absolutely parched. Champagne'd be perfect. Take you to the apartment, but cupboard's bare. How 'bout this place, looks nice?"

This place was a saloon. The proprietor was a spry, balding little man who, as we entered, was busily arranging fresh-cut flowers in a Christmas decoration in front of the mirror behind a long mahogany bar. A classy-looking establishment with a solid air, its elderly bartender looked as if he'd been serving the neighborhood since prohibition's repeal, if not before. He'd been serving Lydia Sands, it developed, for several decades.

"Bottle of the widow, Jim, would be most appropriate. Good and cold. And have some yourself. Just give Otto his usual, please." Otto, I could see, was the bartender's long-haired dachshund that slept behind the bar.

Lydia adjusted her honeyed tresses in the mirror, checking her invisible crown, while taking a seat on a red-leather barstool.

"Gosh, Miss Sands," the bartender turned to us, a sad smile creasing his face. "I'm really sorry . . . about Mister O'Sullivan."

Jim Rose, as Lydia called him when introducing me, pulled a draft Guinness and emptied it into a bowl for little Otto, then opened a bottle of a vintage Veuve Clicquot for us. He set up three long-stemmed crystal goblets on the bar.

This was, when I look back on it all now, the first, and maybe most memorable, of the many bottles of champagne my father's last mistress and I were to share, most of them in the company of others, I might add, in classy saloons like Jim Rose's almost all over the world.

Lydia swallowed a long draught. Relieved sigh, then: "Now, Jim, tell us . . . what's for lunch? And watch Otto doesn't burn himself." The dachshund had polished off the stout in a half-dozen slurps, and collapsed next to a radiator.

Jim Rose put on his reading glasses, a small piece of paper at arm's length. "Smoked salmon, a nice salad, sourdough baguette . . . or some pumpernickel, whichever."

"Fish?" Lydia, lip upturned, ever so slightly. "I'll take a triple order of that nice salad. Please hold the bread . . . and give him my fish. Dan loves fish. You do *eat* them, don't you? I mean, you don't just dissect them or whatever."

"Salmon's fine."

"Don't know what your father ever saw in fish. Tell me: what went on down there with you two? Came home sunburned all over his back, belly white as a dead mackerel's, and simply raving about fish."

"Went snorkeling," I explained. "Around reefs, shipwrecks. Dad floated on his stomach for hours in the sun."

"Well, he never recovered. Thrill simply too much, I suppose. Now wants to spend an eternity with those fishy friends of yours.

Close your mouth, it's unbecoming, you'll begin to look like one."

Lydia popped her eyes, sucked her cheeks in and out, and released a couple of gasping gurgles in fair imitation of a fish. We both laughed, and I began to warm to her, in spite of myself. I suppose I started right then to understand how this formidable woman could bewitch even my father into monogamy.

"I'll explain everything," she continued. "But drink up first. Good for the figure, champagne. Jockeys' favorite tipple, won't put an ounce on you. Learned that when I was nineteen, modeling for *Vogue*. Been drinking it ever since."

I wasn't sure about the modeling part, not yet anyway, but Lydia was as good as her word, explaining all about Dad over lunch.

"Your father developed a fascination," she said. "Got quite taken with underwater scenery, during his brief stay with you down there. So taken, in fact, that, to his last will and testament, he added a codicil requiring that his earthly remains be transported to those tropical isles, back to where he'd spent such a great time with his son.

"And so he insisted, Dan, that you . . ." Lydia paused, dabbing a drop of vinaigrette from her chin. ". . . absolutely insisted you be the one to pick the right spot. Do the honors. He said only you knew where the best wrecks were. Almost his very last words, I'm afraid."

I choked: "You're joking—"

"Death, Dan, is no joking matter."

Know how they say unexpected scares cure hiccups? Well, a scare can just as easily cause them, particularly if you're caught entirely unawares, mid-sip in champagne.

"*Hic*—" Me, straining for coherent objection.

"No back talk, I won't hear of it." She checked the mirror again, to adjust her hair and invisible crown. "And neither would your father," she added, as if lecturing her own reflection. "Can't deny him his dying wish, not that little bit. Not after all he did for you."

"—*huc?*"

"Settled then." She smiled. "Now, there's still a little problem we have to solve first. I've got just enough of the ready to pay off Campbell's, you see. And cover delivery to a location inside city limits. But I can't afford to ship it—him—and us, down to the islands. Not yet, anyway, not until I get back on my feet, cashwise. And I gather you're flat broke. So we've got a problem—"

"But—what—about—cremation?" Me, quickly, in a race with the hiccups, hoping to shrink my filial burden.

Lydia shook her head. "Out of the question, your father'd never hear of it. And I don't know why you're carrying on so, none of this should come as a shock to you. He *was* Catholic after all."

That cured me. "Catholic?" I was getting quite upset with my father: Dad sure had his nerve, even after death. "Maybe in name. But even Catholics can get cremated now, I think."

"Might be right, Dan. I wouldn't know about those things, no more fish on Friday and so on. By the way, that could be the source of your fish fetish."

Lydia enjoyed lecturing and, clearly, she felt I had much to learn, particularly on the topic of my own father.

"Nevertheless, your father took his faith quite . . . well, he took it quite seriously, in his own way. For example, he refused to go to church anymore, because they don't speak Latin. Can you imagine? Even forbade a funeral mass. Hence, Campbell's."

I could imagine all right. I could just hear Dad trying to pass off a cockamamie excuse like that.

"So you see," she continued, "he was really very staunch. In his own way, of course."

"Of course. In his own way. But now what? I mean, you don't have the money—and you're right, Lydia, I'm flat broke—so we got a problem, just like you say. I don't have the money to go anywhere. What are we going to do?"

Lydia proceeded to explain that Dad's plush Fifth Avenue property was protected from creditors' demands on his bankrupt death estate—I'm not a lawyer, thank God, so I had to take her word for this much—and, as his sole residence, the apartment was spared the clutches of the IRS, who otherwise got everything they could trace. The apartment, according to the terms of Dad's will, would now belong to Lydia.

My eyes widened at the news.

"Stop," said Lydia. "I know exactly what you're thinking. But no, our apartment is, well, let's say *my* apartment's ownership is currently under discussion. But don't *let* me get started, since it's quite a heated discussion, actually. Fighting for my rights against a few of his more persistent creditors, some of whom are very shady characters indeed—"

"You're telling me. Met a couple of them, they took my boat." That other major asset, not mentioned in the will, one that failed to catch the government's attention, but not Mr. Starace's. My father's body had barely journeyed its last few blocks to Mr. Campbell's establishment before those thugs turned up at the dock in Cruz Bay to claim the *Madonna Maris*.

"Ah yes, heard about them. The gentlemen from Star Ace Corporation, I believe it's called. But Mr. Starace himself personally promised your father you'd be taken care of. And believe me, Mr. Starace is very much a man of his word."

Lydia was terribly well informed regarding my new circumstances.

"So as I understand it," she continued, "you are going to *live* somewhere. And I mean, really, for the time being at least, until I get the money, it—I'm sorry, *he*—can always stay at your new place of course. The one that goes with your new job."

That floored me.

"Look, Lydia . . ." I began somewhat hesitantly, fearing a hiccup relapse. "Of course I have no objection at all, and so on, I mean I am his son after all, I do understand that much, I accept it, but haven't you thought about . . . about his . . . well, you know, his body, won't it start to—*huc?*"

"Of course not!" Lydia was adamant, her tones chilly as Alpine peaks. "He certainly will not. Not your father. Impossible. Campbell's assured me he got their *crème de la crème* treatment, or whatever you call it. Premium stuff with a lifetime guarantee. Top dollar! Won't even notice it's—he's there. Not a whiff."

My guts groaned.

"You *are* a good son, Dan. I'm so glad you understand. Your father would be enormously proud of you. And he really won't have to stay with you very long. Not to worry, we'll get him down there soon enough, where he wanted to go. You can count on it."

And with that reassurance, Lydia whisked off to the ladies', leaving me to catch my breath. A few quick words and she'd won, stuck me with Dad's coffin.

I'd been soundly licked.

No, never before had I met anyone quite like Lydia Sands.

And what I was to learn next about her really left me gasping for air.

6

Lydia herself, of course, didn't tell me a word about this part. The saloonkeeper did.

Lydia was still in the ladies' room when Jim Rose sidled down to my end of the bar.

"Known Miss Sands nearly fifty years now," he confided, in half-whispers. "Almost like a daughter to me. But a difficult lady, I'll grant you that."

"No kidding."

"Had a helluva life, what does it. Used to be a model, see, when she was still a kid. That'll screw up anyone, what I always say, flaunting around like that, makes you a little cuckoo. Know she was in Vietnam?"

I didn't. I confessed to knowing very little about Lydia Sands.

"Yeah," said Jim Rose. "During the war, she was a nurse there. Red Cross, I think it was. Decorated even. Doesn't talk about it much. And certainly not about *before* . . ."

He leaned across the bar, to assume an even more confidential tone.

". . . not about her affair with John Kennedy, back when he was a senator—I'm talking here, since you're family and all, so I kid you not. Reason she signed up with the Red Cross? Or the Army or whatever the hell it was, for going over there was . . . she flipped out after he was shot."

"Flipped out?"

"Yeah, and he used to sit," said Jim Rose, "right where you're sitting now, son, back before he was president, whenever they weren't together in that rear booth over there. But after Vietnam, never guess where she was living—"

"Europe," I said.

"She told you?"

"No, I guessed. She has a certain style."

"Yeah. She was living with *princes* even, what I hear, Dutch and English and only God knows what else."

"Princes?"

"Exactly. But she got fed up with their hoity-toity, she's no dope. Left the royal riffraff and came home. Decades ago, all that. And then she's nursing your father here these last years. Lemme tell you, boy, it was tough, but she had the stuff all right."

"Guess so."

"So don't go getting Miss Sands wrong, lad, she's got heart. Guts, too. Got to admit, your dad was no piece of cake."

I could indeed admit it, and nodded in agreement.

So far, it seemed to add up, what Jim Rose said. I could see how living with princes in Europe, and all that hoity-toity, might explain the queenly airs and an invisible crown.

"Miss Sands got her strange ways," Jim Rose concluded, "that's for sure. But chips are down? You can count on her, son."

And I would. Although at this point, I had no idea just how much. My mind was now stuck on my new filial obligation.

7

"Don't suppose your father ever told you much about me. He was never terribly talkative."

"No disagreement from me there."

"So maybe we really ought to be getting to know each other better." She put her hand on my arm. "Don't you think?"

"Sure."

"After all, we *are* almost family. I often regret never having children of my own, but it hasn't always been easy, you see."

She paused, violet eyes misting slightly.

"You've come so far, Dan, I really should tell you about myself. After all my years with your father, but never meeting you. You've been *so* understanding. And we are growing closer now, aren't we?"

I nodded.

"You don't mind, do you?"

"Of course not."

"I promise I'll be brief."

As it developed, Lydia wasn't all that brief.

"Where shall I start . . . My parents, why not? I was born in Warsaw," she said, satisfied with my surprise. "Father, Polish: Sandowski. Mother, Austrian: Linzl."

A European background, which went some way toward further explaining her champagne tastes and regal airs. That, and the fact her parents had fled to England with young Lydia, just before the Germans invaded Poland.

"Father enlisted in the R.A.F. And right at the start was shot down by the Nazis over Hamburg. Left Mother and me to fend for ourselves. In beleaguered Britain. *Bleak* beleaguered Britain."

"So you grew up there."

"Fortunately, no."

"Where'd you go?"

"Here. Right after the war, Mother and I got on one of the first ships to America and settled in Westchester. Mother worked as a maid for wealthy families. Never enough money in the house, so right after high school I got a job at a Wall Street brokerage, as a secretary."

"I see."

"And along the way, I guess I acquired some expensive tastes. Living in Westchester, seeing all those rich homes Mother worked in . . ."

"Understandable."

"Well, to make a long story really long, a senior partner at the firm, where I got that first job, spotted my special potential, if you will. Right off the bat. Set me up. An apartment. Colony Club membership. Tiffany's house account. Saks charge. Launched me on life's journey, all right."

"Quite a life."

"Mind you, I'm not bragging, nothing to brag about, actually, but I'm afraid I had few talents for real work. I did model for a couple of years, once made the cover of *Vogue*. And there were no other prospects for leading the kind of life I wanted while taking care of Mother's bills all that time."

"Must have been tough, making ends meet."

"Ends meet?"

"To cover expenses."

"Ah, yes. Expenses often exceeded revenue. So I fell into associated vices of the rich, to supplement my friend's support . . . gin, bridge, backgammon, a little dealing in art and antique jewelry. In my thirties—Mother of course was gone by this point—I decided to do something more meaningful with my life and went to nursing school."

"Really."

"Don't look so incredulous."

"I mean, good for you."

"Actually worked at it. In Asia. Where I also became quite expert in local art and jewelry. Opportunities were rife then. Some friendly U.S. colonels and generals flew out quite a little trove I put together. I was able to live decently enough, dealing off my collection. Still, of course, with supplementary support, I must admit. But I managed to get by for some years, doing that sort of thing . . . until I met your father."

"Where was that?"

"At a dinner dance, at the Colony. Came with old friends, and it was instant attraction all around. So we swapped, and your father and I left together. No looking back after that."

"I see." Boy, did I ever.

"My life may sound like it had a touch of glamour—and I suppose it did at times—but it was too often a hand-to-mouth existence. Until your father came along. As you know, he always had such a generous heart."

"Didn't he, just?" Good old generous Dad, R.I.P.

"Before him, I could never get far enough ahead of the game. And stop worrying about what's just around the corner. How to pay the Hamptons rent. Bills from Saks. Colony dues. Not to mention the Maidstone."

"Adds up."

"Exactly. And I'm no trust fund queen, no J. P. Morgan's daughter. Constantly, I saw golden opportunities all over the place. Could have given me retirement money. Set me up for life. But I could never put together enough capital to be a real player. Know what I mean?"

"I think so."

"What I mean is finally make that big score. Your father, God bless him, changed all that. . . ."

The rest of the afternoon remains a champagne bubbly blur. Lydia herself never actually mentioned Vietnam—Jim Rose was right about her reticence on that point—and she certainly didn't bring up JFK, I'd surely have remembered that if she had. The even livelier chapters in Lydia's life story had to wait until later in our relationship.

But right up front I must say that, however dizzying our first day together may have been, it still couldn't prepare me fully for what lay ahead.

Forget what she'd already done—if merely half of what Lydia would yet do, her memoirs, had she ever written them, would have stocked the supermarket bestseller racks for years. But, as far as I know, this is the only record the world will ever have of Lydia Sands.

Prior to meeting Lydia, my life as a Caribbean charter captain had taught me to remain unsurprised by the antics of the outrageously demanding rich. I'd always made it a point never to look for explanations, but to accept my clients—and their money—without question.

Not exactly the most enriching nourishment for one's inner life, I'll concede that much. But if all this makes me appear a rather shallow individual, please note it didn't thrill me either. Just keep in mind my life's conditioning up to that point: Pomfret prep. Great Blue Mother Yale. Deke brother, tapped for Fly. Those tables down at Mory's. My father. Twenty years of the Caribbean good life.

So. Honestly now: What else could anyone expect from me?

My father's last mistress, on the other hand, had been conditioned by nothing remotely that . . . semi-conventional, shall we say?

Although Lydia Sands looked life square in the eye, she was far from simply accepting all life proffered. Certainly she wouldn't, as I would learn, if life didn't at the same time promise to deliver the goods according to her precise specifications.

I recall that when we parted that day, she kissed me goodbye on both cheeks, promised to pay for our imminent trip with Dad down to the islands, to stay in close touch, remain forever good friends, if not exactly family, et cetera, and so forth.

But it would be some time before I'd talk with Lydia Sands again.

Before our paths would cross once more so unexpectedly.

And so fatefully.

8

A few days later, I was on the job.

Brand new "property supervisor," for Star Ace Corp.

This landed me on Carroll Street, Park Slope, Brooklyn, N.Y. 11215, ensconced in a comfortable groundfloor garden apartment, my primary fringe benefit as overseer of three buildings collectively known as Carroll Estates. The rent was a freebie and the pay seven hundred dollars a week, cash.

All in gratitude for whatever favors my father had once rendered the mysterious Mr. Starace.

I hated it.

Here's why. First, the surroundings I was so keen to flee. Somewhere in this world there may exist a more pleasant neighborhood than Park Slope, but I haven't found it yet.

So a moment's description is called for. The Slope encompasses some fifty-odd square blocks of fashionable nineteenth-century residences—usually brownstone, some limestone—with prewar apartment buildings crowning most corners. Gentrified urban prime. A tree-lined, peaceful preserve along the west side of Prospect Park (greener, grander than Central), peopled with the sort who achieve the sparkling stats of Yale alumni bulletins, people who live the ideal lives that I'd hoped to continue evading forever. The escaped fate: both spouses professionals, married 9.3 years, two children, one au pair, 7.4 plays per annum, Brooklyn Academy of Music subscribers, *Times* readers (daily, Sunday), *New Yorker* (weekly), *Post* never.

That kind.

We could dial HOT-FOOD, and get a sort of Meals on Wheels for yuppies. Dial YUP-PIES, for the freshest sushi this side of Tokyo. CHI-NESE would bring Szechuan and Cantonese to the door.

I should have been, what, pleased?

The chance to get back on my feet. Redeem myself.

But I saw only boredom ahead. A lifetime collecting rents, playing custodian, indentured to eternal mildew. *Is this what Dad thought of me?*

Obviously.

On top of this, my cozy sinecure came with a wrinkle all its own. First day on the job, and another Star Ace employee dropped by the apartment.

"Got a package to leave off," he said. "Keep an eye on it, but don't touch, hear?"

I heard. And watched him place, in the refrigerator, a package neatly wrapped—and sealed—in a plastic bag from Fazzulo's Pork Store, Court Street.

Next day, another Star Ace staffer—"I'm Tony Dee, I do pickup."—retrieved the parcel. Every two days, same procedure.

Deliverymen would differ, but pickup was always Tony Dee.

No sooner was I informed of this arrangement, the day I moved in with my one suitcase, than I began working on a flight plan.

As sterling examples, my neighbors might have been a source of great inspiration to me, spurring me on to ever more strenuous efforts to raise myself, to move up out of there, but—with one special exception—I had no great desire to have contact with the tenants beyond what the job required.

That one exception: the neighbor one story above me, second apartment, rear.

She—it was a she of course, by name Celeste Tranor, I was quick to learn—came home most days around noon. By limo or towncar or, occasionally, by taxi, after being out most nights, all night.

But that wasn't the first thing I noticed about my neighbor that made her, to my eyes, so special.

My first day on the job, the first thing I noticed—I was at my ground-floor window, admiring the view—was her round little bottom, wrapped in a black cashmere number that was tight and short and chic, sashaying up the stoop.

That and her legs—long, slim, to expire for—were the first items to catch my attention.

I slipped out my door, just enough into the areaway to see her without being caught sight of.

It had been cold all morning, yet she was dressed without regard to hour or weather.

The dress had a sort of black furry jacket, but the wrap was more of an indoor accessory than midwinter apparel.

No hat, of course. Her long hair was—I observed, as she stopped to search her purse for keys—so carefully cut, it fell perfectly into place after each breeze. Tresses shaded multiple—henna and black— set off by a few stark streaks of no color at all.

Her nose was bobbed, naturally, it appeared.

Her mouth large.

Sunglasses obscured her eyes, although the sky that day was a lightless, wintry lead. Her skin was tan, maybe lamp-tanned, perhaps even a touch of Asian there. In all, her face was past childhood, but still the other side of womanly.

I say "other," because, from my perspective, still the far side: roughly half my age, my disappointed guess.

(Twenty-two, I would conclude, upon prompt investigation of her tenant file.)

Disappointment, however, did not keep me from improving my knowledge of this particular neighbor's comings and goings. For after that first sighting, my interest—with little else to dwell on, as a Star Ace property supervisor—stayed piqued. Riveted, around noon each day, at my front ground-floor window.

I spied on Ms. Tranor.

On making my duty rounds, perusing the bags she set out for garbage collection, I noted Dean & DeLuca take-out containers. Empty wine bottles, always fancy, once even an Yquem. *People. Vanity Fair.* But no newspapers. Junkmail, mainly from Bergdorf's and Prada. Plus occasional postcards, which—except for discernible postmarks (New Orleans, Galveston)—were torn too small to read.

It was winter, remember, and I was suffering severe withdrawal symptoms from my Caribbean sun addiction. Depression threatened, and my special neighbor promised at least a distraction, if not a total cure.

For I could see no immediate prospect of falling into a better line of employment, one that would let me squirrel away a downpayment on another boat and a one-way ticket back to sunshine—for Dad and me—and then maybe a trip to Europe.

Lydia, of course, never called. And the box? Well, I'll get to the box in a moment.

9

The long-haul view—of saving enough on my princely salary for the permanent powder I began plotting as soon as I started the job—was looking to me increasingly like a life sentence in penal servitude.

My managerial duties included, one evening a week, bookkeeping for Star Ace Corporation.

I set up a computer on the makeshift dinner table-cum-desk that I kept carefully covered with a length of sun-bleached sailcloth, lest this, the living room's largest and most unusual piece of furniture, distress any visiting tenant, who might then feel impelled to inform my employer, and cause me to lose my position before I'd found a more secure way out of my predicament.

The oddity of a wide-bodied coffin, perched on two low saw-horses, as my living room's centerpiece was sure to raise eyebrows, even in Brooklyn.

But there he remained, the filial duty.

Dad.

Bizarre. Over the top, by anyone's standards. But big as life.

My father's coffin.

Big enough for the closed top to hold piles of my magazines, books, the computer, and still leave room for two people to have dinner, although as a newcomer to the neighborhood I was still dining alone, if you didn't count my father. I, for one, did not. We had so little to talk about.

The promised funds—to get us back to the Caribbean, for that last-testamented burial at sea—remained unextended.

It would, in fact, be quite some time before I was in contact with Lydia again, apart from a hotel postcard—an Italian establishment, unknown to me, an inn named after an English poet—mailed from Antibes, promising:

Will write at length. On French R&R. NY apt gone. Have
NOT forgotten you 2! Love you both. A bientôt.

Prohibitive fares to the islands made it impossible for me to fly right down on my own with Dad, before I had enough of my—"hard-earned" might be stretching it a bit—savings, to indulge this last mad whim of his.

Lydia had, nonetheless, been right.

I quickly got used to the box, and I never—just as she'd promised—sensed "even a whiff" of Dad's substantial presence. While Campbell's house prayers may have left something to be desired in the spiritual department, the firm had given Lydia her money's worth on the olfactory guarantee. Not that this made the presence any more appealing.

Like I said, I wanted out.

I became a restless insomniac, generally wide awake when one of Star Ace Corp.'s well-heeled tenants forgot a key in the middle of the night, flushed the paperback she was reading down the toilet and clogged the pipe, or dropped by to pay the next month's rent just seconds before the midnight deadline.

I certainly didn't relish the job for its social advantages. Daytime hours passed without so much as a tinkle of the doorbell. My neighbors were all out working for a living.

Except for one.

But relations with that special upstairs resident made no progress, for she was a model tenant: her rent in cash, in a taped envelope, in my mailbox day before due. She never, much to my regret, rang my bell, a helpless casualty of forgotten keys or clogged pipes. She kept herself to herself, at least as far as I was concerned, only adding to my disappointment. A beautiful young woman of good taste—no tourniquet-tight toreadors for Ms. Tranor, she didn't need them—a figure of consequence, of independence, of the most intriguing routine.

Maybe the older you get, the harder it is turning thought into action, and the more you just think about it. Anyway, about Ms. Tranor I most certainly thought. A lot.

But I didn't let her keep me from my plans.

With no manager on site to order me around, and my duties so untaxing, I set out from the start to give my escape plans specific shape.

First, after doing my duty for Dad, a grand tour of the Mediterranean basin, which I'd never seen but often read about in the yachting magazines.

Then, maybe a modest boat, running day cruises in the Med for sun-starved tourists from Northern Europe.

Gradually, I'd hustle my way up to bigger craft, refitting and selling for a profit, until that point, when one port grew too familiar, I could afford to pull up anchor and cruise to the next.

Such were the limits of my ambition. But the almost four-hundred a week that I was able to salt away from my Star Ace job was, of course, nowhere near enough to make these dreams come true any time soon.

So, at night I scanned the *New York Times* and pulled numbers: How many dead in a plane crash. First digit or two of a corporate merger. Our president's poll ratings.

I wrote the numbers down on little slips of paper, collecting them in my old boat-captain's hat, plucking out five-times-six numbers, which I recorded on a lottery card that I handed over twice weekly, along with five dollars, to Mr. C. L. Krishnaswami of Uttar Pradesh, who owned a newsstand a block and a half down Carroll Street on the corner of Seventh Avenue, right next to Taj Mahal Travel, where posters of sunny places served to goad me on to ever greater, if not exactly efforts, then dreams.

But hey, as they say, you never know, do you?

So if, or rather as soon as, I hit it big on that lottery, then boom: I was gone. Right back to a big boat, a fifty-footer would do nicely, and I'd live on it the rest of my years.

Starting in the Med.

And so it went, day by excruciating day, for the first couple of weeks of my new existence.

Until the events of a snow-stormy night intervened to sort of speed things up.

10

As was threatening to become too often the case, I was all alone that evening.

But I was comfy. Behind barred windows. Triple-locked door. And, under the stoop, a double-locked iron gate.

Outside, New York City was wrapped in the whiteout of a surprise blizzard. I could hear tree branches, just beyond my windows, cracking under the weight of ice. Otherwise, silence. For hours, nothing passed in the street.

It was dreamlike.

I'd started out the night updating a computer spreadsheet on the rent accounts. The job's bookkeeping side—at first tedious and, like the rest of the job, beneath the dignity of an old half-Yalie, one-time commander of a seagoing vessel—grew almost soothing. Indeed, I welcomed it, especially on a bleak night like this.

After e-mailing my report to Star Ace headquarters in Zug, Switzerland, I scanned the *Times'* pages.

I could just feel the pitch and roll of that fifty-foot dreamboat beneath my feet. Hear the steady hum of its twin inboard engines. Taste the first sip of champagne, washing salt from my lips after a long day at sea. Even smell the fish I'd caught that morning, now sizzling on the grill.

And then my eye caught sight of an ad for "Tropical Cruise Wear."

I thought of the *Madonna Maris* and Laffs and red sunsets on the straits. I thought of cocktails on deck and sea-scented nights below with a guest from Muscade, or a Navy nurse on leave, or maybe a woman I'd met the season before who'd fallen for the islands and was back again for yet another fling.

Such memories arouse appetites, and soon I was nosing around in the refrigerator for something to drink, something to throw in a sandwich—there being no take-out place open in the neighborhood at that hour, even if I were inclined to slog through snowdrifts Yukon deep.

A Star Ace delivery had arrived that morning, and a package labelled "Fazzulo's Pork Store" sat there in my refrigerator, all alone on its very own shelf, waiting for Tony Dee to show up. Inside the bag, perhaps a wedge of well-aged provolone, some Parma prosciutto, a loaf of Stromboli bread?

Not likely.

My kitchen ended in sliding glass doors that led out into the backyard, a place I never used. Out there now, under the one lamp I kept on all night (burglars hate light), a thick quilt of snow covered the flagstones, the small rectangles of grass, the scrappy flowerbeds, the gaunt ailanthus sagging under icicles.

From the refrigerator, I retrieved a bottle of Sam Adams, some pepper mackerel, couple of slices of rye, jar of grain mustard. I closed the refrigerator and, at the very next moment . . .

. . . almost like an echo from the other end of the apartment . . .

. . . a car door slammed just outside the building. Not a sound I'd normally notice. But on a night like this, and about 2 A.M. by that point, after hours of whiteout silence, it was like a muffled gunshot right in front of my ground-floor windows.

Such was the moment—and the sound—that I just knew I'd always remember this. But with how much regret or pleasure, I as yet hadn't an inkling.

I peered through a barred front window, out into that snow-bound night, and saw a cab crawl away. Back to Manhattan no doubt, its driver surely of two minds about having had a fare all the way to Brooklyn in a snowstorm.

Under the glare of the streetlamp, a figure, loaded with a pair of canvas travel bags, struggled to the curb, then made its way over knee-high drifts to the foot of the stoop.

She—it was a woman; I could now discern that much through those snowball-sized flakes—paused to catch her breath and look upward. She appeared about to attempt a treacherous ascent of the snow-covered stoop, but then she turned and slogged into the areaway to ring my bell.

"Who is it?" I shouted.

I mean you never know, do you, in New York . . . middle of the night . . . snowstorm . . . each of those bags big enough to hold a machine-gun.

"It's to be!" I swore I heard her cry.

Great—cryptic, possibly heavily armed, probably nuts.

Me: "Who?" I opened the door a crack, inspecting her through the grille of the iron gate.

". . . upstairs," she gasped. "Two B."

The tenant from 2B, rear apartment, second floor, backyard view.

"I'm sorry," she said. "I've lost my key."

I fumbled with the locks and let her and her bags tumble into the apartment. She was sopping wet, almost half-frozen.

Impatient, she pushed her way past me, dragging the bags across the floor. She flopped into a chair at the table, head drooping like a dying swan onto my father's canvas-covered coffin.

"Oh jeeez," she sighed. "I'm so whacked . . ."

Celeste Tranor. Hadn't seen her for a couple of days. Odd to find her now—at long last—actually sitting in my apartment so, of course, I stared at her, shamelessly.

Apart from her strained breathing, silence returned. And at these close quarters, I had a chance to examine my guest intently. She was, most uncharacteristically, a wreck.

Her clothes, tatters. Her face and hands, bruised and bloodied. She looked as if she hadn't merely slogged that short distance over the snowy peaks outside our building, but crawled miles through arctic wastes, before she'd found a cabbie unwary enough to bring her all the way back to Brooklyn.

Entirely my fault—or to her credit—I now became a captive of curiosity, a slave to temptation.

I mean, what could be more—disarming, beguiling, or potent than a dazzling divinity, for whom you have to feel sorry?

A beautiful victim. For whom I would eventually lie, steal, and commit offenses that could have, probably still could, put me in the slams for years.

11

"Guess you're wondering . . ." said my late night visitor, easing back in the chair.

She attempted to smooth that glossy streaked hair into place, but to no avail. Glamorously coifed on every previous occasion that I'd glimpsed her, she now wore her hair hanging stiffly, sticking to her face and neck, twisted and matted with blood and grime. In a word, a mess.

Not a trace could I detect of the aura of urbane chic that Ms. Tranor wore so lightly on her dashes in and out of the building. In her current state, our most glamorous tenant resembled nothing so much as a battered woman-child, a runaway waif, perhaps even a victim of city predators.

I also noticed that her fingernails were gnawed to the nub; that was no accident.

"Want to wash up? I've got some antiseptic. Maybe a little ice on that bump?"

Her jaw was as swollen as a pug prizefighter's. Her hazel eyes—green-flecked, I noted at these close quarters—focused properly, so she didn't seem to have suffered a concussion from whatever hit her. I felt a sudden paternal urge to nurse this child's wounds and give her a square meal.

But I had no wish yet to learn how disaster struck.

I was unprepared for heroics of my own. I heard a distant siren outside in the snowbound streets, but dismissed the thought of calling 911 for help. Star Ace Corp. might not take too kindly to New York's finest nosing around Carroll Estates. Neither might Ms. Tranor think the cops such a hot idea.

"Want to wash?" I repeated.

"Please, thanks, I . . ." She didn't finish her answer, but fainted dead away, toppling over like a broke-back ragdoll.

I sank to my knees, catching her as she slumped off the chair.

The fragrance of expensive perfume wafted up to me, a whiff of luxury incongruous with her tatters and grime. I had no idea how she could account for this present disarray, but I suspected any explanation had to be a doozy.

I set my unconscious visitor down on the floor as gently as I could. She lay stone still. I removed her jacket and sopping wet shoes—high heeled, once elegant, and totally unsuited for arctic trekking—and then put a pillow under her feet to raise her legs, so the circulation could flow back into her brain and revive her. I went to the medicine cabinet for my first aid kit, and some warm water and a face cloth.

As I patted dried blood off her forehead and cheeks, she blinked her eyes briefly, murmuring, "So awful tired . . ." before promptly falling off to sleep.

No question now of risking both our necks, bearing her up that snow-covered stoop to her own apartment, and into her own bed. That left only my bed, a king-size futon couch that I usually slept on unopened because, when extended, it took up most of the living room, with one side abutting Dad's box.

It required some tricky acrobatics to get that couch open, and the bed made, without further disturbing my guest, or knocking Dad off his sawhorses.

I picked up Ms. Tranor (despite the forced intimacy of the situation, I still couldn't think of her yet as "Celeste") and placed her on the futon—a few feet from where I myself would have to sleep—and gingerly covered her with the goose-down duvet I'd given myself for Christmas. I didn't have the nerve to undress—and probably awaken—her, however much my fingers trembled over the zipper on her once immaculate garment.

My eye fell on the two travel bags she'd schlepped over the snow-drifts and into my apartment. I hefted one and was surprised at its weight. It felt full of books and papers. So did the other bag.

I hadn't really thought of my beautiful neighbor as the bookish type. In fact, I hadn't yet figured out what she actually did for a living, if indeed she did anything at all, although I had been nursing some rather defamatory suspicions in that department. A vision of her spending long nights in the library, however, dressed up in Bergdorf's best, had never entered my imaginings of Ms. Tranor's performance on the job, or in any other professional capacity.

I lay on the bed, at a middle-aged gentlemanly distance, still fully clothed myself, and looked over at her face in repose.

The black-and-blue lump on her jaw had stabilized at about the size of a peach. I decided not to apply an ice pack, lest the cold and damp awaken her and bring back memories of what must have been one hell of a nightmare. I left the light on, so if my guest did awake before morning, she wouldn't panic—not completely anyway.

Staring at her battered face, I could only wonder what kind of men Celeste Tranor chose to spend her time with. Apart from her mouth, which was large, she was small-featured, in a delicate Asian-like way—hardly the type, I decided, to provoke anyone to violence. So whoever had done the number on her must have been a monster.

And it was while pondering such lurid speculations that I fell asleep. Surprisingly, given the circumstances, it was a deep sound sleep.

Until a few hours later, when Ms. Tranor's screaming awoke me.

I immediately sat up to find her at the foot of the bed, clutching the sailcloth table cover to her breast, trembling, wide-eyed at the sight of my father's bare coffin just inches from her nose. Stripped of its cover, the grand oak box shone in all its wide-bodied glory.

"Jeeeez!" she shouted. "Hell are you, a vampire?"

"No, no," I said. "That's my father."

"Your *father's* a vampire?" Ms. Tranor looked about ready to pass out again.

"No," I interjected. "He's dead. Totally dead."

My explanation didn't seem to reassure her.

"You keep *bodies* here?" She looked at me with an about-to-faint cloud over her eyes. "Oh God, I don't feel too good—"

"How 'bout a bite, something to drink?"

"Like *what?*" she gasped.

Quickly, I listed my stock of normal breakfast foods.

"Thanks . . . but I don't think I'm hungry."

Given the circumstances, she might have been expecting something more alarming than the orange juice and hot tea I had in mind. I'd run out of coffee.

"Well," she said, "guess tea's okay. What do you have?"

That threw me. Tea's tea, as far as I'm concerned. A&P generic was it for my cupboard.

My guest wrinkled her nose. "I got dozens of teas upstairs. Some black Assam'd go nice now, good and *strong*. But I don't actually feel like being up there, know what I mean? Not yet anyway." She eyed Dad's box. "Can't honestly say I feel like staying *here* either—not by myself."

So we settled for cold Tropicana and some hot generic. Briefly, I explained how Dad had come to a temporary rest in my living room. "Sounds strange," I said, "but you understand, Ms. Tranor, I come from a pretty strange family."

"Celeste," she said softly, accepting a cup of tea. "Least you had a family."

I detected a certain pleading in those last words, an anguished intensity, as in a message stuffed in a bottle by a castaway and thrown into the waves. That entreaty, and her enigmatic look, like the glow of a mysteriously colored crystal held to the light, made my eyebrows rise, questioningly. But Celeste didn't seem at all inclined to elaborate.

As the juice and tea took effect, my guest began to take stock of herself.

"Bet I look even worse than I feel."

She lifted her arm to examine her clothes.

"This Chanel has certainly had it. Want to be a dear?"

My beautiful neighbor looked at me, those green-flecked hazel eyes displaying sudden calculation.

"Don't ask questions," she said, "not yet. Just get me some clothes from my place. Please? I can't possibly step outside like this."

Given her current state, her reluctance to exhibit herself was completely understandable.

"I do believe you have a key," she continued. "C'mon . . . be a dear, pretty please?"

I nodded, but without enthusiasm. Rummaging in a woman's closets and drawers, even at her own request, made me uncomfortable.

Ever astute, Celeste deciphered my hesitation.

"That's cute, I like you. *Most* men I know . . . anyway, here's what I need."

Celeste was coolly precise as to what items to bring back, and exactly where I'd find them. Her instinct for organization surprised and impressed me; apartment 2B sounded positively shipshape compared to my lax landlubbery.

I retrieved my key to Celeste's apartment from the safe installed by Star Ace Corp. in the cabinet under my kitchen sink. The safe's considerable heft, and its unlikely location, bespoke SAC management's unfailing insight into human nature.

12

Outside, in the pale haze that passes for sunshine on a New York winter morning, heavy hills of snow were just melting. Since the storm had stopped, the temperature must have risen a good twenty degrees. Typical New York. The snow might all be gone, I thought, by the time the removal crew got around with their shovels and brooms to clean the row of stoops on our brownstones.

I picked my way through the slush, little realizing, with each step up that high stoop, just what I was getting myself into. I went into the hall and down to the door of apartment 2B.

I didn't need the spare key.

With a simple turn of the knob, the door opened, revealing an interior not remotely similar to the mental picture I'd formed of Celeste's spit and polish quarters.

A scene of utter devastation confronted me.

A jumble of torn-up clothing, broken lamps and scattered CDs covered the floors; every closet and drawer was open and emptied. Even the refrigerator had been evacuated, its few contents strewn around the small apartment. Smashed fruit dribbled juice down the walls and, in the midst of it all, a decapitated statue of Buddha sat in mute blind witness.

A dark layer of tea leaves covered everything.

My first thought was, "I don't have the heart to tell her."

My second thought was to open the windows to let out the smell. In the bedroom, the odor of that seductive fragrance—which had wafted from Celeste's bruised body just a few hours before—was now one of about twenty other smells. The dreadful *potpourri* had me gagging. Bottles of her perfume—not inappropriately labeled *Fracas*—shampoos, face creams, hair colorings, everything lay smithereened across the floor. The place reeked. I hurried to open a window, snow or no snow.

I quickly sorted through piles of clothes, uncomfortable now at seeing what may have been everything Celeste owned in this world spread out on the floor for me to step over and pick through like a rag and bone man.

A cold breeze from the open windows blew tea leaves around the apartment, a squall of black snowflakes swept in on an ill-wind.

I selected whatever clothes looked (to my masculine, what-the-hell-do-I-know mind) still whole and suitable enough for Celeste to wear. There wasn't much in the way of blue jeans and sweatshirts in her wardrobe. I figured she must have put every penny she had on her back, after she paid her exorbitant rent, of course.

What, I wondered, could have provoked this mindless vandalism?

Then again, perhaps it wasn't so mindless. Instead, it seemed more like a raging search for something the intruder valued far more than Celeste's couture collection.

The lady's mysteries deepened for me with each startling discovery. I was about to close the windows before leaving, when a voice at the door intervened.

"The tramp!" a voice behind me croaked. "Look what a slob she is."

I'd left the apartment door open, and Madelaine Hopkins was standing there now, with her Doberman and a copy of the *New York Times*.

Madam Mad, as the other residents referred to 2A's tenant behind her back, was bristling with indignation—a frequent reaction of hers, I'd learned, to anything that didn't meet with approval from the mean-eyed assessor's squint with which Madelaine Hopkins viewed the entire world. Her permanent outrage was reinforced by her steel gray crew cut, always stuck up stiff as a Brillo pad. Madam Mad was enjoying early retirement from a slot as a reading expert at the Board of Ed. in downtown Brooklyn.

This left her loads of time for neighborly chat, when she would generously share her opinions of other tenants with anyone she could cow into listening . . . *guy's depriving a village of an idiot . . . out of his depth in parking lot puddles . . . brains get taxed, jerk next door gets a refund . . . any dumber, have to water him twice a day . . .*

Whenever she spotted me doing my rounds, I was a captive audience.

Madam Mad spent early mornings exercising her brute in Prospect Park's Long Meadow, and performed occasional volunteer duty as a gallery guard at the Brooklyn Museum of Art. I think it was the guard uniform, not the art, that attracted her. She'd never married and had no offspring; only her Doberman was there to continue the line.

"This time, should've got the cops." Madam Mad was thumping my chest with a day-old copy of the *Times* she used to scoop up after her dog. "Filthy tramp. Next time, I'm calling. Six o'clock they woke me up!"

Pete Burns and Mario LaRosa, roommates on the topfloor, came bounding down the stairs for their daily early-morning jog around the park's eight-mile perimeter when she captured them.

"Look!" she croaked. "Isn't it disgusting?"

Pete and Mario were a mixed race couple, who'd met as Green Berets in Vietnam and been together ever since. Maybe the only couple on the block, in all those years, not to get divorced. They stopped and peered in.

Madam Mad's Doberman was gnawing on a partly frozen pizza from the refrigerator.

"God almighty," said Pete. "Celeste all right?"

I nodded, silently, not wishing to enflame Madam Mad with details.

"You want we can do anything," said Mario, "lemme know," and they bounced off down the hall for their run.

Neither gave so much as a good morning nod to Madam Mad.

13

Celeste took the news with amazing sangfroid.

"Yes, well, thanks." She smiled wanly. "Thanks for the clothes anyway. Not what I'd have chosen, but under the circumstances, you did all right."

She gave me a light blow on the cheek with a lacy black bra.

"You *are* a dear. Can I use your shower?"

"Sure."

Celeste wasn't forthcoming on explanations, and at that point I saw no margin in pushing her.

While my guest repaired herself in the bathroom, I made more tea, and pondered further the mysteries that had just enriched my life.

Nothing was ordinary about the beautiful Celeste Tranor, that much I could conclude.

Twenty-two?

This kid was twenty-two going on ageless.

I went out and collected the *Times* from the grated gate just outside my door under the stoop. I tore off the protective plastic and turned right to the sports pages.

I was following the daily progress of an around-the-world solo yacht race.

The lead boats had just left Cape Town, headed out into Southern Ocean storms, en route to Perth. This was the leg where the most accidents occurred—boats capsizing and intrepid mariners hanging on, frozen for hours, even days, until rescued by helicopters sent out from the nearest navy, usually Australian.

I loved imagining myself, Walter Mitty-like, a solo sailor in a forty-knot and rising wind, whipped by rain and hail, up against a powerful current and waves the size of apartment blocks; the main's reefed and the number three jib's up, when a sudden eighty-knot gust turns me over, and I'm stranded on an icy hull, now riding six-story-high swells, and reciting everything I can remember—just to stay awake, keep from sliding off, down to certain death in the frigid black sea—poetry, prayers, songs, recipes, New York City subway stops. That kept me alive in my dreams.

Endurance ennobles? A con, of course. My adventure fantasies remained steadfastly unfulfilled, as I detest cruising anywhere the temperature threatens to dip below sunbathing levels. A warm breeze and a rum cooler are my favorite sailing companions.

After scanning the latest race reports and finding no capsized boats to divert me, I turned to the front page.

Another massacre in the Balkans.

The president and his wife at a White House dinner for twenty-two Oscar winners. Election year, of course.

Twenty-two.

Sounded like a good number. I began searching for my pad on the floor under Dad's box. It was down there, along with the yachting magazines Celeste had knocked over, and my boat captain's hat with all those lucky slips.

I gathered up my lottery tips and the cap, adding the number twenty-two to my investment data.

My eye then caught note of an unusually frightful photo for the front page of the *Times*, the sort of grisly car-accident shot that you associate more with the *Post*'s sensationalism. A sidebar next to the picture indicated it was a late-breaking story, on which limited details were available when the last edition went to press. But what was known about the accident so far certainly seemed worth reporting on the front page.

At around eleven the night before, in the wreckage of a luxury limousine crushed by a trailer truck on the FDR Drive, were found the secretary of the treasury, the recently resigned-in-disgrace U.S. attorney general and . . . Enrico Monteleon of Cali, Colombia—cocaine billionaire, wanted by the FBI and Interpol for multiple murders and other felonies too numerous to list.

All still alive, but seriously hurt, and transferred to NYU Downtown Hospital.

The question raised by Captain Francis X. Murphy, the NYPD detective first on the scene—a question left unanswered in this initial brief coverage in the *Times*—was: *what business brought these three together?*

I turned on CNN for an update on the yacht race, but instead got an excited reporter standing in front of NYU Medical Center. He was giving background details on the car's accident victims.

Toweling her hair, Celeste came out of the bathroom, dressed in the outfit I'd chosen—which looked pretty good to my untrained eyes. Too good.

Twenty-two.

Well, it *is* a lucky number, I'm figuring: gorgeous kid in my living room, and I'm not so old, am I?

Or am I. While I was finding Celeste's revived presence in my apartment such a welcome stimulant, she just ignored me and sat down, silent, her attention fixed firmly on the tube.

She let the towel slip to the floor.

The CNN reporter was jabbering on, a note of astonishment coloring his voice, as the screen showed archive photos of the two American cabinet members, as well as mug shots, full face and profile, of Señor Monteleon of Cali, Colombia. Señor Monteleon had died at the hospital shortly after arrival; the other two were in intensive care.

"Jeeeez . . ." Celeste released a long low sigh.

She shook her head slowly, her arms drooping at her sides. She was deflating like a punctured balloon.

"Can you believe it?" she said, more to herself than to me. "Ol' fickle finger of fate."

Shaking her head, she turned her gaze from CNN and stared off into the middle distance.

Then: "He gave me that." Celeste aimed a kick at one of her black canvas bags under the table. ". . . why the apartment's wrecked. Looking for these." She kicked the bag more forcefully. "Should've left it all there."

She had me hooked. "Where?" I asked.

Celeste pointed her chin at the TV: "On the Drive."

The news reporter was back. "The limousine's chauffeur," he was saying, "a Mister Sonny Fragala, crawled from the wreckage and was found unconscious in a nearby snowbank. Coming out of sedation, after a two-hour long operation, the driver reportedly asked after a young woman who was also in the car. But police sources say no other person was found in or near the accident vehicles. . . ."

"You?" I asked my guest.

Celeste nodded. "They were clients . . ." She shrugged. ". . . new ones. Never did business before. Then bango, that truck falls on us. Next thing, Señor whatsisname there—only one behaved anything like a gentleman all night, I can tell you—he's pushing me out the door with these bags . . . 'Take them, go run,' he's going. 'Take them, get outta here.'"

"Forget run, but I got a move-on, all right. I mean, there was no one else around, anywhere. I must've stumbled two, three blocks, before I shook a leg at this cabbie shoveling himself out of a snowbank. Poor guy, gave him a terrific tip when we got here, but he still looked pretty disappointed I didn't invite him up for a drink or whatever. Want to help me open them?"

I looked at her questioningly.

"You're not curious?" said Celeste. "After all that? I mean like Señor whatshisname gave me the bags, right? They're mine. I want to know what's in them."

"Maybe," I said. "I guess so. Sure, okay."

But I wasn't sure. I recalled the sight of Celeste's apartment and shuddered to think what might have provoked such destruction.

"Might as well," I said hesitantly. ". . . open them up . . . if you want."

"They're locked. Got some kind of tool?"

I did, and went into the kitchen to retrieve a hammer. I returned and smashed the locks. Small locks, they weren't much of an obstacle—considering the lengths someone had already gone to get the bags back—more like discouragements to any passing luggage handler tempted to take a quick peek and snatch at a handful of whatever the contents were.

We set the bags up on Dad's table.

"Open sesame," said Celeste, and she pulled at a zipper. "Oh, God!"

Stacks of money came tumbling out. Bundles, bales, piles of the stuff. We grabbed at the neatly bound packets, flipping rapidly through the bills.

"Hundreds!" exclaimed Celeste. "Nothing but hundreds! Hundreds and hundreds and hundreds . . . holy shit, I've never seen . . ."

Holy shit indeed. Nor had I: I was speechless.

The bills were old and new; some with the big Ben Franklins, some with the old small pictures.

"Jeez," said Celeste, laughing wildly, "must be at least a gazillion here!" Her eyes sparkled at the mention of the luxurious number. Her giggling was infectious, and I started laughing, too.

I began dipping into the bag, methodically emptying its contents. Nothing but money.

Nothing but bundles of well-wrapped cash, all the bundles the same size. We arranged the stacks of bills on Dad's box, in piles of two stacks each, two hundred and twenty stacks, a hundred and ten piles in all. They just about covered the entire coffin. I counted the bills in a single stack: one hundred bills.

In total, we were staring at two point two million dollars in cash.

Ready cash, as my father's last mistress would have put it. If only Dad could open his eyes now, I thought, wouldn't he be pleased.

"The other one," I said, shaking with excitement. "Clear these off first."

We repacked the bag and unloaded the second. With exactly the same results. Celeste's giggling was reaching manic heights.

We were, tattered beauty from apartment 2B and I, now in joint possession of—I dared to think, "joint"—not a gazillion, but four point four million. Of the ready.

And the highly heavy, I might add, heavy and obvious.

My first thoughts, I should be forever ashamed to admit, did not dwell on whatever ethical considerations were raised by this startling turn in our fortunes. Instead, my mind raced through ways of escape: fast, preferably legal ways, of removing the money, Celeste, and myself to somewhere safe.

At this point, up from my subconscious, lottery dreams re-emerged to suggest a whole new life for me and my partner. For, like it or not, this gorgeous kid and I now looked more like partners than anything else.

I found these sudden prospects immensely invigorating.

My neighbor appeared to be contemplating a similar future. "Guess we're stuck with each other," she said, between giggles. "Least for awhile." Her eyes seem to say she could probably think of worse fates. "Any bright ideas?"

I was about to test my Mediterranean-charter-yacht plan, when loud voices out on the stoop made us both jump.

"Get the money in the bag!" she gasped.

I had dark visions of Celeste's apartment raiders coming back to burst in on us. Shouts were followed by an unholy din of banging and scraping.

"Relax," I said. "Just the snow removal guys—"

"Hide the money. Talk later."

The giggling had ceased. Our actions were sharp, silent, automatic, as though we'd rehearsed this job dozens of times before, as though we had absolutely no alternatives, as though we'd already embarked on a journey from which there would be no turning back.

We were in it together. Up to our necks. For better or worse. For me, a leap into the dark, no doubt, but blessedly light years removed from my heretofore vegetative state, a glamorous remedy for eternal mildew, surpassing any of my ridiculously modest daydreams.

Our first step along this utterly uncertain path was to hide the loot. I thought about Star Ace's safe under the sink, but dismissed it as too small for our haul.

I looked down at Dad's box.

"Forget it," said Celeste. "No way. I can't handle creepy stuff."

Celeste, who only a moment before seemed revived by our windfall, now lost all color, save for her bruises, and appeared about to faint again.

"Find somewhere else . . . *please?*"

So I threw the bags into the back of the living room closet, covering them with all my yachting magazines.

Photos of luxury boats, bikini-clad girls sunning themselves on teak decks, dashing captains at the wheels . . . my whole world of daydreams now concealed the wherewithal to make them come true.

As I was locking the closet, my doorbell rang.

We both froze at the sound. And at the sight of someone peering in the window.

I could make out the bulky shape of Tony Dee, and it was obvious he could see us both. He gave me a cheery wave and a knowing wink. It was the first time he'd found me with a woman when he dropped by to pick up the package from Fazzulo's Pork Store.

I opened the door. "Hey, Tony, how's it going? . . ."

"Awright, Danny, awright—way to go, kid." Tony faked a shot at my crotch, grinning all the while. "How's it hangin', fella?" Clearly, my Star Ace colleague approved.

That is, until Mister Dee entered my apartment, and got a closer look at the beautiful Celeste. The bump on her jaw had gone down some, and a little makeup concealed the worst of the bruises, but that fine-featured face of hers still looked as if someone had taken a powerful dislike to it.

And, of course, she appeared to be at least half my age.

"What the fu—" Tony eyeballed me as though I'd done it. His brow wrinkled. He stared accusingly, shaking his head, incomprehension and disgust distorting his features.

Celeste, right off the mark: "He saved me. Some thugs broke in my apartment when I was home. And Danny—"

"Who, goddamnit?" Tony was incensed. "Who's the assholes broke in here? Don't know the hell they screwing with, they break in here. You see the bastards?" he said to me.

"They took off," sniffled Celeste, "when they heard Dan coming, pushed him down the stairs and ran. What a terrible thing to have happen on your wedding day."

That stopped Tony. Not to mention me.

"Hey, you don't say nothin'?" Tony turned to me. "I'm a stranger? You don't tell me nothin'? This is terrific, congratulations, but what about—"

"We're keeping both apartments," I lied. "Nothing to worry about."

"Who's worried? So introduce me. I'm Tony Dee," he said to Celeste. "Congratulations, sweetheart, you got a good man here. He's got a lot of good points, it's just his bad points ain't so good. We're gonna miss him."

I raised my eyebrows questioningly.

Tony shrugged. "Gotta be single, pal, that's the deal. Goin' on honeymoon?"

"Vegas," said Celeste. Me: "The Caribbean."

"Don't mix me up. You arguing already? All I'm asking, how long you gonna be away, I get a sub for you here."

"Couple of weeks," I said.

"Month," said Celeste.

"You two off to a great start. Make up your mind, so's I know."

"Three weeks," I compromised, "if it's all right with you, Tony. I was going to put in a written request for vacation."

"Skip it. Getting married today, unh?"

I was stumped. Celeste looked at me and sighed, her eyes pleading: *Don't be a jerk, not now.* She looked at Tony. "Today," she said, "and we can be packed to go . . . tomorrow, okay?" Her pleading smile dazzled.

"Yeah, go on," said Tony. "You go, and I'll get a sub here. God forbid, those bastards come back, they don't come back no more, not nowheres."

Great, I thought, just started a gang war. Unless the FBI or New York police showed up ahead of Señor's cocaine caballeros.

Tony headed for the kitchen. "Lemme grab my stuff. Leave you love birds in peace." He got his package from the refrigerator and returned. "Bye sweetheart, all the best." He bent down to kiss Celeste on the head, avoiding the bruises on her face. "You take good care of her, you hear." He shook my hand. "And here's a little something for the wedding." He took out his wallet and gave me three months' pay. In hundreds. "For Easter and everything. We'll square up, you get back. Have a good trip."

And he left.

"Oh, swe-e-e-et *heart*," said Celeste. Then, teasingly: "Should've seen your face. Listen, Danny, you're okay, least you didn't panic. That's good. Keep it up, we'll get along just fabulous, I think. Just stop, like, looking so scared, I mean we don't actually have to get married or anything . . . but we *are* going to be joined at the hip for a while, honey, like it or not. So we better get used to the idea. And each other. I mean, like we start telling people the truth, and I think we're both dead, know what I mean? So jeez, you want dead? Or you want to win?"

With a prize this great, with my all-new ambitions suddenly within reach, and the price no more than a lie, I naturally—errant, but true son of Great Blue Mother Yale—preferred winning over losing. I nodded my assent.

And so sealed our fates.

"Gosh," said Celeste, "can hardly breathe in here. He gone?"

I glanced out the window. Tony's car had pulled away.

"C'mon," she said, "let's get some fresh air. After all that, I can't stand being cooped up."

And, after all that, I could only agree.

14

Winter clouds cast a shade over the sun, but the temperature was still rising as we picked our way through slush down to Seventh Avenue.

I stopped in at Mr. C. L. Krishnaswami's to fill out a lottery card. I wanted everything to look normal, just like any other week, in case anyone were ever to come around inquiring after us.

I didn't need my research data any longer, as any numbers I picked now didn't matter, not with that cash jackpot back in my closet. Our loot's security, I must confess, had fast become my main concern; otherwise, I wasn't reflecting on anything much, not even the nature of the new partnership in which I so suddenly found myself.

We crossed the avenue, the Purity Diner our destination, a Greek family-owned place from before the Second World War, when it must have been the only non-Irish restaurant between Flatbush and Prospect Avenue over a mile away. Which is to say, the only place you could get anything to eat, all the others being Irish bars, at least three to a block for twenty blocks or so. Gentrification, of course, changed all that; there are now dozens of decent places to eat in the Slope, but I had a retro taste for the genuine no-frills formica and mirrors of Purity. Payment was cash only, and the prices suited—or had suited—my most recent budget: cheap.

The diner's windows were steamed, and the place was just emptying of the breakfast crowd. Celeste and I grabbed a booth.

"Quite a guy," said Celeste, "your friend Mister Dee. I've known a few gentlemen like him in my time."

We ordered coffees and toasted English.

"In fact, all these Mafi—" She stopped herself and looked around.

The other customers appeared innocuous enough, but you never know, do you, in New York? Celeste was a hot number, I was learning that much, even in her current distress, and clearly she possessed more than her fair share of street smarts, seemingly acquired the hard way.

"Tell you a funny story," she continued, in a lowered voice. "About some people, kind I get to know in my line of work. Like jokes?"

I nodded.

"Good," she said. " 'Cause, you know, I was kind of wondering about you, all those books you got, and you're so quiet, locked up down there, like a schoolteacher or something. You a schoolteacher?"

I shook my head.

"Terrific. This could work out. Since I never much liked school. Anyhoo, you heard this one, stop me. I just it heard last night, one of those creeps on the private plane up from Washington . . ."

Celeste leaned forward and placed her hand on my arm. I thought I could smell that perfume again, but this time it didn't make me gag.

"Seems the—shall we call them the affable brothers of Saint Anthony?" She giggled. "They were looking for a new man to make the weekly supplemental healthcare collections, from some businesses they're protecting. And they're feeling the heat from a D.A. with ambitions . . . so-o-o, the affables decide to use a deaf person—this isn't a very P.C. joke, I'm afraid, you don't mind?"

I shook my head and smiled. Celeste was a beguiling, if startling blend of playful-puppy candor and feline sophistication. She had me entranced. Our coffee and English muffins arrived.

She continued: "So they get a deaf-mute for this job, figuring he gets caught, he can't tell the police what he's doing. Well, first week, the deaf collector picks up over fifty grand. And he gets a little greedy . . . maybe you know the feeling?"

That giggle again. She certainly had me absorbed.

"Anyhoo, our mute friend decides to keep the money and stash it in a safe place. The affables soon realize their collection's late, so they send a couple of enforcers after the deaf guy. The boys find him, and ask where the fu' their money is. The deaf-mute collector can't communicate with them, so the boys drag the poor stiff to an interpreter. 'Ask him where da dough is,' they go. And the interpreter signs: 'Where . . . is . . . the . . . money?' The deaf guy signs back: 'I . . .

don't . . . know . . . what . . . you're . . . talking . . . about.' Interpreter turns to the brothers: 'Says he don't know what you're talking about.' The affables each pull .38s, and place the business ends in the deaf guy's ears. 'Now ask him where da fu' da dough is.' So the interpreter signs: 'Where . . . is . . . the . . . money?' And the deaf guy signs right back: 'The–fifty-thousand–is–in–Central–Park–hidden–in–the–third–tree–stump–on–the–left–just–inside–the–East–72nd–Street–entrance.' And the interpreter goes to the brothers: 'Says he still don't know what the fu' you're talking about, and you schmucks ain't got the balls to shoot.' "

Celeste laughed, and ran her hand down my cheek. "Don't you love it?"

"Yeah," I said, my smile pained. Celeste was an exceptional mimic; she could imitate with the most discomforting accuracy. But hers wasn't just casual mimicry; she delivered her lines with the skill of an accomplished actress. "Good joke, Celeste. Know any more?"

"Tons. Jokes, stories, the tallest tales . . ."

"Maybe something a little less appropriate than the affables. . . ."

"But that's my point." Gingerly, she wiped crumbs from her bruised lip. "You see, what I mean is . . . it's business time, my dearest partner." Her eyes assumed the glint of calculation: "Twenty-five percent."

The sudden proposition stung like a dash of ice water in my face.

"Actually, I *was* thinking more like fifty-fifty," I said, footsying around for a little wiggle room. "There's nobody's name on that dough . . . and it's all sitting in *my* closet now . . . puts my neck out as far as yours."

"But," she said immediately, "not a scratch on it. Not *so* far, honey."

"I know, but—"

"But what? Lookit, let me tell you something. I grew up in Louisiana, I don't want to get started on that now, but I do know some very weird people down there—up here, too, like I said. There was this creep stalking me once? I mean scaring the bejeezus out of me, all over New York, ruining my business, driving clients away. Some of my friends left him in a mailbox, about two blocks from here, part of him anyway, rest was found floating up in the sea lion pool in the Prospect Park zoo. Maybe you heard about it?"

"Incredible."

"Exactly. Now what these people I know wouldn't do for just *one* percent, Mister O, you wouldn't want to know."

Celeste lowered her voice to a whisper and leaned closer to me.

"Listen, honey, you could *try* walking off with all that money, but they won't let you get very far, that's my point. Sixty-forty, final offer. I'm willing to take you on board, since you seem like a very re-spectable person, intelligent, too, considering what you do for a liv-ing. So I'll be up front here: sure, you're right, it'll be easier with you than without you, I can see that, I understand the jam I'm in. Only don't push, please, just count your blessings, Dan, it's lots safer, and it pays better."

I nodded, slowly. Her logic was devastating.

"Good going. Now just think of our little agreement like a kind of pre-nup, okay? Which sure beats being a super, right, a janitor . . . really want *that* the rest of your life?"

Celeste offered little room for negotiation: those green-flecked hazel eyes said simply: *Take it or leave it, honey.*

So what could I say? I said: "Okay."

And battered beauty and I were in business.

Exactly what that would come to mean, I hadn't a clue yet. But, if nothing else, it certainly looked like a way out of eternal mildew, that much was promisingly clear.

A fully financed, if menacing, way out of Brooklyn.

And off to that dreamboat in the Med.

With a twenty-two-year-old beautiful schemer thrown into the bargain.

And so, who? *Who* could refuse all that?

Not me.

15

Celeste and I left Purity. The temperature had risen well above freezing, and the streets were now flooded in ankle-deep slush.

"Okay," I said again, "so that's it, Celeste. You got a deal, we're in business."

I linked my arm with hers, ostensibly to help her through the slush. She moved closer to me.

"Right," she said, "in business." But a hesitant note enfeebled her voice, as if implications were now sinking in, her moxie dwindling, and suddenly my new partner was less than ageless, even less than twenty-two. A scared kid, peering over her dark glasses at me: "Look, Dan, I only hope—"

"Hey, c'mon, don't worry." I felt something like a caring instinct reemerge, a duty to keep us on at least an approximation of an even keel. "I think we just mull it over a little first, okay? Come up with a good strategy, before we take off. Then wherever we're going, get there fast as we can. That's what I think."

"Sure, same as I was thinking," she said, looking even more unsure than I was, peeking into the dark of our partnered future.

"But, you know, Celeste, even if we did change our minds now? Probably too late to turn back. I mean, who'd get the money anyway? Who's the rightful owner? We don't know. Or do we?"

"Didn't even know anyone's real name until they popped up on TV. If the money really is theirs."

"Right, *if*. Exactly my point."

"So in other words—"

"In other words, the unknown persons missing that pile of loot are unlikely to be calling in officers of the law. No way the Secretary of the Treasury, a former Attorney General and a cocaine baron, I mean, absolutely no way on earth a combo like that got involved in anything remotely resembling a legal transaction. Not likely either that it was the cops or FBI in your apartment six o'clock this morning. Puts the bad guys and us on the same side, is what I mean, Celeste, outside any limits of law-abiding behavior. And that makes you and me, kiddo, pretty fair game."

Right, I thought, lay it on the line. An even keel, sure, but with a realistic assessment of the odds on some pretty rough weather ahead.

"Still," said Celeste, "you got to remember, Dan, Señor whatsisname last night, he did give it to me, didn't he, so that has to mean something, doesn't it?"

She looked at me, in her expression a hope that maybe, just maybe, this added up to some sort of dispensation for us, an implied conveyance of title, conferring legitimate ownership over a windfall.

I shook my head. "Let's not kid ourselves. We already know somebody wants it real bad—look at your apartment. Even in these boom times, four point four is nobody's idea of loose change."

"You're right. Okay. Just get out fast as we can. And get wherever we're going, quick. But you got obligations."

"Nah, I'm single, no kids. Just me—"

"—and that box."

Dad. I couldn't run out on Dad like that. Leave him to potter's field? No way. Dad may have kept his distance, leading his merry life, but he was still Dad. If nothing else, I owed him this last one.

"Right, Celeste, don't worry. I'll handle it. I'll handle it, and then we'll vanish. Start new lives, where no one'll ever know us or our pasts."

That felt good, reassuringly decisive. I sensed the momentum building. A plan taking shape.

We.

Our.

Us.

Thinking in the joint familiar, I could discern some powerful upside in that otherwise vague and hairy future we were hurtling toward. Prospects of a second youth with the beautiful Celeste stiffened the old resolve all right.

"Let me make a call," I said, squeezing her arm.

"Sure," she said, squeezing back. My confidence surged, rising like hot lava, driving me into action.

I popped into the nearest bank. And got twenty dollars worth of quarters.

To use in an outdoor pay phone.

A quick call to an old friend, my former agent, the concierge at the eminently quiet—and discreet—Muscade Bay resort.

Lafayette Bramsen.

As I dialed and waited for an answer, Celeste was studying a sign pasted on the phone box. JEWISH WOMEN! it read. DISCOVER THE KABALISTIC SECRETS OF WHAT MAKES WOMEN TICK! EXCLUSIVE AT BETH EL TUES. 12–2. FREE INDIAN FOOD LUNCH!

"Sorry I'll miss it," she said, sounding not all that sorry. Funny, I thought, but she doesn't even look Jewish.

"Laffs?" I finally got through. "How's it going, pal?"

"Dan-*ny* boy!" He sounded, to my great relief, delighted to hear my voice, although I hadn't spoken with him since leaving St. John. "How you doin', mon? Sounds busy like hell up there."

"You're not kidding," I shouted over the din of passing traffic. "Too busy. I need a rest. Listen, Laffs . . ." I swallowed hard, before lying: "Big surprise. Had some great luck . . . on the lottery . . . and met a swell woman. So I just got married . . . and we're planning a honeymoon. For tomorrow. Can you help?"

It was a tall order. The high season would soon pick up again.

"How long?" said Laffs.

"I dunno. Five, six days, maybe less. Got to get back to work. Real busy up here."

"Okay, I squeeze you both in, no problem. We're not full again for a few weeks. Nice and quiet now. You and your bride get a speci-*al* rate."

Perfect, just what the doctor ordered. Next, I alluded to our extra special third guest.

"Your father? On a honeymoon? Thought he died, mon."

"He did."

I explained the situation, as best and quickly as I could. My quarters were running out. Laffs was sympathetic. Islanders were not entirely unaccustomed to strange requests from the grave, and vice-versa.

"But not here, Daniel, can't bring no coffin in Mus-*cade* Bay—shit for business. You know what it's like here, newly wed and nearly dead, not t'other way round."

His description of the resort's usual clientele was accurate: honeymooners and well-heeled seniors. A coffin on the premises might indeed put a damper on all that expensive fun.

Laffs promised to make local arrangements for Dad through extended family connections, shipping him over from the port at Charlotte Amalie on the neighboring island of St. Thomas, then a private boat for burial at sea.

"I fix it up, Daniel, no problem, we take good care of your Dad-*dy*. Happy mon down here."

My confidence magnified.

I nipped into C. L. Krishnaswami's with Celeste. She looked relieved to have a partner who seemed to know what he was doing, who, with a quick curbside phone call, could get her out of the country—or off the mainland at any rate—and, in the same ten minutes, arrange for his father's proper burial at sea.

My thoughts raced.

Tickets to the Virgin Islands, and then on to . . . *where?*

The sight of C. L. Krishnaswami from the great subcontinent reminded me of the tourist agency next door. Taj Mahal Travel, and all its sunfilled posters fueling my daydreams; proprietor, Mr. P. T. Patel of Bombay.

Our very next stop, I thought, after a quick swing back by the apartment. The agency, that is, not Bombay.

From Krishnaswami I bought a dozen large, padded manila envelopes and—for cover-story purposes only, as I had no intention of entrusting anything to the postal services, most certainly not four point four in cash—a roll of stamps. Also, a bag of rubber bands and some Scotch tape.

As Celeste and I walked up Carroll Street, I sketched in a few details to give my plan confidence—let it build shape.

"You *crazy?*" was her terrified first response. "Half a million—on *plane* tickets?"

Her voice cracked. She looked faint again, her frail fledgling hopes sent crashing by this mad stranger she had so rashly linked arms with only moments before. On her face, pain and perplexity exactly reflected.

"Where we going, Mister Spaceman, *Mars?*"

"Please," I said, as gently as I could, angry with myself for mistaking her worldly exterior for worldly experience. "Let's be reasonable here—"

"*Reasonable?* Half a million? Okay, you got forty percent, Dan, agreed. Deal's a deal. But long as we're supposed to be partners, I got a say, too, you know . . ." Her voice had tears in it, exposing a frailty, inducing a butter-hearted sympathy that the dazzle of her glamour did nothing to dissipate.

She made me feel like a bully.

"We're partners, Celeste, honest we are. Please, trust me."

"Sure, trust. Until we each get to do what we want on our own two feet. I mean, I can do lots with that money, once I get out on my own."

"Absolutely."

"But blowing it—on *plane* tickets?—that's definitely not part of the picture. I'm still young. I got a whole life ahead of me, spite of the pickle I'm in now. I want to make up for everything I never had, do something, be somebody. Turn my share into a gazillion, before I call it pension time. I don't have to take abuse anymore, the way my mother did all her life. Don't get me started on that, but I'm not going to spend all my days sitting on airplanes, no way, partner, that's final."

Under her hardness, the spirit of pathos convinced and charmed, the appeal of her circumstance true to fact: she was an orphan, I would learn, in spirit and actually. And she thought like every lonely child must think: trusting no one, not very much, and with one eye always peeled for a fatherly protector. A life-view with which I could empathize. But which I'd failed, insensitively, to take into account.

"Damnit," she said. "I could almost cry, except it's so cold I'd just chap my face. And here I was hoping you knew something I didn't know, that I could count on you for help. Thought you went to college. What'd you study there?"

Ichthyology, I was about to say, but thought better of it. My partner's faith in me was fading fast. It was time to reassure Celeste, not frighten her. Further explication was in order.

"You know what a bust-out is?" I asked her. She gave me a side-long glance of suspicion, her eyes flaring with fear.

"A bust-out," I continued as we walked up the block, "is an old travel agency scam that I heard about when I was a charter boat captain. Working on the fringes of the tourist business, you get to pick up things like that."

"Like what?"

"Like this, just listen. You see, any travel agency that has a license, and a stamping machine to issue airline tickets, also has, you could say, a license to print money."

"So?"

"And so a full-fare, properly issued ticket without conditions is as good as gold. You can turn it in for cash at any airline office in the world. It's guaranteed by IATA, the airlines' price-fixing cartel."

"Hell's that?"

"They're like a very private bank for airlines. Guarantees their whole business keeps moving, otherwise it just grinds down into chaos."

"But what's that got to do with your bust-out?"

"A bust-out is when a dishonest IATA agent with a stamping machine stays up all night, say, issuing himself tickets for which no one has ever paid a cent. Then he buggers off with hundreds of thousands of dollars, maybe millions, in freshly minted money—very compact money, I might add—that he can cash in at travel agents round the world, or sell at a discount, whenever he needs the dough. And all it cost him was a good night's sleep. That's a bust-out."

"And what's all that got to do with us?"

"A variation on that, and somewhat more legal I must stress, is the legitimate purchase of lots of first-class round-the-world tickets. Concorde tickets are even more expensive, and so even better suited to the purpose . . . that is, the purpose of reducing a pile of bulky cash into, shall we say, a more manageable format?"

The penny dropped. A lightbulb illuminated.

"Okay, professor." A note of relief entered her voice. "What else you learn?"

Sensing a small seed of trust beginning to sprout, I held forth: "Travel agencies owned by people from the Indian subcontinent are particularly accustomed to heavy purchases of tickets for cash.

62

Tickets that'll then be turned back into cash somewhere else in the world. In some countries where they've lived, it's a way of beating currency export restrictions . . . or a way of getting around the tax-man just about anywhere . . . you know, with money not declared as income. This can be especially helpful in certain high-tax European countries."

"I know, I've had some European clients, they're like Republicans, all they talk about is taxes."

"And, of course, it's also a way of slipping assets out of a country that's on the brink of war. Like in Latin America or Africa, for example."

"But we live in Brooklyn."

"Same difference, in our current position."

"That's a point."

16

Nine-forty, and we're back at my apartment.

Taj Mahal Travel will open for business soon. And I intend to be there right after Mr. Patel unlocks the door, his first customer of the day, whom he'd be loath to lose, lest this bring bad luck for the remainder of his week.

I had no idea how much more grace time remained to Celeste and me before any one—or several—of those pursuers I was now certain existed would drop in on us.

To retrieve their cash.

And ensure our permanent silence.

I turned on the tube for the latest news. The story, according to CNN, was heating up, focusing now on the mystery woman that the limo driver had mentioned.

That vanished witness, spectator at the summit meeting between our government's highest representatives and a cocaine billionaire.

That lady on the loose, who'd pulled the disappearing act—and whose home address, she and I well knew, someone now had.

I put Celeste to work tearing out the center pages from every book in my apartment. We labored methodically and, after I explained the point of our efforts, in silence.

Into the empty pocket now formed in each volume, I taped two or three packets of hundred-dollar bills—twenty, thirty-thousand a pop—then wrapped a stout rubber band around each of these collector's items. Ensconced in murder mysteries and Stephen King classics, our nest egg must have felt right at home.

A half-million went into four of the large padded envelopes I'd just bought.

And what was left over I taped into yachting magazines.

We then loaded our little library into my L. L. Bean backpack and a Patagonia carry-on bag. When we got to an airport, and our hand-luggage passed through an X-ray machine, the shadowy outlines of our books and magazines would mark us as no more than a couple of serious readers.

The canvas bags the money originally came in were nondescript enough to be safely used again for our own very ordinary clothing; those bags, we'd check.

And all that time we worked, CNN droned on.

I was zipping up the Patagonia carry-on, when a picture of the limo's chauffeur appeared on the screen.

". . . Sonny Fragala," the newscaster announced, "was found dead in his hospital room an hour ago, the intravenous tubes meant to keep him alive now torn from his body. Police believe Fragala may have actually been the victim of suffocation, since they also found a pillow over his face. . . . Round-the-clock guards have now been placed on the rooms of the two remaining survivors, Secretary of the . . ."

"We got to move," I said.

"No kidding." Her breathing was growing more rapid. "No round-the-clock guards for this place."

We returned the packed baggage to the closet, where I carefully arranged the bedding on top of our haul.

And then we headed straight back down to Seventh Avenue, carrying the envelopes stuffed with cash for our plane tickets, our own personal but legal bust-out.

"Look, honey," said Celeste, "I got to have at least a thousand now. And please don't look so shocked. I need a whole new wardrobe, something more suitable for the tropics we're headed for than the clothes you picked out. Need some makeup, too, cover up traces of my big night on the Drive."

I peeled off a thousand from Tony Dee's "wedding present," and suggested meeting back at the apartment, right after my transactions at Taj Mahal Travel.

"You're dreaming, Daniel," said Celeste. "This much money wouldn't last me ten minutes in Bergdorf's, but we're in Brooklyn. It'll take some time. And far as I'm concerned, less time I spend near that apartment of mine the better. Creeps might come back any minute. Say we meet in Purity around two, okay? Grab a late lunch? Shopping always makes me hungry."

As for my own purchases, I as yet had absolutely no idea of what other destinations to book beyond the Virgin Islands. With first-class tickets, of course, we could always make up our minds whenever we felt ready, and even then change plans as often as we liked.

Staying loose, our key to survival.

17

At Taj Mahal Travel, my hand was surprisingly steady as I counted out the money for Mr. Patel.

He and I were seated behind a large screen, hidden from the rest of his small office and, more important, from the busy thoroughfare of Seventh Avenue right outside his shop window.

I'd briefly introduced Celeste to Mr. Patel as my new bride before she scooted off to assemble her casual-wear trousseau. God is in the details, and I was determined to give our story at least a touch of normalcy.

Mr. Patel didn't raise an eyebrow as he counted out the money and then put it all back into the padded envelopes. He had the tranquil, reassuring face of a Hindu priest.

Our conversation was brief and businesslike. He recommended open legs—that is to say, the intermediate stops left unspecified—interspersed with major airport hub destinations. These arrangements were quite typical, he assured me, not at all unusual for world travelers in this class. It would take him about an hour to make out all the tickets, he said apologetically, and would I care for a cup of tea while I waited? He even offered me a choice of teas, including Assam, the only name I recognized. I chose it. Celeste would have been pleased, I thought. Off to a promising start.

Mr. Patel extended an invitation to browse the agency's small library of travel magazines. While he worked, I scanned tables of contents, looking for stories about Mediterranean cities. Rome was the first to catch my eye. Photos of the Vatican, the Forum, and Colosseum glowed with allure. Old churches, great pasta, warm people.

And didn't all roads lead to Rome?

Once there, I could take more time plotting my course to a nearby Mediterranean port, one blessed with a reliable supply of sun-starved visitors from northern Europe, all panting for trips on board that charter boat of my dreams.

But first I'd have to figure out how I'd float Rome by Celeste and get her hot for the idea.

Managing the beautiful Celeste, I realized, was clearly going to take up a big part of the days ahead, but it was an effort vital to our survival.

Then I remembered something.

When I interrupted Mr. Patel's ticket-stamping to air my concerns, the special request for shipping Dad to his final resting place in the Caribbean deep now brought out all of the travel agent's Hindu respect for the departed, no doubt recalling ashes of deceased family members lovingly conveyed to the waters of the great Ganges.

"Yes, sir, I quite agree," he said. "It is certainly a family's deepest obligation. I can fully respect your wishes. In fact, we have excellent freight handling connections, sir, if you don't mind my referring to . . . as freight. But even with a first-class baggage allowance, sir, that would be most prohibitive to ship as luggage, sir, you do understand, don't you?"

I did. Checking Dad in as luggage was the attention-getter we didn't need. So I was greatly relieved to learn that Mr. Patel's freight connections were all family relations and equally understanding. Someone could be at my place that afternoon for pickup and delivery to the airport; similar arrangements could be made for the other end of Dad's last trip.

Plus shipping charges, that would all come to $4700.

For a paltry share of my windfall, Dad was about to get his wish. And I, at long last, would be absolved of further filial duties.

Family circle closed.

"Fortunately," Mr. Patel concluded, as he handed over a simple manila envelope stuffed with our half-million in first-class and Concorde air tickets, "the Virgin Islands are U.S. territory. If this were a foreign shipment . . . of that special nature, there'd be many, many papers to fill out. We are lucky, sir, are we not?"

"Very lucky," I said, shaking his hand. "And I'm very grateful." Wishing him a week full of customers like me, I left for the apartment to stash the tickets.

18

Striding purposefully back up to the brownstone, I could feel my heart already taking flight for points south.

We'd be off soon.

Or so I imagined, until I reached the house and spotted someone in the vestibule at the top of the stoop, holding the front door open with his foot and inspecting the names on the letter boxes.

In his midthirties and broad-shouldered, he appeared intense, deliberate in his movements.

His cheap pale gray cotton suit and ill-fitting thin black sweater looked subtropical in midwinter New York. A man of color, a kind of milky cappuccino to be precise, he appeared to have no intention of actually ringing anyone's bell, but was just checking for someone's name.

I decided against going into my apartment, and instead crossed the street, heading back down to Purity to wait for Celeste.

Before I'd walked more than a few yards, I realized he had fallen in behind me and, as I listened to his footsteps in the slush, my heartbeat quickened.

I was even less prepared for what I heard next.

He was humming. The tune: a familiar old Creole melody that I'd often heard in the islands. His humming continued all the way down to Seventh Avenue, where I stopped to wait for the light to change.

A damp mist hung in the air, and the voices of a few children who romped high on the mountains of gutter snow sounded breathless and tired. Out of the side of my eye, I caught a glimpse of him gently warning a little black kid not to stuff a handful of slush down his sister's collar.

"She your sister, boy," he said in a gentle drawl. "You oughta take care of her." And then he laughed.

Purity was almost empty at that late hour of the morning. The lunch crowd had yet to materialize.

No matter, my tail took a seat right next to me at the counter. He gave off surprising odors of sea and diesel oil, familiar smells I could swear by. He ordered a Coke, but barely sipped at it. Instead, he just stirred the crushed ice round and round, staring at my reflection in the wall mirror.

"Want something?" I finally said to his reflection.

He smiled at the mirror, seemingly relieved that I spoke first. "Yeah," he said. "Help. You live there, doncha."

A statement, not a question.

He reached into his jacket pocket, and removed a worn and yellowed envelope. It was covered with smudged fingerprints and creased as if it had been opened, its contents studied and replaced, a thousand times. The newspaper clippings he showed me looked just as worn.

"Check this," he said. "Just check out my gal."

The clips were photos, headlined and captioned. Several were of young girls in tutus. And one shot of a somewhat older girl in a flouncy dress, who was singing at a microphone. *Li'l Sweetheart Celeste Makes Big Debut Splash*, read that head. All the photos were clipped from New Orleans neighborhood papers.

"Li'l Sweetheart Celeste," my countermate said, "that's the name she used to go by back home. I'm Bill Smalls." He smiled shyly and offered his hand to shake mine, a grip of steel.

I did just as he said, and checked out "my gal."

No question: she was certainly even younger in the pictures, and clearly not in Bergdorf's best, nor did her hair look as if she treated it to weekly visits at the hairdressers back in New Orleans. Otherwise, it was her all right: my new partner, the beautiful Celeste Tranor.

And Bill Smalls?

I checked a picture more closely. Celeste couldn't have been more than thirteen or fourteen; but then again, that *was* the South, and Bill Smalls was one good-looking guy.

"Her husband?" I asked.

He laughed, and slapped my back so hard I thought my spine would crack. "Brother," he said, "but that's a good one. Big brother. Same momma, different daddies."

". . . her brother . . ." I said, hesitantly, not wishing to offend.

"That what troublin' you?" Bill Smalls smiled. "Okay, I under-stand, look strange maybe. Our Momma white, and her Daddy white. Maybe all white, maybe not. Like lotsa people."

True enough. "Hey," I said, "doesn't worry me. Really, Bill, I be-lieve you."

And it fit: it could explain what I'd thought of as a touch of Asian beauty about her eyes and dark hair wasn't Asian at all. The beautiful Celeste descended from centuries of rich mixing in New Orleans. Couldn't blame me for not figuring that out.

I was drained by all that had happened in what wasn't even half a day gone by yet. I tried to sip my coffee, but my hand now shook so violently, I spilled some on my lap. We were supposed to be taking a permanent powder, and here was her brother showing up right in the middle of our dash.

"Whoa there, nuthin' be scared of." Bill Smalls put his arm around my shoulder, as if he were *my* big brother. "Nobody accusin' you a nuthin'. I jes' wanna see my sister, that's all, ain't seen Celeste since . . . family got all split up. Sent me a postcard, says she's doin' real good up here. In the 'entertainment sector.' Always knew she had it, all them lessons I paid for. Now's her turn, invest in me."

"Invest?"

"Yes sir, looka here."

He pulled a final picture out from his envelope. And, so help me God, it was a boat. A Gulf Coast shrimp trawler.

"Outta Langtree, Texas, west of Galveston. Been workin' that stretch since the family split up, me and Celeste all what's left. This boat my big chance. Celeste say she doin' real good now in a enter-tainment sector, and I believe her. She is one phe-*NOM*-enal woman, you listen to me. And I'm her brother, ain't nobody know better than me."

But it was the boat that now riveted my attention. Bill Smalls—of New Orleans, then Langtree, Texas—and I seemed to have dreams not all that dissimilar.

"Tell me about the boat," I said.

"That's my baby," he answered proudly. "Live alone down there, every penny I make socked into that boat. Don't own it outright, not yet, that's the problem. Pollution."

"Pollution?"

"Yeah, all that crap from refineries in Galveston killing shrimp beds. Catch is down. Can't meet the payments, even if I don't have much left to pay off. Bank wants the boat, I don't come up with money. So I hat it up here. Lookin' for Celeste. All those lessons I paid for? All those years? 'You gonna be a movie star,' I tell her, she musta been eleven. 'Movie star, Brother Bill?' she goes. 'I ain't never been a movie star before, think I can do it?' I jes' laugh and laugh, and pick her up, dancin' her all over the place . . . *never been a movie star before* . . . you imagine?"

I could. Every bit of it. Bill Small's story dovetailed neatly with what little I had observed of my new partner's life, those few crumbs of her history and hopes that she dared share with me so far.

"Guess that what done it," he continued, "what send her up here. All them lessons, picture in the papers. I heared her singin' all the time, all the time after she left, all time I'm workin' boats, savin' up. I heared her singin', and it keeps me goin'. I got her somethin' to live by, till that pollution come, now she get me somethin', that's how I figure it. So here I am. Gotta pay off the bank, and move more west, way down the coast, farest away from Galveston I can get."

I could understand Bill's dream. It certainly mirrored my own, not least because we were both counting on fresh financing to get us as far away from "pollution" as we could go.

"How much you need?" I asked.

He eyed me cautiously. "More'n I got."

He hunched over his Coke and took a long slow pull on the straw, nearly draining his glass. He poked at the ice and fell silent, as if listening to that young girl's voice long ago, singing, singing still. The silence between us continued, until I spoke up: "Well, you said you need my help. What do you have in mind?"

"Not sure. Help me talk to her, I guess, know where she is? Don't seem home much. I know she'll help me out, wanna do her best. Always did."

The thought of bringing Celeste together with her brother, on the eve of our great escape, had its unsettling aspects, I must admit. But looking at Bill Small's earnest eyes, hearing the pride in his voice as he talked of all he'd done for his sister, of the life he'd built for himself and now hoped to salvage . . .

. . . well. It all stirred the first faint feelings of shame for the fears I had about his sudden appearance screwing up our departure.

"How I look?" he said softly, concentrating on his reflection in the mirror, smoothing the wrinkles in his ill-fitting cotton suit. "They got a men's room? Wanna clean up first."

Bill wasn't in the restroom a minute before Celeste materialized, peering in Purity's window. Her arms were full of packages, and she was wearing a new pair of even larger dark glasses, presumably in anticipation of our sunfilled destination the next day. The huge glasses also helped conceal some of her bruises, as did the makeup she'd already begun to apply in the drugstore where she stocked up.

She spotted me and, with great vigor, nodded and came bouncing in.

"Howdy, partner," she said, playfully dumping her packages on the seat next to mine. She glanced at the Coke glass on the counter and seemed irritated. "Don't let me break up your party."

"Li'l Sweetheart Celeste," I said, "is always welcome at any party I throw."

She removed her dark glasses and eyed me cautiously. Her hazel eyes seemed even more flecked with green than I remembered, as if speckled now with shattered glass, her voice a cemetery hush: "And *who* told you that?"

I didn't have to respond, as at that very moment, right on cue, Bill appeared in the back of Purity. At first Celeste recoiled, as though she were retreating into some sort of shame. Then Bill Smalls was standing right in front of her, towering above a suddenly very little girl.

"Damn, sister!" he whooped, and scooped her off her feet. He held her in a bear's embrace, her feet off the ground, while she touched his hair as if to confirm the truth of what was happening. He put her down, and stared at her face. "What happen to you? Who did that?"

"Nobody," she said. "Just a car accident. I'm all right, Bill, really. C'mon." She took him by the hand, and turned to me. "Did you tell him?"

I shrugged my eyebrows, unprepared to make up any more of our story than she wanted Bill to know. She got the message.

"You're right on time," she said to her brother, "almost. We just got married, and we're going on honeymoon. I was going to write you soon as we got there."

"Oh sister," he said, his voice cracking with joy. "I'm happy for you, Li'l Sweetheart. Brother—" He extended his hand to me, that steel grip again. "Congratulations."

And not a word about that twenty-year spread between Celeste and me. It just didn't seem to faze brother Bill Smalls.

19

I paid the check and we headed back to the house, brother and sister walking arm in arm up ahead of me, jabbering away nonstop, while my arms embraced Celeste's shopping.

Damn, I thought selfishly, this family reunion is all very sweet, but we got to get moving, kiddo.

As we entered the areaway, they didn't even notice Madam Mad and her monster Doberman marching down the stoop.

"Tramp," I could hear Madam muttering. "Look what a slut," she hissed, as though lecturing her beast. "See what she runs around with?"

Well, madam, you'll soon be relieved, I thought, when you learn this particular bête noire is exiting your life forever. On second thought, I reflected, Madam Mad might actually be disappointed, one person less to rage over in her empty angry life.

I was not going to miss Madam Mad.

"Well, well," said Celeste, back in the apartment, "my first big investment. A shrimp boat."

She had the good grace to laugh.

"You get it back, sister, all fifty-two thousand," said brother Bill. "Payin' interest forever, long's people eatin' shrimp."

"I don't doubt you," said Celeste, digging around in the backpack on the closet floor. "And I do love shrimp."

I could only admire this devotion to her family, itchy as I now was for Mr. Patel's relatives to pick up Dad and his box.

Celeste gathered up a couple of issues of *Cruising World*, glanced inside the magazines to count their contents, and passed them to her half-brother.

"Being a boat lover, you ought to enjoy reading these, brother Bill. Have a look inside."

Bill did, and whistled long and low.

"What you doin' with all that cash, girl. I didn't plan carryin' no cash."

"Good as money, isn't it? Don't be so choosy." Celeste looked at me and grinned sheepishly. "Toward my first gazillion."

At that point, the doorbell rang.

Bill looked around frantically for somewhere to put his shrimp boat money. I gave him one of my padded manila envelopes, and I answered the door to let in two gentlemen from Patel Brothers World Wide Freight, their aging truck double-parked in front of the building.

"Bill, could you give us a hand, please?" I removed the sailcloth cover from Dad's coffin, and Bill's eyes widened. "I'll explain," I said.

It took all four of us men to move Dad, who was still no lightweight. I could see him settling speedily to the sea bottom in the Virgin Islands scenery of his final wish.

"My father," I said to Bill, as we strained at tilting the coffin to get it out the door. "Been staying with me . . . until we could get him to the place he wanted."

Bill looked as if he might be nursing a few doubts about his new brother-in-law. We slid the coffin into the back of the truck, and I gave it a small wave. "See you soon, Dad," I said to myself, surprised at just how much I looked forward to seeing my father again, just as soon as possible, with us out of New York and under Caribbean sun.

Brother Bill, it developed, had come up to the city on a last minute el cheapo flight from Houston, and had to catch the return out of Newark that afternoon.

Celeste and I were, to be sure, equally eager to get out of town, but had to wait until early the next morning for our flight to the islands. My apartment, without Dad and his box, might have been a bit more spacious now, but my partner and I had no intention of hanging around the targeted premises of Carroll Estates any longer than necessary.

I called a car service—not one from the immediate neighborhood, lest anyone was already nosing around—and ordered two cars. One for brother Bill, to Newark airport, and one for us. Celeste knew a hotel in Manhattan she and I could stay at that night.

"Hotel?" said Bill. He whistled. "You really must be loaded, when you got a perfectly good apartment here."

"Nothing's too much," said Celeste, "when you're going on honeymoon, brother Bill, you'll learn that one day. Besides," she added somewhat mysteriously, "no one would ever think of looking in a place like the Hotel Aïda, not for a couple with our resources."

Hardly a promising note, I reflected, at this first mention of what, precisely, Celeste had in mind for our first night. I'd never heard of the Aïda.

The cars arrived, and brother Bill went off first, with a big hug and kiss from Celeste, and her promise to write from every place we visited.

"We're taking a very long honeymoon," she told him. "God only knows when we'll be back."

Watching Bill ride away, I wondered if I'd ever be seeing him again. But see him again I would one day, and once more under circumstances no less surprising.

Celeste and I rode along Prospect Park West. The backpack and the carry-on bag, stuffed with cash and air tickets, lay at our feet in the rear of the car. We were taking no chances.

"Sweet, isn't he?" said Celeste, staring out the window into the nothing-in-particular of middle distance. "After Momma died, Bill pretty much raised me. Bill ever needed it, I could buy him a whole shrimp fleet after this. So, Daniel, guess you know my secrets now. Some of them, anyhoo."

Tip of a whole iceberg of secrets or not, meeting Bill Smalls revealed for me—families can be so enlightening in that way—probably as important a truth about Celeste as I would ever learn in all our time together. And with her heart surprisingly as big as the Ritz, I began to wonder just how my new partner intended to get closer to all those gazillions she craved. As for her trove of hidden mysteries, I doubted that I knew, or would ever know, the real heart of her enigmas, some of which, I suspected, might yet prove rather less benign than half-brother Bill.

So an uneasy feeling began worming its way back into my gut . . .

. . . until I caught a glimpse of Madam Mad, jogging with her Doberman along the parkside, and my heart took flight, soaring off into the blue.

Good-bye to you, Madam! Adieu to Star Ace! And good riddance to mildew forever!

But most of all, good luck to us.

We were off.

With that creepy, clammy, queasiest of fears still sticking to me like white on rice.

20

The Hotel Aïda was on Second Avenue, somewhere in the twenties between Murray Hill and Gramercy Park, the district a dismal limbo of dusty shops peddling home furnishings and secondhand clothing, where I knew not a soul.

I hesitated at the Aïda's check-in desk.

Two singles? Or a double? I hadn't planned this far.

Celeste, to the rescue: "Double, please, twin beds."

"Credit card?" said the clerk.

Again, I hesitated, not wanting to leave a paper trail for snoops to follow. Plane reservations to the islands were bad enough.

"Cash," I said. "I'll pay in advance."

The clerk didn't blink, seemingly familiar with visitors desirous of anonymity. I signed us in as Mr. and Mrs. D. Rhodes, the name no doubt suddenly inspired by thoughts of *Aïda*, Egypt, the African continent.

We struggled with our bags across the lobby and stumbled into the small elevator, a snug but comforting fit so close to our cash.

"Jeeez," said Celeste, "never thought I'd stay in this dump again."

She didn't, as we ascended, elaborate on her prior visits to the Aïda, and I was reluctant to probe. Those defamatory suspicions I'd nursed about her occupational activities oozed back into my consciousness.

Our room had only one window, and that opened onto an air shaft. On the sole chair, I piled our bags.

During my weeks with Star Ace, I'd grown accustomed to little sleep. But now I felt so tired, so drained, I just flopped on a bed, and as a small cloud of dust rose around me, I stretched out my limbs for a snooze.

"Don't get too comfortable," said Celeste. And her voice suddenly sounded like Lydia Sands, disturbingly so, in her tone the rhythms of command natural to majority rights. "I think we got work, partner."

"Like?"

"Like, I mean, at least *I* can't start fooling around with all this money, without some research first, something professional. You ever handle this much money before?

"Not quite this much."

"Didn't think so, not in your line of work."

I could sense disappointment: she was hoping for sensible perceptions from me, pragmatic insights, pristine advice that would clarify her own half-formed ideas about how to handle so much cash.

Celeste, I felt the urge to tell her, *I've been around some pretty big bucks in my time, used to captain fancy yachts, rub shoulders with the rich, grew up on Fifth Avenue*. But all that, I concluded, was probably a story better off waiting.

My thoughts about our money had yet to assume the form of concrete investments. The specter of my father's bankruptcy made me leery of running financial risks—beyond the petty fling of a lottery ticket—and playing with our loot on the market certainly held no attraction. Conservative bank accounts, an offshore mutual fund, perhaps a personal portfolio eventually entrusted to a professional, these were the limits of my fiscal expectations. But blow it all in a day? Broadcast online directions to wherever we might end up? No way.

"Well," said Celeste, "you *are* older than me. So I thought you might have a little *experience*, an educated person like you. You might know something about investing. Don't you always do some kind of research or something first?"

"Some kind." I was too ashamed, "educated person" that I was—*forget* older and experienced—to mention my numerical data retrieved from the *Times* each day. "I suppose so. Sure, do some research."

"Big help *you* are," she sighed. "Got to talk to Wolfie about this."

"*Who?*"

I shot bolt upright on the bed.

"Hell's Wolfie?" I feared a double-cross. "Thought this is just you and me, Celeste. I don't think we should start dragging in other people. That's not such a hot idea."

I could just see my forty percent further diluted.

Or Wolfie whoever-it-was blabbing away for a fat reward.

Maybe sticking the business end of a .38 in my ear.

"Amanda Wolfe," said Celeste, calmly. "That's who. Got me my first job up here. Wolfie used to be very successful, repped a lot of us in New York. These days she does professional advice and stuff, now that she's sort of semi-retired. Like all I'm saying, Dan, is I'm saying Wolfie's real smart, *and* she's my good friend. Almost a mother, way she treated me. So at least I ought to say good-bye before we leave. Okay? Now relax."

"But you realize—"

"What *I* realize, darling, is I'm not telling Wolfie zilch about *our* money. Wolfie won't screw us. Like I said, she's practically my mother in New York, know what I mean? I can't just take off, God knows how long, maybe forever, without seeing her, at least saying good-bye. You know, just like you have to say a proper good-bye to your father."

"Look, Celeste, let's not argue, we're just getting started here. Makes you feel any better, sure, talk to her, say good-bye to your—" *Friend? Business agent? Madam?* Whatever Wolfie meant to Celeste, I saw little margin in probing, and even less in arguing. "—just don't go blabbing, all I'm saying, don't go telling her any specifics."

"I *heard* you, no details. Don't insult my intelligence."

"Great, keep it general, like with Tony Dee. You were terrific there, Celeste. So now, what kind of business is Wolfie in that can help us figure out what to do with our money?"

"Fortune-telling. And she's really good at it. Tea leaves, mainly."

"Oh, God."

We were a right pair: me with my *Times*, Celeste with her fortune-telling agent or madam or stepmother or whatever Amanda "Wolfie" Wolfe used to be.

"Listen," I said, "why don't we have a bite to eat first? And think this over, okay?"

Stall for time, that's the way.

"I could pop out now," I proposed, "buy some sandwiches, and then maybe we could even consider calling it a night, how's that? I'm not so sure fortune-telling is exactly what we need right now, Celeste, know what I mean? Sure, give your friend a ring, absolutely, say good-bye. But we got an eight A.M. flight from JFK, which means up by five."

"*Sandwiches?*" Mournful sigh. "You mean I'm stuck with a party pooper for God knows how long?"

"Just being practical, Celeste."

"Don't you feel like *celebrating*? We're rich, Mister O, we're alive, we're going on a *lo-o-o-ong* vacation. Okay, maybe tea leaves aren't exactly what we need right now, *that* was just an idea, more than you had. And I could try calling Wolfie later, but she never answers anyway. Has a phone service, so it sounds like a big office. I mean, we got brand new lives ahead of us, Danny Boy, and now all you want to do is lie on this?" She pounded the bed for emphasis. A dust cloud rose, then settled. "And eat *sandwiches*?"

"It's the money, Celeste." I despaired of her impracticality. "Have to schlep it with us, we go out. We can't just leave it here, *no way*."

"Only across the street. That Italian place, Pete and Paulie's."

I'd spotted it. The kind of place where you're well advised to eat with your back to the wall, where we could easily run into a Tony Dee, if not the Cali caballeros.

"Forget it," I said.

"Then I got a whim." That unnerved me; whims often lead to disaster at sea. "Union Square Café," she explained. "It's not far, and I know somebody there, we can get in without reservations. I call, it's set. This somebody owes me big time . . . and you *don't* want to know the details."

Correct, I didn't. And I'd never eaten at the famed Café, not on my Star Ace Corp. salary and layaway plan. Moreover, it was unlikely to be a place Tony and the caballeros would frequent.

". . . and the money?" I said again.

"We can afford it, don't be so cheap."

"I mean, all the money, the cash. I'm not leaving all *my* money in this rathole."

"Rathole, says he. Your high-rent brownstone wasn't so hot either, Mister Building Manager, look at all the protection I got there for my monthly dues."

Celeste had me. "So that was there, now what about now?"

She took about two seconds to think it over. Then: "Put the pack on your back . . . and that carry-on there turns into a pack, too, right?" I nodded. "Great, we'll look like a couple of fresh air freaks out for a hike. No one'll ever guess."

21

Humping a few million in cash around the streets of Manhattan wasn't quite how I envisaged my first day as a rich man.

But I wasn't about to leave our nest egg anywhere out of my sight. Certainly not in our hotel room nor in the Aïda's safe deposit boxes. A haul the size of ours would have filled at least every drawer in the hotel vault, and raised enough eyebrows to attract a few dozen of New York's finest, if the Cali caballeros didn't beat them to it.

A pair of backpackers, I rationalized, wouldn't be a New York mugger's first choice of victims.

Hiking down Second Avenue, looking for a cab, we passed a used-book shop. In the window was a dusty model of a sailing ship, a splendid old windjammer surrounded by the complete series of Captain Hornblower novels. The books had their original jackets, yellowed with age, but still powerfully redolent of romance and adventure on the high seas.

I stopped to look, and warmed to it all immediately. Seaborne memories and daydreams returned. I wanted to buy the entire collection, even the old ship model, and have it sent to me.

But sent where?

I no longer had an address. Utterly homeless, for the first time in my life, I felt oddly liberated.

We caught a cab.

$ $ $

True to her word, the beautiful Celeste got us into the Union Square Café.

At a quiet corner table, in the soft light that hid what could still be seen of bruises through her makeup, she looked self-possessed, lovely, and completely at home, resplendent in the clothes I'd rescued from her apartment's chaos.

But before feasting on this vision, my eyes roved the room, quickly checking over every guest, until completing their inspection tour by glancing under our table, where I furtively ran my hands in a anxious search for . . . microphones?

My fears were slow to settle; but if Celeste had any willies, she kept them well hidden.

She promptly ordered champagne cocktails.

She winked at me, and we clinked glasses; I found the bubbles soothing.

This was the first chance we had to catch our breaths, our first calm moment together and, in a weird way, I began finding it more exciting than anything that had happened so far.

And, between us, in the corner on the floor, four point four in ready cash.

So.

Me, plus twenty-two-year-old beauty.

How to describe the beautiful Celeste at that moment, so anyone would know what I was starting to feel?

Every minor detail of her shape and color might guide an art director reconstructing the ambience, the magic overwhelming me, but that would hardly convey my strange mix of emotions.

Maybe better just to paint one's own picture of a shrewd, beyond-her-years young woman, with a demeanor as vulnerable as she could be hard; wisecracking and wistful; grasping yet openhanded, seasoned pro and naive dreamer.

Preposterous, in other words, but never really absurd.

No better than I can explain it now, I certainly couldn't find the right words to tell Celeste my feelings.

"You're looking a lot better," was the best I could muster. "In fact, you really look great, Celeste."

The swelling in her jaw had subsided. And, thanks to the champagne cocktails, her spirits were now buoyant as a bird in flight.

"Thanks, that's sweet of you, I'm feeling tons better already. God, don't you just love this place? I used to come here a lot, for breakfast at the bar."

"They're open for breakfast?"

"No. But it was breakfast for me. They got these great cajun shrimp sandwiches on sourdough baguettes, just remind me of home, you can get them at a place in the French Market near Jackson Square. The gay bartender here was from N'Orleans, too. Everyone who came in, he used to tell them his N'Orleans Jesse James story . . . ever hear it?"

I shook my head, welcoming the chance to get my mind off ever more mischievous stirrings.

She commenced: "Seems the James boys were once in the French Quarter, partying all night? And they stumbled onto a morning train to stick it up, and Jesse shouts—he's still half in the bag, of course—'we're the James gang, and we're gonna rob all you women and rape all you men!' So one passenger pipes up, 'Excuse me, sir, don't you mean the other way round?' And this sweetie on the train gets all upset, and he shouts: 'Mind your own business, Mr. James *knows* how to rob a train.'"

I applauded. Champagne. Celeste. The loot and our laughter. The moment lightened beyond cares.

She winked at me and, tilting her head back, finished her champagne cocktail in one smooth swallow. She did this with a beguiling grace, an agility that revealed her full lovely throat.

I winked back and smiled, feeling the air between us turning wonderfully erotic.

"Now, that's better, Dan. You do look cute when you smile. I don't know about you, but all this excitement we've been through makes me hungry. We owe ourselves—C'mon, let's celebrate like kings."

And she proceeded to order royally. Foie gras poached in bouillon. Pheasant risotto. More champagne.

I, on the other hand, knowing little about fancy food except that I like it, ordered the special fish menu as a matter of principle, and couldn't resist the opportunity to show off my knowledge of matters piscatory. I thought I'd charm my lovely partner with descriptions of the beautiful fish we'd be seeing down in the islands.

"Yes," she said, patting down a yawn, "by now I guess brother Bill's back on his shrimp boat."

In vain, during my discourse on underwater life, she tried blinking away the frost forming over her eyes.

But while we waited to be served, I persevered in holding forth, nervousness and vanity pumping my blabber.

Celeste examined her fingernails. Fiddled with her knife and fork. Stared thoughtfully into the middle distance as if trying to decide whether or not to buy a dress she'd recently seen in a shop window.

Then the foie gras arrived to recapture her attention. My first course was fresh crab salad.

"Gosh," she said, her spirits reviving. "This looks great, honey."

Watching her dig in, I puzzled over how, with such an appetite, Celeste maintained her model's figure. And I hopefully interpreted her enthusiasm as yet another promising sign of a healthy libido.

With my gift for flawless timing, I thought this might also be a good moment to ask how she'd made her debut in show business.

"What kind of gigs did you get," I asked, showing off my small reserve of the jargon, "when you were in the entertainment sector?"

Celeste just looked at me, blankly, and stroked the remnant of the lump on her jaw, as though it still hurt: a reaction that I came to identify as a Do Not Enter sign. As with many people who display a bent for at first boldly volunteering personal data, anything like a specific question, a nailing down of details, got Celeste's guard up, and off she'd slip into self-protective detachment.

She polished off the champagne in her glass. "So what've you got in mind—" She tapped a backpack with her toe. "—for your share? Tell me *your* dreams, Mister O."

Few daydreamers have the nerve to reveal their secret desires. And I was no exception. Deep down within every escapist lies the dread that some hidden wish will be exposed, setting in motion its destruction.

To kill time, I refilled our glasses and offered the beautiful Celeste a second toast.

The first toast had been hers: "May all our dreams come true." I had no cavil with that.

Now, my turn: "For brother Bill. And for all his dreams."

"That's sweet," said Celeste. "Thank you. But haven't you given it *any* thought?"

I looked over at our backpacks, lying in the corner, stuffed with loot. Humping this haul through the streets of Manhattan gave me a few thoughts all right.

"One thing's for sure," I said, "I'm not schlepping that around forever. We bank it, in a special sort of bank. Then when we need it, we transfer it."

"And what—" Celeste eyed me, a surgical glance of precise incision. "—just what do you *know* about these sorts of banks?"

"They're around," I said. "The British Virgin Islands aren't that far from where we're going. They got Swiss banks there. I gather they're pretty good with cash, especially large amounts."

I more than gathered. I'd known some boat captains in the islands who made a very nice living just running cash into the BVI. I'd even done it myself a few times, during off-seasons, when I needed the money to keep the boat in shape and pay for fuel and mooring fees.

Our main courses arrived. Celeste's swanky pheasant risotto with truffles (the superior white, not the black, as our server enthusiastically noted), and my fish, an honest broiled scrod, accompanied by a bowl of garlic mayonnaise. Now I love the stuff, but felt obliged to ask: "Celeste, you mind garlic?"

"Hate it."

"Then I won't," I said, pushing the bowl aside.

She eyed me with amusement and giggled. "Very gallant of you." She reached over and touched my arm. "Guess I ought to be flattered."

Is it possible to fall for a woman—go tumbling, totally—over a bowl of garlic mayonnaise? Seems unlikely, but I swear that was the exact moment I took my all-out swan dive.

Twenty-two. Or no twenty-two.

Of course, it wasn't just her accommodating interpretation of the sacrificed garlic. It was her humor, her frankness, the same airy candor that would so often make me happy.

And so miserable.

"So now you're not," said Celeste, dipping into her risotto, releasing a fragrance of autumn woodlands, "you're not just handing me another plate of happy horseshit, are you, Mister O'Sullivan?"

I felt like my swan dive just landed me in arctic waters. "What do you mean?"

Her eyes grew coldly surgical again, incisions neat and probing. "I mean, you're not trying to play macho man of the world with me? With these banks? Taking advantage of . . . my age?"

I was flabbergasted.

" 'Cause if you are, if it turns out you don't know what you're doing with these banks, Daniel, then you *really* don't know what you're doing. You'll never live to regret it, so help me."

She gazed into her wine, watching its bubbly flickerings, like a gypsy consulting a clearing crystal, peering into cold ghostly glass.

"What do you mean, Celeste?"

"I mean, Mister O, I've had more opportunities—than you got hairs on your head—screwed up for me. By guys who weren't even wacko." She raised her wineglass to her lips, and again drained it in one luxuriously graceful gulp. "And you're wacko. Living with a coffin?"

"It wasn't my choice."

"Okay, and we're partners, I know, for better or worse, you don't have to remind me. We're glued together at the hip for awhile. So you better hear *my* dreams. I know you don't believe in fortune-telling, it's just a lot of old bull for someone like you, but it's true bull for people like me, know what I mean?"

Did I. "And?"

"And my friend Wolfie also believes in all that bull she believes. In fact, she told me she once saw gazillions in my teacup, and now look what happened. See?" She eyed our backpacks. "Also, Wolfie always said that with the right push, I could really take off. And fly. A serious performer. Sing. Act. Dance. you name it. *Real* entertainment, that's my dream. I mean, I know I'm gonna do it, I really am, and you know why?"

I shook my head, fearful of any explanation justifying dreams of *public* performance.

"I'll tell you why: because I don't even *think* I might fail, that's why. You start thinking about failure, know what happens?"

"What happens?"

"Fall flat on your fanny, guaranteed. Imagine the worst, you get the worst. So here's my secret."

She paused for dramatic effect and took another long sip of champagne.

"Con–cen–tration."

"Concentration?"

"Exactly. Stay concentrated. Just on what you want? And you'll get it. Don't believe me?"

"Well—"

"Don't believe me. I'm not out to prove anything to anybody but me. Some people, they land in this kind of money? They do something dumb, like run out and buy a dozen Rolls-Royces or something. Not me.

"So please don't think I'm just another New York geisha, Dan, some expense-account armpiece, one of those nightclub cuties with a string of stolen husbands. I want my own life, I want a career, and that—" She poked the packs again. "—that's a lot of push in there."

Strong emotion, compulsion edging toward obsession, can demolish logic, even in so shrewd and seemingly commonsensical a person as street-smart Celeste. I wasn't prepared to argue with her, not in her present delusional humor, but I thought it advisable to introduce at least a small modicum of prudence into her dreaming.

"Well," I answered, "if you mean you got a real entertainment future ahead of you, I don't doubt it, Celeste, believe me. But maybe, for awhile, with other people looking for the same 'push' in those packs, maybe you'd do better just lying low a little, know what I mean, if you don't want—"

"Who's got forever?" she snapped. She knocked back a dazzling dose of champagne, sniffled, wiped her eye. Then: "I'm not *that* young." Her mood, up to now bird-buoyant, suddenly crashed to earth. "I have no intention of retiring like a high society call girl, some trust fund queen. Seconal to sleep? Speed to stay awake? The Upper East Side is crawling with women like that. *And* their doctors, who'll sell you prescriptions for anything you want, if you can pay the right price. No, thank you. I respect work."

She picked at the grains of her ritzy risotto. I said nothing: my mental eye was still elsewhere; still, in fact, watching her lovely throat swallow more champagne.

"Done enough *lying* low in New York," she said darkly. "Know where it's got me?" She grew grimly subdued. Then answered her own question: "Lots of 'bookings.' Zero career." She contemplated her empty glass: refilled it, swallowed, stared at the bubbles. Dim though the candlelight was, the hurt in her eyes was clear. "I didn't go to college like you, Mister Smart Guy, I was kind of hoping you had some encouragement to give me."

At which, she grew as silent as a solitary child hiding in a dusty closet. It took some guts, I realized, for her to make such revelations, to expose such grandiose dreams, and who was I to measure another's hopes?

As for my own, I wasn't in the mood for confessing what more I had in mind for my future, beyond what I'd already said about fulfilling my promise to bury Dad in the waters of the Virgin Islands. Exposing myself as a secret dreamer of modest pleasures—for whom her celebrity hopes threatened disaster—would have been an invitation for the beautiful Celeste to take sudden flight all by herself, the public plumage of her showbiz ambitions attracting God-only-knew-what predators to the money's trail. But, I feared, the shifting instabilities of her character—insecure orphan, determined performer—would have made it impossible for her to admit this.

And so my dread now was that, while "glued together at the hip" as she put it, we might easily end up devouring each other.

Stark choices: grim visions of losses as sudden as our windfall, the damned-if-I-do, damned-if-I-don't dilemma, the pity and the fear, all combined to make me miserable, and my spirits plummeted.

That mountain of lucky loot began to look increasingly like a poisoned chalice.

In silence, we shared dessert, a plateful of the Café's richest and darkest chocolates. When I paid our whopping bill in cash, the waitress was surprised, but pleased: always a thoughtful gesture in the service business, as I well knew, letting the waitress pocket her healthy tip without leaving a record for the taxman.

$ $ $

As we walked back to the Aïda, snow was falling in a swift screen, footprints vanishing as soon as they were printed.

Celeste took my hand. "Hey, promise me, Dan, c'mon, promise you won't screw up? You really know what you're doing with these banks down there?"

I stopped, and bent to kiss her forehead.

"Look, I trust you, Celeste." I crossed my fingers. "And you have to trust me. That much has to be fifty-fifty."

And that much, at least for the moment, seemed to satisfy us both.

We reached the Aïda. At the desk, I ordered a wake-up call for five A.M.

Celeste groaned.

Upstairs, while she was in the bathroom, I undressed and slid under the Aïda's dusty bedcovers. At least the sheets were clean and fresh.

When she returned, Celeste turned off the light and began removing her clothes. In the faint gray from the airshaft, I could see her nakedness in dark outline. My imagination filled in the remaining details, and I became aroused. Pleasurably, but with growing regret for the late hour.

"G'night," I said, ever so tentatively, hoping for just a single encouraging word after she got into bed.

But instead: "'Night. Sleep well." She sounded even more tired than I was, rolling over, her back to me, the dark outline of her hip rising in a graceful curve.

Our second night sharing a bedroom, and we'd met barely twenty hours before.

But what a twenty hours.

Fueled on Union Square champagne, on food fit for kings, my head began to spin with images of Dad's coffin and Lydia Sands . . . Celeste's ravaged apartment and that car wreck on the Drive . . . murky hints of her past . . . millions in cash plus Mr. Patel's good-as-gold air tickets on the floor between our beds . . . mobsters, bent politicians, cappuccino-toned brother Bill and a whole gulf swimming with shrimp . . . all that . . . and a beautiful twenty-two-year-old's mad showbiz dreams.

A witch's brew.

A headfull.

But certainly not the eternal mildew I dreaded as an indentured servant of Star Ace Corp.

I soon fell asleep, dreaming of dark tea leaves swirling wildly in a winter wind.

22

It's just before dawn, and our yellow cab moves out into traffic, thin at that hour. We're headed uptown, across the 59th St. Bridge to the great sprawl of Queens, at first light the borough gray as a graveyard, a monotonous vista of endless slush.

Great day for a getaway.

At JFK we check in at curbside, handing over only the black canvas travel bags containing our clothes.

"Check the backpacks, sir? No extra charge in first class."

I decline politely, tip the man generously, and we go inside to face security, a semi-comatose guard staring at an X-ray machine's monitor screen as our backpacks, concealing millions, pass under his nose.

Before proceeding to the gate for our flight to St. Thomas, I have a letter to mail.

With a phony return address, in Australia.

A brief resignation, a parting gesture I've written Star Ace Corp., a final communication with my mysterious employer: I thank them for all they've done for me, noting how glad Dad would also have been.

There's a PS:

> *Ms. Tranor in 2B won't be returning to her apartment either. You may retain her rent deposit and accumulated interest, in lieu of any expenses the company may incur.*

Still that mess in Celeste's apartment; someone will have to clean it.

Succumbing to a sudden twinge for closure, the feeling that I just simply have to say a personal good-bye to someone, I make a call to Pete and Mario, my topfloor neighbors.

No answer.

Already gone, no doubt, for their early morning run around Prospect Park.

So I put the quarter back in and, on a crazy whim, dial Madame Mad, that other early riser; she can at least pass a message to them.

"Yeah?" In one word, Madelaine Hopkins's voice managed to convey her total displeasure at human contact, her intense disapproval of all the world.

"Ms. Hopkins?" I ask, as if there's any doubt. "Dan O'Sullivan here."

"Jesus *Christ!*" she shouts. "You alive?"

Not what I was expecting.

"Yes, Ms. Hopkins, I'm fine, thanks—"

"Hell happened?" Her voice quivers with anxiety. "And no cops? You need 'em, hell are they? Kid killed every day in this town, all cops do is give tickets."

"Those're traffic cops, not criminal," I reply, angry with myself for ever making this call. ". . . you know bad drivers kill more people in a year—"

"Just jaywalkers. Thought they goddamn murdered *you* ferchrissakes. Hell's all that noise, middle of the night?"

"What noise, Ms. Hopkins?"

"You don't know, you weren't on duty? No wonder this place is bedlam. Not even on duty. No one's there, serves you right they trash your apartment, and I'm thinking: *me next!* They could've killed *me*, you lazy son of a bitch! You won't get away with this, O'Sullivan, I'm complaining to the management. I'll get a lawyer. First the tramp next door, that slut and her riffraff, then *you?* I never expected it of you, Mister O'Sullivan, you ought to be ashamed of—"

I hang up on her in mid-sentence, and return to Celeste at the gate.

"Pardon the expression," she whispers, "but you look like death, and I don't mean warmed over. You're all pale."

I shake my head. "I'm okay, just tired and hungry."

The latest news—that they, whoever "they" are, have discovered me, too—can wait. At our very gateway to escape, I'm not about to risk sending Celeste into a panic.

"Get some of that great airline food in me," I say, "and I'll be set for anything."

We board and take our seats in first class. Celeste picks up *People* and *Vanity Fair*. I grab the *Times*, hoping for more news on the East River Drive crash, maybe even a hint at the identity of whoever wrecked our apartments. The backpacks are locked in a closet right in front of us. We're the only passengers in first class; economy is barely half full: the islands' high season has yet to resume.

The fasten-seat-belt sign lights up, and we taxi from the gate.

A few minutes later we're bouncing through thick cloud cover. Then we break into dazzling sunshine, a couple of miles above the Jersey shore.

My eyes focus intently on the *Times*.

Some little kids in Alabama shoot up a PTA meeting. Several teachers and parents killed. A too-familiar photo is also there, young people hugging each other, grieving.

Cigarette companies get nailed again—TOBACCO EXECS FLEE RICO CHARGES—this time for funnelling huge insurance premiums to brokerages owned by senators and members of the House— specifically, legislators opposing FDA regulation of tobacco, but supporting subsidies for cigarette exports. A companion piece announces a major cigarette manufacturer moving headquarters from New York to Switzerland . . . PRESIDENT SAYS GOOD RIDDANCE, MAYOR OFFERS TO MATCH SWISS TAX DEALS.

Knicks cream Celtics at the Garden, a big turnaround for them.

And the White House—since the matter is now a subject of FBI investigation—refuses all comment on the Secretary of the Treasury's apparent involvement with a cocaine billionaire.

I race through the long front-page article, then continue inside the paper.

No mention of missing money.

Or further deaths.

Or of the beautiful Celeste.

Certainly no mention of a break-in at a super's lowly apartment in Carroll Estates, Park Slope, Brooklyn.

Our pursuers, I conclude, could be associates of any of the big shots in that limo, with the dead cocaine baron still prime candidate. His body has undergone autopsy, according to the *Times*, and is en route to Colombia, our mysterious benefactor's last journey home.

I ask for a phone, to call Lafayette Bramsen at Muscade and confirm our arrival time. The flight attendant looks disappointed when I don't want to pay with a credit card. Grudgingly, she accepts my cash.

Laffs isn't there, so I leave a message on his voicemail.

Some of the great airline food arrives. We drink the orange juice, leave the rest. Celeste nudges me. A whisper: "Ever been on honeymoon before?"

I shake my head.

"Good." She smiles. "So neither of us knows what we're doing. I love surprises."

It's too encouraging.

I'm ecstatic.

And conflicted. I don't have the heart to disenchant her with news of the latest incursion back at Carroll Estates.

"You know," she says, "this is the best—but scariest—thing ever happened to me."

"Me, too."

"Want to know the second scariest?"

"Chopped-up guy? In the mailbox, the stalker."

"Bad. But this other one's worse."

"Could anything be worse?"

"I was just a kid. Time Bill and I moved into—jeez, what was the name of that neighborhood? Blocked it out, I guess. Somewhere in N'Orleans anyway. And certainly not the Garden District.

"I must've been about ten. And we were near busted. Bill found a room at Ida May's, only boarding house around. More dogs than boarders there, Ida May was always scared to death of burglars. What boarders she did have were mostly older black folks. And a high-yaller widow lady with a small boy, Jasper Stiles, seven years old.

"Except for Jasper, no one was too pleased to see a white-looking little girl moving in. Not with a handsome young colored man, sister and brother or no sister and brother. They didn't want trouble.

"Ida May told them they shouldn't go on like that about a young child. But they weren't paying Ida May a mind, especially the women. Said they knew better, and Ida May wasn't old enough to remember what could happen in N'Orleans."

"Yes, I can understand," I say. I hear the hiss of the air-conditioning and the engines' drone, but in my mind, Celeste has transported me back to her childhood in New Orleans. "I guess it used to be pretty bad that way."

"Don't kid yourself, Daniel, still is, and just about everywhere. Anyway, Ida May'd planted her yard thick with sweet roses and mulberry trees and lots of red and yellow tulips along the borders where the sun was strongest. And after it rained, you could smell sweet right into the house. In the middle of the yard was a birdbath the dogs used like a johnny-pump.

"But it was the tulips that caused all the trouble."

"Tulips?"

"Tulips. And poor little Jasper. Thin as a stick. With kind of reddish hair, so he also stuck out as mixed. And then those green eyes, even worse.

"Jasper's mama, Arabella, had a phonograph, and I would practice dancing to it, out in the yard whenever the weather was fine, round and round, the phonograph at the window and Jasper on the steps, clapping and singing right along . . . *a-tisket, a-tasket, a green and yellow basket, wrote a letter to my auntie* . . . Best audience I ever had, little Jasper."

"Who could blame him?"

"Thanks. But his mama could. One morning Ida May went out in the yard and found half her tulips gone, cut off. Went berserk, called the cops. Cops came, and I piped up: 'Nobody stole your tulips. Jasper give them to me.'

"True enough. Chopped off half and gave them to me, his little sweetheart, one great big beautiful bouquet. And right in front of the cops, Arabella gave that boy a whipping like I've never seen before or since. Beat the bloody blue blazes out of him. She's the one the cops should've arrested. But they left, sort of disappointed Jasper was just trying to be kind. I could've died, and even Ida May felt rotten since she'd made all the stink.

"Little Jasper felt so bad, he wouldn't go to school for a week."

"Truant officer come around?"

"For a black boy? Not in N'Orleans. Nobody cared."

"Poor kid. I can see how you'd still remember that."

"But that's the not scariest part. Scariest part was when I won my first wee folks talent contest. Half the boarding house was there, Arabella and Jasper and Ida May front row and center with Bill.

What a show! Everybody all dressed up and soapy smelling. Ida May had made my dress, and Arabella put vanilla behind my ears, first perfume I ever wore. Jasper couldn't keep quiet, waiting for me to come on. Even backstage, I could hear Arabella shushing him.

"And when I did come out, singing and tapping—I forget what song I was singing—but I'll never forget Jasper clapping and whooping: 'Cee–leste! Cee–leste!' And when they turned on the applause meter and I won, it didn't hurt that I had the audience stacked with all those fans from Ida May's. Especially Jasper, who made more noise than the Fourth of July.

"Won a hundred dollars. And Bill took me out for my first restaurant dinner. Crab cakes. When we were getting off the streetcar across the road from Ida May's, there comes Jasper running down the steps of the house, great big bouquet of tulips Ida May let him cut for me, all hiding his face. The streetcar we just got off was pulling away and making a racket, and you could see what was going to happen. Everybody on Ida May's porch was shouting—there were roadworks and a manhole was uncovered—but Jasper, his arms full of flowers, couldn't see a thing, and then all that streetcar noise and his head and heart so full of me, he just couldn't hear a thing. Fell straight down that manhole and into the sewer."

"That's horrible."

"Even worse, poor Jasper drowned. And that's when I learned little kids could die, too. Cried for weeks. Still makes me teary every time I think about it. That was the scariest thing in my life, up to now."

"Helluva story."

"And all true. Bill wrote it up, you know, sent it to the biggest paper in N'Orleans, *Times-Picayune*, as a sort of tribute for Jasper.

"And the editor sent it back, saying, 'So what, every contest has a winner. This would've been a story if the little girl became a TV star.' Not a word about Jasper. And I'm still not a star—not yet, anyway—so it's no kind of story to make up.

"To this day, whenever I have bad dreams? Little Jasper's in there somewhere, disappearing into the middle of the street."

23

I keep my own fears to myself as Celeste nods off over *People*, the magazine falling shut in her lap.

She looks contented, beautiful, dreamless.

I smell her perfume, real perfume, not vanilla. Feel the warmth of her closeness and, through no fault of mine, I'm aroused. In vain, yet again. For not even in first class is sex an item on offer.

I let her sleep for a few hours. As the verdant hills of the Virgin Islands come into view, I take pleasure in stroking her cheek until she awakes.

She blinks her green-flecked hazel eyes.

And I point out the extinct volcanoes, and some of the highlights we'll be seeing close up. White ribbons of private beaches. The Muscade Bay resort on St. John. And, not far from there, the small town of Cruz Bay, my old home port.

My brief history of the islands captures her interest, which is no surprise, given her Louisiana heritage.

"St. John is U.S. territory," I tell her. "St. Thomas and St. Croix, too, all the U.S. territory of the Virgin Islands. The historically anti-colonial United States owns the islands, by right of purchase from Denmark during the First World War.

"The islands' earliest known inhabitants Carib Indians who migrated a millennium ago from what is now Venezuela to the West Indies. But now there's hardly a trace of these peoples or of the forests that covered their islands."

"What happened to them?"

"The Europeans arrived. They made fast work of the people and the trees. They killed off the Caribs and set African slaves to clear-cutting the forests. Then they planted sugar cane in the stripped land, sugar then being an almost addictive luxury for Europeans.

It was the cocaine crop of its day. Sugar made fortunes for European plantation owners."

Celeste listened intently when I went on to tell her the results in Europe of centuries of easy wealth. It built fine townhouses in Copenhagen and London, *hôtels particuliers* in Paris and Madrid. It clothed cool white owners in silks while hot black slaves sweated in near nakedness, cutting cane and distilling rum. Generations of black women gave birth to children sired by white overseers.

Caribbean life was like this until the mid-nineteenth century, when cheap European sugar beets, easy to farm in colder climates, ended the whites' reverie, and made the abolition of West Indian slavery a painless option.

Bankruptcy followed throughout the Caribbean, including the Virgin Islands. The bankrupt whites abandoned the Caribbean to the blacks. They returned but only as tourists, after the Second World War.

"Bet you my sixty percent," says Celeste, "black folk nowadays don't own much of those green volcanoes down there."

"Not like fifty years ago," I say. "But people who actually come from here do all right. Lots of federal jobs, so not many gripe about getting ripped off for their land. Migrants from other islands do the work locals don't have to do anymore."

"Always the way."

"Yeah, it's a pretty quiet place," I say, "especially St. John." I repress all thoughts of the thugs who took my *Madonna Maris*.

$ $ $

"O Lord, summer!" says Celeste, as we step out of the plane, packs on our backs, first passengers to disembark.

When you arrive in the islands straight from the frozen north, you step into a sauna, embraced by the hot salt-rich air.

"Heat!" she cries. "What a relief. Feel it? Smell it?"

I can: I'm back in paradise.

While we're waiting at the luggage carousel, the Virgin Islands Board of Rum Distillers hands out free cool drinks to arrivals.

And an elderly local man, half-hidden under a battered, wide-brimmed Panama hat, sidles up to me.

"Dan O'Sulli-*van*?"

I don't recognize him, and decide to ignore him: I don't want to identify myself. I concentrate on my free drink.

"Got yo' dad-*dy*," says the stranger, softly. "Arrive yesterday night, on a freight flight." He smiles, a broad toothy grin flecked with gold. "Me and Laffs take care of everything, don't you worry none. Bobo Bramsen."

He extends his hand.

"Uncle Bobo, everybody call me."

We shake, and a great wave of relief washes over me.

"Nothing be feared of. We gonna set yo' daddy down nice and easy."

Uncle Bobo removes his hat. He's almost bald, with a thin coronet of white hair adding a princely touch to the gentle grace so clearly his nature. He shakes Celeste's hand. "Hello, young lady."

"*Enchantée,*" she says, and truly seems so.

"*Par'ment, madame. Moi'si. Quel île?*"

"N'Orleans," she replies, laughing. "And my Creole's good as your Chinese."

Nevertheless, a distinctly different way of speaking, an echo, a back-bayous accent seeps into Celeste's voice.

Uncle Bobo smiles. "Gonna like it here, Madame, gonna like Carib-bee-*an*." He turns to me. "Laffs meet you t'other end. I see you later. No problem now, mon, yo' daddy all safe."

24

Celeste and I ride a taxi into the St. Thomas town of Charlotte Amalie, a quaint, quiet place in its day, now an overbuilt muddle of tourist boutiques and fast-food joints, wrapped in a haze of exhaust fumes turning toxic in the sun.

At regular intervals, a private launch from Muscade picks up arriving guests at Charlotte Amalie's busy harborside, then runs them back across the strait to the hotel's estate on St. John, less than an hour away. There's little left to compare between the two islands. St. Thomas enjoys progress, St. John retains exclusive beauty. Pays your money, takes your choice.

But before heading for the launch to Muscade, Celeste and I have some errands to run in Charlotte Amalie.

First, to get our passport photos.

While the pictures are being printed, Celeste dashes off to the tax-free shops. "I need something special, Brooklyn didn't have much choice. Be right back, meet you at the post office."

Right back? I doubt that: she has several thousand in cash. But she overcomes the challenge and sashays into the post office, arms full, in time to sign her passport application.

Laffs has a cousin I know who works as a postal clerk, and she promises us that she and some of her relatives, all on the federal payroll around town, will get the passport paperwork processed in a couple of days, record time by government standards.

Fine by me, but my mind is elsewhere. I'm still thinking of my wrecked apartment, and how little time it took "them" to track down the dough to yours truly.

So how long before they show up in paradise?

On leaving the post office, I feel it's time to broach thinking about our next stop.

"Ever been to Rome?" I ask Celeste.

"Well, there's Rome City, about thirty miles outside N'Orleans. Two all-night saloons—one black, one white—a 7-Eleven, and a trailer park. Guess you don't mean that Rome."

"Rome, Italy."

"Like in the old movies on TV? Like in *Ben-Hur*? Oh my God, Dan," she squeals with delight, "you're *kidding!*"

"You liked *Ben-Hur*?"

"Liked it? Cried my eyes out. Least ten times. Charlton Heston breaking up with his boyfriend Messala, he was so cute, they looked so young. Didn't you just love it?"

"It's okay. If you like corny old movies."

A distinct chill enters the balmy air of Charlotte Amalie. Celeste shifts the weight of her backpack and looks straight ahead.

"So happens, Mister College Boy where I couldn't go, I adore horses. And that race with chariots was to die for. I'd give your left one to go to the races in Rome."

"It was just a movie."

"They still make movies like that over there, it's my first push, get things really rolling. Look what it did for Heston, he got to be famous, and that guy's a whole lumberyard. Tell me: who you know in Rome?"

I don't have the nerve to suggest, at this tender moment, that launching a movie career may not be the best way of keeping a low profile, at least not for a while. Perhaps our cocaine baron's boys, even the FBI, go to the movies, too.

"Don't know anyone in Rome."

"Never mind, I'll make my own contacts." Celeste displays an unnerving confidence. "You book our flights?"

"Not yet."

"Then c'mon."

She grabs my arm, and we march off to a travel agency. I cash in some of our tickets, and while we're waiting for our business-class bookings to Rome via Atlanta—business class to save some of that cash, and round-trip lest anyone sniffs around—Celeste admires the travel agent's hairdo. In a couple of minutes, she's booked a session at the travel agent's hairdresser for the day we pick up our passports and leave town.

A few days is all the safety margin I give us, and even that I'm not sure about. But we've got no choice. No skipping the country without passports.

"Can't go to Rome," Celeste explains her appointment, "looking like a beach bum. All business for me, once we're there."

My guts groan. Still, I feel it's premature to start debating the pros and cons of her putative celebrity versus the reality of our pursuers. Once we reach Rome, I figure, I'll reason with her.

At the harbor, the hotel launch to Muscade has just left, so we board the hovercraft for the run over to Cruz Bay.

Before departing, I call Laffs from a public phone; his assistant says he'll meet us down at the dock in town.

The hovercraft ride across the strait is always boring. Passengers have to sit inside, and the spray makes it almost impossible to see the scenery.

So Celeste dozes off again, leaning on my shoulder, as I scour the remains of the *Times* for distraction.

By this point, I've worked my way down to the obituaries. Since Dad's departure, and its intimations of *your turn next*, these notices are not totally devoid of interest for me. Someone named Mortimer Townsend III, age eighty-six, is the star death on this otherwise slow day. A Princeton man, Cottage Club. No military service, but retired as president of a CIA-sponsored nature group, after what appears to have been a luckless run at a string of ad agencies. Member of Union Club and St. Nicholas Society. Not married until late in life, and then to an oil and mining heiress, Daphne Devereau, by whom he'd had one son, Mortimer IV, a labor lawyer and dispute mediator in New York. So no doubt a busy man, Mortimer III. I wonder if IV ever mediated disputes between my father and his building crews. Dad was forever damning unions, always ready to go to war to stop a dime more in overtime.

The peaceful Caribbean is a long way from the battlefield of New York construction sites. Dad's desire for the sun-dappled, watery grave is an unpredictable break from all that went before in his life, his one small act of social deviancy. In Dad's circles, financial shenanigans and collecting mistresses certainly pass muster as conventional, maybe even admirable, behavior. But burial at sea does not.

The hovercraft slows for our approach to Cruz Bay harbor, and

I catch a clear first glimpse of familiar waters. My heart leaps. I have to admit that, in spite of all the inconvenience, Dad's last call is a good one.

At dockside in Cruz Bay, Lafayette Bramsen is waiting for us. I glance around for the *Madonna Maris*, but she's gone.

Laffs greets us like returning family, with big hugs. He's laid on a driver and car from the resort.

"The lottery, mon?"

"And then some gambling. Just so it's all in cash." I pat the backpacks and he nods.

I do not tell him exactly how much. And he's too smart to ask.

"Soon's we get there," he says, "we lock it up. Tomorrow's all set, you go over to *Tor*tola. See my banker."

Just as he arranged my tourist charters, Laffs also sent me, during summer lows, the few clients I took on cash-run cruises to Tortola, British Virgin Islands. But the open sea could be choppy now, with the seasonal winds, so I didn't want to risk a cruise that far, not with our precious cargo. Instead, Laff has booked a sea plane hop for us, over and back in half a day.

"Everything arranged," says Laffs. "I fix the works. Got a new lawyer in Tortola, set you up proper, with a bigtime Swiss bank. I'm taking care of my Danny boy, just like fami-*ly*." He puts his arm around my shoulders and hugs me. "Know I feel like yo' Daddy, now yo' Daddy gone. That so funny?"

His broad smile, which is, of course, meant to be warm, makes me laugh, it's so full of new gold teeth, like a burst of heartening sunshine after an icy rain. He notices me looking at his mouth.

"I don't win no lottery," he explains. "So that's my pension, extra gold teeth I got put in for Christmas. Only jewelry a man can wear that women really love him for."

"I think they're beautiful," says Celeste. "I can't *wait* until I'm old enough to get some of my own."

"Your Swiss banker likes them, too, he *never* take his eyes off my gold teeth!"

After locking our backpacks in a closet safe meant for guests' minks, Laffs gets us squared away, like a proper pair of honeymooners.

We have a private cottage—at ordinary room rates, since it's not otherwise rented—hidden in a palm grove, with a perfect sea view, far from the main buildings.

"You always live like this down here?" Celeste asks me, looking around our classy new digs. "Why'd you ever leave?"

"I told you, I was busted. Flat broke. No boat, nowhere to live. I had nothing after my father died."

"Except your father."

"Except my father."

"Gosh, I can see why you started playing the lottery. Desperate. I'd have found something, anything, to be able to stay in a place like this. You know, Mister O, I'll bet losing my keys and ringing your doorbell must have been the luckiest thing ever to happen in your life. At least in New York."

She looks at me, a calculating glint returning to her eyes.

"And don't think I don't know it, Celeste, believe me, I'm eternally grateful. But stop and figure for a minute, if you hadn't met me, where would you be now? Hardly here."

"A point. I might've otherwise had the pleasure of meeting the gentlemen who trashed my apartment. In fact, I might also be dead. So, you're right, I guess we're even."

We go for a swim. We chase seagulls. We collect shells. We lie, thigh by thigh, on the beach.

Celeste snoozes. And I dream—alas, not about life with her. In my dreams, apartment wreckers still star, their faces masked.

25

Dining at Muscade is magical.

The restaurant terrace takes on a special charm at night. Acres of crisp white linens cover the tables, crystal bowl centerpieces overflow with great sprays of fresh-cut flowers: yellows, crimsons, every shade of blue. Dozens of candles flicker in the warm salt breeze, and special lighting on the hotel lawns catches the phosphorescent sparkle of sea swells breaking along the shore.

Beyond that, the Caribbean lies black when there's no moon, otherwise a white lunar light like tonight's flickers romantically across the sea's surface.

All in all, honeymooners' heaven.

Only a dim glow from Cruz Bay farther along the coast serves to remind us we're not alone in this paradise. And as for those few lights seen on the horizon from St. Thomas, they may as well be distant stars.

Celeste looks radiant. She's wearing a pale lemon-yellow silk caftan and pale lemon-yellow silk slippers with pearl buckles, part of her afternoon haul in Charlotte Amalie.

Swept away, I put my hand under the table and place it on her knee. Her hand comes down to hold mine in place. We finish the bottle of Montrachet the house has treated us to.

"Great wine," I say, and order a second.

"And isn't this terrific lobster," I add.

Then, like music, her reply: "The best."

And so, without another word, we rise, and leave half the terrific lobster on our plates, the second bottle of great wine untouched.

No pursuit, no seduction.

We're serious now about playing honeymooners.

Sex, fast and furious, becomes our magic medication, restorer of my youth.

Twenty-two.

Sex, that feel-good tranquilizer and cure-all, at least temporarily banishes all nightmares of apartment plunderers in hot pursuit. My fears of middle-age mildew are now as distant as those stars.

Sex double-quick-fixes our life on the run.

And afterwards, lying in each other's arms, exhausted, Celeste teases me. "So when did you first feel like it? C'mon, Mister O, fess up, the exact moment."

"Last night, at dinner," I answer honestly. "At the Union Square, when you said I was being so gallant about the garlic."

"*Garlic?*"

"Garlic."

And so this becomes our code word for passion.

Garlic.

Making love becomes *garlic.*

As in: "How 'bout some garlic in the shower?"

Or: "I could go for a little garlic before breakfast, you?"

At the end of our first night full of garlic, she asks: "Feeling better?"

"Better?"

"Now that your daddy'll be down where he asked to be."

"Certainly a relief."

"Least you'll always know where he is. More than I can say."

"You don't know—"

"Not my daddy. I don't mean to spit on his grave, wherever that is, but he wasn't much of a dad, anyway. Just boozed and played cards, all I ever heard about him. Southern white trash."

"I'm sorry."

"Not your fault. Cops in Miami found him dead on the beach, mainly empty bottle of Wild Turkey lying on his stomach. Only ever drank the good stuff. Can't say I'm glad he died, a terrible thing to say about anybody, but he never did much for Mom and me, except cause pain. Mom went before he did, that's when Bill took over. We got the phone call from Miami at Ida May's—don't know how the cops found us, but they did. Bill told me the news, and only thing I could picture was a body all dressed and lying on the sand in the early morning, and that was just so sad, I cried and cried. Owed him that one good cry, I guess, since he gave me life. Also owed him a swift kick in the butt."

I do not probe further. Celeste soon falls asleep and, probably to reassure myself that this young beauty is indeed now truly mine, at least for the moment, and that we might even be safe, at least for a couple of nights in paradise, I give her one last kiss, thinking she's out for the night.

"What's the matter?" she murmurs.

Even in her groggy state, she's quick to read the meaning behind a kiss, that small whisper in the brain.

"Nothing," I reply. "Sleep well."

And we do. It's not until just before dawn that the bad dreams hit me again. Masked plunderers invading our hotel cottage, tearing us from bed, drowning us in the sea, our bodies found washed up on the sand.

The room is air-conditioned, but I awake with the sweats.

26

Our seaplane hop to Tortola in the morning may be scenic, but the view is lost on us honeymooners.

Garlic-stuffed, we doze almost all the way.

Once there, in the offices of Nigel Plumm, solicitor, Celeste and I complete forms setting up shell companies for transferring our money as we need it. Park Slope Co., our Lichtenstein base. Mardi Gras Investments in Panama. Madonna Maris Management for Monaco. The law's magic works its worldwide funding wonders.

Our lawyer then leads us and our cash over to the bank.

On the way, he brags about how the Caymans and BVI have one bank for every fifty-seven inhabitants.

"With so much competition," he assures us, "service stays first-rate." Solicitor Plumm is alarmingly frank: "The States may have the world's toughest anti-laundering laws. But that's no surprise, since your countrymen," he explains, with self-satisfied British smugness, "are the world's leading consumers of illicit drugs."

The matter-of-fact way he delivers these home truths, in broad daylight, makes me distinctly uncomfortable. The Caymans and BVI, I'm reminded again, are a couple of those many sunny places in this world called home by far too many shady people.

These are not the sorts of ports I want to linger in.

"Nervous?" asks solicitor Plumm.

"Little," I answer.

"Lots," says Celeste.

"Needn't be," he replies. "Nowhere do laws—not even in your law-ridden country—hold decent white-collar professionals criminally liable for what goes on way up, or down, the line. You're solid company owners now. You'll only ever have to deal with other professionals—bankers, and lawyers like me."

This is meant to reassure us. But I remain far from convinced it's the end of our cares, up or down any line. Our haul might soon be safe, but as for us, my fears remain on a steady boil.

The Swiss Trust Bank maintains its BVI offices in a tree-shaded faux-colonial shopping center, a warren of swank boutiques and casual but expensive restaurants, stretching along the edge of a golf course with an expansive view of sea.

One flight above a real estate office, off a veranda overlooking an inner courtyard of palmy cafés, the bank's premises aren't remotely as imposing as one might expect for an institution rumored to have reserves of a half-trillion dollars—rumored only because nothing for certain is ever known about Swiss banks.

Our lawyer informs us how Swiss law—that magic wonder worker—allows Swiss bankers to keep their vast reserves a secret, even from shareholders.

So you bank with the Swiss strictly on faith and, at least in the Caymans and BVI, at the Swiss Trust Bank by referral only.

If not for solicitor Plumm, we'd have a hard time even finding the bank's offices. The discreet, small brass plate on the door simply reads: STB BY APPOINTMENT ONLY.

We ring the bell and an armed guard admits us.

The reception room is minute. A reassuring sign, Plumm tells us; the bank doesn't believe in throwing away money on rent.

Celeste and I eyeball the place.

In a corner, a tennis racket, worn leather golf bag, drivers and putters.

Bare walls, save for a couple of framed diploma-like awards to the local branch manager, a Professor Doctor Peter Fuchs. One diploma, from the Geneva Red Circle Masonic Lodge, praises lodge brother Fuchs for unspecified "services to humanity." The other award, emblazoned with a rather sinister-looking cartoon panda, lauds his "support for wildlife worldwide." Our Swiss banker appears devoted to life in all its forms, but there's no indication of what he is a doctor of or a professor in.

We wait only a moment before three large Russians in wrinkled linen suits come rolling out of the inner office.

Professor Doctor Fuchs bids them good-bye in their own language, then greets us in English. Perhaps he has taught linguistics.

The professor's accent, the kind of Swiss-German sing-song that provokes giggles, I'd normally find funny coming from a man his size—about six-five and broad as an Alp—if it weren't for his grand titles, service-to-life awards, and that half-trillion holding him up.

He eyes our backpacks.

Plumm whispers to us to pass the packs to an assistant in the inner office, who straightaway begins counting the contents.

Handing over the loot of your life is not a comfortable situation. My stomach rolls.

Our professor doctor's face glows with pleasure.

"Hikers?" he asks. "I too hike, when I am home in the mountains. I miss the mountains. Please to be seated." He sighs, a heavy wistfulness coloring his voice. "These days we go so far from home for business. Much easier before. But you know Swiss banks have acquired, shall I say, a peculiar notoriety? Completely unsought, unwelcome, and, I might add, unearned. Certain laws forced on my country require us to ask insulting questions of clients who come to Switzerland. For this, I apologize. It only frightens away business. But that's human nature, no? So we're here now, in the sun, where all our competitors are, too. Global economy, yes?"

He shrugs his eyebrows.

"One adapts." He explains his business philosophy: "At the end of the day, the best advertisement"—our Swiss banker slips in the cliché like a thermometer, one more service to humanity—"is a satisfied customer."

I smile politely, but am suddenly aware of Professor Doctor Fuchs staring at my mouth. Nervous, I run my tongue over my front teeth, with a chill remembering Laffs's warning about this Swiss banker's tooth fetish. Perhaps the professor's doctorate is in dentistry.

Solicitor Plumm passes the banker a copy of our papers, which he barely skims.

"As usual, all in order, Mr. Plumm." He cosigns the documents, inserting some account numbers, returning our papers to the lawyer. "I thank you. And I congratulate you people on your good fortune. And your new businesses. Best of luck to you both. Interest is variable, two and a half net at the moment, it will be transferred monthly or quarterly, as you wish, to whatever account you tell us is most convenient. Your preference?"

"We don't know yet," I say. "We'll inform you shortly."

"No problem."

And we're finished. No further questions.

Celeste and I take ve-e-e-ery deep breaths.

The professor doctor stands to shake our hands, and we're gone. The brand new owners of several far-flung paper companies and, I pray, the bulk of our fortune safe in Swiss hands.

Time now to grant Dad his final wish.

27

We're back on St. John that same afternoon.

We've picked a gorgeous spot for Dad, near a couple of my favorite wrecks, home to thousands of beautifully colored fish.

Dad ought to love it.

Laffs and Uncle Bobo have everything arranged for the burial. Celeste and I are traveling by bush taxi, Laffs driving, all the way up-island to Dead Frog Cove, to rendezvous with Uncle Bobo who's bringing the coffin around by boat.

Island bush taxis are hardy open-back trucks, fitted with bare benches in the rear for passengers. This one has an open cab. No limo for Dad's burial.

St. John is almost all hills, so level land is such a rarity that any flat plot commands a huge premium. For cardiac-arrest-style riding, the island matches any roller coaster, but at least roller coasters have no oncoming traffic. The spectacular panoramas only add to a driver's distractions; they are everchanging, from the dense towering greenery of St. John national park to sudden bright expanses of azure sea and precipitous red ochre cliffs.

The road to Dead Frog Cove grows more winding the farther away we get from Muscade Bay, the scenery wilder, the forested hills and valleys plunging to crags and down to the breaking sea. After mounting an especially steep peak, we round a high sharp curve, and stall for a second at the top.

Celeste peers over the side down at the sea. "That's a long way. Gosh, but I do hate funerals."

"Funeral was last month," I note. "This is just the burial."

"Right, I forgot. It all seems the same to me. Glad I won't have to go to my own funeral. Except I don't even want one. My kids can just scatter my ashes, I ever have any—kids that is. They can scatter me off the Brooklyn Bridge, make it easy for them."

"We gettin' close," Laffs calls to us. "Hold yo' heads!"

"Hang on!" Celeste is shouting as we turn off the paved road, bounding down a dirt trail, through tangled woods of wild palms and kapok trees, swollen burls and termite nests.

We're laughing now, our mood jolted out of the funereal.

The road to the cove grows steeper and stonier, entering a different climate of dry hot wind, as the car kicks up a cloud of acrid-smelling red dust.

Cactus plants appear: clumps of tall spiky tubes, barrel cactus, prickly pear. The trail turns to hard stone rubble. Increasingly, trees yield to cactus, thorn bush, the spikes of century plants.

We jolt forward over the stones. Long thorny branches rake the sides of the truck, and we duck down on the floor, as there are no windows to close.

The open-air taxi bounces.

Shudders.

Groans. Its axles and underside pound rocks with teeth-shattering blows. The plunge lasts about three minutes before we break through the cactus and are at last on hard sand, relieved to see Uncle Bobo standing at the water's edge farther down the empty beach, an open motor launch moored in the pale blue shallows about seven yards offshore, carrying Dad in his great oak box, one end of the coffin projecting about a foot out over the stern.

Only a couple of days have passed since I said good-bye to Dad, entrusting him to Patel Brothers World Wide Freight, up in wintry Brooklyn.

But that time and place could just as easily be two decades ago, and my Star Ace indenture as distant as outer space.

Uncle Bobo points to a clearing in the forest. We purr along the hard sand and pull up in a grove of tall coconut palms.

Laffs has brought along an ice cooler and a jug full of sundowners. We toast Dad and his coffin bobbing offshore in the launch.

"Well, maybe your dad knew what he was doing," says Celeste. "It's a beautiful place, beats a New York graveyard. Even beats the East River."

"Yo' daddy," says Uncle Bobo, "he get around."

"Guess so, least now he has."

"Always a travelin' man?"

"Sort of. Never really left New York though. Just kept going from woman to woman, for years."

"Yeah," says Uncle Bobo, "kinda like travelin', ain't it?" We all laugh at this. "New sceneries all the time, always different ways a doin' things. Must've piled up lotsa memories, like a tourist goin' round the world. Enough last a dozen lifetimes."

"You must've had a great teacher, Danny," says Laffs. "No fact a life yo' daddy don't know."

Facts of life: I smile at the memory.

"Yeah, I must have been about three or four, and my mother was still alive, and we were living across from Central Park. Dad and I went out for a walk, and we saw two dogs sniffing around each other, and then one dog mounts the other and starts in.

"'What are those dogs doing?' I asked him.

"'Well, Junior,' Dad began very slowly, 'that first little dog there, you see, she's all of a sudden gone blind, and that other little doggie is very kindly pushing her all the way over into the park, where there are no cars, and it's much, much safer.'

"It was an old joke, but of course I didn't get it at that age. I was just deeply moved by such an act of kindness on the part of one dog for another. I became silent and thoughtful for the rest of the day. At supper that evening, I related all this, almost word for word and in great wonder, to my mother, who burst out in uncontrollable giggling. I suppose it was from that very moment that I took to doubting every word my father ever spoke to me."

Sitting on the hard sand, under the palms, we share another laugh, watching that great oak coffin bobbing gently in the launch just offshore.

Then the four of us wade out to the boat.

Slowly, we motor to a spot not far from Dead Frog Cove.

Uncle Bobo and Laffs mumble some juju prayers, begging the sea spirits' protection—I recall Campbell's generic invocation on Madison Avenue—and we slide the coffin off the stern of the launch, very nearly tipping ourselves into the sea.

Watching Dad's coffin sink, I reflect: If ever I meet Lydia Sands again—which, in this moment of heightened sentiment, I have an ominous feeling I just might—I'll offer to take her back to this un-marked watery grave, so she, too, can say farewell.

Otherwise, at his depth, Dad'll probably rest undisturbed for-ever, among the fish he took such a surprising fancy to, those sub-jects of my studies at Great Blue Mother Yale that he'd paid so dearly for. Down there with leopard rays and groupers and parrot fish, the octopus and eels, Dad is at rest.

My duty done.

And so, by this point, of course, I'm envisioning a similar end for myself. The bottom line is we all have the same percentage of salt in our blood as does water in the sea—sweat, blood, tears: every bit of us just as salty as oceans.

We return in the launch to the beach at Dead Frog Cove, and leave off Laffs who drives the taxi back up that jungly hill. Then Un-cle Bobo, Celeste, and I head for Cruz Bay by the sea route.

Celeste snuggles up to me, and we bask in those final warm rays of setting sun.

"Nice," she says. "Nice if it's this peaceful forever."

"Yeah, forever," I say, and I mean it.

Even if I don't believe it.

28

The next morning I got hit by the feeling you get when you're reluctant to leave somewhere, a place you really love.

But you know there's no choice.

And you're afraid you'll never come back.

So you feel like throwing up.

Celeste—lying there in bed, right after garlic, watching the dawn—looked just as melancholy as I was about departing.

"Do we have to?" She stroked my hair. "One more day, what do you say?"

Tempting, but what I said was: "Night before we left, Celeste, they tore up my place, too. I called from the airport and got the news, but didn't want to upset you."

She bolted out of bed.

"*Upset* me?" she shouted. "I'm terrified! Don't ever hold out on me again. They're on to you? They'll be down here in no time, if they're not already. Get dressed, let's get out of here!"

At the checkout desk, I paid our bill with an embarrassingly large wad of cash.

The sleepy clerk smiled, and presented us with an envelope. Inside was a picture postcard of St. John from the air. *Merry Marriage & Happy Travels!* read the handwritten message, *Laffs & Uncle Bobo.*

"That's sweet," said Celeste. "I'm going to miss them. But we got to move."

I wrote a hasty note on hotel stationery from the desk clerk, thanking Laffs and Uncle Bobo for all they'd done, and promising we'd be back. Celeste planted a great red-lipsticky kiss on it.

First, a quiet plane hop up to Atlanta from St. Thomas, then we boarded for the next leg of our escape—on Alitalia to Rome—all of it, so far, blissfully uneventful.

Which didn't keep us from worrying. While trying not to.

"Okay," said Celeste, "so maybe we're not in the clear yet. Not completely. But I think we're all right on the plane, don't you?"

I nodded. I saw no one suspicious seated near us. And no one appeared interested in a middle-aged man and his youthful companion.

"Good," she said. "And Rome's pretty big, isn't it?"

"Must be, it's the capital."

"Great, New York without winter."

"Or Broadway or skyscrapers or Gray's Papaya."

"We'll manage. Least I won't have to start work right off the bat, way I did when I got to New York."

The opening was too wide to resist. After the plane took off, I asked: "What did you do, when you first got to New York?"

Celeste began rubbing her chin where it had been swollen, the Do Not Enter sign. Then she shrugged, as if it didn't matter anymore. "Market research."

Not quite what I was expecting.

"And don't," she said, "look so surprised."

"Well, you said you were only sixteen—"

"I was big for my age. But I was still innocent, sort of, almost a virgin, kind of. And I met this tall advertising guy, Brendan, and he hired me. He had a beard, so he was very creative, talked a great line of blarney."

"Big agency?"

"Wouldn't know. I worked at home. He got me the place at Carroll Estates. He'd come over and pay me to tell him my daydreams, and he'd take notes. Starkers, the both of us, but he was Irish, so he never touched me. And don't look like that."

"Sorry."

"It's all true, I swear. He said I had the perfect consumer mind. But I know he did it with other girls, too. Also boys, I bet, to cover the whole market. His notebooks were bulging."

"Weird."

"Still, it paid. 'What do you really, *really* want?' he'd ask me, in this deep, whiskey-hoarse voice. 'Tell me all your secret wishes. Add them up, and that's who you are.' So I told him. And told him. And told him. Started making things up, stealing stories I got my other clients to tell me, anything just to keep him taking notes. And paying me."

"Keep the client happy."

"Exactly. It spoiled me. Spoiled him, too. Shot right up to the top of the agency. Still see him all the time in '21,' but he pretends he doesn't know litle ol' me."

"Typical, I guess, from that kind."

"Guess so. Anyway, I'm not complaining, my other clients were lots more demanding than he was. Made the mistake of bringing some of them round to the apartment, too. That's when Madame Mad got on my case."

"Ah, my favorite friend."

"Likewise."

"So she told me."

"Well, our favorite friend finally called the cops on me. And they're pulling up, just as I'm leaving with a client, and Madame's waiting on the sidewalk for them. I had to think fast, so I point at her and start crying: 'She's the one! She's the one who's molesting little kids!' "

"You're amazing, Celeste."

"What's amazing was how loud she started screaming. Let loose like an opera star on speed. Then she grabs me, starts throwing punches, and then the cops grab her, and I go, 'Careful, she's a wild one, might have a knife.' That did it. She goes ballistic with the cops, who are trying to hold her back against the squad car. And so I just kind of strolled off down the street, not being much of a fight fan. Never saw that client again. And our good friend got off with just a fine, but still she's had it in for me ever since. Anyway, after that, I stopped working at home, pretty much."

"Don't blame you."

Celeste yawned. "Think I got time for a little beauty rest?"

"Sure, it's a long flight. Pleasant dreams." I was amazed at her focus. Daytime napping had clearly become a matter of daily routine, a way of life for Celeste.

I put my arm around her as she snuggled up and dozed off. And although I tried, I still couldn't sleep. The steady drumbeat of concern kept me wide-eyed.

So I buried my nose in a newspaper.

Surprisingly, that morning's *Times* carried only an op-ed piece about "Crashgate," as the smash-up on the Drive was now known—Safire dilating again upon the prospect of yet another good reason to topple a Democratic president. Nor were there any new details on the accident itself, not in the paper or in *Newsweek* or *TIME*, although the magazines ran several photos of the accident scene.

And no, not a word, not a hint anywhere, about money missing or the beautiful Celeste.

A blessing?

I had no idea yet, but my crazy mix of emotions—of fear for our lives and of melancholy over leaving St. John—was subsiding, replaced by relief at just getting away from the dear old U.S. of A., saying goodbye to all that, our loot safe and the two of us still intact, putting many thousands of miles between us and them, our pursuers, whoever they were.

Once settled in Europe, I resolved, I'd lead a simpler life, one of far fewer complications, an anonymous existence in quiet comfort.

So I hoped I wouldn't have to be taking any further great pains to stay in daily touch with events back home. Apart, of course, from keeping track of Crashgate; struggling to divine, from its twisted entrails, just what, if anything, lay in store for Celeste and me: how low should we lie? for how long? and where?

But if things worked out the way I hoped—and we weren't doing too badly so far—if the heat cooled off and we found a refuge, then even my daily newspaper fix wouldn't have to be more than just an every-other-day event and, as our luck grew, finally a mere weekly indulgence.

I fantasized long Saturday mornings with a weekend paper. Over several cups of cappuccino. On sun-filled terraces, overlooking the Mediterranean.

Or lazily turning the pages, sprawled astern on my new boat, rocking gently at an anchorage in a quiet bay . . . evenings swinging in a hammock, between a pair of palms, under the light of a storm lantern . . . and, on winter nights, during rare chills, staying warm inside smoky seaside saloons, where the ice and the bar dice click . . . until that news from back home becomes just a small voice, so remote and irrelevant, the facts pass straight through my brain, like so much chat freely exchanged between strangers on a plane, leaving not a trace.

Nothing will matter then.

We'll be safe. My concerns limited: boat, weather, the next day's charter . . . and, of course, Celeste. If Celeste is still with me.

Still with me. When, I wondered as we approached Rome, will she pack it all in? Start counting the years between us, grow restless, itching to bolt, to start on her own ambitions?

But in the meantime, all it was really boiling down to for us was . . .

. . . *when the hell would our pursuers grow weary, and give up their hunt?*

29

On reaching Rome, Celeste and I made sure we were among the first passengers off the aircraft.

No waiting for luggage; all our belongings were in the backpacks that we'd carried on board.

Our brand new passports worked just fine, and we cruised straight along the green line, through the unmanned nothing-to-declare customs door, and out into the arrivals hall.

Unstopped.

Italian officials are so charmingly tolerant of visitors, I was pleased to note, a refreshing change from any U.S. port of entry.

I grabbed a wire cart and piled our backpacks on it. But before we could head for a taxi, I had to book a hotel. I hadn't dared make reservations from the islands. When planning a permanent powder, your trail better peter out early.

"Someplace *bella*," I told the female clerk at the accommodations desk. "Tranquil, charming, not too expensive."

"And with great food," added Celeste.

The clerk eyed Celeste's confection: toe-to-throat Gucci from Charlotte Amalie's tax-free boutiques, topped by the classiest hairdo St. Thomas could concoct. Then she glanced at our humble back-packs, and shrugged. Strange Americans.

"No problem," said the clerk, "not so many tourists. Too chilly." She consulted her hotel list. "Honeymoon?"

"Is it obvious?" Celeste peered over her dark glasses at the clerk.

"You look so sleepy," the clerk explained.

"Think we smell of garlic?" I whispered to Celeste.

She giggled. "Won't matter in Italy."

"You like poetry?" said the clerk.

"What kind?" I asked, perplexed but charmed.

"Romantic, *molto romantico*," she replied. "Lord Byron Hotel, near the Borghese. *Che bella*. Not cheap, not expensive. *Mezzo, mezzo.*"

$ $ $

The small Lord Byron Hotel—that was indeed its real name—graced a quiet posh quarter, just northwest of the Villa Borghese and gardens, in the old Paoli district of Rome.

A palazzo of a place, it had a vaguely familiar look about it, but for exactly what class of clientele the rates were meant to be *mezzo* I could only wonder as we checked in. It was in a league with Muscade Bay.

"This place costs a fortune," I muttered to Celeste as we followed a porter up to our room.

"So what, we're loaded. It looks fantastic."

And it did, right out of a movie. All burnished woods, bouquets of fresh flowers, marble floors and oriental carpets, dark paintings and polished mirrors.

An expensive hush prevailed.

I resolved we'd be guests only long enough to find somewhere more reasonable, for a longer stay of who knew how long. My mind wasn't fully adjusted to being rich, and blowing a lot of dough on fancy hotels was never my idea of fun.

But some serious contemplation of our futures was in order, and what could be more conducive to calm reflection than a quiet stretch in this city of churches and ruined temples.

I was happy to be in Rome.

Our room at the Lord Byron was, as advertised, *molto romantico*, with a view over the trees and gardens of a row of neighboring villas, all painted in warm colors reflecting the pale midwinter sun. A far cry from our airshaft at the dusty Aïda. The site looked poetic enough to inspire the romantic Byron himself. And probably had: the quarter would have already been a few centuries old when that dashing revolutionary stayed in town.

"I approve," said Celeste of our accommodations. She glanced at herself in the mirror. "But not *that*," she said of the reflection. "My God, talk about shagged out honeymooner. Can't audition looking like this." She yawned. "Think I'll shower, get some rest."

Auditions. Show business. Movies. Celeste's ambitions scared the hell out of me.

"What about you?" she asked.

It was no time to argue. But I was too nervous to snooze. "Think I'll play tourist for a couple of hours."

"Okay, just don't forget."

"What?"

"To bring back some garlic. *Ciao, bello.*"

At the hotel desk, I picked up an admission ticket and guidebook for the nearby art galleries, and strolled over to the Borghese gardens, surprisingly green in spite of the season.

I ambled through the park and ended up at a building that the guidebook said had originally been Cardinal Borghese's personal casino, now a public *galleria*, filled with sculptures and paintings.

I wandered around the museum—Bernini. Botticelli. Caravaggio. Rubens. Titian. Veronese—until my head spun.

I needed a drink.

On the way back to the Lord Byron, I stopped at a news kiosk to pick up a copy of the *International Herald Tribune* and a few postcards. It wasn't until I paid and put the postcards in my pocket that I realized I didn't know who the hell I could safely send a card to any longer. That realization really cheered me up.

A large *aperitivo* was in order.

$ $ $

The Lord Byron had its own swank bar and Michelin two-star restaurant, *Relais le Jardin*. French name, Italian menu. The hotel garden outside the bar was small, but still green and lush as the Borghese park.

I entered the bar: a quiet, soothing place compared to most Roman establishments, as it boasted neither neon nor pinball. Rare hardwoods and long polished mirrors reflected sunlight from the garden.

I sat back and ordered a Campari and tonic, then scanned the restaurant's menu for that evening. The special was *trittico* followed by a *pollo al diavolo*. Devil's chicken.

Looked good.

Gulping my drink, I ordered a second, and opened the *Trib*.

Nothing grabbed me on the front page. But inside, about six column-inches—from the *Washington Post*—captured my attention.

Headline: "Crashgate."

The speaker of the House was calling for a special prosecutor—eighteenth, for this president's administration, almost a record—to investigate the Secretary of the Treasury's connections to Colombian cocaine. The secretary himself, it appeared, was now on the mend.

But still nowhere in the piece a mention of missing money.

Or of Celeste.

So the coast, as they say, looked clear, at least on the Washington front. I figured that if anyone in Our Nation's Capital had an inkling of four-four in cash changing hands in that wrecked limo, the tale would have surely leaked by now. It was too juicy by half.

Hence, our pursuers probably weren't the Feds. Not yet, anyway.

Relief seeped into my soul.

I was reaching for the second drink when, out of the corner of my eye, I caught sight of an unescorted woman entering the room.

Elegant, in a tailored beige tweed suit, she strode, with regal bearing, straight up to the bar. She was, at the very least, a known entity there, for the bartender was already pouring his guest a glass of champagne before she'd sat down or spoken a word.

She accepted the proffered glass with the air of a woman accustomed all her life to the swank and posh.

But when she began to exchange a few pleasantries in Italian with the bartender, her clear American accent made my blood freeze.

Her no-nonsense tones had a ring much too familiar.

And I lowered my paper to inspect her more closely.

No: this was not just a case of jet-lagged brain playing tricks. For when this queenly figure looked at her reflection in the mirror behind the bar, there was no confusing her at all with anyone imaginary.

And then I remembered why the Lord Byron had looked so vaguely familiar to me when we pulled up in the taxi.

I'd seen the place, just a few weeks before.

On a postcard.

And that elegant apparition at the bar was none other than Lydia Sands—Dad's last, her regal self—in the well-preserved flesh.

Mounted on throne. At the bar, Lord Byron Hotel. Paoli district, Rome.

30

To leave.

Or not to leave. To stay, and take it like a man, or flee for the sake of my life.

The question barely posed itself, when: *"Madre di Dio!"* Lydia exclaimed at her reflection. But she wasn't talking to herself. "What the devil are you doing here?"

She spun on her barstool.

"My God," she said, "the resemblance is amazing. You do look *so* like him. Taller, of course, a ton lighter. But no question, your father's son, all right. How'd you ever find me here? So thoughtful! Come, kiss kiss . . ."

Arms outstretched, violet eyes pleading, Lydia made kissing sounds in my direction. Me, whom she'd met but once, from Dad's funeral to the bar on Madison Avenue. Me, her long lost—whatever you call the son of your late lover.

And so, trancelike, obedient as a dog, I came as summoned.

We kissed, European style, one cheek, other cheek.

Lydia placed her hands on my shoulders and frowned slightly, those violet eyes fixing me squarely in their gaze. "Tell me, Dan, *how* . . . no, *where* is he now?"

"Not with me."

"Certainly not." She shivered slightly.

"Where he wanted to be," I said. "Dead Frog Cove, down about a hundred feet."

"Dead Frog? He asked for live fish."

"They're there," I said. "He's by a wreck. Very colorful. If you want to go down sometime, I'll—"

"Your word's fine. Colorful, yes, I'm sure. Someday I must, meanwhile . . . how *did* you find me?"

She had me there. I stalled. How could I tell her the truth? I was far too flustered to compose a good lie. "Have to get my drink," I said, turning toward the window table.

"That silly looking red thing?" Lydia wrinkled her nose. "Allow me." She raised a finger to the bartender.

"*Prego?*" An accommodating smile brightened the bartender's otherwise expressionless face. He'd surely overheard, and understood, our bizarre conversation, but pretended not to. Very European.

"*Per favore,*" said Lydia, "*ancora un champagne.*"

"*Si Signora. Molto grazie.*" The sudden bright smile again.

"Your Italian's impressive," I said to Lydia, stalling for time.

"So's his English," she answered in a low voice. "So let's sit at your table. We have a lot to talk about. Private talk."

The bartender brought my champagne over, and removed my disgraced, outclassed Campari.

"*Cin-cin,*" said Lydia, as we touched glasses. "So, tell me: how long have you been here?"

"Just arrived."

"Really? Don't you just love the Lord Byron?" She paused. "*That's* how you traced me, isn't it, my postcard. You look sunburned. Been to the beach at—"

"—came straight from the islands. Buried Dad a couple of days ago."

"Oh dear, if only I'd known," said Lydia, her face collapsing like a Roman ruin. "You make me feel so awful. How *can* you forgive me? No: you can't, it's unforgivable," she answered her own question, dabbing at her eyes with a cocktail napkin. "But nothing to be done. Too late."

"Yes, well, he's down there now. He's okay."

She sipped reflectively on her champagne. "And all this way, just to tell me. How sweet of you, your father'd be so proud. You must join us for dinner."

Us?

Her eyes now dry, Lydia perked up. "Flamed chicken tonight, Ernesto's favorite."

"Ernesto?" I said.

"*Si,* Ernesto. Ernesto Cardinale Tovini. I couldn't bear being a widow, in a manner of speaking, not forever, not Lydia Sands. After all, you know me. And I'm sure you'll love his *eminenza*, charming, cultured. His English is impeccable. London School of Economics. Brilliant financier."

"Eminenza?"

My Italian was less than rudimentary, but I could figure out enough to question an *eminenza* succeeding my father in Lydia's bed.

"Yes. *Cardinale*. On leave of absence, I suppose you could say."

"From church?"

"Well, sort of. They had some trouble at the Vatican bank, during his watch as director, so Ernesto had to resign. All a big misunderstanding, of course. Some rogue options trader, if that means anything to you. He didn't listen to Ernesto, and the young Jesuit know-it-all cost them a few hundred million."

"Lira?"

"Dollari. The Holy Father was not amused. He's quite miffed at the Jesuits these days."

"Who could blame him?"

"But poor Ernesto ended up with most of the blame. No throne of St. Peter for him now, I'm afraid."

"Too bad."

"And certainly not his fault. He advised them of sophisticated accounting practices that could make the loss immaterial. But they said they weren't looking for miracles, they just wanted their money back."

"I can understand that."

"Anyway, please, don't *let* me get started, but—a nice *but* this time—the Vatican's bad luck turned out to be my good fortune."

"How so?"

Lydia beamed. "They recently went long on the new Euros, and I stayed short on Ernesto's advice. Then Euros took a nosedive, just like magic, a *real* miracle. Even now, I swear I don't understand exactly what Ernesto did. But I absolutely cleaned up."

"I can see why you're grateful."

"And, of course, we do love each other. Never underestimate the power of love, although we can't actually live like man and wife. So no, he's no Roncalli, I must admit."

"Pardon?"

"Oh dear," said Lydia, "you do make me feel old. Roncalli before your time? Who'd ever guess . . . the yuppie generation missed him, didn't you, your generation X, Y, Z or whatever it is. Not to worry: Ernesto should be much more your type than any Roncalli."

The alchemy of living in the Eternal City, plus Lydia's natural talents, seemed to have turned her, in a matter of weeks, into an expert on ecclesiastical affairs. Her recent fiscal renaissance would explain her residing at the toney Lord Byron where, it developed, she was ensconced in their exclusive garden suite.

"Right over there." Lydia pointed across the interior garden to an arbor-covered portico. Beneath the bowers, French doors led to her suite.

"It's quite discreet," she said, in a low voice. "Ernesto hates parading through the lobby, if he can avoid it. This *is* Rome after all, so one has to maintain *una bella figura*."

"How'd you meet Ernesto?" By this point, I'd become quite curious again about Lydia's personal history. "That before, or after, my father died?"

"Ah, yes . . ." Lydia was trying hard to recollect. I became aware of her age. ". . . let me see . . . after, of course. Definitely after. So much has happened since. So much to tell you. . . ."

31

The sunlight was fading in the hotel garden.

I should have been exhausted, thoroughly jet-lagged. But sparked by champagne, and my curiosity now inflamed, I felt strangely energized.

"So you met Ernesto here in Italy?"

"Oh no, not at all," said Lydia. "I really knew very little about Italy before, nothing at all actually. Never been here. We met in the vestibule of Saint Patrick's Cathedral. In New York."

I raised my eyebrows.

She shrugged. "It was raining. But you know, I did think about becoming a Catholic once. Not because of your father naturally, he never minded, but because of the Kennedys."

I recalled my conversation with the bartender in the Madison Avenue saloon, and gingerly asked: "And how did they, I mean, what did they—"

"They were simply so enchanting, that's all. And I was so young then, so impressionable. But after two of them were shot, and then Teddy nearly drowned, I thought being a Catholic might be bad luck."

I blinked.

"Anyway, it was raining in Manhattan the day I met Ernesto, torrents positively *pissant* out of nowhere—typical New York weather, one extreme to the other. I was in midtown for the post-Christmas sales, and I'd have floated away just trying to reach Saks, so I nipped into Saint Pat's. Divinely ordained, I suppose. Ernesto came over and offered me the most beautiful linen handkerchief to dry my face. He was in civvies then, absolutely immaculate. *Che bella figura*. With the most gorgeous red silk tie, the same shade as those little scarlet beanies they wear. It was right after that unfortunate bank misunderstanding, and Ernesto was taking a busman's holiday in New York. The Federal Reserve wanted a word with him. Well, it stopped raining as quickly as it started, so there was no point staying indoors any longer. We strolled over to the Plaza for aperitifs in the Oak Bar. I hadn't been there in years. Your father and I always had tea uptown at the Lowell. It's such a disappointment now, the Plaza, just another dreadful tourist trap, I'm afraid. Ernesto, however, was anything but disappointing; charming, witty, urbane. So the awful surroundings didn't really matter, even if I was still in mourning, you understand, quite distraught, after being forced to sell the apartment on Fifth to Mr. Starace. For twenty cents on the dollar."

"What—"

"An offer I was *not* allowed to refuse. But Ernesto, sweet man, he raised my spirits. Right up to the heavens, you might say. Did the same for my investment portfolio, too. *Such* a clever man."

No doubt, and while I certainly wanted to learn more about Ernesto by this point, my curiosity spiked at the mention of Dad's palatial digs.

"And what," I inquired, in as nonchalant a tone as I could muster, "was the apartment worth?"

"Five, so I got one. Deposited directly in Geneva—all net, no tax. Nothing to sneeze at, I know—and I don't wish to sound ungrateful—still and all, one million is not five million."

"I'll say."

"Even if only one *is* enough to live on—modestly of course, for a couple of years—I've never really been overly wild about modesty. Life would have just gone on, drearily predictable, if Ernesto hadn't appeared like a vision in my life. But don't *let* me get started. Just thank God, I say, Ernesto's been such a help. I knew next to nothing about investing in markets before I met him."

Five.

Got one.

I got none.

Lydia's inheritance deposited in Geneva, no less, maybe even at the headquarters of the same Swiss bank as our limo loot.

But don't let *me* get started.

I struggled to maintain self-control. Champagne with Lydia

invariably seemed to end this way. She was concluding her revelation when I choked on my drink, and the hiccups struck.

"Try drinking from the far side of your glass," she advised. "That usually works."

I tried one sip that way and felt like an absolute fool.

"So what have you seen of Rome?" she asked.

"Pai-AINT-ings. Bor-GHE-hese."

"All those naked women?" Lydia smiled slyly. "Quite a collection, isn't it? But don't look so bashful. In this country, they say a filthy mind is a perpetual feast. That's exactly how Ernesto got the crook."

The shock of the unexpected worked, my hiccups cured.

"Crook?" I asked.

"Bishop's staff of office," Lydia answered coolly. She sipped her champagne.

"Actually it all started in the Borghese," she explained. "Great art can prove very hazardous for some, you realize."

"I'm not sure I understand—"

"*Alora*, this story goes back quite a few years ago now, when a poor impressionable young art student was spending months in the Borghese, simply months studying all those sumptuous nudes, and then he suddenly snapped, lost his mind completely. Quite dangerous for the suggestible, as I said."

"But what's that got to do—"

"Well, the poor boy went out on a rampage, raping and murdering plump young women all over Italy. But just plump ones, that was the criterion. You were damned if you were young and plump, like those Borghese nudes. Panic ensued. Women's magazines sold millions of copies touting crash diets. He would stalk his chosen victims on trains all around the country. That's where he did it, in the train john, while the train was moving fast, so no one could hear the victim's screams above the din. The '*rapido* john killer,' they called him. He was finally caught by a mob on the *rapido* between Roma Centrale and Genoa, dragged off, put in a sack with stones, and thrown over the cliffs at Cinque Terrae, to drown in the sea. An elderly woman, who sold smuggled cigarettes in the Piazza Navona for the Franciscans, was praying for his salvation, in the little Roman church of Domine Quo Vadis—the one where they keep Christ's footprints, embedded in a slab of marble . . . I don't know enough about theology to see the connection there—"

"Neither do I."

"—but this old woman was praying for the *rapido* john killer's soul, when she claimed she saw a vision of the Virgin Mary, who said to her: 'And the violated shall be whole.' Which the old woman was certain meant the *rapido* john killer had repented while in that sack with the stones, before he hit the water of course, and so his soul was saved. Imagine! Ernesto was still a young monsignor then, attached to an almost bankrupt diocese down south, in their accounts department, when he heard the story . . . and, appreciative as he is of the overwhelming power of art and the eternal possibility of redemption, Ernesto immediately realized that what the vision said was revelatory proof . . . of the killer's grief, not for himself, but for his victims. Isn't that *such* a lovely thought?"

"Amazing."

"So Ernesto began preaching this on Sundays. And a following for 'the good rapist' sprang up all over the *Mezzogiorno*. Ernesto had retrieved the sack, you see, and put it on display in the diocese. Hordes of pilgrims began to flock there every year on St. Valentine's Day, when a face miraculously appears on the sack shedding tears of real blood. *And the violated shall be whole*. Any defiled girl seeing those tears of blood is said to have her virginity restored. A miracle that's really worth something in southern Italy, I can guarantee you. There are already calls for 'the good rapist's beatification. The pilgrims rescued diocesan finances, in spades, so Ernesto was promoted to bishop. And to think, it all started in the Borghese art galleries. Just goes to show, I suppose. . . ."

"Show what?"

Lydia shrugged her eyebrows. "Power of art, I guess."

"That's what makes people believe all that?"

"Oh, that? Quite honestly, I've always believed that for people who *really* believe, no explanation is needed. And for those who don't believe, no explanation's ever good enough."

"And you," I said, "do you believe?"

"Me? Guess I'm an atheist. A person with no invisible means of support. Everything I ever need is, as you can see, always highly tangible, *very* much of this world." She drained her glass. "Another? Hours until dinner, everyone eats late here. You'll have to get used to that, too."

"Why not?" I said. "Let's."

It struck me, witnessing Lydia's performance, that in a couple of decades or so, this could be Celeste, in her own personal version of the happily ever after.

And me?

I felt numb: how would I end up?

32

Two glasses of champagne appeared, unsummoned.

The bartender seemed well acquainted with Lydia's routines.

"So, if it hadn't been for Ernesto," Lydia continued, "I'm not sure you'd have ever found me."

"Probably not," I replied, reluctant to reveal what actually brought me to Rome.

"Men," she sighed, generally. "And what about you? Sleeping with anyone lately? Want to meet some Italians, Ernesto and I can—"

"Thanks, but . . ." Lydia had a most unnerving way with questions. ". . . actually, I'm here with someone."

"Really?" Her face lit up like a Roman candle. "How absolutely delightful! Brought someone all this way, just to meet me?"

"Sure."

"I'm deeply touched, Dan, truly I am. Now that I know your father's at peace—for which I'm so grateful, I can't even begin to tell you, but don't *let* me get started—I'm absolutely dying to meet your lady friend. Excuse me: woman friend. Is a woman, I trust? I can be awfully old-fashioned, so easy here in Europe, where habits die hard. Now, tell me *all* about her. No: don't. Let her tell me. We'll all have dinner together tonight, like a family foursome. I so regret never really having a family of my own. Hasn't always been easy, you know. But then you do know, don't you, I've already told you all about me once before, haven't I? I'm afraid I don't always paint the prettiest of pictures . . ."

"But, Lydia, we all have to do what we can," I said, "to survive. So of course I understand."

Boy, did I just.

"Know what I'd really like?" said Lydia. "What I'd like really most of all?" She was reaching across the table to hold my hand, locking onto me with those vital eyes. ". . . is for you to believe and trust me. And Ernesto, too, of course. That's the one way I can truly repay your father for all he did."

Repay. Yes, that idea certainly thrilled me.

Listening to Lydia hold forth in the Lord Byron bar—on Ernesto's financial genius—I'd begun to marvel at this sudden turn of luck, envisioning Celeste's and my little nest eggs flowering under the pastoral ministrations of Lydia's financier cardinal. Here was a man who seemed to know what he was doing.

Nothing miraculous, mind you.

No tears of blood for us. Just some sober bankerly advice.

"Lydia, you don't have to feel you owe me anything," I demurred, ever so innocently. "I believe you. And of course I trust you. In fact, now that you mention it, about repaying and so forth, Celeste and I have put together a little nest egg, and I'd like to feel we could turn to you, and maybe Ernesto, for some advice—"

"Celeste!" Lydia suddenly exclaimed. "What a heavenly name—that's exactly what it means, you know. Heaven."

"Appropriate."

"Ernesto will be over the moon, absolutely over the moon. Of course, you can turn to us, you *must* turn to us. Trust us."

"Thank you."

"Ernesto can be so helpful, an absolute saint of a man, in some ways, even if he's unlikely to be one of the *papabili* after what happened at the bank."

"Unfortunate, that."

"Quite. And you can think whatever you wish about gullible pilgrims, and all those bloody tears, but men like Ernesto are rare, I tell you, incredibly rare. They rise above simple honesty, the way a great general must sacrifice an army to conquer a nation. Look at that other great Roman, look at Julius Caesar!"

"Caesar?"

"Caesar. Greatness like that is incompatible with petty scruples. Greatness like that is an art all its own. Trust us, Dan, no one said it better than Shakespeare himself. About Julius. '. . . *why man, he doth bestride the narrow world like a Colossus!*' Or something apt like that. But you do get my meaning."

I now concluded Lydia was thoroughly sincere. Misguided.

Perhaps even insane. And highly talented at elevating half-truths into universal laws.

As if on cue, at that very moment, a darkly elegant figure appeared, slipping through the open French doors of Lydia's suite and into the garden.

He wore a beautifully cut, gray—nearly black—flannel suit, a luminously white shirt, with lots of high custom collar, and a scarlet silk tie, the same princely red that I thought I glimpsed flashing from his socks as he walked over the moss-covered paving stones.

I waited with growing curiosity and excitement to meet his *eminenza*, Ernesto Cardinale Tovini: investment genius, irresistible preacher, churchly colossus on leave of absence. Not many men receive such a loving and indulgent introduction from a woman, particularly not from a woman of Lydia's wide experience.

His eminence was as aristocratic in his bearing as I expected, with the lean physique and erect posture of a cavalry captain. But he was so short that, in a dark room, he could probably pass for an adolescent boy. This may, of course, have only augmented his attractions to women beyond a certain age. A giant among men he may well have been. But it wasn't thanks to his physical stature. Ernesto's colossal qualities, so it seemed, lay well concealed.

"That him now?" I asked.

Lydia turned. "Who else?" Her voice grew warm, her eyes glowed. "Think I keep strangers in my bedroom?" She laughed. "No, Ernesto feels perfectly at home in the Lord Byron. It used to be a convent."

Ernesto entered the bar, and Lydia introduced me. He held out his hand, and revealed an enormous jeweled ring, symbol of his professional status. I wasn't sure if I was expected to shake his hand or kiss the ring.

He had soft almond-brown eyes, enlivened with a steady twinkle. You could read into those eyes whatever you liked. If Lydia read love and good counsel, I thought more along the lines of wily and amused. I'd never met a cardinal before, and his *eminenza* didn't remind me at all of any banker I'd ever known, not even the unctuous Professor Doctor Fuchs of Tortola and the Alps. But then I'd never encountered a banker who was also a cardinal, absent on leave or otherwise.

"What a surprise," said Ernesto, "and what a pleasure to meet you at last." He spoke cultivated English with scarcely a trace of accent. "Lydia speaks so warmly of you, and of your late father. Enjoying my country?"

"Just arrived," I said. "Haven't seen much yet."

"Then we'll have to show you some highlights." A waiter placed a glass of champagne before him. "*Salute*! I love Rome. Lived here all my life, except for studies in London, and a few assignments in the south. Italy will grow on you, you'll see. You must visit the Borghese, it's just nearby. That today's paper you have there?" Ernesto nodded at the *Herald Tribune* by my elbow. "May I? Haven't seen yesterday's closings yet. Usually read the *Financial Times* every morning, but missed it today. Follow any favorites?"

"Nothing special," I lied. "Usual blue chips." I could just about tell a blue chip from a potato chip, but I wasn't about to launch into a discussion of my advanced number theory for winning lotteries.

"I'm a Dow dogs man, myself," said Ernesto, displaying his skill with the universal language of money. He opened the paper and turned to the stock listings. "Fat and slow, ripe for the kill, know what I mean?"

Hadn't a clue: mere terms of art, I concluded. I found myself thinking only of those fat Borghese nudes, and the *rapido* john killer's poor victims, too ripe and slow to get away, when my eye was attracted by a small photo on the back page of the paper Ernesto was holding.

The picture was down in the "People" section, a daily column relegated to the tail end of the *Trib*, a reservoir of gossipy snippets about the great and infamous.

The photo so startled me, I forgot myself and reached across the table to steady the paper, so I could examine it more closely.

A mistake.

For now not only could I see the picture better, but both Ernesto and Lydia were aware of my intense interest in its subject.

A young woman, stepping from a limo, so it seemed. Her head was down, her face only partly visible in profile. A photo most likely taken with another subject in mind, and this beautiful young woman caught by chance in the frame.

And now she herself was the focus of interest.

"Crashgate Socialite Sought," read the caption, and went on to quote the upcoming issue of *TIME* magazine, reporting this months-old picture as a rare sighting of "that mystery woman about town, lately rumored to have been in the recent limousine crash with . . ."

Well, I didn't have to read the rest.

Her name was there, too. Spelled incorrectly—Trabor instead of Tranor—but close enough.

Socialite sought.

"Friend of yours?" asked Lydia.

The good Lord giveth, I thought, nodding slowly, *and the good Lord taketh away.*

We're goners.

Trapped prey.

Toast.

33

I began to shake violently.

Cardiac arrest imminent, I was sure.

Now it's a whole new ballgame: The Media. The bloodthirsty, sex-hungry, maniacal media. With a worldwide, round-the-clock, insatiable appetite for scandal.

And hot on our trail.

Plus the Cali caballeros, or whoever they were.

"May I?" said Lydia, taking the paper. She eyed the photo. Scanned the caption. "Oh, her. Saw it before. Bit of a jam, poor kid. Without my reading glasses, can't make out her name."

Lydia squinted at Celeste's photo.

". . . looks like she might be quite pretty, too, although hard to tell from this picture. Lady does get around, I'd say. Were you close?"

I was speechless.

"Looks like you still can't get over her."

"Lydia, you might say . . ." My options, such as they were, appeared limited. ". . . yes, I think you could say I just can't get over her."

And so, I proceeded to preempt the situation—with some trepidation, and much doubt, but figuring they'd find out soon enough anyway—ever so cautiously explaining our predicament to Lydia and Ernesto.

Just the basics, of course.

Certainly not the whole story. I stayed highly selective on certain specifics.

Like how much money, exactly.

I dwelt on the ransacked apartments.

Drew a picture of Celeste's and brother Bill's disadvantaged past. Her victimization by evil elements in New Orleans and New York.

Recounted our close-call escape together from the city. And Dad's burial at sea.

Even touched lightly on Celeste's entertainment sector career, the particulars of which, by necessity, still remained foggy even to me.

I hinted at uncertain motives behind our troubles—but most likely jealousy, with undertones of revenge and sadism, of course—and then embroidered crimes of extortion and explosive violence into the lurid backstory.

So that by the time I was finishing my tale, Lydia and Ernesto were clucking sympathetically, shaking their heads, and wiping their eyes. But they were far too discreet—because too experienced, no doubt—to probe for further details.

"So now you know . . ." I was saying to wrap it all up, when Celeste entered the bar. ". . . the other reason we came here."

There was no time to warn Celeste.

"She know yet?" said Lydia, nodding at the paper. I shook my head. "Don't worry," she added quickly. "We're here to help."

But seldom has a more loaded promise ever been vowed.

$ $ $

Yet that evening, wouldn't you know, but help they did.

My three dinner companions hit it off like a family reunited. (Without a peep from anyone about a wrecked limo, cocaine mobsters, or bought politicians.) You'd have thought Celeste was their own daughter, the way Lydia and Ernesto carried on over her, their only child just returned for vacation after her first year at college.

His *eminenza* was positively fatherly.

"You must allow me to escort you through Rome's splendors. I know secret sights tourists never get to. But I can slip you in."

"And," said Lydia, "I know all the best shops in town. Can save you days, Celeste."

My young beauty was, in turn, grateful, charmed, and charming. At one point, Celeste even asked (ingenuously or not, I couldn't tell) about chariot races, further enchanting and encouraging Lydia and Ernesto. Her love for *Ben-Hur* proved inspirational.

"I, too, was once moved," said Lydia, nostalgia dimming the violet vitality of her eyes. "Moved by history. I was so young. *Lady of Fatima. Song of Bernadette. The Robe* . . . I cried, quite literally, every time I saw them."

"Ah, the movies." Ernesto nodded, his smile bestowing a warm indulgence on us, his small congregation. "I think our lives may be formed more by movies and by television than by anything else, don't you? Maybe even more than by other people."

"I love movies," said Celeste.

"Who doesn't? Movies and television teach us so much about so many things. Love, for example, if we're ever lucky enough to fall in love—" The amused twinkle in his eyes grew stronger. "—it's often because we're conditioned by what we've seen, don't you agree? And if we're not lucky, and we don't fall in love . . ." He shrugged. ". . . maybe it's just because we don't see the right movies. Or TV shows."

"What a beautiful thought," said Celeste.

"So you understand my meaning?"

"Oh, exactly."

Notwithstanding those sly eyes, Ernesto's voice remained so reassuring, with its smooth rumble of authority, so sweet in its tone of reasonableness, I could just picture his *eminenza* moving hordes of pilgrims in any direction he chose, grinning to himself the whole while.

But for all Ernesto's soothing tones, by the time our little dinner party had drifted back to the bar, for espresso and *disgestivo*, my anxieties were beginning to reappear like a case of heartburn, stubbornly resistant to Ernesto's antacids, however sweet and reasonable.

Celeste had to learn, sooner or later, about the latest pickle we were in, this media debut of hers, and now was as good a time as any, surrounded, such as we were, by family.

I produced the *Herald Tribune* from my jacket pocket and handed it to her, the paper folded down to her photo on the back page. I had a short speech all prepared for this moment.

Celeste glanced at the paper, just long enough to absorb the gist. Then: "Sooner or later, I guess it had to happen."

Cool as a clam.

Her sangfroid put me to shame. There's a lot to be said for growing up the way the beautiful Celeste did. Prepared you for life's harder knocks better than any New England prep school or Great Blue Mother Yale.

She tossed the paper on the table. "Too bad it's a lousy picture."

"Maybe it's not *too* bad," I said.

"Just don't panic." She sounded sweeter than reason. "Know what they say in show business, no such thing as *bad* publicity."

Again, a groaning in my guts.

"And you know," she continued, on a philosophical note, "I've been thinking a lot, since we got here. I'll bet we can come to terms with whoever's after us. Eventually. We just need more time. Nobody knows we're here. Not yet anyway. Sorry to bore you." She turned to Lydia and Ernesto. "We got our little problems, nothing very serious."

"I've already explained to them," I said, "most of the essentials."

"And we're here to help," said Lydia, reaching across the table to hold our hands. "Think of us, please, as family."

"Yes, as family," said Ernesto, his soft brown eyes now moist with emotion, his voice choked. "And as a priest, I do, of course, accept people's frailties. While as a European—a Roman especially—I'm too tired to expend energy on matters I can't possibly change. So now looking at your current predicament, in which I can see love has worked so well to bring you together—just like in the movies—if I were you two, I wouldn't panic unreasonably. You have each other. And, of course, you can always count on us."

"Thank you, Ernesto, and Dan and I are really, really grateful."

"I feel like you're the son and daughter I never had. You make me want to be a simple pastor all over again. I'd be so honored to help. Blessed even. *Grazie, molto grazie.*" He raised his glass of *grappa* to us; candlelight refracted through the jewels on his big ring. "So think of us, please, as your virtual parents."

A half hour later, Celeste and I were in bed.

Jet lag. Alcohol. Sheer fear had numbed my mind to all thought. Several times during the night, I awoke, haunted by angst-driven dreams, and I remembered my resolution on the plane coming over.

How, once safely in Europe, I would restrict myself to a simple life. Of few complications.

Some hope.

34

For the next few days, our lives often went separate ways. Lydia and Ernesto took over the Roman education of Celeste, while I prowled bookshops, hunting for sailing charts and maps of the Mediterranean basin and its ports: cradle of civilization, or so I'd been taught.

At night we reunited for yet another magnificent dinner, and afterwards the beautiful Celeste and I would ascend to our room, for a round of garlic and then sleep.

Anxiety stayed at bay, barely.

We went on pretending we were safe. That no one would ever guess. But I had no idea what our real margin of safety was. How much lead time we had. So we imagined we had at least a few weeks of catching our breaths, seeing the sights, making plans, since—being newly rich—this was anyway all somehow rightfully ours to enjoy. I'd hoped to begin my book and map research enraptured. Hunting for a permanent refuge promised a welcome, almost scholarly diversion from the merely mundane concerns of murder and larceny.

But now the combo of snooping journalists *and* determined pursuers restored urgency to finding that sanctuary.

And so I resolved that we would, after two weeks max, be saying farewell to Lydia, Ernesto, and Rome.

And take off for that remote hideaway of my dreams, wherever it was.

The Adriatic initially tempted me as a place to settle down quietly into a boat charter business.

Split. Or Dubrovnik, perhaps. Both were ancient Roman and Venetian towns, and they certainly glowed golden in guidebook photographs. Favorites for decades, I learned, with Germans and Austrians, and where mooring and outfitting costs were less than half what I was accustomed to in the Caribbean. Cheap living along those Balkan shores had its sound reasons, of course, the threat of war among the Yugoslavs being always a constant.

The other side of the Adriatic, where Italian ports faced inundation with refugees from Balkan wars, was equally unappealing. I already had enough on my mind as it was.

And so maybe the Greek islands?

But similar life-and-death scrutinies applied there as well. Our allies, the Greeks and Turks—armed to the teeth, and feeling forever deprived and aggrieved—hadn't had a really good go at each other in much too long.

History: Europeans are forever lecturing Americans: *You know nothing about history.*

When what they really mean, I was discovering as I attempted to plan my new life in the Old World, is that Europeans always have perfectly good reasons to hate and kill each other, reasons given them by a history that fresh-faced, corn-fed, simpleminded Yanks are simply too untutored to grasp.

I turned my focus to the coasts of Spain and France and the islands in between.

Forget Corsica, where terror bombings are as frequent as soccer matches.

Sardinia maybe—until I learned that kidnapping was its major industry.

So perhaps the Balearics, famed for tourism, and not much else as far as my research revealed. Palma de Mallorca loomed as a likely prospect for further exploration.

But how amenable to all these plans would Celeste be?

We had so little time in Rome, between excursions with Lydia and Ernesto, and long meals, then bouts of garlic and sleep. The present was far too diverting to bore her with the future.

So I thought I'd wait a few days before lowering the boom.

While I continued to anguish: how long *would* it last?

Just how soon before we would reach the point, where we had to go our truly separate ways. The months, maybe the years, adding up. My garlic losing its strength for her. And her thoughts turning to livelier elsewheres?

145

Not to mention, I told myself, that was *her* picture in the newspaper, not mine.

Celeste was the far more obvious target: my chilly observation.

So maybe, just maybe—the cowardly thought wormed its way into my consciousness—I'd actually be better off. With the beautiful Celeste gone from my life, rather sooner than later.

A realistic, if caddish, conclusion for which I would soon feel thoroughly ashamed.

$ $ $

After dinner one evening, Celeste and I went out for a stroll, tipsily wandering the charming backstreets.

"There's someplace I want to show you," she said. "It's just down this alley. Ernesto took us here."

Someplace, to my surprise, was an ancient chapel, pinched into a corner between a pair of gracefully sagging apartment buildings.

Inside the chapel were two narrow rows of kneelers, a small altar with a medieval crucifix suspended above it on chains, and an even smaller side altar topped by a statue of the Virgin, a wormhole-pocked, wooden image bearing only the faintest traces of color. An odor of burning candles dominated the gloom, the lights fluttering like spirits in flight.

We were the only visitors.

Celeste led me to the side altar, and she knelt before the Virgin. From her purse, she produced a rosary. "Ernesto gave me this. Showed me how to use it. If I got it right, these few big beads are for your own special wishes. And on all the little beads you pray for other people. Isn't it nice?"

To my unpracticed mind, this instruction didn't ring as quite fully compliant with accepted procedure, but in spirit sounded more or less substantively correct. The big beads on Celeste's rosary were twenty-two carat gold, she told me, the small were solid silver.

"Ever use one?"

"No," I said. "I think I remember my mother had a rosary, but that was a long time ago. Certainly never saw my father use one."

"First time I'm using it."

Celeste's lips moved as she began whispering her prayers, the scent of our dinner's wine still strong on her breath.

"Please, God, and please, Mary, and please, sweet Jesus, please take care of little Jasper wherever he is. And please don't let Madam Mad go picking on people anymore, it's no good for her or them. And if Ida May's still alive, please remember her. And Jasper's mamma, too, Arabella, don't forget her. And—here's a big bead—please, please help me make it someday, you know what I mean, after everything's safe again. And please do take extra good care of my brother Bill, and Dan, too, they're both so sweet. And, of course, remember my mother. And Ernesto and Lydia, they may seem strange, but they're good people. Wish us luck, please . . ."

I was entranced, as her list of people went on and on, her many pleas for their sakes, and hers, as touching and as fervent as the candles' tiny flames.

She turned to me. "Aren't you praying, too?"

"Yes."

"I don't hear you."

"I'm praying for you, Celeste. That all your wishes come true."

"Thanks. You *are* sweet, exactly like I just said to them. And now don't forget to pray for *your* mother, too. And especially your father, I think he needs it. All those poor souls wandering around alone out there, gives me the shivers. Wandering around like my father, for sure. Yes, my father, bless him too. . . ."

35

My first inkling of how some of Celeste's fervent wishes might be granted came after we'd been in Rome about a week.

Lydia, Celeste, and Ernesto were returning from a shopping spree, arms laden with gaily beribboned packages.

I met them in the bar of the Lord Byron.

The extravagance of their purchases made it obvious Celeste had dipped into our cache of flight tickets. The mounting costs of our stay at the Lord Byron were making me nervous enough about our finances. So this splurge failed to cheer me.

Lydia motioned to the bartender for the usual. A bottle of champagne appeared. Celeste snuggled up to me.

"Smile," she said, "we got gifts for you, too. So don't look so glum. I got good news."

"Can always use some."

Lydia and Ernesto looked on like proud parents. All seemed eager to give me the glad tidings.

"Just made our first business investment," said Celeste, a chirp in her voice. "First one, if you don't count my fling with Bill's shrimp boat."

"You mean you cashed tickets?"

"Put them to good use."

"For what?" I snapped at her, the bile of fear rising in my throat.

"Daniel," said Lydia, "don't be so rough. It's good news, not bad. Ernesto is advising us very well."

I held my breath, all ears, and turned to Ernesto, who was smiling like some inscrutable mandarin. Something sober, a little bankerly advice was what I'd hoped for.

Instead, he said: "Venezuelan bolivars."

And not a word more, as though that were enough to put all doubts to rest.

"What about them?"

"Silly boy," said Celeste. "We went long. Don't you see? Didn't you read today's *FT*?"

What I could see was that, under her new tutelage, Celeste's reading habits had expanded dramatically. The *Financial Times* was making her an expert in currency trading.

Ernesto explained: "I was talking just the other day with our papal nuncio in Caracas, and he told me there'd be a military coup, since their socialist president was dying of cirrhosis of the liver. An alcoholic. Everyone else was shorting the bolivar, because the Nigerians and the Saudis are breaking OPEC quotas, overproducing oil, and Venezuela is totally dependent on oil money—if you don't count dirty business. Falling oil prices means falling Venezuelan bolivar. So, of course, the market shorts the bolivar: plain common sense. But, I reasoned, just as soon as the socialist dies, and the military takes over, there'll be a quick resurgence—however unreasonable and emotional—in international investor confidence, that should give the bolivar an unexpected boost, albeit shortlived. So, go long was my advice. And then, day of destiny, realities converged last night: the president died eleven o'clock, Rome time, and the military did indeed take over. Markets opened in London this morning . . . with a big jump in the Venezuelan bolivar."

World-bestriding colossus, indeed.

"How much?" I asked.

"We invested a couple of hundred thousand," said Celeste, "just the other day."

"We did?"

"Uh-uh." She nodded, proudly. "And it all moved so fast, we were able to cash out our options this afternoon for eight-fifty. Net-net."

"We made *that* much?" I said.

"Clear," said Ernesto. "After commissions, of course." Part of which, I assumed, went for his sage advice. "And naturally no tax," he added, cheerily. "We did it *all* through your company in Lichtenstein. I congratulate you on your foresight. Nothing to be upset about, getting rich. Wealth in pagan Rome, back in the old days, was necessarily something cruel, but not any more. To get rich today is certainly no sin."

"Okay, great." I swallowed hard. "But, please, not again, not without first letting me in on what you get up to. Now, may I have *my* share, so I can settle our bill here, and start looking for someplace more in line with our situation—"

"It's not quite that simple," said Lydia.

"Well, we have the money," I said. "Or we don't . . . don't we?"

"Have some champagne," said Lydia, topping up my glass. "We all have to learn to trust each other, certainly in matters of investments."

A sharp pain shot through my head. "While we're on the topic, are there some other 'investments' I ought to know about?"

Celeste rubbed her jawbone where it was once swollen, her usual Do Not Enter sign.

Lydia lifted a finger for the waiter to bring a second round of champagne. The first bottle was empty.

Lydia and Celeste had apparently bonded like two bars of molten steel. I shuddered to think of their strength together as one cold hardened beam, the devastation they might wreak as a team.

To steady my nerves for the next revelation, I was gulping champagne, when the clerk from reception stuck his head into the bar and motioned to me to come over.

At first I thought he might be wanting a healthy installment on our astronomically mounting bill. Our windfall on the bolivar was about to come in handy.

But no.

"Courier letter, sir," the clerk whispered to me, as I stepped out into the lobby with him. "Just arrived, for you and your wife."

He handed me an envelope that was, in fact, addressed only to Celeste.

From Amanda Wolfe, Gramercy Park Square, New York, N.Y.

I grew faint.

Wolfie?

Celeste's surrogate mother in New York. Agent. Madam. Seer. That farewell encounter I'd so narrowly talked Celeste out of back at the Aïda.

My fear and self-pity now linked arms like a couple of sociopaths without a keeper, and propelled me straight into a chair in the lobby.

My stomach was in turmoil.

As this was now clearly a matter of life and death, certainly to me, I had no trouble overcoming any chivalrous hesitancy about opening a lady's private mail.

Thanks for the postcard, began the message on Amanda Wolfe's classy linen letterhead.

So.

That was it.

That's how Wolfie found us: Celeste, my beautiful traitor, went ahead and blabbed.

> Then: *Helluva time finding your hotel, kiddo, but I got what looks like THE alltime break for you. PUSH? You won't believe! This is it, the career break everyone's always looking for. After I saw your pic in TIME (not a very good one), figured I owed you, and got through to an old client at Vanity Fair—Eddie Schirmer, remember Eddie? Eddie the mouth? Guy could go for hours. Anyway, Ed's way up there now & can offer high five figures + four-page story guarantee with FULL PAGE pic! And maybe— just maybe—ya sittin' down, kiddo? The COVER! My comm, just the usual 15%. But VF wants exclusive, honey, you can't go yakkng to anyone else, and they're willing to go to Europe for the shoot—beat that! (I haven't told them exactly where you are, yet—it gets out, exclusive dead.) They'll book a photographer who usually works with Armani. If he's good enough for Gior- gio, hon, GRAB THIS OP! But you have to make up your own mind. Just lemme know soon, I can't keep this secret forever.*
>
> Ciao, bella!
Wolfie
Encl.

> *PS VF falls thru, maybe get you People, ok?*

The attached letter was from Edward J. Schirmer, a senior editor at *Vanity Fair* editorial offices in New York.

> *Dear Ms. Tranor*, it began, *We'd have preferred to call you di- rectly about such a matter, instead of going through your agent*

like this, and I've tried to find your whereabouts and number, but without success. As you've no doubt heard by now, an explosive story is heating up about your involvement with the three men in a limousine crash a few weeks ago on the East River Drive. We're now trying to package the most rounded, most informative and fairest piece possible (perhaps even an instant paperback) about this whole remarkable affair. The public has a right to know, which we recognize, and we're looking for people who know, or rather knew, these three gentlemen as a team, you might say, and you appear to be well situated to share some very interesting memories of them together. Our photo editors are particularly looking for pictures of them with you, to help illustrate the article(s), and possible book, for which we are prepared to enter into further negotiations, should you be in possession of such photos. We, of course, agree with all your agent's conditions for photographing you as and where you are now. We have reason to believe you will find these conditions equally acceptable.

We have all been caught off guard by the shock of this story, and we appreciate that the first human impulse is to be defensive and protective. That's how I felt about it, too, for you, when your agent first contacted me. Then I thought some more, and realized that if the stories are to be accurate, they need your side of it also. If they are to present a fuller picture of all the people, and especially of the poor victims—not to mention you yourself and the possible impact on your dreams and plans— then we need the help of people who have been caught up in this vortex and have the facts and background material.

So please, think a little about this, Ms. Tranor. We would like very much to hear from you as soon as possible. Thank you . . .

. . . etc.

There was a PPS scribbled by Wolfie on the bottom.

My old nose tells me you know lots, kiddo, and there may be more than a book in it—MOVIE, too! Hope you're scoring over there. Knowing you, bet you are! But nothing lasts forever, hon, *remember that. So what I can offer you, on top of this op, is 20% equity in the production company I'm forming, to make sure this story gets developed in every possible way it deserves. We're talking TRUTH, not make-believe fiction. Sorry, can't offer up-front $$, but you know how things are. I've done some thorough research & forecasting on this with the leaves—prospects look FABULOUS! Love & XOXO, Wolfie.*

And that was it.

Cat right out of the bag.

Suspicions confirmed, insecurities reinforced. Everyone, but everyone, had big plans.

And all of them insane.

If there were any question remaining as to the margin of safety we now enjoyed in our little Roman hideaway, Celeste—with her thoughtless postcard to Wolfie—had blown away all doubt.

And I was now certain we had no choice left.

We had to get the hell out of Rome.

The very next day.

36

Later, up in our room.

"Understand you got a thing about writing postcards, Celeste."
She looked puzzled, until I added: "Amanda Wolfe."

"What about her?"

I produced the news from Wolfie.

Celeste sat down on the bed and skimmed the letter's contents.
At one point, she laughed: "Eddie *Schirmer*? God, I'd almost forgot-
ten that guy . . . but Wolfie's right, Eddie had a helluva mouth.
Clearly doesn't remember me."

"Do you mind?" I asked, but I really didn't know what I meant. I
think I was expecting some expression of remorse. But, unlike most
of us, Celeste was undaunted by guilt. In her view, what's done is
done. Me and my insecurities? Unreasonable. The beautiful Celeste
was a woman of few doubts: only the moment mattered.

Then: "Wolfie still barking up that *movie* tree? She's serious,
should come to Rome, work with me here. But she's got a point,
though: I ought to be thrilled. Who wouldn't? Cover of *Vanity Fair*?
But don't worry, Dan, I don't want to die, least not yet."

"Relieved to hear it. We're getting the hell out of here. Tomorrow."

Her face sagged. "I understand. And I'm sorry, honey, I'm thinking a lot straighter now. I swear, never in a million years did I ever figure, just from a lousy postcard, Wolfie could track us down here. I
mean, you kidding: Rome, *Italy*? Ain't Rome City, honey, Deep
Bayou Parish, Louisiana. Got to hand it to her though, Wolfie's one
determined woman, she sets her mind to something."

"Some mind."

"Okay, Dan, I'm sorry—bigtime screw-up. You're right. I'm
wrong. Had to show off, had to let Wolfie know I'm on a roll."

"Anybody *else*?"

"My brother, Bill. But I told him to write back care of *poste restante*. Forget it now. And as for getting a movie job, under *any* name, we'll forget about that, too, for a while."

"That's a relief. For a while."

"Just don't get me wrong, Dan, I don't mean I don't want rich and famous *some*day. That's still on *my* agenda. Only right now, you're right. We're getting richer than I ever figured, and famous can just wait. Least ways till our situation simmers down, and we can go off on our own. Maybe I'm crazy, but I'm not dumb, darling. Not ready for the angels, not yet anyway. Forgive me? C'mon, Mister O, what do you say . . ."

"Let's get some sleep. Got a lot to do tomorrow."

Again Celeste displayed, to my amazed eyes, a certain grace under pressure that only humbled me. I couldn't expect her to say anything more than the truth—which certainly did not include *our affair will last forever . . . don't you worry . . . one day we'll become just like other folks, settle down in a house with kids.*

Forget that.

But even if she had promised me all of it, of course I still wouldn't have believed her.

I might have liked, at that tense point, to have heard something more soothing, something that meshed more with the outlines of my own escapist dreams. But Celeste confined her brand of make-believe to her peculiar vision of success, which, in its way, was perhaps as narrowly conceived, and as ultimately selfish and lonely, as my charter boat fantasy.

Nevertheless, her cold-blooded premise—that one day our relations had to end, that eventually we'd go our separate ways—made me even more miserable.

Forget that I had recently entertained the very same thought.

I didn't say anything until we were in bed, side by side, both staring up at the ceiling. Then: "Know what this means, don't you?"

"Can just guess . . ." she sighed. ". . . where to next?"

"Exactly. Where to. Wolfie found us here, anyone can. They'll be after us sooner than I figured. Whoever's money it is—or whoever thinks it's theirs—won't take *them* long. Soon as Wolfie blabs to *Vanity Fair*—and she will—the whole world finds out. So hate to hit panic buttons, but you're right, Celeste, we have to find someplace else."

"Know what?"

"What?" I said.

"I hate Amanda Wolfe." Celeste reached over and stroked my arm. "So where do you think?" she asked softly.

"Someplace with boats. Maybe Palma."

"Where's that?"

"Mallorca."

"Which is?"

"An island. In the Mediterranean."

"Tell me all about it," she said, "tomorrow. I'll be packed."

And she reached over to pull me to her, and we made love for the last time in Rome.

After, she whispered: "Know what?"

"What?"

"I don't think I've ever made love to the same man as many times as I have with you, you add it all up. And I don't know if I ever will again. Somehow, no matter what happens, I kind of doubt it."

That made me feel happy, kind of. Even if I knew she was only playing the same game of make-believe I was.

After that, I slept for about an hour, I suppose, before I awoke, drenched in sweat.

Dreams again.

I was being stalked.

Hunted.

Would it always be like this?

Phantom pursuers slipping in and out of our lives, for an instant of violence, and then, terrified, we run once more, as they fade away, unidentified still.

An unending cycle?

I had no answer. No solution but running.

Hours passed before I fell back to sleep.

37

Our last day in Rome.

Packing quietly, I let Celeste sleep. In a wastepaper basket, I spot a postcard torn in half, addressed to Bill:

> . . . *Dan's the sweetest . . . Honeymoon terrific, highly recommend . . . Rome so nice, might stay . . . Remember my career? Could start again here . . . BIG hugs! BIG kisses! BIG love from Yr Sis, "The Come-Back Kid."*

My innards twist. I swallow hard. Amazing what dreams will do to logic.

Celeste snoozes on until lunch, not the best head start. Lydia calls on the phone: they'll meet us downstairs in the restaurant.

Celeste is crying softly.

"What's wrong?" I ask, knowing full well what's wrong.

"Just as I was getting to love Rome," she sniffles. "Now we'll have to tell them, won't we . . ."

"Yes, we will."

And it won't be easy.

As we walk to the restaurant through the bar, the unsmiling bartender follows us with his eyes. He stops in mid-conversation with two men in dark glasses, whom I have not seen here before. I feel their eyes on my back the whole time.

Suddenly, all three start whispering, simultaneously, great billows of chat in endless Italian paragraphs.

Lydia and Ernesto are waiting for us at what has become "our table" in the restaurant. We have a lovely view of the garden and, on the other side, of the porticoed French windows to their suite.

Lydia is wearing the smartly tailored beige tweed suit she wore the day I first encountered her in Rome; Ernesto sports gray flannels and a cashmere blue blazer, a red silk tie. He's also got on the big ring again.

Lydia is reading to Ernesto from the Italian supplement of the *International Herald Tribune*, and they're both laughing. The atmosphere is gay, partylike.

I feel like a heel.

Kisses all around.

Then, Lydia: "Listen to this, it's so wonderful . . ." And she reads to us from the newspaper: "Headline, 'Have I Got a Deal for You!' Dateline, Rome. 'More than 600 people in Italy wanted to ride in a spaceship badly enough to pay ten thousand dollars apiece for the first tourist flight to Mars. According to the Italian police, the would-be space travelers were told they could spend their "next vacation on Mars, amid the splendors of ruined temples and painted deserts. Ride a Martian camel from oasis to oasis and enjoy the incredible Martian sunsets! Explore mysterious canals and marvel at the views. Trips to the moon also available. . . ." Authorities believe that the con men running this scam made off with over six million dollars . . .' "

Lydia is delighted by the story, her violet eyes sparkle.

"Oh Lord," she laughs, "what a marvelous country!"

Ernesto smiles, his eyes glow, his voice indulgent: "Yes, we're a believing people, you're right, a nation of great faith."

Lydia: "Looks like we're all in the right place, I'd say . . . wouldn't you?"

Clearly, Lydia's time in Italy has served only to reinforce her years in New York. She turns to us for agreement, and Celeste begins to sob.

"Sweetheart," says Lydia, "what's wrong?"

"It's too . . ." And then Celeste really starts to bawl. I chicken out and look blank; uncomprehending Celeste, crying, to me: "You tell them, honey, it's your idea . . . that we have to leave."

And that does it: Pandora's box wide open again.

Only this time out come *all* the demons, the whole four-point-four parade's worth.

As we eat, we tell our entire tale.

Unabridged.

No need this time for deletions or embroidery.

I describe how we really scraped together the little nest egg they've been so gaily investing.

And now they know everything: how we actually got ourselves into this pickle, and why we have to get the hell out of Rome.

Immediately.

Soon all three of my lunch companions are teary-eyed.

At one point, Ernesto regains his composure to taste the wine he's ordered, rejects it, and a new bottle is brought. He approves of this one, and resumes his silent weeping.

Afterwards, he folds his handkerchief carefully, arranging it in his blazer's breast pocket to show just a monogram, *una bella figura* regardless.

The waiter observes our entire performance with the indifference of a movie projectionist to a film he's been showing for at least a month.

Out of the corner of my eye, I see him enter the bar and whisper with the bartender and the men in dark glasses. Endless Italian paragraphs again, more furtive glances in our direction.

"Ernesto," sobs Lydia, "is so charming when he cries. Don't *you* ever cry?" She looks at me, her eyes misted over.

"Not really," I say, adding for accuracy, "at least not in public."

I'm so intent on wrapping up my explanation of our predicament, making it clear we need a secure refuge now, that by the time dessert arrives, I'm struggling, in conscientious pain, to report each last harrowing detail, listing every suspect in the rogues' gallery of who might be pursuing us.

I eye the three characters in the bar, but dismiss that thought.

A contract, I conclude, couldn't possibly be out on us here this soon.

Dessert arrives, a well-iced *zabaione* and, *presto*, everyone cheers up. The *dolce* vanishes quickly.

Ernesto smiles, a shy boyish smile.

"And now if you'll all please excuse me," he says, almost bashful, as if apologizing for ruining a good cry. "But actually I do have some good news. The bolivar again. The papal nuncio in Caracas tells me the military will fall in a week. So this time we've gone short. I estimate we'll at least quadruple what we made before. Which is the next investment we meant to tell you about, Dan."

Ecstasy reigns. There is, as I learn one says in this business, not a dry eye or seat in the house. But this time, our tears are joyful.

"Oh my gosh!" Celeste, gushing: "It's just like that story in the Bible."

And, suddenly, we're silent.

"Which one?" asks Ernesto, baffled.

"You must know," she says to him. "The bread and fishes one? Isn't that what you do with money—"

More laughing.

But by this point, I'm also counting: at this rate, we'll double our original nest-egg in a matter of weeks. Maybe days.

Jubilant, forgetful for a moment, I order champagne. Our mood is celebratory, and I push to the back of my mind thoughts of imminent flight.

"Ernesto," I say, "you're amazing. So much good luck, it just seems unnatural."

"But I'm a Roman. And we Romans aren't subject to every law of nature."

" 'Finders keepers, losers weepers,' " I almost blush to confess. "It's starting to seem like a biblical commandment for us."

More laughter; no dissent. Lydia, smiling: "But what isn't lost, my darling Daniel, can never be found again, can it? I assure you it won't."

Yet rarely has a more inaccurate prophecy ever been prophesized.

And this time, my laughter is nervous, for I know, deep down, someone, somewhere, certainly considers that nest egg as lost.

And damn well wants to find it.

"A little expropriation," sermonizes Ernesto, "never hurt anyone. Money has to be kept at work. Take the grandeur that was Rome, for example. The Roman Empire would've fallen far more quickly if the barbarians and the Church hadn't been there to keep a healthy proportion of its silver and gold in wider circulation. And while we're on the subject," he adds, "you two do have a philosophy of money, don't you?"

Celeste looks at him as if Ernesto wants to know if she has a philosophy for breathing.

I answer: "Not a real philosophy, I guess not . . . should we?"

"Might help, at this point, considering your circumstances."

"What kind of philosophy?" I ask.

"*Alora,*" Ernesto begins, "not the scholastic kind, nothing abstract. After all, money doesn't exist by itself, in a vacuum, does it?"

"Hardly," I say.

"So you need a philosophical system to fit it into, something that takes account of the whole struggle to survive. It's in that dense, overflowing crucible that your ideas about money get formed. For example, from what you just told us, Dan, you and Celeste both immediately decided to change your lives, totally, the moment you opened those bags and found all that money. Correct?"

I hesitate, almost ashamed. But: "Correct."

Celeste nods, cautiously.

"And so, would you say," Ernesto continues, "before that moment, you had a dramatically different philosophy . . . of life and of money?"

"You could say that," I concede, "to an extent, but I can only speak for myself."

"I don't know about me," Celeste sighs. "Money and survival are the same thing, you can't have one without the other. Okay, guess you could say, in our case, keeping one could cost us the other. That's a big switch, I'll admit. But we're kind of stuck. So what's *your* philosophy?" she asks Ernesto.

"Quite simple," he answers, his eyes a-twinkle. "And quite complex. Poverty, I think we all would agree, is slavery. Money buys freedom. Provided—and here's the complexity—you don't upset others. That could be costly. It's all a question of balance, what we Romans, have always called the golden way: *aurea mediocriter,* the golden mean. In other words, don't—as I believe you Americans say—go bananas. Don't rub it in, announcing yourselves *urbi et orbi,* as we say here—which is to say, all over the place. It could kill you."

"Bravo, Ernesto!" Lydia whoops. "To each, his or her own pleasures. But upset no one. Simply live and let live. That's certainly my philosophy, which, alas, too few others share. Had to learn that the hard way at times. But it doesn't really mean I'm still not totally and utterly absorbed by, absolutely *driven* by my own satisfactions. Selfish and banal, I grant you. And while I'm certainly not a slothful person, I simply abhor normal work. I adore elegance. Travel delights me no end, especially when I can stay in the Lord Byrons of this world. I love beautiful things. None of this may be particularly edifying, but then I've never been a candidate in the admirability sweepstakes.

"And do you," Lydia asks me, "do you consider yourself a moral person?"

38

I reflect on Lydia's question, pondering how to answer it more or less honestly.

"Can't say I ever gave it much thought."

"A precarious position." Furrows of concern are now wrinkling her brow. "Must be more sure of who you are, Daniel, if you're going to survive and enjoy what you're risking your life for. What is it the Italians say . . . 'he without teeth has no toothache'? Something like that. But you get my point . . ."

Haven't a clue actually, and I shake my head.

"Well, what I mean is . . ." She pauses, attempting to clarify. "What I mean is . . . do you *sincerely* love money? I know I do. And at the same time I'm bored past extinction by people who devote their lives to amassing it. I don't belong to that species. And I don't feel bound by any pretensions to their particular brand of morality. The denizens of that dreary world are there strictly for picking and plucking."

I nod, hesitantly.

"But don't get me wrong. Your found money—honestly found money, I must stress—has helped give me—give *all* of us—a new lease on life, has it not? Together, I'm convinced, we've done quite well so far. And together, I believe, we can continue to do well . . . indeed, to positively thrive. Provided you agree, of course."

"Agree?"

"Yes. There's something about you two young people that makes me feel, well, so protective—motherly would be too strong a word—but you seem such neophytes at this, lacking any clear direction, if I may be so impertinent . . . Or am I simply mistaken?"

"Mistaken," says Celeste. "At least I know what I want. I just can't put a definite label on it yet . . . takes time, and we got a lot of other things sort of on our minds now."

"I'll say," I say.

"Money can buy time," says Lydia. "Isn't that right, Ernesto?"

He nods, a sage nod.

"And so first," he intones, "first you must build up enough capital, so that no one ever questions your beginnings. You simply are . . . you. Rich. At this point, your instincts are correct: you may be discovered here in Rome after this magazine business. That cat's out of the bag, as you say, and there's no telling where it will pop up next. So at the moment you have no choice . . . on this count, you're right: you must flee. But may I propose you choose a quieter venue next time . . .

". . . for a little tranquil reflection . . . yet near sufficiently modern communications, so that we can stay in touch with the means for growing your capital. Then, who knows, with luck someday you may be able to make a deal, and buy your way out of this—how do you say—pickle? I mean, pay them back eventually, with interest. It's only fair. They simply want their money, they don't want you. But *prego*, Celeste, don't go asking your agent to line up any work for you, not right away at any rate."

I'm intrigued by Ernesto's suggestion.

"How do we pay them back," I ask, "when we don't know who they are?"

"Good point," says Ernesto, sage nod again. "But they, as you might imagine, probably have ways of making themselves known. Still, if they don't find you first, would you consider finding them?"

"Not really . . . and I wouldn't even know where to start, if I did."

"Excellent point. That might put them on your scent even more strongly than they already are . . . they could find you before you're in any condition to be found. Wouldn't want that to happen now, would we? So tell me . . ." Ernesto pauses, as if searching for just the right words. ". . . before all this . . . has either of you ever had any business dealings with . . . the underworld?"

I think of the thugs who repossessed my boat. And Mr. Starace. And Tony Dee. But somehow all that doesn't seem to really add up to "business dealings."

So I fib: "No."

And Lydia doesn't correct me.

"And you, my dear?" Ernesto to the beautiful Celeste.

"Not really dealings," she says, caution constricting her voice. "Social relations perhaps. I've known some men from that economic sector socially, yes, you could say that."

"I see, just as well, I suppose. If you don't know how criminals think, you won't be tempted to outwit them at their own game . . . at least, I trust you won't. So you're on the right trail, best to simply keep moving for the time being. You do enjoy traveling, don't you?"

"Love it," says Celeste, "long as it leads somewhere."

I begin to have the disquieting feeling Ernesto is spinning a very comfortable web around us, leaving little room for movement, nothing for Celeste and me to think or say or do on our own that would alter our dilemma . . . without Lydia and him at our sides to guide us.

"Precisely, Celeste." Ernesto resumes, confident, reasonable, persuasive. "It should all lead somewhere. But all on your own, where can you go?"

"Well . . ." I begin, and then run out of words.

"And how long would your money last you? Two, three, perhaps four years? If you're very lucky, and they don't track you down first. I gather you have little experience in, let's be frank, concealment."

"Well . . ." Again, I'm speechless.

"The Swiss bank in the islands was a good start. So were the foreign companies. And those plane tickets may be a masterstroke, one I must remember."

"Thank you."

"Of course, someday, if you ever get up into serious money— nine figures or so—you should consider opening your own little bank on one of those islands. Nothing physical, naturally, just paper. It can exist in your laptop, with the real money all in a correspondent account at a major money center bank. No records, no taxes, no problems. All strictly discreet, and fairly common practice these days, when you get up into those numbers . . ."

"That's *really* interesting," says Celeste.

"But no more hotels." He shakes his head. "Hotels can be terribly public hiding places . . . all this constant coming to and fro in front of staff and perfect strangers. . . ."

"You're right." Celeste is nodding, looking contrite. "You're absolutely right, Ernesto."

"And as for postcards to old friends and family? *Alora*, for the time being, you should perhaps forget you ever had a past. Only a present and a future. It's safer that way. Then someday when, as you Americans say, the situation simmers down, and you're out of the pickle, you can settle your debts and live more normally."

"I can't wait," I say. And I cannot.

"*Bene*. So for the moment, may I suggest—with *Vanity Fair* sniffing around—that you consider a quiet stay in the country? A secluded private house, from which we might, together, make the occasional necessary foray? To invest, of course, get you that total security I mentioned."

The web grows tighter, more comforting. In no position to demur, I remain silent.

"As you see, Lydia and I," Ernesto expands, "have more than a little experience in these matters. I have over thirty years in private banking, dealing with extremely large sums, while Lydia is quite the connoisseur in so many matters, from paintings to jewelry to . . . to simply the fine art of living very well indeed. Together, we, all four of us, could profit and find pleasure in each others' company, for a time at any rate. Whereas on your own . . ."

Ernesto pauses, to let it all sink in.

"He's not," says Lydia, in an effort to reassure us, "trying to pull any wool over your eyes."

"I beg your pardon," says Ernesto, looking slightly confused, almost affronted.

"Wool over their eyes," says Lydia. "What do you say in Italian?"

"Ah," he says, grinning, "we say 'don't hang spaghetti from my ears.'"

Lydia looks askance. "But that's meaningless."

Ernesto shrugs. "So's wool over your eyes."

"Please, Ernesto," I say, "continue."

"Well, given our performance together so far . . ." A calming smile, then: "I wouldn't be at all surprised if you didn't end up with, say, something in the neighborhood of, roughly, ten or eleven million in a year or so . . . all of this, of course, after commissions and expenses, so I'm talking net–net here."

Ernesto's soft, persuasive voice has an hypnotic effect on us.

The luxurious numbers intoxicate.

We say nothing.

"As you're both American citizens," our prudent *consigliere* continues, "we'll have to consider carefully the tax consequences of all this. Your government's fiscal spies and informers are ubiquitous."

Now we're a captive congregation.

"Eventually, you'll need a functioning business, somewhere, through which to funnel your gray profits and turn them into sparklingly white assets. It can be done. Fine art and antique jewelry are often perfect catalysts for that sort of alchemy. Lydia has a good eye for both, I'm not inexperienced, and you . . . you could be making people happy, spreading beauty."

Ernesto's logic may be circuitous, but it is seductive. And he makes questionable dealing in art, if done on a swell enough scale, appear not only to sound like a business, but a boon to culture as well.

"And what," I ask tentatively, "do you mean? Exactly?"

"Staying alive is, of course, uppermost. But I mean you wouldn't want to put yourself in legal jeopardy with the American government, if you can avoid it. In the long run, governments can be worse than any underworld. So don't hand the Americans anything they can ever pin on you, taxwise. . . ."

Our glasses are empty. Another bottle is ordered and poured.

". . . run-ins with governments," Ernesto is summing up his homily, "is what you must be most careful to avoid. Governments carve away at our freedoms, little by little. Even in Italy, not only in America: nowhere is truly free any longer. It used to be they only *asked* how much money you had, now they go off nosing around all over the world into your affairs. If there is one quality I truly *detest* in any person—and I must confess to just this one prejudice—it's mistrust. Utterly contemptible."

"I have an idea," says Lydia, her eyes glowing with maternal concern. "Ernesto and I rent a quiet country place. An exquisite villa, on a hill near Florence . . . we were hoping you'd join us, least for a long weekend . . . but the situation, it now appears, may call for you to be out of sight somewhat longer. And a bit sooner."

"This afternoon," I suggest, "wouldn't be too soon."

"We'd love to join you," says my beautiful partner.

Join them. Another snap decision. Another die cast.

Celeste looks delighted, her spirits greatly revived after all that crying and more champagne.

Ernesto's sermon seems to promise salvation, if not exactly redemption.

39

We're packed and ready to leave an hour after lunch.

The front desk has been notified to have our bills prepared.

I have a stack of cash at the ready.

Celeste seems wistful, an unusual mood for her. She's looking out the window of our room, her gaze lingering over the neighboring villas and gardens.

"Guess you never forget the first place you stay in Europe." She sounds dreamy. "Least I won't. Someday, think I'd like to come back here. Show my grandkids Rome, same way Lydia and Ernesto took me around."

Grandkids? The image, at this moment, is difficult to visualize.

"C'mon," I say.

We kiss, grab our bags, and go downstairs.

I pick up the bill and hand over the wad of cash. While the clerk counts all the money, we join Lydia and Ernesto in the bar where they are having a final champagne. Ernesto has changed his outfit and is, for the first time that I've known him, wearing a clerical collar. His black vest has a discreet trim of purple piping.

His usual traveling outfit, I learn.

"One more for that road?" says Lydia. "We'll need it, the way they drive around here."

The usual unsmiling bartender is not on duty. She motions to his replacement, but he's too preoccupied on the phone to notice, too deep into another endless paragraph.

At that moment, our chauffeur appears. Ernesto has arranged for a car and driver to take us to our Tuscan hideaway.

He introduces him to us as "Pedue Ambrosiano, an old trusted friend. Pedue and I go way, way back, don't we, *dottore?*"

The *dottore* speaks no English, all broad smiles and energetic handshakes. He's a small man who appears permanently nut-brown, the descendant of generations of ancestors toasting in Mediterranean sun, knotty with muscle and full of spirit.

The *dottore* once worked for Ernesto at the Vatican bank, we learn, but was dismissed by the Curia when they placed Ernesto on that indefinite, involuntary leave of absence he seems to be so enjoying.

The trunk of our large comfortable car, a black Mercedes S600 with Milan plates, barely contains our luggage. Lydia does not travel light.

Half the hotel staff seem to have emerged to wave us good-bye. Tips have been very generous, so even our usual bartender materializes.

So much for a secret getaway.

Lydia and Celeste sit in the back with me. Ernesto is up front with the driver, the two of them waving and jabbering away.

As we drive north out of Rome, Lydia points out some sights, but I've grown too apprehensive again to pay much notice to scenery. The wine from lunch has ceased to cheer; a bilious feeling creeps up from my stomach, my head grows leaden. I'm starting to doze, another way of escape, when Ernesto turns around to me, and says: "Who are they?"

He's pointing at the rear window.

I turn to look. Two men on a motorcycle are about a half-block behind. On the wide boulevard at this hour, no vehicles are between us and them, most of Rome still dozing after its long lunch.

"They've been in back of us almost since we left," says Ernesto, not unduly disturbed, but an emotional notch or two above his usual calm. "Hold on, we take a roundabout route, see what they do—"

And we make a sharp turn off the boulevard, without signaling, roaring up a side street . . .

. . . as behind us the motorcycle does the same . . .

. . . . so we careen into a street on our right, and just as we do, I get a better look out the side window at the motorcycle's riders . . .

. . . helmeted, so I can't see their faces, but they're wearing suits which, in that split second, strike me as sickeningly familiar . . .

. . . I wouldn't bet on it, my head may be spinning too fast, but our tails look to me like dead ringers for the hotel bartender's two friends in dark glasses . . .

. . . and they seem not the least bit interested in the sights . . .

. . . but they're gaining on us . . .

. . . as one of them signals for us to pull over . . .

. . . and I shout this to Ernesto, who then urges the *dottore* to re-double his efforts.

"Who are these *salopardi?*" Ernesto is shouting now, his bankerly demeanor crumbling. "What in hell do they want—"

"Guess!" I shout back.

And Ernesto shouts: "Faster!" And bursts into laughter, a long cynical cackling sound that seems to me as ancient as Rome itself.

We're pulling out of the side streets now, approaching a ramp out onto the *autostrada*, slowing down just a fraction to make the ramp . . .

. . . when the motorcycle pulls up right alongside my window . . .

. . . the riders' helmets have tinted plastic shields over their faces, so I can't distinguish any of their features . . .

. . . but I do see the rider behind pull a gun . . .

. . . and I spin around to throw myself over Celeste and Lydia . . .

. . . as I hear two shots explode through the window . . .

. . . and the calf of my right leg is now burning . . .

. . . burning with a fire that races, as fast as our car flies up that ramp and out onto the *autostrada* . . .

. . . the fire racing right up though my leg and into my groin, as I slump to the floor . . .

. . . smearing blood on Celeste who is now crying, while Lydia tears open the leg of my trousers.

"Christ, you're lucky," Lydia says, as she pulls off my belt, tightening it around my thigh. She ties a knot. "Passed right through you." She presses several lace-trimmed white handkerchiefs to my burning calf, and asks Ernesto for his belt. She uses this to bind the bandage of hankies to my calf. "Probably find that slug on the floor somewhere. . . . Keep it as a souvenir, darling. You'll live."

And these are the last words I hear before passing out on the floor of our racing Mercedes.

I slip in and out of consciousness, until we finally stop, an hour? two hours later?

We're in a small town, behind a *pharmacia* where I learn Ernesto and Lydia are buying morphine and syringes—you can get almost anything you want in Italy without a prescription, particularly if you're a *cardinale*—as well as sterile compresses and everything else Lydia knows she needs to nurse me back to health.

My head is resting on Celeste's lap, she's stroking my face. I can't see her face clearly, but I feel like I want to sleep with my head in her lap for a long, long time.

"Trust me," says Lydia, as they get back into the car. ". . . I've patched up hundreds worse than you in Vietnam. You'll be dancing in no time. Find the slug?"

I certainly haven't, it's the farthest thing from my mind. But Lydia's mention of her nursing days in Vietnam—the first I was to hear from her lips—reassures me: she probably knows what she's doing.

And now I close my eyes, praying that we all know what we're doing, and cursing myself for not reacting sooner to my unease with that bartender and his friends.

Clearly, Wolfie has talked. To *Vanity Fair*. Or to someone else. It doesn't matter now, as the word—the contract—is out.

My suspicions and warnings all confirmed.

But I can hardly feel victorious. My delayed victory is as painful as any prolonged defeat.

40

I arrived at our destination, the Villa Giulia, in a morphine dream.

My first look at our new refuge was hazy: a vast mausoleum, my hasty conclusion. The journey's too-permanent end.

But of the doctor who came to the house to suture my wound, I have no memory at all.

When I finally came around—in what I could then observe was a large and splendid bedroom—my first thought was amazement at being alive.

And then wonder at landing in a *palazzo*.

My leg throbbed.

"How bad?" I asked Celeste.

"You've been out for two days."

And she'd been sitting or lying next to me almost the whole time that I was fading in and out of consciousness.

"But it could've been worse," she laughed. "Could've been my leg."

She kissed me. My return to a waking state delighted us both.

"How'd it get fixed?" I asked, referring to the stitches in my right leg, two long raw and ugly scars running down the sides of my calf.

"Suture self," she answered, laughing and kissing me again. "That's Lydia's joke. The doctor's a friend of Ernesto and Pedue. Lydia says he's very competent, didn't ask a single question."

"Competent indeed," said Lydia, entering our bedroom. "And highly experienced. Only good thing to be said for age. Patched up resisters during the war. Fascists, after peace broke out. Business is rarely bad for combat surgeons in Italy. Our patient hungry?"

My stomach felt hollow, I was about to say, when a flurry at the door intervened.

An older woman scurried in, bearing a tray filled with goat and sheep cheeses, olives, Parma ham, dried tomatoes in oil, fresh bread, an apple and a pear, a triangle of *panforte*, and some grilled oval objects I couldn't identify.

Behind her followed a beaming Pedue with glasses and a bottle of red wine.

It was a party to celebrate my revival.

"So we're safe?" I said.

"We're safe," said Celeste.

"Completely," said Lydia. "No one could ever find you here. Ernesto guarantees it. We're very well protected. These hills are as silent as a tomb, if you'll pardon the expression."

"Where's Ernesto?" I asked.

"Biziness," Pedue answered. His English thus exhausted, Pedue smiled warmly and introduced his wife. "Signora Graziella."

His signora, my angel of mercy, was as nut brown in complexion as Pedue; less muscular, to be sure, but no wimp. She whipped that heavy tray around with all the practiced ease and grace of a feather-waving ballerina in *Swan Lake*.

Setting up a table next to my bed, Signora Graziella spread cheese and ham on the bread, arranged olives and tomatoes on a plate, sliced the apple and pear. For a moment, I thought she might even chew it to save me the effort; Graziella was the Italian grandmother I never had.

Pedue poured the wine: *"Salute!"*

And salubrious it proved. Food, wine, company: my spirits were now buoyant as a bird in flight.

"What are these," I asked about the grilled oval objects before me.

Pedue, proudly: *"Tordi, allodole, pettorossi, merli . . ."*

"I don't know the English names," said Lydia. "They're all small birds."

"Really small." I held one on the end of my fork. "But tasty," I added.

Pedue laughed, and said something in Italian.

"If it's bigger . . ." Lydia translated, slowly, ". . . than an olive . . . and it flies? In Italy, we say . . . shoot it."

Time to change subjects. "What's Ernesto's 'biziness'?" I asked Lydia.

"He's at a monastery."

I raised my eyebrows.

"Buying art," she explained.

"What kind . . ." Me, tentatively, suspicions growing. ". . . of art?"

"Old, probably even genuine. But let's not discuss business, this is a party. Our patient has revived."

"It's almost like that story," said Celeste, "about the poor burned man? And the beautiful nurse taking caring of him in a villa. But you don't look at all like Ralph Fiennes," she sighed, "even after he was burned. Go ahead, say it."

"Oh," I said, "the movie."

"Snob."

"Perhaps we should let you two rest," said Lydia, making moves to leave, as Pedue and his wife slipped out quietly.

"Please stay a minute," I said to Lydia, keen to learn more about this latest 'biziness' of Ernesto's. "We got another investment I ought to know about?"

The beautiful Celeste looked guilty. "I voted our share of the bolivar profits—"

"—by proxy for you," explained Lydia, "while you were less than *mens sana*. A thing of beauty is a joy forever, and I'm sure you'll be pleased with Ernesto's taste in art."

I groaned. "Art, this time."

"Dan," Lydia asked me, "don't you like Ernesto?"

A note of appeal colored her voice, almost begging me to feel kindly toward our clerical money magician. This was surprising, because Lydia wasn't a woman given to begging for approval on anything.

"I certainly appreciate Ernesto's help," I said. "But it's kind of strange, actually a little hard for me to grasp. Art. And, I mean, he's not really much of a cardinal, is he?"

"And if he were," Lydia laughed, delightedly, "you really think we'd be lovers? If Ernesto were typical—at least I gather from what one reads in newspapers these days—it would probably be more a case of him and you. But, no: Ernesto is most definitely not your typical cardinal, and *Deo gratias* for that, I say. Now I, for one, am just so happy we're all together. Maybe I'm simply feeling my age, but I quite enjoy a little quiet family life in the country . . . for awhile . . . just the four of us—"

"—all dealing in shady art?" I said.

"Shady?" said Lydia. "Who said anything about shady? And as long as it's beautiful, and makes people happy, that's what's real."

"I don't want to always be on the run," I objected, "just one step ahead—"

"Oh, Dan," Lydia sighed. "I understand what's happened has taken the wind out of you, but you'll bounce back. Don't be so dull. I certainly wouldn't want *my* life to just dribble away—do you, Celeste?—day after day, no excitement at all."

"I'm talking about balance," I said, "something more stable."

"Stable? Vegetables are stable," said Lydia. "Stability may be fine for turnips, but not human beings. Look on the bright side of our situation!"

"How much," I asked, "are we in for this time? And what can we expect back?"

"Don't know yet," said Celeste.

"Ernesto's still negotiating," Lydia explained. "That's why he's in Florence."

"Why didn't you tell me—"

"You *were* out a long time," said Celeste. "Enough morphine in you to sedate an elephant."

"Okay, so somebody fess up, what are we in for?"

"About two million," said Celeste.

"*Dollari,*" said Lydia. "Not euros. And certainly not lira."

I grew faint.

"Have some wine," said Lydia, holding a glass to my mouth, ever the good nurse. "A proven restorative, good red wine. Great art doesn't come cheap, you know."

I felt too tired, too weak to argue further. And there was nothing more to do now anyway but wait for Ernesto to return.

41

Celeste and I spent much of those first long days inside the walled garden of the Villa Giulia.

A word about that *palazzo*.

Our refuge was an enormous ochre-colored house, with Doric columns and rows of windows framed by fading green shutters, standing at the peak of a hill with a splendid view of the Arno river plain and the hills surrounding Florence, a city that, from our upper floors, we could just about glimpse on the horizon.

The hills near us supported villages and small towns. Our hill was more modest and isolated, its slopes covered with orchards of olive, apricot, lemon, and peach trees, the fruit trees denuded of their leaves now in midwinter, standing guard like an army of dark skeletons around the hill's sole house, the Villa Giulia.

Wide stone steps led up to the villa's porticoed entrance that looked out over the plain.

Stands of oak and chestnut trees guarded two sides of the house, and in back was a large walled garden of at least an acre. The garden's high walls were of ancient stone, blotched with lichen. Within this enclosure were rows of fragrant herb bushes and a vast vegetable plot.

Winter in this garden was brief and benign.

Protected from the winds, and catching the sun, I spent the days hobbling on crutches up and down the paths between the vegetables and the herbs, back and forth in endless laps to strengthen my right leg.

Beneath the Tuscan sun, Celeste and I were turning almost as nut-brown as Graziella and Pedue.

If it hadn't been for the urgent circumstances of our sojourn at the Villa Giulia, I think I might have been tempted to stay on forever. For the garlic, too, was wonderful.

As I became stronger, our walks took us beyond the garden walls. Up and down and around our hill a dozen laps a day, and in no time, I felt, I'd be fit for travel again.

I was soon enough fit for dancing.

"A little music is what you need," Celeste said one evening. "Like at Ida May's." She set up a radio outside on the villa's portico, and fiddled with the dial until she found a station lulling us with mandolin music. "Now watch. Then you do it. Dancing's perfect exercise, almost as good as garlic, for whatever ails you."

And then her hips take to the offensive, and her hands undulate.

Celeste is abandoned to the music, yet she is elegant, all intriguing sensuality, dancing her secret choreography with a ghostly partner.

Celeste is magic.

Her youthful body responds to the Mediterranean melody, the music shapes her to its rhythms. She moves as if in a trance, a saint lofted on a vision.

And soon through me, too, the music is flowing like a wonder drug, every plucked string ringing with the clarity of a Tuscan church bell at dawn.

I drop my cane, and I slip into her arms, and we match each other step for step, swaying, giggling, crooning in each other's ears, and even when the music is interrupted by an announcer speaking Italian as soothing as the evening's breezes, we dance on, the mandolin in our brains now, as we become tethered to each other, in our laughing, our dancing, our embrace.

And so with all the walking and all the dancing, and those many nights of garlic, Celeste and I were growing closer and closer, or so I thought, and together we were soon plotting the fulfillment of dreams, those Mediterranean boat captain fantasies so carefully nurtured during my lonely nights of indentured service to Star Ace Corp.

Convalescence was sealing our partnership, at least for the foreseeable future.

And, to my relief and surprise, not a mention of show business, at least for the time being.

We agreed that, as soon as I was fully fit for travel, the two of us would make our way to a town on the coast of France, someplace where they had a busy drydock, and I'd buy a boat—the best deal I could find—before one of our investment schemes went belly up on us, and we might find ourselves bankrupt just as suddenly as we'd found ourselves rich.

We pictured ourselves cruising together from the coast of France down to Palma de Mallorca.

And in these plans our dreams were meeting.

Melding.

Multiplying.

42

Ernesto stayed away much longer than expected.

Lydia began to grow concerned.

And to fret.

Then, abruptly one evening at dinner, she said: "Ernesto's just like Jack Kennedy was, you know. That's why I'm so worried about him."

"How's that?" I asked, doubtful at the comparison.

"Well, Ernesto has the *exact* same problem Jack had," she declared, as if that settled everything.

"You knew Kennedy?" said Celeste, a touch too worshipful, I thought. In the art of high living, she was now fully Lydia's amanuensis.

"Well, knew and knew. In New York, I had a small apartment at the Carlyle for a few years—I never dreamed of working in Washington, beyond boredom, that place—Jack stayed at the Carlyle, too, even when he was a senator. Occasionally, we'd meet."

"So?" Celeste, all ears: "What was *his* problem?"

"Jack used to get these terrible migraines," Lydia explained, "if he had to go without a woman for as long as three days. *True* fact. He complained about it to everyone, even to the prime minister of England, I'm told, who was British, of course, so he hadn't a clue what Jack was talking about. That's why I'm beginning to worry about Ernesto. He gets migraines, too."

♯   ♯   ♯

While we waited in suspense for Ernesto to return, my own convalescence continued to progress.

Lydia played physiotherapist, and taught Celeste some helpful, even interesting, massage techniques to restore my strength as well as my spirits.

I was certain Lydia could work similar wonders for Ernesto's migraine, should he come back with one. The wonderful, restorative properties of garlic.

After dinner, near the end of our second week at the Villa Giulia, Ernesto finally returned. He was beaming.

Not a trace of migraine in evidence.

Lydia appeared quite concerned.

"No headache?" Her first words after Ernesto kissed her.

"We've been blessed by the gods," he offered by way of explanation. "The ancient pagan gods."

And he proceeded to push aside the dinner dishes to clear a space on the dining table for his suitcase, which he then opened to reveal wads of chamois cloth.

He carefully extracted one wad and opened it.

Inside was a gold hair comb studded with precious stones.

"Etruscan," he said, placing it before us, "and very genuine. All of it is." He waved his hand over the chamois wads. "Italy is so rich, look . . . *look!*"

Ernesto busied himself unwrapping his art purchase, arranging over a dozen works of gold on the table.

"A king's treasure," he exclaimed over the display of plates, bowls, drinking cups, knives.

I picked up a knife; it must have weighed five pounds.

"Oh, Ernesto!" said Lydia, kissing him. "You *are* forgiven. Presents do make the heart grow fonder."

"All of it comes from a royal tomb," he said. "Discovered only weeks ago. Unfortunately, the monks had to bulldoze the tomb to get at the treasure, but we have so many tombs in Italy, it doesn't matter. I bought these directly from the excavators, the Capuchins. A young novice found the burial place on the monastery estate. He didn't know what he'd stumbled on, of course, but the abbot did, immediately. He'll use the money we paid him to restore a priceless Giotto mural of the Cana wedding feast in the abbey refectory; it was crumbling from mold. One has to chose between patrimonies in our country, and so we sell the pagan. But Italy is so rich, so blessed—"

"How much?" I asked.

"Almost four," said Ernesto. "Half yours, half ours."

I closed my eyes. I had no idea how much this treasure was worth. Or if, indeed, any of it was genuine.

"There was no time to quibble," said Ernesto. "The abbot made a take-it or leave-it offer. How could I leave that?" He opened his arms as if to embrace the display of ancient gold before us.

"But how do we know it's genuine?" I said.

"The Capuchin abbot," said Ernesto, his voice hushed and reverent, "is a highly respected man. An Etruscan expert. And an honest monk. He's made many finds like this. We'll have no problem placing these in Geneva, with a specialist dealer I know, after we legitimize it all first—for export and resale purposes, not authenticity. The Swiss have very efficient ways of legitimizing art, entirely legal under local law and custom, which will then make this eligible for legal transport and sale anywhere in the world. We'll just have to exercise a little caution first, exporting it from Italy. We are rich here in Italy, yes, but we can be very greedy, very selfish with our abundant treasures."

"And what," I inquired, "will we be asking from this dealer in Geneva?"

"Why, at least eleven. Million dollars, of course. He won't quibble. Our dealer friend will surely get fifteen or even twenty when he sells it. But that's only fair, as even I don't have access to such specialist collectors."

"Bravo!" rose the cry from the rest of us investors.

I raised my glass, with its remnants of dinner wine. "*Salute,* Ernesto."

At this point, the idea crossed my mind that I was being corrupted perhaps beyond redemption. Life was moving so fast, and we'd had such extraordinary luck up to now—except for my bullet wound—I didn't have much reason to gripe.

In fact, I was feeling quite fortunate that we'd run into Lydia and Ernesto.

I was thinking that, before not too long, Celeste and I would end up behaving pretty much like our beguiling and stylish mentors.

In past times, heroes were celebrated for bravery, magnanimity, shrewdness, loyalty. Pious Aeneas. Wily Odysseus. Yet the ancients' admirable virtues rarely included, as far as I could recall, style.

And whatever their faults, whatever their personal shortcomings and ethical imperfections, whatever the size of their personal spreadsheet's deficit, Lydia and Ernesto most assuredly enjoyed a whopping great surplus of style.

"*Salute*, Ernesto!" I said once more. "*Mille grazie.*"

$ $ $

A few days later—days of tramping up and down the hill, nights of wonderfully restorative garlic—I graduated from crutches to a stylish ivory-handled cane. Lydia and Ernesto presented me with this dapper gift the night of our last dinner at the Villa Giulia.

In the morning we departed for Switzerland, leaving with some sadness but in high style, ensconced this time in a '59 Bentley. Its vast interior, Ernesto boasted, was as "luxurious as a first class stateroom on the QE2. It once belonged to Sophia Loren and Carlo Ponti. Pedue picked it up at a bankruptcy auction, paid peanuts."

I no longer had reason to doubt Ernesto, about anything.

I just sat back and enjoyed the luxury. One of the many special touches gracing the passenger compartment of this magnificent vehicle were crystal vases, filled by Graziella with fresh cut blossoms from the garden.

Pedue was at the wheel.

Our Etruscan royal treasure was tucked away neatly in its suitcase up front under Ernesto's seat.

And we were headed off for the Alps.

Ernesto was wearing his black clerical suit and vest with bishop's purple piping, our divinely sanctioned passport through any police and customs checks. An effective precaution, it developed. For wherever we encountered officialdom, they simply waved us through, often bowing out of respect for his *eminenza*, utterly unsuspecting of the haul leaving Italy after millennia in residence there.

En route north to the Swiss border and the Mont Blanc tunnel—unfollowed, to our enormous relief, by pursuing motorcycle or car—we detoured for a pause at Cinque Terrae.

Here Ernesto pointed out the exact spot on the cliffs above the Golfo di Genova where the enraged mob tossed the good rapist in his burlap sack over the edge and down into the Ligurian sea, launching that obscure art student, so maddened with lust, on his transforming journey to repentance, then perhaps beatification and, who knows, maybe even to sainthood itself one day.

"A fortunate turning point," said Ernesto, "that fateful toss, for my career as well."

We stopped nearby for lunch, on a sun-filled terrace overlooking the sea with a view of those famous cliffs. Ernesto's suitcase, full of the Etruscan treasures, remained at all times by his side.

Ernesto ordered an enormous seafood risotto for the five of us, and bottles of the local white wine. "Quite drinkable, but overpraised and overpriced," he noted, "like so much else nowadays."

I had no complaints.

The view was grand, company splendid. I could hobble around on my cane now quite effectively. And we were all about to become truly rich.

Or richer.

Our *vita*, in my undemanding view, was now almost only *dolce*. Almost only, because I couldn't entirely erase from my mind the thought of desperadoes somewhere hot along our trail.

But if such fears troubled my partners, they didn't show it.

Lydia positively reigned over our lunch table; you could almost see the dazzle in her imaginary crown.

The beautiful Celeste was beaming, enraptured as much by being on the road again, I suspected, as by the prospect of soon becoming wealthy, the gazillions of her dreams just rolling down over us in reliable green waves, as steady as the sea lapping at the foot of the Cinque Terrae cliffs below.

Our final meal in Italy was a memorable celebration of all our good fortune.

For the moment, fear of that fortune's costs, like the ebbing waters below us, receded. But its return, for me at least, would prove as inevitable as a tide.

43

We crossed the Swiss frontier into the canton of Geneva, through a border checkpoint in—Ernesto noted with a smile—"a Catholic neighborhood."

"Geneva remains sensitive to such distinctions," he explained, "although, mind you, it's hardly Belfast."

The distinction had its advantages. When Ernesto stepped from the Bentley to show his passport, and waved his hand with the big ring at the border guards, the Swiss officers nearly fell over each other urging us through customs, with nary a glance at our baggage.

"When such distinctions help business," Ernesto continued, as we rode into Switzerland, "everyone here is happy. But if faith gets in the way, the Swiss are far too prudent to insist on prejudice. They become refreshingly tolerant. To Swiss eyes, hard currency is unblemished by religion, nationality, or ideology. Cash is simply a virtue in and of itself. Their firmest belief, I'd wager, regardless of denomination. Sound, practical people, the Swiss.

"And so, of course, quite humorless, not unlike—if you'll excuse me—many Americans I've done business with. Usually pleasant enough, and quite often down to earth, if not exactly its salt."

We drove across the quiet suburban plateau of Pinchat, overlooking the city, beneath the hulking presence on the east of the Salève mountain, just beyond the border in France, and the snow-covered Jura range to the west, another protective French barrier, on the far side of Lac Léman.

Geneva, a conveniently enclosed crossroads; city of religious reformers, UN bureaucrats, and banks. A great multitude of banks.

As we arrived, the city was wrapped in cold fog and rain, secretive and aloof. Its charms, if it had any, stayed concealed in heavy gray mists.

Pedue drove us and our Etruscan gold directly across town to the Geneva Freeport, near Cointrin airport, an anonymous, light industrial district of several dozen warehouses, displaying no discernible distinction or character, no external hint whatever that four of the warehouses are home to one of the world's great entrepôts for art on the run.

"What attracts the murkier elements of the global art trade," Ernesto instructed us, "to such dreary premises as these, is the legitimization Swiss law extends to any art sold within these confines.

"Of course," he clarified, "first you have to get it here, which is often the hardest part. But once here, like us, it's perfectly proper to place your trove on auction in one of these warehouses set aside for such purposes. And then immediately buy it back. All for an agreed upon price with the commissionaires, of course, who'll issue you the necessary sales documents, entitling you to legally export the art from Switzerland to wherever. France and Monaco are close and convenient destinations. Museums much prefer your taking this route, instead of simply walking in their front door, a hot pot in your arms, fresh from a secret midnight dig in some country rich with archeological sites. Like Italy. So as far as hot pots are concerned, the Geneva Freeport is, as it were, the cooler.

"There's little incentive"—we were relieved to learn—"for anyone involved in the whole long art business chain to demand a burden of due diligence placed on buyers. Least of all on the world's museums, and certainly not on the Geneva banks that handle much of the cash."

"And on sellers?" I asked.

"If your treasure requires a more detailed pedigree, that provenance, too, can be arranged here. For a price. By proving a work of art you possess was traded anywhere in the world before 1970, you'll be covered in just about any court anywhere, immune from either criminal prosecution or civil suits by allegedly rightful owners. Such documentation is available in the Geneva Freeport. In the form of blank contracts. For example, from London and Paris auction houses and galleries, some long extinct. But the papers are convincing enough, when filled out properly, to document your current purchase as having transpired ages before you may have even been born, if that's what it takes."

Lydia: "The Swiss do sound accommodating."

"Just don't ship your precious object wrapped in, say, last week's newspaper from its country of true origin. But otherwise, we're in good hands with the Swiss."

"So you're sure, Ernesto," I said, "we won't be landing in a Swiss jail?"

"Here," he replied, "read this."

Ernesto handed me his breviary, the prayer book he perused for a quarter-hour each evening.

On leave of absence or not from his vows—whatever those vows may have been—Ernesto retained certain admirable habits of his profession beyond mere clerical garb.

In this sturdy leatherbound volume I found a small collection of clippings, including an article entitled "Fine Art & How to Sell It," from the *Traders Tips* monthly newsletter. As frank and businesslike an introduction to the art trade as any aspiring dealer could wish for.

It confirmed everything Ernesto said.

"There isn't a major museum in the western world," he went on, *sotto voce*, as we entered a Geneva Freeport warehouse, "that doesn't have something that has passed through these hallowed halls. And everyone in the business knows it. We are in highly distinguished company today."

Our transactions at the Geneva Freeport, although involving millions, were completed in a matter of minutes. What's never ceased to amaze me, then and now, is how little time it can take for vast sums to trade hands and get pocketed.

Especially where art is concerned.

Most people will slave a lifetime and not have saved even a tiny fraction of what we cleared in just a single Geneva afternoon. Not to mention all those risk-free commissions the Swiss made from us right along the line.

"Our good Swiss friends, of course, complain," Ernesto said, as we drove out of the Freeport, with our now legitimized Etruscan gold collection. "They constantly moan and groan about the offensive criticism they receive for simply having the wit to be so accommodating and realistic. These insults hurt them—very much, so they tell me—and at the end of the day, they go sobbing all the way to the banks they own."

From the Freeport, we drove into the heart of Geneva and up around the Old Town section to a hill overlooking Lake Léman.

We arrived at a relentlessly sterile quarter of eighteenth-century limestone townhouses, *hôtels particuliers*, where no one seemed to live, judging by the endless rows of discreet brass plaques on the facades, each quietly announcing private banks, insurance companies, and lawyers by the brigade. An entire district of buildings like monumental bank vaults, stuffed with stock certificates, bullion, the tainted loot of a million shady deals.

Switzerland washes whiter, the brass plaques proclaim.

M. Albert Gassmann, our private art dealer, had his offices in a building overlooking, appropriately enough, the Museum of Fine Arts. M. Gassmann was also, Ernesto told us as we crossed the street, a lawyer and a professor, lecturer at a Swiss institution dedicated to teaching democracy to eager politicians from Eastern Europe.

"What does he teach them?" Celeste asked.

"Where to sell art. And what banks to put the proceeds in. It's not listed in the official syllabus, of course, but everyone needs a pension someday."

The four of us trooped into the building and up the marble stairs, Ernesto bearing his suitcase with the utmost paternal care. Pedue stayed outside in the Bentley.

On the wall in M. Gassmann's reception room hung rows of diplomas, one of which I recognized immediately. It was a near duplicate of the one in the reception room of Herr Professor Doctor Fuchs's bank office, back on Tortola, BVI. My affable Swiss banker with the gold tooth fetish possessed a similar award for unspecified "services to humanity," bestowed by the same Masonic Red Circle Lodge of Geneva. I began to suspect this particular Swiss honor might be the local equivalent of a Harvard M.B.A.

M. Gassmann, the high-class art dealer (but no, let's be frank: fancy fence) for our trove of Etruscan gold, was a self-perfected presence: a slight, elderly Alpine pirate in Saville Row worsted. His oft-lifted face resembled nothing so much as finely cracked porcelain. His voice—as he welcomed us into his office salon, with its grand view over the Musée des Beaux Arts—was, at first, teacup-timid with deference and age, but his mahogany eyes had the 20/20 iciness of a Gestapo interrogator.

His office furniture, save for an extravagantly severe Bauhaus desk, was covered in crisp linen, white as the snowy walls adorned with a single painting each. But all Franz Kline, all opulently spare. Nothing ostentatious, a milieu as altogether lacking in surplus luxury as our swanky art broker himself.

Except . . . on his wrist, an almost square, large old gold watch with Roman numerals. M. Gassmann was perhaps the most tastefully groomed and accessoried man I'd ever seen, save for this singular ornate quality, his chunky gold watch.

(Jack Kennedy, Lydia told us afterwards at dinner, had a Swiss watch just like it. Lydia knew, because she'd given it to him in 1959. She'd bought it at Van Cleef & Arpels, when that store was still on Fifth Avenue, and it cost her two thousand dollars, a lot of money then. Which was half the value of the engraved gold and emerald brooch—*Dearest Lydia, Love Jack*—JFK had given her in exchange. And which Lydia was eventually forced to sell—"Lucky buyer!" said Celeste—a memento of their first rendezvous at the Carlyle.

Or so ran this *sportif* chapter of Lydia's life narrative. One may think it's all a load of bull, but I had no more reason to doubt Lydia on her affair with Jack Kennedy than on any other luxurious episode from her past. Lydia's present circumstances provided persuasion enough for me.)

M. Gassmann rolled his double-barreled eyes over us.

"Antiquities, this time?" he said to Ernesto, voice warming to the subject at hand, smile razor thin. "Your taste in ancient art has always been impeccable. All that classical training, no doubt."

Ernesto opened his briefcase and unwrapped from chamois cloths each piece of worked gold, placing the collection on the snowy linen of the office table.

Combs. Daggers. Bowls. Rings.

The gold glowed, a warming presence in that chilly office.

"*Parfait,*" said our fancy fence, breathless at the view. "Precisely as promised. Congratulations. My preliminary quote stands."

Eleven million. Not lira, not francs, not euros. But dollars. Yankee greenback dollars.

If I'd nursed any doubts before about my good fortune, such hesitations evaporated on the spot.

My mind now adjusted firmly to the indisputable: I was, by my standards, a wealthy man. And Great Blue Mother Yale could, at long last, be proud of me. With the right-sized donation, properly timed, I might even get that belated degree.

The pirate shook Ernesto's hand first, then pressed the cool flesh with Lydia, Celeste, and me.

"Alors," he said, aiming at us those shotgun eyes, so like the business end of a Purdey twin special. His voice, in an instant, cold steel: "There are certain rules the three of you must now abide by— Ernesto, I know I can trust. But you three must never, not under any circumstances whatever, ever attempt to contact the eventual buyer of these objects. Since you're Americans, and the buyer may well be one of your countrymen, you might learn that person's identity one day. And perhaps sooner than later.

"So let's be candid here. Unlike Europeans, who are always fearful of burglars and thieving tax authorities, American—and even British—buyers of such quality rarely wish to remain anonymous. You Anglo-Saxons do have your strange ways. For the same reasons, I suppose, the wealthy everywhere buy big yachts. To announce themselves.

"American and British owners often lend out such possessions as these—I'm speaking of art now, not yachts—temporarily displaying their treasures in museums. Such generosity, of course, increases market value. And, perhaps just as importantly, such gestures also endear a donor to museum boards. Trustees melt, extending blessings of social acceptance, where they might otherwise be loath to even acknowledge existence.

"So I must warn you. If any of you ever see or hear of these objects again, do not attempt to contact the owner. With another offer perhaps. Or, even worse, to embarrass the person. Yes, I'm talking about blackmail. Behavior like that will result in the most severe retribution. And, by this, I do *not* mean just that we'll simply never do business in the future.

"If ever you wish to divest yourselves of an acquisition again, please contact me first, not the buyer. I am, of course, always at your service.

"Now I would prefer," M. Gassmann concluded his lecture for us, "if you three would leave, while Ernesto and I settle details. Public display is alien to my nature. I wish you a pleasant good afternoon."

And, as we left his office, he bowed to us, ever so slightly.

44

With all the necessary banking transactions for our new millions completed, we headed straight for France, maybe the happiest people ever to exit Switzerland since Hannibal and his elephants made it out over the Alps.

That night we stayed in Talloires, at the posh Auberge du Pere Bise, on the lake of Annecy.

We dined like Lydia's old royalty. *Gratin de queues d'écrivisses, tatin de pommes de terre au foie d'oie et truffes, poularde de Bresse braisée.* The memory lingers, the mouth still waters over the elaborate meal.

Not to mention the ensuing night of glorious garlic.

In the morning, we took the winding *route Napoléon* south, dipping down through the Savoie and into the Haute Provence, curling up to the mountains past the town of Gap, and descending into the flower fields surounding the perfume center of Grasse. Finally it followed the toll road behind the coastal hills for the run into Monaco. And then lunch, at a restaurant overlooking the Mediterranean.

Lydia, Celeste, and I ordered simple seafood salads, nearly a fast by the standards of our recent indulgences. We were on a terrace perched in the hills near the botanical gardens, overlooking the Princess Grace Hospital. Pedue had driven Ernesto off to yet more "biziness," buying or selling an apartment, in the almost Miami-like ambience of tax-haven Monaco.

From our table, we had a splendid view of the palace on "The Rock" down below, the cramped city state stretching downhill to the sea, the Côte d'Azur's ochre and red cliffs above us.

"See that villa up there?" Lydia was pointing to a grand edifice at the very peak of the cliffs. "Used to be a circus, of sorts."

"I've never been to a circus," said Celeste.

"It's always fun to visit a great circus," said Lydia. "But imagine having the good luck to actually live in one. Well—" The gleam in her eyes grew brighter, another tale to begin. "—I did, right up there. With princes."

"Really?" said Celeste. "How amazing . . ." The tone in her voice—the awed pupil, so captivated and curious—disturbed me. It was as if Celeste now had her own personal Geraldo, entertaining her snooping, scratching her voyeur's itch. For Lydia's take on the great and glamorous may not have been as romantic as what's on *Current Affair*, but at least her version—we now had more than ample reason to believe—had the merit of hard-won experience and cold-eyed truth.

"Princes," mused Celeste. "I've met all kinds, but never a prince."

I fully expected her to whip out a pen, start scribbling her amanuensis notes on a napkin. Celeste's keenness to learn about Lydia's exploits with other men—rich, royal other men—left me feeling chilled on that sunny terrace.

"Dish it, Lydia, what kind of princes—"

"Old ones." Rueful sigh. Then: "Well, not so old, not back then. Today, you'd hardly recognize them, they must be so shrunken with age, and in more places than one, I bet. Wish I could say the same, but when I was staying in that villa up there—"

Lydia pointed her chin in the direction of that magnificent pile looming above the cliff edge.

"—I was still young, and that villa was run by a man named Charlie de Haitter. A South African de Haitter, by way of the Belgian Congo, son of minor—very minor—Belgian aristocracy. But then everything's minor in Belgium. During the war, the de Haitters ran a minor *maison privée* in Brussels. For German officers. After liberation, not too popular a profession, procuring for Nazis. The de Haitters had to hotfoot it down to the Congo. When Belgium got booted off the dark continent, they went slithering into South Africa and bought a farm in Natal. Young Charles apprenticed himself to the richest arms dealer in that benighted land. Selling weapons to dictators, in jungles everywhere. A born dealer, which is how he ended up there. In that villa. With his circus."

Lydia paused to shade her eyes, squinting up at the villa, as if trying to see the past more clearly.

"Took after his parents. Naught if not a pimp, please pardon my French. But there was *so* much promiscuity around that circus in those days, I'm afraid even I got drawn into it. I came here for R and R, after Vietnam where I was a nurse, and I wanted to sell some ancient art I'd collected out there. Got rather more recreation than I bargained for, but did get some excellent prices here in Monaco for my collection."

Lydia's reference to Vietnam was fleeting—only the second I could recall from her—and again no mention of her wartime conduct, the decorations saloonkeeper Jim Rose had told me about back at that memorable first meeting after my father's funeral. Lydia's thoughts this sunny afternoon remained up at the villa.

"So what went on up there?" said Celeste, egging her on.

"Hot and cold running royals, chasing an endless string of sequined sorts from the casino chorus line. These ladies certainly raced their Monte Carlo motors in the grand prix manner. Amateurs, of course, exaggerated and overly eager, they'd break all speed limits for royalty, absolutely out of control, those girls.

"But they kept the princes amused. Except for sporadic negotiations with a simple sailor trade, from the port down there—a Danish consort particularly comes to mind—royals are pretty much single-gaited ponies. Anyway, it wasn't much rest, but tons of recreation. Just like a circus should be. Princes do love their wildlife—great naturalists, you know."

"So I've heard," I said, unable to warm to her tale of upper-class louts. "But I don't believe a word of it. The wildlife part, I mean. Worthless sentiments from heartless people, in my opinion. I've seen firsthand too much destruction, wreaked by their kind, all over the Caribbean, to give royalty any credit as champions of wildlife."

"Oh, my dear," said Lydia, shaking her head. Sly grin, then: "You are a harsh judge, Dan O'Sullivan."

"Not harsh, just accurate, their hypocrisy is so obvious."

"Well, you didn't inherit that from your father. Had his faults, dear man, but he was never a harsh judge. And, by the way—pardon me for asking—but where would we jolly three be now, if we judged ourselves so harshly?"

I shrugged and tried, but failed, to force a yawn.

Celeste, awed pupil, was nodding in agreement with Lydia, mental lightbulbs illuminating her face. I got the uncomfortable feeling that, in the bright dazzle of Lydia's life narrative, my brand of garlic might soon begin to look tasteless.

"But I'll forgive you your stern opinions, Dan," our teacher continued, "since you do, after all, practice what I preach."

Lydia reminded me of the Edith Piaf song, *Non, je ne regrette rien*. Always defiant.

"But people like that," I limped to rebut, "must really have a lot worse on their conscience. Far worse than anything we're up to."

"But people like that, Dan," Lydia laughed with delight, "don't have a conscience. Half the misery in this world is caused by people whose only talent is worming their way into positions for which they otherwise have absolutely no competence. And princes don't even have to worm, remember. All they have to do is drop out of some queen's womb. Bred like prize poodles, and that's exactly how they behave. No surprise there. Anyway, it's all over now . . ."

She cast a nostalgic glance up at the villa.

". . . vanished into history." In the hard afternoon sun, the vitality fading from her eyes, Lydia now looked old and vulnerable. "That was eons ago. So here's to us today." She raised her glass. "And to all our good fortune."

Exactly how good that fortune had grown to be, I was attempting to compute, as we polished off lunch with the last of a second bottle of champagne. The numbers went spinning wildly in my mind, too lavish for spreadsheet precision. Somewhere upwards of four million, I reckoned, my final share from all our deals.

My ticket, at last, to dreamland.

At last, because I resolved then and there, while absorbing Lydia's tales of exhausted luxury, that I wanted no more of her kind of life.

No princes. Or Charles de Haitters. And no more M. Gassmanns.

Playing footsie with such fancy vultures wasn't for me. I knew my limits; and they really didn't extend much beyond the modest plans of my daydreams.

Which fantasies I could now easily afford.

I was on the shore of the Med, and somewhere just down the coast, I was sure, waited the boat of my charter captain dreams.

The peaceful, simple life.

Thus, my resolution that afternoon in the Monaco sunshine: *No more shady business*.

But how to break the news, my biggest challenge.

That, and confronting the ever youthful enthusiasms of beautiful Celeste.

45

Later that afternoon we all joined Ernesto, who was looking quite pleased with himself, the day's transactions done.

We were strolling around the Monaco port, ogling the grand yachts of billionaires, when I thought I saw my opportunity, an opening for my retreat from *la dolce vita*.

"You know, I was just sort of thinking . . ." I began, ever so tentatively, as we sauntered down a quay, ". . . that maybe we, or at least I, really have enough money now—"

"Enough?" said Celeste. Calm, not hostile, curious even.

"You know, for that new life we talked about? And I was thinking, maybe it was time to sort of, well, chill it a little, find a quiet place, somewhere out of the way—"

"Out of the way . . ."

"Right, I mean, where no one's likely to think of looking, where I could start hunting around for a boat—"

"A boat."

"What a great idea!" cried Lydia.

That stopped me cold.

"It does get tiresome, doesn't it? All this money-grubbing. You're right, Dan, somewhere nice and quiet, and start thinking about what to do next."

What to do next. I feared a parting of minds on this point.

Not to mention hips.

"And I believe," Lydia volunteered, "I know precisely the place."

No one had asked her advice. And I certainly wasn't expecting what came next.

"I have the sweetest old friend who lives right over there—"

She pointed west, into the horizon. A stretch of sea, a few boats, the sky. I couldn't imagine where she meant.

Or whom.

But I feared the worst.

"Stop squinting, Daniel, unbecoming for a man so young. Gives you wrinkles. I mean the *vieille ville* over there, the old town in Antibes. It's not that far. And Elisabeth LeBoeuf, my friend, has been pelting me with invitations ever since her husband died. Poor dear is so lonely. And her house is s-o-o-o big. Tante Elisabeth is such a darling, I just know you'll love her, seventy-five now if she's a day.

"And Antibes, of course, is crammed with yachts, Dan. Not like *these* grand tubs, far more modest, but I'm sure you'll find your dreamboat there."

"Thanks, but I really don't want to intrude on anyone I don't know." I was assessing risks.

"Oh, but you'll adore her. And she'll adore you both, she'll love having us all for company."

Us all?

"I'll call Tante Elisabeth at once. What a wonderful idea, Dan, you're absolutely right, of course, I can't wait to get you both settled into a nice quiet place. After all, it's the least I owe your father. And you, too, of course, Dan, that bullet could have hit me. You saved our lives."

True: Antibes *is* a great yachting center, I knew that much from all my magazine reading. Dry docks, several yacht brokers, boat chandlers. All true and tempting about old Antibes, but . . .

False. It was never my idea that we should all, one big happy family, hunker down anywhere together any longer. No three- or foursomes peopled my daydreams. I wasn't sure if even the beautiful Celeste would still be up for joining me in the low-key life I had in mind.

Well. Surprise, surprise. Lydia was determined to mother us both into a nest before returning to Rome.

Only Ernesto escaped. Something about the terms of his leave of absence, after that Vatican banking scandal, making his presence outside Italy, even for this short time, a violation of parole or something similarly dire. He had to go back before his absence was discovered.

With a few phone calls, Lydia arranged everything.

A rental car for us.

Her Tante Elisabeth alerted in Vieil Antibes.

Pedue at the wheel of the Bentley, for a ride with his eminence across the French-Italian border to Ventimiglia, then points south, and presumed legality in Italy for Ernesto.

Lydia and Ernesto parted sweetly at the quayside in Monaco, their arms around each other as if in a slow waltz, like an elderly couple celebrating a golden wedding anniversary, two old people still bound in passion for each other.

To my surprise, the moment touched even me. Have you ever seen faces from your past suddenly materialize right in front of you—so intense is the pitch of present emotion?

Well, at this point, the setting sun lit up Lydia's face with such a warm glow that, just for a moment, in Ernesto's arms she seemed a young woman again, and the vision resembled for me nothing so much as the last dim memory of my own mother...back, back... when I was nine years old.

And then the sun dipped below the horizon and, in evening shadow, Lydia again became the older woman of queenly airs who'd left me with my father's coffin.

As we drove away in our rented car, Lydia at the wheel, Ernesto lingered by the quayside to wave goodbye. He raised his hand, tentatively, as if he were uncertain of ever seeing us again. Then his shoulders slumped, as though the air were leaking out of him, and Ernesto suddenly looked a sad and solitary man, a lonely figure on a dock waiting for a ferryboat to come in.

This melancholy image seemed so out of character, so unlike him, it unnerved me for a moment, since Ernesto was not a man I could envision as destined for loneliness, a monk's cell or hermit's cave never his fate. To my eye, he was always that outrageous combination, forever fascinating, of brimstone behavior and undaunted adherence to faith.

This assessment may be a bit unfair, for in truth, although I wanted to break free of our tutors, I admired Ernesto, in a way I even envied him: his savoir faire and self-assurance, his culture, his almost instinctive good judgment and luck, his nearly effortless success.

And now I realized why I held him in what may seem such odd esteem.

Although an Italian, Catholic and a cleric, Ernesto so clearly embodied that Yalie ideal I'd always missed winning for myself.

46

Our drive along the coast—up the winding road from Monaco to the *corniche*, west past Nice and down to the Antibes peninsula—dispelled a number of illusions.

For starters, in the land of anything goes, everything is gone.

The famed Riviera of Maugham and F. Scott fable today looks more like Los Angeles than this side of paradise, only with much less room, and the sea its sole grace.

"So where is it?" Celeste popped the question, as we toodled past Biot.

Lydia: "Where's what?"

"The Riviera."

"You're on it."

"You're kidding."

"No," said Lydia, "it's not everyone's bowl of *bouillabaisse*, I'll grant you that, not any longer. But you can still get lost in comfort down here, considerable comfort. Lots of people do. Long as you know where to hide."

Approached at sunset, the old town of Antibes—our next hideout—looked like an exquisite piece of cubist sculpture, in tones of gray and beige, mysterious, almost Levantine, fleetingly illuminated by shards of the orange and gold light flashing across the ancient ramparts that loomed above the *Baie des Anges*.

Bay of Angels. A misnomer, I'd soon learn.

For if there are any angels left on this celebrated coast, they must all be fallen. Virtually every foreign Riviera seems to have hunkered down here for at least one, if not all, of five reasons: outmoded snobbery, the easy availability of prostitutes (F and M), tax dodges as twisty as the *corniche* roads, business scams of every imaginable skew (yes, I know: look who's talking), and all sanctioned by an extravagantly indulgent criminal justice system (criminal, oh yes; but justice? system? I'd soon have abundant reason to doubt).

At the time of our arrival in Antibes, however, I had only the usual glamorous ideas about the Riviera, misconceptions formed by nostalgic novels and travel-page hype.

And so as we entered the old town of Antibes, the shock of the nearly unrelieved and surprisingly modern ugliness of the coast evaporated, and those dreamy expectations revived.

Nestled in the nook of the cape bearing its name, buffered by a brooding ancient fort and a port chock-a-block with pleasure boats, old Antibes presented a welcome full of promise for us—so we thought—a refuge and respite for three decidedly unangelic fugitives.

We arrived at dusk and parked on the old town's ramparts.

"Leave nothing in the car," Lydia warned. "Thieves *own* the Riviera. It's almost like Rome."

Almost, but not quite, I prayed, my leg throbbing at the memory. While my bullet-torn limb had nearly recovered its full strength, the cane now more of a fashion accessory, the stitches from my wound remained to be removed.

We walked along the top of the high sea walls, up the Promenade Amiral de Grasse.

Lights were now appearing in houses on the seafront, the few small places that hadn't been shuttered for the winter. Once the cottages of goatherds, these old seafront buildings had been windbreaks for the ancient nobility's far larger residences just behind in the Rue Saint-Esprit. The location enjoys a grand view of the bay and the Maritime Alps, and so, with the advent of central heating, the site has been born again as prime realty.

Although the air was cooling, the buildings' old stones still gave off the warmth of the day's sun, even in February.

Our *châtelaine*—Lydia's old friend, whom she called her Tante Elisabeth, although they couldn't have been more than ten years apart—lived on the promenade in No. 10 *bis*, a three-room house—one room on top of the other—a tiny well-kept garden out front.

"Thought you said it was big," said Celeste, looking up at the small building. "The three of us'll never fit in there."

"There's more," said Lydia. "She's got a big place just behind. Old money tends to hide itself around here."

On the door of the unassuming, almost miniature seafront house, our hostess had left a note indicating that, right after our call, she'd scurried off to the *traiteur*—that wonderful French version of a delicatessen—to pick up our suppers.

"Walk in my old town, while you wait," her note urged us.

A perfect invitation, it developed.

For as evening closed around, we killed time strolling up and down the small backstreets. Overhead, in some places, we saw the day's wash being pulled in. We caught glimpses of small rooms with artisans' workshops: bookbinders, framers, leather workers, silversmiths. We admired the ancient stone scrollwork that adorned what had once been the homes of aristocrats. We peeped into kitchens overflowing with children and grandchildren. The air filled with the first smells of dinner preparations, peppers and onions sautéeing in olive oil, and of course, the fragrance of garlic, real garlic. Large wine barrels, and small boys playing soccer, now made the cobble-stoned streets even narrower. In a small room adjoining an antiques store, a man sitting in the yellow light of a single lamp entered numbers on a computer, and I suddenly grew homesick, absurdly so. I began to long for that quiet undisturbed existence I, too, had once had, all those lovely evenings on the *Madonna Maris*, even my indentured nights back in Brooklyn, all these memories returned and made me wistful.

But in front of me, Lydia and Celeste—bonded sisters, teacher and avid pupil, heads together—went chattering on, another lesson for Celeste, drawn from Lydia's long experience, the homiletic an *aperçu* on French lovers.

"*Ecoute, ma cocotte*, no woman in her right mind can be serious about anything a Frenchman ever says. Invariably ridiculous, always falling for their own lines. French love, you see, is merely self-love."

And . . .

"But we must get up to Paris for the shows."

Celeste: "What shows?"

"Couture, of course. And soon, I believe. Want to go?"

"You kidding? I'd kill for it."

They stopped to purr over all the charming little things they spotted in the windows of artisans' workshops, treasures they conspired to acquire as soon as we were settled in.

Settled in.

My dreamlife at the seaside.

Paris held no attraction for me. Quite the contrary, big cities meant big risks. I remained convinced that only a boat of my own would erase my anxieties.

Tante Elisabeth found us wandering up the Rue Saint-Esprit.

47

Our silver-haired *châtelaine*, looking warm in tweed trousers and sweater, might have been that commonsensical lady of advanced years you'll encounter early mornings striding over a private golf course almost anywhere in the world, if it weren't for this lady's distinctly unladylike voice, of indeterminate accent and a range stretching all the way from a middle-C cackle, when something amused her, to an alarming shriek when she became excited, a voice that could open oysters at twenty meters.

Shrieking, Tante Elisabeth embraced Lydia.

"Come, come!" the old woman admonished us, her voice echoing off the stones. "We must go inside. It's getting dark. You shouldn't be out after dark. They found a body on the beach!"

"*Babette, ma chere,*" said Lydia, "what *are* you talking about?"

The old woman's voice dipped to a cackle. "Politics." With a conspiratorial wink, she grinned and shrugged, as if her answer explained everything. "*C'est normal dans le coin.* Here, you live here."

We stopped in front of No. 9 in the ancient Street of the Holy Ghost, our refuge at the foot of a narrow passage, a stone's toss from the bell tower in the old cathedral.

Tante Elisabeth handed me the shopping bags she was toting, extracted a ring full of keys from her trouser pocket, and opened the immense wooden door to a stone building: shuttered, of no special distinction, a late medieval structure that the three of us had passed without notice only moments before.

"We moved down here ten years ago," our hostess explained, as we entered. "From Paris. My late husband was a stockbroker, and we sold our apartment on the Parc Monceau, *très high standing*, to buy this place."

Inside, this place was a marvel. Nothing of its anonymous exterior gave any indication of the richness within. The ceilings were high, the rooms large, light, and airy. Embedded in the walls, every five feet or so, were segments of Roman columns, traces from an earlier edifice on the same site. Between the column remnants hung dozens of modern paintings, all oils, and all somehow—but not entirely—familiar. And in a corner, a large Marino Marini horse that even I could now identify.

"Soon after my husband died," Tante Elisabeth went on, "I was burgled, of course, and they beat me, an old woman, quite severely. Took everything except that horse, too heavy for them to carry. It's genuine. And so then I bought that small place on the ramparts, hoping it would be too modest to attract the attentions of thieves. I live there, and I let out this large house, at very kindly rates, to friends on vacation. And every year I absolutely skin some movie people who come for the Cannes film festival."

She shrieked with pleasure over this little bit of larceny.

While our hostess busied herself building a fire in the hearth, Celeste and I laid out supper on the dining table, a long oak affair from a monastery refectory, worn smooth by centuries of feasting monks.

Lydia grew engrossed in the paintings on the walls. Examining one signed "Miro," she gasped, and then laughed.

"Well, I'll be damned," she said, "look at this." She was pointing at the painting's signature.

I scrutinized it, and saw beneath the famous script of the painter's name, in much smaller letters, invisible to the casual eye, the words *de l'école du maître* . . . from the school of the master.

Tante Elisabeth noticed our curiosity and cackled. *"Pas mal, eh?"* Her grin grew wider, her eyes sparkling with mischief. "You like my art? They're almost real, aren't they." Not a question, more an admission. "All my *real* paintings were stolen, when the burglars came. Everything! Picasso. Miro. Braque. They took everything." She shook her head in disgust. "Politics," she spat out the word. "Like that body on the beach today."

I failed to see the connection, but thought it rude to probe. I could, however, just imagine what fancy fence might have ended up selling Tante Elisabeth's real paintings. In a few years, if Tante Elisabeth were still alive, she might even get to admire her assets again, on loan at a museum in New York or Los Angeles.

"Who painted these?" I asked of her current collection.

"My friends!" she laughed. "Wonderful painters, they live up behind the hills. It's cheaper for them back there, and so much quieter. You like art? My friends are very talented. You can buy pieces just like these, you know, at gentle prices. I have a gallery near here. It's my pension. But tell me, honestly, you don't find these too kitsch, do you?"

"Not at all," said Lydia, "I think it's a brilliant idea. You can hardly tell they're not from the masters' own hands." As Lydia's glance swept over the collection, a familiar—and disconcerting—gleam returned to enliven the violet of her eyes. "Anyway," she said, clearly intrigued, "at least I can hardly tell."

"Thieves can tell," said Tante Elisabeth. "They'd never touch these." Then, alarmed: "Your car, where is it?" Tante Elisabeth had a gift for non sequitur.

"On the ramparts," said Lydia.

"Move it!" Tante Elisabeth became greatly agitated. "Right now, move your car. Come with me." She grabbed my hand. "Ladies stay. I need a big strong man. I don't want to end up on the beach tomorrow."

Tante Elisabeth had me drive the car from the ramparts, and down to an underground garage nearby, where she kept hers. She was certain that, if left outdoors, our car, being a rental, would be broken into and trashed by disappointed thieves.

"My husband used to pay the right people every year," she explained, as we walked back along the Rue Saint-Esprit. "At Christmas. But I don't have enough left to pay them, even if I knew who the right people were. That's why they broke in and robbed me. Beat me up, an old lady. I haven't slept in that big house since. Didn't even bother telling the police, no point. Politics," she said, with a shrug. "That's the way it is down here. C'est normal. So I live in my small house now. I feel safer, and they think I have nothing. What's wrong with your leg?"

"Politics," I explained, "in Rome."

"So, you know." Tante Elisabeth cackled. "You understand what I mean."

Which I did. Or thought I did. Moreover, I suspected that— should Tante Elisabeth's fears prove founded in fact—after I got my seaworthy boat, I'd probably be drifting away from this seductive place and its "politics." Still partnered with Celeste, I hoped, just the two of us, cruising southward, to safety and anonymity, in the more plebian ports of a touristy Mallorca.

That night, after dinner, after coffee, after Armagnac by the fire, Tante Elisabeth offered Celeste and me the bedroom she'd shared with her husband.

She and Lydia remained downstairs, watching the two of us ascend the winding stone steps. As we opened the bedroom door and turned on the light, we heard Tante Elisabeth shrieking with laughter below.

The bedroom ceiling, we saw, was entirely covered in mirrored glass. A lively old gal, Tante Elisabeth.

"How would you like your garlic?" I asked Celeste.

"Frenchly," she replied, turning on all the lights.

That night, and again the next morning, we put Tante Elisabeth's mirrors to good use, the sea air invigorating our appetite for all tastes French.

48

The hour was still early when Celeste and I left our mirrored chamber.

We let Lydia sleep, and the two of us went off to find a café for breakfast, and to explore our new refuge.

Old Antibes in winter. Free of tourists. And picture-postcard perfect.

I have a weakness for seaside resorts off-season, the island of St. John being just one good example.

Once the tourists leave Antibes, its more modern sister town of Juan-les-Pins, just over the hill on the other side of the cape, becomes as sad and tawdry as a carnival gone bankrupt.

FERMETURE ANNUELLE signs in the bar windows. The *Concours Mondial du Crossdressing* suspended at Le Voum-Voum until next summer.

But with the leaves all gone from the plane trees in the squares of old Antibes, a country market town comes to life again.

The Cameo *auberge* is packed once more with locals eating *grand aioli* and *brandade du morue*, the air fragrant with real garlic. The town's pensioners are out sunning themselves, sipping pastis around the *Marché Provençal*. In front of the Oursin fish restaurant, in the Place République, oysters on the frosty half shell and spindly sea urchins split open like eggs, their flesh a vibrant orange, all nestle in beds of glistening seaweed; red *langoustes* bask on beaches of flaked ice.

This has to be the best time of year.

In the public garden on the ramparts, among the stunted palm trunks wrapped in browning fronds, old men are playing *pétanque*. Long past unnecessary motion, they retrieve their steel *boules* with magnets suspended on the end of strings, hauling up the balls like fish on a line.

The sun is crisp and clear. The burning glare of summer has subsided. The sea is cool, the port nearly tranquil.

Hidden away in old Antibes, *hors de saison*, you needn't have a clue or a care that the rest of coast is malled over and car-bejammed—year-round—with or without the seasonal hordes.

"After breakfast," I said to Celeste, "let's go buy a boat."

"You buy one. I'll watch," she replied. "Everybody owes himself at least one dream, Danny boy. Go for it. But not me. I don't want to own anything that big yet, not before I know exactly where big things and me go together. Might be here. Or somewhere else. Maybe Mallorca, I'm not sure yet. St. John was nice—I could see what you see in it—but that's not for me either. Haven't seen my kind of place yet. But when I do, I'll know it. Ever get the walking blues?"

"You mean depressed?"

"Not really." She shook her head, slowly. "Depressed is when you just don't like yourself, because you're too fat or a flop or you think you're lazy or even crazy. Walking blues is different. You get the walking blues when you feel you're caught where you don't belong. And you don't know yet where you really do belong. So you just keep on going. Ever feel like that?"

"Sure. It's called restless."

"Mmm, maybe. So what do you do about it?"

"New job, new lover . . . that helps."

"Tried them. Pills, too, but that was just kidding myself. Know what seems to work for me? Night. I get off on night. Perks me up. The way flowers open up to sunshine? That's what night does for me. I don't mean dark, I mean the *things* that go on at night. If I could find a real-life career, and a real-life place, that could just let me live all night? That's where I'd settle down. Buy all my big stuff and move right in. Like Bill on his shrimp boat. Maybe like you and the Mediterranean. I thought New York could be like that for me. But maybe, someday—you think it'll ever blow over? You know, all of it just fade away?"

"The walking blues?"

"No, dummy, those creeps who want their money back."

"Oh, them. Well, look at it this way, Celeste: how long would it take you to forget someone ran off with a few million of what you thought was your money?"

"Okay," she sighed. "Go buy your boat. God knows you earned it, that bullet in your leg. Just let me warn you, hon', I do get seasick. And I don't swim too good either."

"I'll teach you."

"Thanks. Only don't expect me to become completely like you, my darling Dan, because I do not wish that either. I'm a landlubber, not a sailor. And I got enough faith in me just as I am. I got some talent, and don't laugh. I'm not *only* some lucky piece of fluff who fell in it, you know. And so that's not how I'm going to spend my life, a lazy leech living off lucky bucks. I don't mean you, of course, you've earned it, like I said. But I mean like a lot of people I think you can meet around here on the Riviera. I know this might make me sound like a terrible narcissist, but I'm a born narcissist—and I know I have talent, so that's where my obligation is. Sure, you can teach me how to swim, soon as the water's warm enough. And I'd love to help you out on your boat, honest, long as the sea stays calm out there. But tomorrow morning, first thing, I'm finding the best voice coach there is around here and start singing lessons again. Practice dancing, too. You and me, well, you really *are* sweet, Mister O—I mean after my brother Bill maybe the sweetest guy I ever met—and I think that's the problem. Because like I said, I got this other obligation. Only I won't just walk out on you, so don't worry. It'll be mutual, when we both walk out on our own two feet. I can feel that."

Although stung—and once more counting those years between us—I had no chance to rebut her chilly forecast, for at this point I noticed that an old woman was following us.

49

She must have been close to eighty, but the crone still made me nervous.

At the Cameo in the Place Nationale, Celeste and I stopped for café au lait and croissants. The sun was warm, so we sat outside.

The old woman took a table right next to us. After we were served, she asked Celeste a question, which Celeste couldn't understand, and I couldn't make out.

"Je suis désolée," said Celeste, *"je parle pas français,"* a phrase which Lydia had taught her. This scrap, however, was enough to encourage the old woman.

She began at once to lecture Celeste, while removing from the pocket of one of her voluminous skirts—she was a gypsy, I now realized—the lens from a magnifying glass. She placed the glass on our table as she moved her chair over between ours.

The old woman waved to the waiter to bring us all another round of café au lait, and she helped herself to a croissant from our basket.

I motioned to pay the check, hoping to make a quick getaway.

Our visitor grasped Celeste's hand. Celeste could see that I was annoyed and tried to pacify me. "She only wants to read my palm."

The old woman smiled triumphantly, and began speaking to me so I could translate for Celeste.

"She says," I began, haltingly, dusting off my college French, "her hobby is reading hand lines. She says she's never had the chance to read an Englishwoman's hand."

I turned to the gypsy. *"Mais elle est américaine."*

The old woman shook her head and muttered.

"She says," I said to Celeste, "'Anglo-Saxons are all the same.' C'mon, Celeste, let's go."

"No," said Celeste, holding out both hands. "I want to know."

The gypsy woman chose Celeste's right hand and, squinting through her frameless lens, began examining palm lines.

I wanted to leave and head for the port, check out the boats.

The gypsy woman gave me a sharp poke with her elbow. "Translate," she said.

I was beginning to regret ever taking French.

"Look, Celeste, you really want me to do this?" I tried appealing to her bent for secrecy. "It might get very private, you know, highly personal."

Celeste shrugged. "I don't mind."

"Okay," I began, "so she says, 'You come from far away.' So what else is new—c'mon Celeste, let's pay up and go."

The old woman eyed me sharply.

"And now she says . . . get this . . . she says your foreign travels are almost over, and you'll be going back home soon. See? She's full of it, Celeste, we just got here. And she claims she even sees your mother going back with us. Now that's really crazy."

"No, it isn't," said Celeste. "Obviously, she thinks Lydia is my mother."

"She also claims you have a lot of money coming to you . . . but some other people want to get their hands on it."

"There you go. She knows what she's talking about."

"She sees death, too . . . but not whose exactly . . . it's not near your lifeline, so it won't be you or a relative of yours."

"Well, if she thinks Lydia's my mother, then maybe it's—I mean, we're as close as we can get right now, you and me, but that doesn't mean we're related, does it? And if we are, and we don't know it, maybe we shouldn't be doing what we're doing, I mean all that garlic and everything . . . should we?"

"Thanks, that's great. Thanks a lot, Celeste. You don't really believe all this stuff, do you?"

"Well, I didn't go to college like you, Mister O. I have to believe in something. Of course I don't *want* you to die. You're not all that old."

The crone was smiling, watching us argue. Clearly satisfied with the results of her predictions, she pulled at my arm.

"And then she says, you're the four thousand seven hundred and twenty-second hand she's read. Claims that's a lucky number." I was reminded of my investment research in The *New York Times*. Yes, we were quite a pair, all right, my young beauty and I.

Celeste handed the fortune teller a fifty-franc note.

Getting up to leave, the old woman grabbed another croissant and slid the magnifying lens back into her skirts, like a dagger into a sheath.

All this talk of dying was disturbing me. As we strolled through the old town, toward the gate in the ramparts that led to the harbor, I tried to dismiss it.

"What a hustle," I said, "conning people like that."

"Don't be so hard on her. She has to make a living too, you know. And she's an old lady."

"Still."

"Well, go think whatever you want about fortune-telling and prayers and stuff like that—"

"Okay, okay. You win." And again, not a peep out of me about research in *The New York Times*.

"But, you know, where I come from, we think all that stuff works. In fact, we know it does. That's why Ida May could work magic. We believed in it."

Her tone was so serious I didn't dare raise a question or lift an eyebrow.

"Remember what I told you about Ida May?"

"Ran a boarding house."

"Did magic, too. That's why lots of people called her a witch. With respect. And out of fear. And greed. Which is why they all went to see her. Only two reasons: they were either scared of something—mainly somebody, actually—or they wanted the sun, the moon, and the stars. And Ida May was a witch who could make your wishes come true. She could take water and make silver, mud and make gold. That's why I went to see her. I had a giant big wish, but I couldn't tell anybody about it. I was even afraid to tell Ida May."

Although the temptation, so professionally produced for me by Celeste, was irresistible—to ask, just what was this giant big wish? And what did Ida May do for it?—Celeste's New Orleans witchcraft revelations made me reluctant to expose myself as being too curious. I didn't want to stir any hopes that magic might be just the ticket to get us out of our jam.

"Yeah," I said, "but you were just a kid then."

"That's what I mean. Because if Ida May could do what I really wanted her to do, then maybe she could help Bill and me. And if she couldn't, then where would we go? Would it be any better? Or the same as before? This was all driving me nuts because, like you say, I was just a kid. Only ten years old. So first I thought I really must've been wacko thinking Ida May could do what I wanted, so I didn't tell anybody my wish. I didn't want to get sent away. Or even worse, maybe get locked up in a looney bin."

"Sure, I can see that."

"So could Ida May. She didn't miss me mooning around. Me trying to eavesdrop, spying, always watching her clientele, just who came slipping in and who went sneaking out. 'So?' she says. 'So what are you looking for, child? Am I supposed to do something for you? Want me to read your mind? Or are you gonna tell me?'

"Scared my soul out of me, for sure. So I go: 'Make me a movie star, Ida May. Please.' And she starts eyeballing me so hard, I felt naked. Even more naked than I really was with that advertising guy who bought all my daydreams. 'I want to be the best singer and the best dancer and go to Hollywood and be a star, Ida May.' Which was true, I did. But that wasn't what I *wasn't* telling her."

"I don't follow you."

"I wasn't telling her what I really wanted. I was afraid to, just too ashamed to. So she goes: 'And what would your mamma and daddy think about you going off to Hollywood? And being a big star?'

"That knocked me on my fanny. So she knew, she knew all along what I *really* wanted. 'Can you do it?' I started crying. 'Can you really do that, too, Ida May?'

" 'That *what*? Now stop crying, child, people'll think I'm whipping you.'

" 'Bring back my mamma. Bring back my daddy, too. Bring them both back alive. And living together. And living with me and Bill, so they can see me be a star. *That's* not crazy, is it, Ida May? Am I crazy?'

" 'Course not, girl, everybody wants that. Nothing to be shamed of.'

" 'Everybody wants my mamma and daddy?'

" 'No, child. Their own mamma and daddy.'

" 'You, too?'

" 'Me, too.'

" 'So why don't you do—' But I stopped. Because that's when I knew, right then and there, there's no point praying for the impossible. Just pray for the possible. Pray hard enough, and even if you have to go to a witch, you'll get it. So I said: 'Make me win that talent show, Ida May.'

" 'Child, you got a deal.'

" 'And she did, and I won it, didn't I? And that's why I've been believing *all* that stuff ever since.' "

And since beliefs that strong are too strong to argue with, I kept my peace with Celeste, and left her to cherish her superstitions.

$ $ $

We strolled in the early sunshine out to the port.

Passing a news kiosk, I stopped to pick up *Newsweek* and the *International Herald Tribune*.

Coming out into the harbor, we sat by the water to take in the view.

Boats. *Alpes Maritimes*. The old fort. Cloudless sky. And just a whisper of sea breeze.

The morning was clear, crisp, invigorating. If it hadn't been for the fortune-teller, I'd have said the day was off to a promising start.

I handed Celeste the magazine. "See if they got something in there, you know, on your old clients. From the Drive."

I scanned the *Trib*.

Neither of us came up with anything.

I wanted to believe the story had ceased to be a story, just another hot flash across the national consciousness, one more scandal gone down the American memory hole. But for our money's mystery claimants, of course, the story still surely had legs.

At least four-point-four-million's worth.

I looked out over the port. Along the quays, hundreds of motor and sailing yachts were bobbing at their moorings.

My first goal: chat up some boat people. Then learn the location of their favorite bar. And find the most reliable ship's chandler. Potentially, these were my best leads to a deal on a dreamboat.

Yacht people are a clannish lot, gossipy among themselves, especially about boat business. But they tend to get tight-lipped, even with each other, if talk turns too personal. A lot of them are on the run from something—or somebody—in their pasts, and they prefer forgetting to reminiscing.

Which suited me just fine.

Ask no questions, tell no lies.

50

After our first morning tour of the port, Celeste, true to her word, found a music school in the old town and hired a voice teacher to occupy most of her daylight hours.

Lydia spent the days with her friend Tante Elisabeth, dealing in fakes at the art gallery.

And my instincts proved correct.

Casual conversations on the quays eventually led me to *Le Bar du Loup*, a warm beery place tucked just inside the old walls and run by a Swede named Ulf Axen, a multilingual amiable old salt who lived on a boat in the port.

Ulf Axen had spent years skippering large yachts back and forth across the Atlantic for wealthy owners and was semi-retired in Antibes. After my first visit, I began to drop by his bar every afternoon, as well as most evenings with Celeste.

After not very long, I hit upon what I was looking for.

Talkative and friendly for a Swede—and, even more surprisingly, warm and generous—Ulf soon sized me up as just a serious but harmless boat nut.

"You two seem legit," he said to us one evening, with a big wink. He was pulling out a loose-leaf binder from under the bar. "Here's what's around."

The book held photos and detailed descriptions of dozens of vessels on offer, sail and motor, all moored in the Antibes port. Many I recognized.

"Gosh," said Celeste, "looks like everything's for sale around here."

"At the right price," said Ulf, opening a couple of bottles of Beck's for us. "You can buy almost anything. I just can't put all this up on a bulletin board, nothing public. So keep it to yourselves, or you'll end up paying sales tax, seventeen percent, and I'll have the locals all over me, screaming for a cut. I kick back enough on the bar." He shrugged. "Politics."

"I understand," I said.

"A lot of these boats in the port," Ulf continued—real sailor to real sailor—"are what we call barnacle boats. Never go anywhere. Most of the owners got no real money left after buying them. What I'm saying is they got gypped. These vessels need a helluva lot of work, if you want to make them seaworthy enough to run a charter business. But check out the *Emma K*. She's a beauty."

He showed me a picture of a forty-seven-foot motor yacht in dry dock. There were no details, however, on the *Emma K*.

"Just got the picture the other day," he said. "Boatyard over there is stuck with this one." He nodded toward the far side of the harbor, where a row of dry docks thrived. "Owner died," he explained. "Heirs can't pay the yard's overhaul bill. How's your French?"

"Passable."

"Then maybe you can weasel around and do a deal for yourself. Yard's hard up for cash, like always. Want me to call, tell them you're coming?"

The call would, of course, cement Ulf's commission, if a deal were done.

"Sure," I said, "give them a call. She looks good in the picture." Should the *Emma K* turn out to be my dreamboat, he'd have earned his cut.

The next morning I inspected her. The *Emma K* had beautiful lines and came fully loaded with every desirable device and gadget: radar, satellite navigation system, telecoms, two heads and a shower, even stereo and TV. A new generator, galley, and twin inboard one-hundred-horsepower motors. She'd just undergone a complete overhaul and refitting.

A palace afloat, to my eyes.

But closing the deal took a few days of haggling with the boat-yard owners (this time, I was grateful for my college French). I finally landed the *Emma K*, at a bargain price, provided I could pay in cash and pitch in my labor for her final polish and launch.

The boat slept four in great comfort, six at a squeeze, and as I worked on her in the dry dock, I was already fantasizing my new life aboard, sooner the better.

I'll admit I didn't see any particular woman in these daydreams, as I'd already begun to resign myself to Celeste's taking off eventually for more rewarding points on the compass. Singing and dancing, without me, in that perpetual nightland of her youthful dreams.

And Lydia would be rejoining Ernesto once she saw us, her small brood, relaunched on life's seas.

$ $ $

To get the stitches removed from my leg I had to take a day off from my boatyard labors. I checked into the private—very private—Clinique Saint-George in Nice.

Best on the Riviera, Tante Elisabeth assured me.

The clinique insisted on keeping me overnight for this minor procedure, to run up the bill no doubt, which they also insisted I pay up-front in cash. The cash economy in this part of the world is extremely lively; fortunately, I was able to stay flush with bank transfers from my bulging accounts.

After ascertaining that I could pay cash, in full, the Clinique Saint-George staff showed not the slightest interest in learning how I came to have my leg shot up.

And so this, my one and only encounter with French medical practice, passed entirely without incident.

I walked out of the Clinique Saint-George with a cautious bounce to my step. My sole impairment, that gnawing anxiety, that someday, somewhere, they—whoever they were—would find us. My anxiety a scar for life? Like the red gashes down the sides of my right calf? I repressed the thought.

For the mimosa was coming into bloom, great yellow clouds of it everywhere.

And the *Emma K* was a few days away from launch.

Carpe diem.

Celeste certainly seized it.

No matter what—my anxious nightmares, the mistral winds, or her winey hangovers—each day she worked at her singing, hours up and down the scales, learning to breathe and hold a note, while vocalizing to Sinatra and Billy Holiday tapes. Her voice coach, who, for an extra charge, came to the house, was a former singer at the Paris opera. Madame Mouftard, a muscular, late middle-aged woman, maintained her wind, and kept herself in fit shape, rollerblading along the ramparts.

Celeste practiced dancing in front of, and under, our bedroom's many mirrors.

In the evenings, Celeste, Lydia, and I regrouped for dinner at Chez Felix, a restaurant built in the old town's walls with a fine view of the port.

Afterwards, we would sit by the fireplace back in our house and read.

Lydia was working at her French. "Listen to this," she said one evening, smiling with delight. "Here's a beautiful quote from Baudelaire, about a story he wanted to write. 'In my novel,' he says, 'which will show a scoundrel, a genuine scoundrel, assassin, thief, incendiary, and pirate, the story will end with this sentence: "Under the trees which I planted myself, surrounded by my family which worships me, by my children who cherish me, by my wife who adores me, I am now enjoying in peace the recompense of my crimes."' Now, only a Frenchman would dream up something like that . . . but I ask you, isn't it *such* a lovely thought?"

At night, in bed, Celeste would sing for me, before and after garlic.

So it was getting to be a great life, our cozy seaside hideaway in old Antibes.

Until the day we got a phone call from Rome.

219

51

That morning, we attended a funeral procession.

By mistake.

The three of us were on our way to the Cameo café for breakfast when we encountered Tante Elisabeth at the foot of the Rue Saint-Esprit, and we all got swept up by an angry crowd in front of the cathedral.

Demonstrators were carrying placards with photos of a woman's face, framed in black bunting. An odor of incense and burning wax filled the air. Many in the crowd had candles, the flames fluttering like the sleep of fitful spirits.

We pushed through the crowd to a corner of the square.

"Political trouble," said Tante Elisabeth, explaining the rancorous mood around us.

"What happened?" I asked.

Tante Elisabeth shook her head. "Hard to explain. But it's serious. See those pictures? Well, there she is now." She nodded at the casket on the cathedral steps.

"Looks awfully young," said Celeste, "in those pictures."

"Young and very honest, a prosecutor here. Only law she ever tried to break was the law of gravity. Six stories—" She made a swan-diving motion with her hands. "—onto the pavement." She shrugged her eyebrows. "A political accident. She was prosecuting a politician from the National Front. Our fascists. He built a bridge in this *département*. Bridge fell down the day it opened, and killed fourteen people. But what can you do?" Tante Elisabeth waved her hands as if to banish the thought. "I'm glad I found you. This morning you got a phone call at my house. From a Cardinal Tovini in Rome. I'm very impressed, I didn't know you were so religious.

He said please call back, it was urgent. He sounded *très charmant*."

Directly, the three of us made our way around the edge of the indignant crowd. We headed up the steps for the post office on the Place République in Antibes' more modern quarter. From here, Lydia was accustomed to placing international calls to Ernesto.

She booked a telephone *cabine*, and waited for the clerk to signal that our call had gone through. Through the glass, I watched that familiar vital gleam returning to Lydia's eyes, as her facial expressions passed from looks of schoolgirlish delight—decades vanishing at the sound of Ernesto's voice—to wide-eyed absorption in his message.

She began waving to Celeste to join her in the *cabine*.

A long haggling session ensued on the phone, with the receiver passing back and forth from Lydia to Celeste. There was much serious gesturing and head shaking, while I watched from outside, an increasingly curious spectator.

At last, Celeste, with a get-down-to-business air, took over the phone entirely. A minute later, she and Lydia were nodding to each other in agreement, a pair of co-conspirators, bonded steel on steel. They emerged from the *cabine* looking positively victorious.

"You tell him," said Lydia.

"Good news, darling," Celeste chirped. "Ernesto's meeting us in Paris for the shows."

"Paris? How'd he get out?"

"Of where?"

"Rome. He's still on parole, right?"

"Not completely," said Lydia, beaming. "That's the next part of the good news. The Vatican's giving him some time off for good behavior."

"Good behavior?"

"Don't look so surprised."

"But . . ." I still saw little cause for rejoicing. ". . . fashion shows are highly public gatherings. There are photographers. They'll take pictures."

The women's faces remained radiant. Unmoved. A united, unbending will confronted me.

"So you want to leave?" I said. "Take off? Just like that?"

"But wait a minute, sweetheart, there's more—"

"I can imagine."

"No, you can't. This is really terrific. Listen—Ernesto's lined up a job for me, he thinks. Two weeks' work. Maybe more. And it's completely safe. A musical comedy—"

"A what?"

"A movie."

"*Movie*? That's insane."

"You calling me crazy? This is my break."

"Look, Celeste—"

"You look. The director is Claude Borri, an old friend of Ernesto's. He's supposed to be famous; he's French. And I'll be all made up, in a costume even, so relax. It's about a convent of singing nuns, that's how Ernesto got involved. He packaged the deal, so the Vatican's a backer. These nuns time-travel all the way back to the twelfth century. *Sound of Music* meets *Camelot*, Ernesto says. He figures we can cash in on the nostalgia craze."

"For the twelfth century?"

"For musicals, silly. I'll even get a chance to dance. If I'm a nun, no one'll ever recognize me, since it's all in French. I can start practicing the numbers down here with my coach. This is it, honey, my lucky break. Aren't you going to congratulate me, aren't you happy for me?"

"*Happy*? That you can go flaunt yourself? Maybe get killed in Paris?"

A hot wave of shame hit me. I felt like a school kid caught cheating on an exam. My tranquil dream of running a charter boat—the only dream I could ever come up with—paled next to this extravaganza. Irrationally, I blamed Ernesto and Lydia; I was incensed at them for not producing a more sober blueprint, crestfallen that their dreams weren't at least as prudent as mine. I'd trusted them, the two professionals, and now I felt miserable, my trust teetering in the face of such a mad concoction.

But from the look in my opponents' eyes—steel-on-steel—I could see that there was no point in further debate.

"Dear Daniel," said Lydia, her voice chilled as arctic night. "You just don't get it, do you?"

My spirits plummeted.

"Sweetheart, just relax." Celeste tried a conciliatory tone. "We'll only be in Paris, nobody knows me in Paris. I've never been there before."

They both smiled at me, pityingly at first, and when I failed to come up with a better argument than mere death, they looked triumphant at the prospect of more travel, bright lights, high fashion.

And the big break.

"The producer's paying all our expenses," said Celeste. "He and Ernesto go wa-a-ay back. And I get three hundred a day walking-around money, plus a suite for all of us at the Ritz. Ernesto's arranging that part. Beats *anything* I ever got for a booking in New York. But you don't have to come, Dan, you feel that way about it, you can stay right here. All by your lonesome, Mister O."

"The *Emma K*," I countered, lamely. "We were going to launch her. All of us together, remember?" They hadn't. And so for the moment I was forgiven, almost. To bolster my position, I added: "And I still got work to do on her."

They were unmoved, that inflexible, bonded steel beam again.

"Okay, stay." Celeste, with unnerving cool: "Skip Paris, miss the Ritz. We'll catch the fashion shows. I can work without you around."

"And if you're spotted?"

"I won't be. We're incognito, Ernesto guarantees it. He's even given me a stage name. Gina Lasagna. Like it?"

"Love it." But what else could I say? It was clear they would remain undeterred no matter what I said.

As for me, I just didn't want to die, that's all. Call it unchivalrous, cowardly, selfish, whatever—but I refused to budge.

And they refused to listen.

Nevertheless, for my sake, Celeste and Lydia did postpone until the weekend—the extent of our compromise—their departure for Paris. They booked seats on the deluxe *train bleu* from Nice.

That afternoon, true to her word, Celeste began practicing songs in French—none of which sounded particularly spiritual to me—and Lydia scoured the latest fashion magazines for the Paris show schedules.

On launch day, the ladies joined *Bar du Loup* proprietor Ulf Axen, the dry dock owners and workers, Tante Elisabeth and myself for a brief ceremony in the boatyard.

Lydia and Celeste, each with a hand on the neck of a champagne bottle, smashed it against the vessel's prow. With a cheer from us all, my dreamboat now became a floating reality, the *Emma K* rolling down the rails into the water. Celeste and Lydia gave me a captain's hat that they'd bought at a chandler's and which, with pride, I wore all day.

After a tour of the *Emma K*, and drinks on board (more champagne), we returned to the Rue Saint-Esprit.

The women were departing for Paris that same afternoon. So while I sulked, they packed their bags. Tante Elisabeth drove us all to the train station, where I kissed Celeste and Lydia goodbye.

"See you in two weeks," I said, expecting to welcome them back on the same platform.

"Maybe three," Celeste cried from the train window, as *le train bleu* pulled away.

No more arguing now.

That evening, after dinner at *Chez Felix* with Ulf Axen, I retired to the *Emma K* for my first night on board my dreamboat. Ulf helped me tie her to a quayside mooring, which he'd secured for an unlimited term, greasing the harbor masters and their associates with ten thousand dollars of my cash. On top of that, of course, was my annual rent for the mooring.

All politics, as per.

52

With Celeste and Lydia away, the *Emma K* now occupied most of my time.

A boat can be just like a possessive woman, becoming histrionic after being left alone for only a few days. Or even hours. The deck starts to crack in the harsh sun. Below is always in need of a good airing out.

From my years in the Caribbean, on the *Madonna Maris*, I knew the exact routine to follow after breakfast each morning.

Water the deck.

Open the hatches.

Clean the heads and galley.

A stroll around the quays, then over to the *Bar du Loup* for a sandwich and a beer, and the latest rumors about charter clients for the approaching spring season.

Antibes was starting to grow on me, and I began entertaining ideas of trying it out as a base until I tired of the place. And then moving down to Palma de Mallorca. Ulf Axen encouraged me in the Antibes part. He would play the same role on my behalf that Laffs Bramsen did in St. John. Mister Ten Percent, a man I could rely on.

My afternoons were spent working on the *Emma K*, before heading off for a shower, dinner at *Chez Felix*, sometimes with Ulf, then back to the house in the Rue Saint-Esprit, since it was still too chilly for me to sleep on the boat most nights.

Some nights the mistral wind was blowing and, as I've said, I'm a softy at sea. I like to fantasize transoceanic crossings, through storms and boat-crushing waves, but sunny days and calm warm nights are my climate of choice. Back in Brooklyn, when I was worried about being bored for the rest of my life, I'd dream of solo round-the-world yacht racing—when what I really should have been concerned about was a lifetime on the run with a couple of charmingly mad women.

In that light, my new daily routine started to look pretty good to me.

But then almost a week passed, and when still no news reached me from Celeste and Lydia in Paris, my routine failed to soothe.

I was loath to put out too many feelers, lest I alert Cali caballeros, the CIA, the Cosa Nostra, God knows who. The multiple causes of my headaches were more than the simple lack of garlic at bedtime, however painful that particular loss.

The beautiful Celeste, although a long way from movie stardom, was no longer an entity entirely unknown, thanks to that mention in *TIME* the Paris *Trib* quoted.

And then there was her agent Wolfie's big mouth.

In the protective covering of the freshly baked Gina Lasagna I placed little faith.

More days merged, and I began nursing far-fetched resentments toward Celeste and Lydia, as if I'd been abandoned by wife *and* mother.

A disquieting loneliness overtook me, but still I had no urge to make new friends in the port or at Ulf 's bar. The expat characters on the barnacle boats moored near the *Emma K* were as attractive to me as a wineless, low-fat, salt-free, sugarless dinner from *Chez Felix*. Simply impossible.

During the day, I kept myself busy on the *Emma K* until the sun started to dip into the horizon behind the Cap's hills.

After dinner in *Chez Felix* each evening, I walked home through the old port gate and the narrow streets. Sitting in front of a few fragrant logs burning in the fireplace, sipping Armagnac, I'd try to amuse myself with Maigret novels. But they lacked the spice of life with Celeste and Lydia, I had to admit.

As both ladies predicted would happen, I was regretting their absence, torn between fear of exposure to further danger, while missing them and envying their high life at the Ritz, all those nights and bright lights in Paris.

I found myself—when I waited for my dinner at Felix's, or when I let a Maigret novel fall shut in my lap, or when late at night I still lay wide awake—living with memories of Uncle Bobo and Laffs,

Ernesto Cardinal Tovini, Tony Dee, and the shooter on the motorcycle. They populated my loneliness.

When almost ten days went by, with still no news, I grew anxious. Horrible images of death haunted me. An intentional auto accident in Paris. A fate like that poor limousine driver's in NYU Downtown Hospital. Another shooting.

I even took the risk of phoning the Ritz, from the main post office on the square in the new town, the first time I dared call long-distance to track them, that's how fearful I'd become of being traced again.

I tried to disguise my voice, stumbling along in phony German-accented French, and didn't ask directly for either Celeste or Lydia, but for Gina Lasagna.

The hotel clerk told me Claude Borri and his group weren't at the hotel any longer. And weren't expected back. They were filming at a medieval chateau in the Loire valley.

"Loire valley?"

"*Oui, monsieur, les deux dames et le cardinal aussi,*" I think the clerk was saying, as our poor connection faded into complete static, before I could ask him when they'd left Paris.

Loire valley.

To my ears, the lap of luxury. I grew afraid my partners might skip out on me altogether, if, miraculously, Celeste's career suddenly took off.

Gina Lasgana: superstar.

And then they—we—would surely be traced.

Lydia and Celeste had entered my life only to completely overturn it. Forgetting our windfalls, I grew cross with them.

I began to lose my love of the sea, my appetite as well. As their days of absence added up, I spent less and less time on the *Emma K*, and even began to pass up meals at Felix's, instead just grabbing some sandwiches at a supermarket.

Once—and against Ulf's advice—I even accepted, desperate for diversion, an invitation from a barnacle-boat's Norwegian owner to join a backgammon party on his yacht. It turned out to be a gathering of Scandinavian tax exiles, who sat around all night complaining about back home, and getting obnoxiously drunk on vodka. *La fatigue du Nord.* Sitting among them, not speaking their languages, resented and then ignored as the only person sober, I felt like a transparent ghost.

Returning home to bed in the Rue Saint-Esprit, I went upstairs and was almost surprised I could still see myself in the mirror.

Maybe it was just to prove that I was still functional—but also because, by this point, I was finding it increasingly difficult to fall asleep—that I began writing a letter that same night, to my former upstairs neighbors back in Brooklyn, Pete Burns and Mario LaRosa, the ex-Green Berets.

A mad idea perhaps, but I felt compelled to tell somebody I was doing okay now. I was also pained by a gnawing guilt for skipping out on my Carroll Estates neighbors without saying good-bye, even if I hadn't known Pete and Mario all that well.

I wanted to apologize for anything untoward that may have happened after I left. Madame Mad's telephone rant now echoed back to me off the Roman columns and medieval stones of my Antibes hideaway.

"... *you oughta be ashamed* . . ."

I wrote several drafts of the letter before I got it all out of my system, and the final draft, the one I'm copying now, I never did get around to mailing.

"*Salut* Pete & Mario!" I began with unnaturally good cheer for me at that low point. "I feel like shit that I didn't get a chance to talk to you guys before I had to leave so suddenly . . ."

I'd crossed out the last *I* and written *we* in my final go at the letter.

"... but you know what it's like, eloping on honeymoon and all that."

I thought about changing this, that maybe I was being too presumptuous, but then I left it in, ashamed at my doubt. Just because they were gay, why the hell shouldn't they know what a honeymoon was like?

"I hope all's well with you two, that nothing was disturbed for you by my abrupt departure. I've been leading a rather unusual life lately, ever since we ran into my father's last girlfriend. The three of us make quite a combo here in Europe. The ladies are off now on a long business trip, so I've got time to write at last, down here in the quiet South of France. . . ."

I bragged, to boost my spirits.

But I purposely omitted the name of the town, and planned to mail the letter from a place farther down the coast, which may be why I never sent it.

"We even made it to Rome," I went on, "where I was quite surprised at how unholy the Holy City could be. The day after the ladies get back from their business trip, the beautiful Celeste and I will be taking a cruise ship from Barcelona across the South Atlantic to Buenos Aires, for the next stage of our honeymoon . . ."

I lied, just in case: to throw off our tracks anyone they might talk to, anyone who might really care about where we were headed.

"I don't know when we'll get back to Brooklyn, but it won't be too long, and then I swear we'll all . . ."

But that's where I left off, and I can't recall now what it was I was about to promise or propose.

53

Easter week arrived early that year, signaling the end of Lent in late March.

But with still no news from Celeste and Lydia, not even a simple postcard.

I didn't know where the hell to contact them in the Loire valley, and I wasn't about to file a missing persons report with the *gendarmerie*.

Finally, an envelope came in the mail.

But when I saw the postmark was from Antibes, and that it was addressed to me, I became alarmed.

Who knew me well enough here to be sending a letter?

It turned out to be only a pocket chart of the bay—just what I needed—plus a small *tricouleur* French flag, to fly from foreign-owned vessels when in French waters, an Easter gift from *Chez Felix* to all their regular expatriate customers.

A card noted that the restaurant would be closed for a few weeks. The picture on the reverse side was of the yachts in the port, with *Chez Felix* featured in the background, a harborside view of the old rampart walls, which was now as familiar to me as anywhere I'd ever called home.

Since I had no desire to cook an Easter Sunday meal—and eat it all by myself, feasting on self-pity—I reserved a table at one of the few restaurants offering a special holiday lunch, *Le Dauphin* in the Royal Hotel, with a view of the Bay of Angels, Nice, and the still-snow-capped Maritime Alps.

I booked for as late in the afternoon as possible, in the hope that Celeste and Lydia might yet show up to surprise me, and that, after eating Easter dinner together, we'd all go into Nice to watch the passing parade.

The first person I encountered upon entering the hotel was a wailing infant in a baby carriage, her accusing cries echoing off the marble walls. A pink pillow in the carriage was embroidered *Julia Claire*. Apparently, lunching parents had relegated poor baby Julia Claire to the attentions of a hotel maid, who was rocking the carriage desperately but to little avail. A young couple sat near the dining room door, rushing through their dessert, while casting guilty looks toward the hotel lobby. I was hoping they'd pay their bill soon and leave, reuniting with their baby, before I was served. Although I did empathize with the abandoned child.

The baby's parents left with her as I was ordering my meal, and the restaurant, nearly empty at this late hour, suddenly grew hushed except for an occasional clink of cutlery on china.

I ate my meal quickly, my gaze wandering miserably over the mauve and yellow crepe streamers strung around the dining room for the holiday. The decorations did nothing to resurrect my spirits.

The food helped a bit, the wines more so.

The Easter special was *gigot d'agneau à la provençale*—grilled leg of lamb encrusted with local herbs and extravagantly spiked with real garlic, an unnecessary reminder of what I really needed. This was preceded by *foie gras*—fresh duck liver paté—and followed by green salad, a *chariot* of cheeses, and another cart bearing three shelves of creamy, sinful desserts.

My appetites revived. I finished the meal in silence, washing the feast down with a bottle of Cornas, a muscular red Rhone, splurging on a glass of Château d'Yquem with the *foie gras* and once again with the dessert. Falsely economizing, I skipped coffee.

A mistake.

The walk back home along the ramparts was a drowsy shuffle. A cold wind was blowing by the end of the afternoon; not the mistral, but cold enough. For shelter, I wandered off into the narrow backstreets. Trash bins were out, filled to overflowing with holiday refuse, dogs had done their business on the cobblestones, children had peed in the gutters. I passed the scrawny statues on the terrace of the Château Grimaldi, all looking as bleak and chilled and forlorn as I felt.

Once back in the house, I lit a fire and collapsed on the sofa in front of it, immediately falling asleep.

I dreamt that Tante Elisabeth was taking my pulse, and telling Lydia and Celeste, "He's drowned in all those liquids!"—whatever that meant.

I tried to speak out, to prove I was still alive.

But Tante Elisabeth ordered some shadowy figures in the background to carry me over to the cathedral at once, so I wouldn't be late for my own funeral. Celeste followed, fingering her gold and silver rosary, her brother Bill holding her arm. Ernesto in full clerical regalia stood waiting for us on the steps of the cathedral.

I tried to cry out to my mother and father—they were now back together again in my dream, side by side in a pew right in front of my coffin.

And then I awoke, gasping for air, and for the right words to save myself.

I could smell the embers in the fireplace.

I looked at my watch, and saw it was nearly six in the morning. I'd been asleep for over twelve hours. At first, I felt quite elated not to have drowned . . .

. . . but then skidded abruptly into an anxiety attack, seized by an eerie premonition that I was nearing the end of my stay in Antibes, that my daytime dream of skippering a charter yacht around the Med would turn out to be as cold a comfort to me as the ashes in the fireplace.

I went upstairs to take a shower, to wash the bad dreams from my head, the fears from my heart. But I believe even then I already knew nightmares would always be part of the price I'd have to pay for staying alive.

I got dressed and went out, heading for the Café Cameo and a bracing black coffee to banish my hangover and start the day on a stronger footing.

The early morning air was warm. The wind had ceased. Easter holiday tourists were beginning to fill the old town's narrow streets.

After breakfast at the café, I walked to the port and out along my quay, where I found a uniformed policeman, accompanied by a dour-looking type in plainclothes, both poking around the *Emma K.*

They were searching for a way to go below, but I'd been careful to lock everything. This appeared to disappoint them.

"May I help you?" I said in French, stepping aboard.

"*L'Inspecteur Mondésir,*" the plainclothesman introduced himself. "English?" he said to me. He had a face like a fist, tiny features tightly bunched together, eyes hard and dull and contemptuous.

"No," I answered. "American."

He gave a low grunt that didn't sound in the least friendly. "Why haven't you paid your mooring fees?"

"But I have." I was certain Ulf had paid the fees with the money I'd given him, as well as greased the palms of whomever it was who had to be greased.

"Rates have doubled, *monsieur*. You owe more."

At that very moment, the unfortunate mix of winey remains, acrid morning coffee, and gut-churning anxieties made me nauseated. I felt the bile surging up the back of my throat, and I reached into my pocket for a handkerchief, but instead pulled out the miniature *tricouleur* flag from Chez Felix.

I brought up a bit of vomit into it.

Another mistake.

Now I found myself handcuffed, and the uniformed policeman calling on his cell phone for assistance with an unruly foreigner, who was moored illegally.

And who had just insulted France.

"This is an unfortunate mistake," I said.

"Unfortunate for you," the plainclothesman growled. "Not for me." He spoke with the thick accent of the *Midi* that Parisians laugh at; I found nothing funny in it.

At the police station in the new town—built like a fortress, more to keep people out than in—a group of policemen, in and out of uniform, all at once began questioning me.

I didn't know quite what to say.

I thought of demanding to see the U.S. Consul, but quickly dismissed that idea.

I kept repeating "*Je suis desolé,*" I'm sorry; but I wasn't sure what for.

My apologies were useless anyway. The policemen all rattled on at the same time, mainly at each other, turning to me as if on second thought to occasionally hurl abuse.

The recording officer on duty looked concerned; I think he was having difficulty learning the precise nature of my offense. The *tricouleur* was passed around, and the bit of vomit pointed out to him.

"*Vos papiers!*" he snapped. Your passport.

Yet another mistake, a possible flouting of French law: I wasn't carrying official identity papers.

"Look, I'll gladly go back to the house where I'm staying, and get my American passport. This is all a misunderstanding."

At once, they began shouting at me.

And next thing I knew, I was on the floor. One of them had punched me in the mouth; my lip was bleeding.

"When we ask a question, *then* you may talk," said the officer at the desk, now on his feet, his face red with rage. "Don't interrupt us. We misunderstand nothing." He was waving the soiled pennant at my face. "THIS is evidence!"

The realization struck me—*So it doesn't really matter what I say*—and I at once felt an odd rush of absolution.

Then I truly blew it.

For some strange reason, my thoughts flew back to Brooklyn. To my life of indenture with Star Ace Corp. and my fear of death from boredom. To my escapist dreams of courting disaster in round-the-world solo yacht races. And above all else, back to that fateful night the beautiful Celeste showed up to deliver me from eternal mildew.

Fear of *boredom?*

I laughed at the absurdity of it all, and my laughter was like gasoline on the fire of the French policemen's wrath. I was ridiculing them, again, the impudent foreigner who'd puked on their flag.

They pushed me down a flight of stairs and into a holding cell.

The small cell was empty, with nothing to sit on but the damp cold floor. There was no window to let in light, just a single bulb overhead in a wire cage, and a small grille in the door through which the guards could keep an eye on me, lest I attempt suicide, I suppose.

But they'd taken nothing from me, and now stood outside my cell door arguing with each other about what to do with me next.

Someone suggested releasing me into the custody of their friends.

This met with laughter, and the comment that it was unfortunately too late, now that the recording officer had already made an entry. They were stuck with me until a higher-up authorized my release.

And none of them wanted that responsibility.

54

On the wall of my cell—*my* cell, as I was already thinking of it, however brief I hoped my tenure would be—someone had scrawled a lengthy graffiti in Arabic script, perhaps a prayer from the Koran for salvation, or an obscene curse on the writer's oppressors . . .

. . . French sons of camel-whores and sheep-buggers . . .

To make my own mark, and to kill some time, I took out the keys in my pocket and scratched the date of my incarceration and my initials in the wall: *D.O.* A call to action.

But do what?

This question was at once followed by another—from l'Inspecteur Mondésir, the plainclothesman who'd brought me in—a voice through the small grate in my cell door: "So who do you know?"

Good question. People who own fancy motor yachts like mine, you never know who they know. A mistake may have indeed been made with me.

Taking time-out from shouting at each other, my jailers were now clearly beginning to put two and two together, and adding it up to maybe millions. I could have been their mayor's favorite foreigner, for all they knew, a prudent and generous donor to the last campaign. Their pitch for a bigger payoff might yet backfire on them.

My brain raced for a reply to the plainclothesman.

Who *did* I know?

Tante Elisabeth came first to mind, but was swiftly rejected. Her words came back to me, *I don't know who to pay even if I could pay.* She'd been robbed once, that was grief enough for the old woman. My keepers wouldn't be very impressed with her name dropped, if indeed they truly thought she had nothing left worth stealing.

"Monsieur Ulf Axen," I answered, "le patron du Bar du Loup."

This time my interrogator's grunt sounded slightly less hostile.

My hopes soared.

About an hour later, the door to my cell opened, and the plain-clothesman carried in a stool. I was getting up from the floor to thank him and take a seat, when he pushed me back down. His face reclenched into a fist.

Ulf Axen entered behind him. He looked pained. "You're in a mess," he said, sitting on the stool.

"Only a misunderstanding. I was hungover and sick, and just threw up a little—"

"A little all over a French flag. In front of two cops."

"But it was a small flag. And I thought it was my handkerchief."

"You're in deep shit now."

"Looks that way."

"They could've beat the hell out of you. And would've, if you were an Arab."

"So I gather. Now what?"

"Another thirty thousand. That's what they were on the boat for. Price is up this season, it seems, more palms to grease. I'm sorry, the people I paid said it was enough. Then there's twenty thousand for the flag, so they'll drop all charges. They want to see your passport and ownership papers. And they don't much like your landlady, by the way, called her a big mouth. They've also got some information on your friend Lydia Sands, but they don't want to push on that, until they've checked some more. Seems Madame Sands once had rather powerful protection in these parts. They think you must be mixed up in some kind of crooked business, if you're hanging around with her."

"But she's over sixty years old," I protested, "almost seventy." I, too, would once have thought Lydia's business shady, criminal even. But after what I'd seen the past few months, her resumé didn't look much worse to me than any other highly successful investor's. "Why are they dragging her into this?"

"People talk, this is a small place. If they think there's something in it for them—"

"When can you get me out of here?"

"Few hours. I'll advance you the money. Where's your passport and papers?"

I gave Ulf the keys to the Rue Saint-Esprit house and instructed him where to find what he needed.

My jailers left the stool behind after Ulf went. And they brought me some mineral water. I took these as encouraging signs.

Oddly, I wasn't bored now, sitting alone there in my cell.

I began to summarize the situation, whiling away the time composing a letter in my head to that old Carroll Estates harpy, Madam Mad, a complement to the letter I'd begun writing a few days earlier to Pete and Mario.

"... as you might have guessed, Madam, I just barfed all over the French flag, a serious offense, at least here in France. And because, since leaving Brooklyn, I've also been partner to some extremely profitable criminal undertakings, the sum total of my recent activities might keep me in my present abode—the slams—for decades. Maybe even cost me my life. I've already been shot in the line of business, you'll surely be pleased to learn, but only once so far. Sorry about that. And your old buddy Celeste, my current half-my-age girlfriend but not my wife, is about to launch her professional career as a movie star—surprise, surprise, playing a nun no less. Singing and dancing. Gina Lasagna. That's her business moniker, so keep an eye out for her. As for me, pretty soon I suppose jail may be the safest place, since I don't know what the hell is going to happen when—and if—they ever spring me from this cell. But I have to admit, Madam, life sure ain't dull now. I don't even think about Brooklyn anymore. . . ."

This exercise boosted my spirits a notch or two, but did nothing to answer the question—what the hell *would* I do when, and if, I finally got out of there?

55

Night had fallen by the time Ulf Axen returned to arrange my release.

A policeman led me back upstairs to the front office. Ulf was waiting for me at the check-in/check-out desk.

So was Lydia Sands.

She held my U.S. passport. It was no time now to ask her how she got there, but I was certainly never happier to see her.

Before we left, the policemen on duty—a group I didn't recognize, the new shift I suppose—took turns shaking my hand in quite a friendly way; they even bowed slightly to Lydia. I thought the oldest was about to make a pass at kissing her hand, but Lydia just gave them all a regal wave, adjusting her invisible crown as she strode from the station, a queen taking her leave.

The one-two combo of Lydia's Riviera reputation—whatever it was (and I could just imagine)—plus my latest financial contribution to the powers-that-be appeared to pack a potent punch. I was a free man again, in a manner of speaking.

"Can't leave you alone for a moment, can we," said Lydia, delighted. "You're such a naughty boy, Daniel. The shame of his son in jail would have killed your dear father." She sounded amused by that preposterous thought.

Lydia and Celeste, it developed, had just returned, filming finished, when they'd encountered Ulf at the house in the Rue Saint-Esprit.

"He gave us the fright of our lives," said Lydia. The three of us were entering the old town quarter. Her eyes resumed the familiar gleam. "Thought he was a burglar, nosing around upstairs. Celeste very nearly stabbed him."

Ulf smiled nervously. "She's quite handy with a knife, isn't she, surprising really . . ."

"Wouldn't want to cross her," Lydia said to me, "not if I were you, Daniel."

"You could have called," I said. "I was worried sick about you and Celeste."

"I'm very touched," said Lydia, with credible sincerity, "and very sorry. But Paris was too much fun, I confess, and as for living in a real castle, even a medieval one, well, Celeste was brilliant, absolutely marvelous, her voice, her dancing, she made a perfect singing nun. Audiences will love her. You ought be very proud of her, Dan, you'll never recognize her. But," Lydia turned to me, and lowered her voice so Ulf couldn't hear, "we have some serious talking to do, I'm afraid. Later."

The concern in her voice disturbed me. But it was nothing compared to the alarm I was feeling since we'd left the police station.

Someone was trailing us, of that I was now quite certain.

And it wasn't the old gypsy fortune-teller, not this time.

Either the police were taking no chances with me, I concluded, impudent and unpredictable foreigner that I was, or, worse, in the course of their day's investigations, someone on the force had stumbled across the contract out on our heads, and was now interested in cashing in.

As we entered the Rue Saint-Esprit, our tail followed.

Smells of suppers cooking filled the air of the narrow street. After a day on an empty stomach, I was beginning to feel quite hungry, tail or no tail. The lights were on in our house. Tante Elisabeth opened the door. She waited until we were all inside, door firmly shut, before shrieking. "They could have killed you! Left your body on the beach!"

Not what I wanted to hear.

But I refrained from mentioning our shadow. I didn't want to start a panic.

Celeste embraced me, whispering in my ear, "Scared the bejeezus out of me, you in jail."

I hung onto her, savoring her warmth, a closeness I needed after all that time apart and the day's events. I surprised myself at just how reluctant I was to let her go. The years between us just peeled away.

Lydia produced a magnum of champagne. "We all need something to calm our nerves."

We toasted our continued survival. And Celeste's incognito movie debut. And my saviour Ulf. Lydia called a restaurant in the Marché Provençale a few streets away and booked a table for everyone.

Walking over to the restaurant, she and Celeste took my arms.

"Your timing," said Lydia, half under her breath, "left much to be desired this morning, Daniel. That was a most unfortunate cough. The policemen were terribly upset when they told me about it. I assured them it was all an aberration, that you're truly a great Francophile—why else would a foreigner bother to learn French? Now don't turn around."

I didn't have to.

It's impossible to follow someone through those narrow streets of old Antibes without being noticed. But being noticed may have been our shadow's intent, if indeed instilling fear was his motive. He certainly did little to conceal himself, maintaining a distance of barely minimal discretion.

Standard French precaution with troublemaking foreigners?

Or something worse.

My mind—and heart—raced. I wished I'd been able to whistle a tune, something jaunty and happy, but I've never had much of an ear for music.

"Does your boat work?" Lydia whispered to me.

"Does it what?" Surprised by the question, I was somewhat offended at the idea of the *Emma K*'s being less than seaworthy after all the effort I'd put in.

"I mean, my dear, can you get us the hell out of here? Say, around dawn tomorrow?"

My heart sank. Worst suspicions confirmed. "If no one's screwed around with her, yes. But why tomorrow?"

"And where to?" said Celeste. "We just got back."

"Tell you later," replied Lydia. "After dinner. I need time to think. This is all just falling into place, you see. Thanks to our gentleman trailer. From the local *gendarmerie*, I suspect, but I really can't tell."

Whoever he was, he took a seat in a café on the other side of the marketplace, opposite the restaurant where we ate. We had a table by the window, so his view of us must have been as clear as mine of him.

In the company of Ulf Axen and Tante Elisabeth, we avoided referring to our tail. We pretended all was well. I'd been freed, intact.

Amnestied for my grievous transgression. And this dinner was meant to be a celebration.

Celeste entertained us with details of her screen life as a nun. Her thoughts waxed philosophical: "I think the film was deep in the way that it was actually very light, know what I mean? I think lightness has to come from a very deep place, if it's true lightness. Don't you?"

She may have known what she was talking about, but no one else had a clue. Without much prompting, she even sang for us, a spiritual in French from the movie.

To any onlooker, we must have seemed just another happy family, and all happy families, so it's said, are alike.

When we left the restaurant, it came as no surprise that our shadow exited the café. He was on the far side of the square when we were leaving Ulf at his bar.

Behind us, as we were accompanying Tante Elisabeth back to her little house on the ramparts.

A dark presence, lurking at the foot of the Rue Saint-Esprit, when we went inside for the evening.

The brief good-nights to our friends were warm and grateful, without a hint that this was probably *adieu*, and not merely *au revoir*.

56

"I thought it might take a few more weeks," said Lydia when we were back in the house.

Celeste: "Few more weeks for what?"

"To get spotted. But sure as God made little green apples, the local *gendarmerie* and their bosses must know by now that my princely connections down here ended years ago."

"So?"

"So that's got to be the police sniffing around. You didn't notice? You're having too much fun, Celeste. Not your fault, you're young. You don't deserve this."

"Deserve what?"

"French justice. The cops must want to know what we're really up to. They smell a slice of whatever pie they think we've got our fingers into. I know them all too well. And poor Tante Elisabeth, now they'll make life miserable for her again. But even if we do slip away, the local boys are still ahead—"

"Tens of thousands," I said, doleful at the thought.

"—and so perhaps they won't be excessively interested in us. Not until word catches up to them. From your friends in Rome or Brooklyn or wherever. Good God, if it hasn't already."

Me: "If I only knew who the hell—"

Celeste: "Who the hell what?"

"Wants their dough back. It's driving me crazy. I'm almost ready to do a deal, if we only knew who they were."

Lydia: "Let's not get overly philosophical. Or defeatist. Precise identities don't matter. They've got tentacles almost everywhere, obviously. Whoever they are. So I propose we head"—Lydia took a deep breath—"right where your friends would never think of looking for us. Now that they'll know we're running all over Europe."

Celeste: "Where's that?"

Lydia looked us straight in the eyes. "Somewhere in the States," she said, calm as an oyster.

Me: "Impossible. Forget it."

"Please let me finish, Daniel, you do have a terrible habit of interrupting. Somewhere *quiet* is what I'm thinking. Somewhere comfortable. Yet very out-of-the-way. In other words, somewhere not at all to your friends' tastes."

"Whatever they are."

"Somewhere they'd never think of looking for you is what I mean. Somewhere they'd certainly never think of going themselves. Some utterly unexciting spot, where you can still play with your boats, if you wish. And where Celeste can just catch her breath. After all this, you can't just wander off anywhere. I feel a responsibility for you both. And to your father as well, of course. Let's not forget your father."

"Let's not change the subject."

"What I mean to say, if you'll just let me finish, is you'll both need something to do while you're in hiding. A legitimate front. No?"

"Like?"

"Like perhaps open up a little art gallery somewhere. Selling all these lovely paintings from down here. Something to keep from going mad with boredom, until all this at last blows over. And I can help you get started, just the three of us together."

Three of us?

But instead I said: "For how long?"

"Until it blows over. Time *flies*. I've been doing a lot of thinking, you know. Of maybe getting something going with Tante Elisabeth's artist contacts. Something we could do with all these marvelous paintings." Lydia waved her hand at the dozens of would-be masterpieces that covered the old walls in our refuge. Her violet eyes gleamed.

"You really think so?" said Celeste. "Sell Tante Elisabeth's fakes?"

"Not fakes. Quotations, homages, tributes. Wouldn't it be fun to run a gallery like hers? Full of look-alike Picassos and Miros. Maybe even cultivate some of my old jewelry contacts. I've got a good eye for antique jewelry, and there's lots of it around in Europe. Not as much as after the last war. But there's a strong market for that sort of stuff anywhere you've got pots of money. No traditions to speak of. And people with all the time in the world to spend. And spend. And spend. Somewhere like . . . Martha's Vineyard, say. I have an old friend there. And it's certainly unexciting."

"Martha's *Vineyard*?" I shouted. I was pacing back and forth in front of the fireplace, circling the large room one end to the other. No one outside or next door could hear me raise my voice, not a sound escaped those ancient stone walls. "Martha's Vineyard? But that's *crazy!*"

"Please don't make it sound as if it were somewhere in Patagonia, full of old Nazis on the run. It's just a few hours from New York, but still light years removed from anywhere. *Almost* like Patagonia."

"We'll get killed. If we don't freeze to death first. Ever been up there in winter?"

"Of course not."

"Got to be murder in winter. No pun intended, but I know what I'm talking about. All those years at Yale, freezing my buns off in New Haven, that was bad enough. And then what the hell do we do with ourselves, if do we get there?"

"I told you, run a little gallery or something. Or maybe Celeste and I will just sit around reading paperbacks, sipping champagne, while you work your buns off for us. That'll keep them warm."

I snorted. They grinned. That single steel front was forming again.

"Sweetheart," said Celeste, "I got to agree with Lydia, it's the last place in the world those gorillas would ever dream of looking. Around here, we just stick out like that lighthouse down the road."

"I'd hoped we would learn to blend into the background. Somehow."

"Forget it," said Celeste. "Barfing's not blending."

"Have to bring that up? I didn't *mean* to get sick, you know. I'm sorry, it was a mistake. But I'm not the one whose kisser is going to be on movie screens all over the world."

"I'm a nun, remember. A singing nun. So who's going to recognize me? And anyway, we're talking Martha's Vineyard now, not Hollywood. I'm willing to make career sacrifices. Why aren't you?"

"What career?" I said. And regretted it at once. "Okay, I'm sorry, I didn't mean that. But Martha's Vineyard, what an awful idea, that's crazy—"

"Oh please," said Lydia. "It's not Siberia."

"In winter, it is."

"It's one of the poshest places—"

"Could be. But not in winter."

"The Clintons go there," said Celeste.

"Hardly makes it posh. And I bet they don't go in winter."

"Come on, be reasonable," said Lydia. "Isolation is what we need, isn't it? Isolation and anonymity? It's certainly not like here. People mind their own business over there. Long as you two can say you're married, that is. New Englanders are a bit starchy, I'll grant you that. It's definitely not the Hamptons, but the Hamptons aren't what we need now. Actually, have you two ever really considered it?"

"Considered what?" said Celeste.

"Getting married."

I stopped pacing. I was about to say, look who's talking about marriage, but bit my tongue.

"It's that bad there?" said Celeste, her tone turned hesitant. "We got to get married?"

To my surprise, I felt hurt. Rejection stung, the years between us sliding right back into place.

Attempting to shift the focus of debate—away from marriage—I said: "Lookit, there's got to be somewhere else just as good for us, right here in Europe even. Aren't American women supposed to really like living in Europe? Men here pant after you, right into your eighties, from what I hear. Especially the French and Italians."

Well, that did it.

"To be truthful with you," said Lydia, her tone icy as Mont Blanc in February, "I don't wish to live in Europe, not any longer. I've lived in Europe before. And I'm not nearly as impressed as I once was, nor as you are now. Nothing on this earth strikes me as more pathetic than people playing at exile, people who make a career out of being abroad, because of money problems—admittedly yours are special— or sex problems, or out of warped vanity, or cheap artistic posturing. Exile isn't quite the achievement they'd have you believe. And the expats realize it. By and large, they're a miserable bunch. They know damn well their little overseas paradise is never more than background scenery for them. And often tromp l'oeil at that. Spend the rest of my life—however long or short it may be—as an exile? Think

I'll pass on that one. Not a life I can recommend for you two, either. And, moreover, Daniel, please note: I have no need to be panted after, thank you very much."

And to all of which, all I could say was: "Forgive me, I'm really sorry."

For I was truly ashamed.

"But what about Ernesto?" I added.

Lydia smiled. "He loves the States. With his talents? He fits right in. I'm sure he could swing it with the Vatican. He's up for retirement soon anyway."

But the prospect of returning—under the noses of the gorillas—set my stomach to lurching and pitching with ocean storm aggression. A cascade of nausea rose from the realization that I, in truth, had little choice. I was outvoted, out-reasoned, coerced into returning, unless I wished to strike out entirely on my own. A future that I found, for a whole head and heartful of reasons, even less enticing than a winter shivering on Martha's Vineyard.

An absolute nonstarter.

I'd been figuring all along we could never reenter the States until we'd first done a deal with the original owners of the four-point-four. Yet the owners, whoever they were, didn't strike me as being in the mood yet for negotiating—the scars on my leg a reminder of their recalcitrance—and, although we could now certainly pay them back, even with fairly extortionate interest, how could we communicate that message safely to them?

With a classified ad in *The New York Times*?

Ask the local police to act as go-between?

Not likely.

"How'd I ever get involved in this?" I groaned.

"You wanted to," said Celeste. "Remember? You wanted your dream life, all paid for, the easy way. Just like us. So stop complaining. It'll work out. You want something bad enough, just keep plugging, that's all. You'll get it back. But it takes patience. I know what you're thinking: *look who's talking.* But we all have to grow up sometime, Dan, even I'm resigned to that. And we're not exactly paupers, you know, we'll manage."

I stopped pacing. "So what kind of escape have you got in mind? You mentioned the boat."

"Just before dawn," said Lydia, slowly, carefully choosing her words as if putting together our flight plans for the first time. ". . . you pick us up . . . somewhere around here . . . and we all slip away quietly. How's that?"

"And then what?"

"Then we get to an airport, that's what. However seaworthy the *Emma K* may be, we're certainly not cruising across the ocean. No reflection on your abilities, Daniel, but I suspect you're not up for that either. Or are you?"

I shrugged. "We could make it. But it'll take several hops . . . out of the Med . . . to the Canaries, then the Azores, across to the Bahamas . . . And then, if you still insist, on up to Martha's Vineyard . . . up the coast, taking the inland waterway as far as possible. But every port we pull into, we do run a risk. If there's a price out on us—and they can't find the boat anywhere around here—someone along the way will spot us, and the word could get back. Staying with the boat, we're just leaving tracks. So maybe you're right," I sighed. "Maybe the sooner we get to an airport, the better."

"And just leave the boat," said Celeste, tone blunt, ultimatum delivered. "Look, Dan, I'm sorry, really I am. We'll split the loss. I know it'll break your heart, after all that work, but—"

"I'll live." I saw no perfect choice. But, yes, I was heartbroken. "Maybe we could try selling her first." I tried to sound game. "Cheap, of course, but it beats abandoning her. Sell the boat somewhere not too far away, where they're unlikely to spot us for a couple of days." I was not overly sanguine.

"There used to be," said Lydia, "a place just like that. Hyères, farther west, near Toulons. But I don't know about today. Hyères was fairly clean, by local standards, almost an oasis. Maybe still is, but I wouldn't run the risk of sticking around too long anywhere on this coast."

"And so?"

"And so we could pull into Hyères, rent a car, then drive up to Toulouse. Catch a flight to London from there. Avoid Marseilles, could be spotted too easily, a snakepit at least since the Greeks ran this part of the world. In comparison, Toulouse is fairly civilized. And from London, we'll catch a flight to Boston. Then Bob's your uncle, as the Brits say. We're home free. By the time anyone gets around to looking for the *Emma K*, most of our tracks will have vanished."

57

And so the next morning it came to pass that I was preparing to leave the house before dawn, shortly ahead of Lydia and Celeste.

Lydia was writing a note to drop in Tante Elisabeth's mailbox. It didn't say where we were heading, but promised we'd be in touch soon. I wrote the same to Ulf.

To avoid the appearance of escape, we agreed to carry no luggage other than the one backpack I'd hump down to the boat. Most of those gorgeous rags Celeste and Lydia had bought in Paris would have to be left behind. A small sacrifice, in view of the whopping loss I'd be taking on the *Emma K*. But the losses wouldn't bankrupt us, and the sacrifice might save lives.

The commission on the boat sale that I offered Ulf in my note was generous, a quarter of the proceeds for himself—on top of re-paying the thirty-five thousand he advanced me the day before— with the remainder forwarded to the Swiss account.

I told him there was a sudden career opportunity for Celeste in Paris that prompted our leaving, that I didn't want to do any more business in Antibes anyway (he'd understand why, and I believed I could trust him just the way I could always trust Laffs Bramsen). I promised we'd be calling later in the day, to tell him where to pick up the *Emma K*.

The Rue Saint-Esprit was dark and empty when I stepped out into the street just before dawn, the only sound a continual rustle of the small surf below the ramparts. I saw or heard no one as I strode toward the harbor, pausing only at the *Bar du Loup*, where I slid my note to Ulf in the door's mail slot.

Lydia and Celeste were supposed to give me a few minutes head start, then slip out onto the ramparts. When they saw the *Emma K* poking its prow out of the port, they would head along the shore in the same direction as the boat, toward the Cap and the beach at la Garoupe, where I was supposed to pick them up.

The idea was, we would then cruise out to sea, well past the end of Cap d'Antibes, before turning west to Hyères.

But if, after waiting on the ramparts for a quarter-hour, Celeste and Lydia didn't see the *Emma K*, that meant she'd been tampered with.

And I might need at least a day to get her back in shape.

Harbor noises at dawn are not unusual; sailors are rarely late sleepers. But the port was still lifeless when I walked out on the quay; the only sounds my footsteps and the mast cables rattling in a slight breeze, the bare masts of the yachts a forest of dark toothpicks in the dimness. A thin line of light was forming above the eastern horizon, outlining the Maritime Alps.

Fortunately, nothing appeared to have been disturbed on the *Emma K*.

She started up with a turn of the key, the earliest of the early birds that morning. A minute later, she was putt-putting her way down the quays and out past the old fort.

As I turned to starboard, the dawn's first rays, shooting out of the horizon just above the dark outline of the mountains, were starting to illuminate the old town and ramparts. Above the town, to the west, glowed the last pale radiance of the moon, a full moon rolling like a white wheel; or a mask, a colorless mask without features, observing our escape.

In the almost blue light, I glimpsed two figures hustling along the Promenade Amiral de Grasse.

Lydia and Celeste.

No other signs of life yet. No windows aglow in any houses.

On the water, the *Emma K*'s tiny red running lights were all that could be seen moving.

I maintained a slow cruising speed, to keep the engine noise down, and to allow Celeste and Lydia time to reach our rendezvous.

At the beach at la Garoupe, our destination about a quarter-mile out on the Cap from the end of the old town, was a small dock. I would wait for them there.

But just as I was passing the back of the cathedral, I realized I'd screwed up. It was unlikely I could get close enough to that short dock without running aground.

In any case, this was a risk I was loath to run. If I tried and failed, the racket we would end up creating made for excellent odds someone would spot us.

So. I decided Celeste and Lydia would just have to swim for it. A bracing start to the day.

I cut the engines as close to the end of the Garoupe pier as I dared, about ten yards off. I had enough dawn light by this point to make out two dark figures scurrying along the beachside road. As soon as they reached the dock, they broke into a run.

Celeste was first to the foot of the pier, waving madly at me. I waved back, making swimming motions.

Celeste shrugged as if to signal she didn't understand.

I risked a shout. "Get in and swim. I don't have enough depth."

"Jerk!" she screamed.

At that point, I spotted a police car, its rooftop lights illuminated and moving slowly along the ramparts in our direction. I calculated they would reach us in about two minutes, max, if we didn't arouse their curiosity even sooner.

It was my turn now to wave madly, pointing at the patrol car.

"Oh shit!" I heard Celeste cry. "I can't fucking swim, he knows that."

I did, but I'd forgotten. And it didn't matter now. I waved more frantically.

I could see Lydia take a step back from the edge of the dock and, in one swift movement, push Celeste into the drink.

Splash.

Then a bigger splash, as Lydia jumped in behind her. They could just about touch bottom at that point and were at once back on the surface.

As soon as Celeste popped up, Lydia positioned herself behind, spun her around, clamping one arm across Celeste's chest and stroking with the other. It looked as if Lydia's nurse training, or whatever she'd done, had included lifesaving.

In a matter of seconds, they were alongside the boat, just as the police car was gliding to the end of the rampart, where it disappeared for a moment in the gardens around the traffic circle.

Celeste and then Lydia scrambled up the ladder.

I started the engines again and maintained a calm five knots until we rounded the first point past Garoupe and were out of view of the police.

Then I opened her up full throttle and headed straight out to sea, just as the sun was rising, strong and whole above the horizon.

It looked as if it would be a glorious day, weatherwise.

With no more complaints from either of my soggy passengers.

58

That afternoon, in Hyères, we found a three-day berth for the *Emma K*.

I called Ulf Axen and concluded the deal on his commission to sell her, with detailed specifics on how to transfer my share of the take. Ulf had knocked around enough ports to know not to ask for more than I was willing to tell him.

My heart was breaking, losing the *Emma K*, but my trust in Ulf was implicit. And should that trust prove misplaced, I wouldn't exactly go bankrupt. Not with our bankroll.

Moreover, Ulf still hadn't a clue where we were ultimately headed.

And where we were headed first was Toulouse.

We rented a car and drove up, booking rooms at a small country inn outside town.

First thing, Lydia called a real estate agency on Martha's Vineyard owned by an old flame of hers, a guy named Wally Converse.

". . . a man as far removed from the underworld as we'll soon be from the Riviera." A retiree to the island, it developed, who also ran a local bar.

"Yes, Wally dear," she explained to him over the phone. "I know it's off-season and the weather's rotten. That's why we're coming now. That's why we expect a bargain rent, darling, long-term and starting immediately. . . . Yes, Edgartown would be perfect, nice and starchy. . . . I know it's the last place you'd ever expect me to stay, but that's the whole point. We need the rest, sweetie, so don't *let* me get started. It's a family vacation, you could say . . . in a manner of speaking. . . ."

She signaled thumbs-up to us.

"Toodle-loo, dearest."

$ $ $

Early the next morning, I found myself locked in a toilet stall with Lydia.

In the ladies' room.

At Toulouse airport.

A not-so-long story.

We'd made flight reservations the night before under assumed names. When we got to the departure hall, not a large place, and were picking up our tickets, we spotted them.

At the gate, for our flight to London: a pair of cops.

At least we thought they were cops.

They weren't dressed like cops. They weren't in uniform. But they sure looked like cops.

And they were eyeballing passengers.

We stopped and turned our backs.

Celeste: "Think they want us?"

Me: "Maybe. Maybe not."

Lydia: "If they do, they're looking for a man with two women. Let's go."

It was a fifteen-yard dash to the ladies' room, and Lydia propelled us straight to it.

"Wait a minute," I objected, as we swept into the *Toilette pour dames*.

"No back talk. You take that one, Celeste—next one's ours."

Lydia meant the stalls.

"I got some clothes for you," she said to me. "We're about the same height, it'll be a tight fit, but put this pants suit on." She pulled a garment out of the backpack. "And please be quick about it."

My squeeze into a pale green ladies' suit was not easy, and we concealed the bulging result with Lydia's Burberry raincoat.

She was repacking the bag with my clothes, and Celeste was passing me dark glasses—plus a long silk scarf to wrap around my head and across my face—when an agitated knocking shook the stall door.

An elderly woman's voice, the toilet attendant: "*Q'est ce-qui passe lá?*"

Lydia: "*Rien, ma chère.*"

"*Rien? Je vois quatre jambes! Un, deux, trois, quatre. C'est pas normal, quatre jambes!*"

Celeste: "Oh, shit."

"*C'est dégoûtant!*"

Me: "Oh, Christ . . ."

"*Quatre jambes, deux femmes? C'est pas bien, pas du tout, c'est interdit!*"

Having completed my abrupt sex change, I felt the confection didn't look totally incredible. But I suspected the sight of the two of us exiting from the single stall might soon produce a stunning effect on the toilet attendant.

And, as we emerged, the expression on her Provençal peasant's face confirmed my expectation.

Lydia: "*Pour la service.*" Then, the breezy drop of a five-hundred-franc note into the woman's outstretched palm.

The attendant's unbelieving eyes stayed glued on the money. "*Merci bien, mesdames, vous êtes tres gentilles. Bon voyage, mesdames.*"

We were out in the departure hall, heading for the gate.

Celeste preceded us, as if not part of the party. Lydia, behind sunglasses, took my arm to steady me. My bowels felt loose. My nerves sizzled like a cat just struck by lightning. But as for my guide, the qualities that had so often alarmed me about Lydia—the steely will, the verve, the sheer chutzpah—were flowing from her now with a force like Niagara.

The cops hadn't budged. But they were looking sleepy-eyed, sort of bored. They might have been stationed at the airport all night.

"Pull the scarf up to your nose," whispered Lydia. "And don't breathe a word. Lean on me, like you're sick. Look at the floor. Let me lead."

I shuffled alongside her.

"*Your shoes!*" she gasped. "Hide them, quick."

With my hands in the pockets of the raincoat, I gripped the pants' waistband—all the while limping like a lame centenarian—and wiggled the pants down to midbutt to let the cuffs droop enough to hide my men's shoes. All the way I had to hang on to the pants, or they'd have slid down to my ankles.

"They're glancing our way, darling, so just keep shuffling. You're very convincing. . . . Celeste is passing them. . . . They're turning, eyes glued to her bottom, typical Frenchmen. . . . She's laying it on thick and heavy, good girl. . . . And now they're swapping remarks about her. . . . We're almost there. . . . Keep it up, *garçons*, great billows of your manly chat. . . . Then we give this nice lady here our boarding passes. . . . *Et voilá* . . . We're in like Flynn. Didn't give us a glance. Bravo, Celeste."

We flopped into our business-class seats; I by the window, Celeste in front of us.

"*Champagne? Jus d'orange?*" The flight attendant extended a tray of drinks.

Lydia snatched four glasses of champagne and passed me two. We gulped, the dizzying events since the previous day at last presenting their bill. Lydia motioned for another round, and we all began to relax.

"London," I mumbled through the scarf. "I can't get off in Heathrow looking like this. Brits aren't like the French, they'll nab me."

"For what?"

"Dressing like a woman."

"In London? You're joking."

"Still, I won't do it."

"Then change after we take off. In the john."

"By myself this time."

"I should hope so. Uh-oh, this doesn't look good."

"I know, Lydia, that's what's I'm trying to tell you."

"I mean they're opening the door again."

"What door?"

"The one they just closed. The *airplane* door."

"Mother of God . . ."

"Keep your head down. One of them's getting on. Pull that scarf over your eyes, you'll look like a Muslim. They won't dare touch a Muslim woman."

"Mother of Christ God . . ."

"Quiet. Put your head on my shoulder."

She began to stroke me and hum a lullaby, rocking slightly, like a mother soothing a frightened child. Another kind of humming swept around us, other passengers buzzing with concern.

What's happening?

Why aren't we taking off?

Who's this man marching down the aisle, pausing here and there to scrutinize?

I counted off the seconds.

The minutes.

Then Lydia stopped crooning. I heard the plane door shut. The aircraft began to roll.

Airborne.

Lydia summoned another round of drinks.

Outside: a purple sky, the last stars, a pale sliver of white moon.

"A miracle," I said.

"See?" Lydia replied. "Even you're a believer now. Won't Ernesto be pleased. Which reminds me, I must call him, soon as we get to Heathrow. Our hideaway destination ought to cheer him, it's so dull and safe. Though God knows how long we'll have to be apart. I already miss him so."

Her eyes lost their energy, a mist formed.

"What I'd really like to know now," I said, "is exactly who the hell were those guys back there at the airport."

"Well, my dear Dan, they did look like cops, although you can hardly tell the difference anymore."

"No, I mean, if they were really looking for us, then who tipped them off to start out with—in other words, whose money is it really? Whoever they are, these characters have an awful long reach. I'm not so sure even about this dull safe place we're headed for."

We planned to be on Martha's Vineyard by late afternoon, local time.

"It's beyond them," said Lydia. "Believe me, the Vineyard's totally out of it. It's nowhere."

"But like Celeste said, even the Clintons go there."

"Exception proves the rule."

In the plane john, I changed back into my own clothes from my shoulder bag. The flight attendant gave us a series of harsh assessing squints.

But no questions were asked.

59

At Heathrow, with a couple of hours to kill before the midday flight to Boston, we had nothing to do but stroll the transit lounges and tax-free shopping zones, bazaars the size of football fields.

Tin Pan Alley tunes, written before Lindbergh crossed the Atlantic, floated in the air of the cavernous halls.

Easing their way along marbled alleys were swarms of travelers, from Bombay to Buenos Aires, Tokyo to Topeka, gliding past rows of boutiques, roving from counter to counter, stopping to snap up pricey Pink's shirts, tweeds from Harrods, single malt Scotch and Cuban cigars.

Lydia placed a phone call to Ernesto. Celeste and I waited just outside the booth.

"*Urbe Vaticana?*" Lydia half-shouted. "*Urbe Vaticana? Cardinale Tovini, per favore. Si, precisamente, il Cardinale.*"

Then, to us: "They put me on hold. They're playing the *Ave Maria*, listen."

I put my ear to the phone. It was true. An organ played. A choir sang.

Lydia sniffled. "Makes me miss him even more." The phone again. "*Si?*" Her voice trembled. "*Si? Si. Si. Si. Capisco. Che meraviglioso. Grazie, sorella mia, grazie mille.*"

Her face sagged like a Roman ruin.

"What's wrong?" said Celeste.

"Please," Lydia sighed, "don't *let* me get started. The nun said they've just sent him to a monastery. On a spiritual retreat. Must have overstayed his leave in Paris. Let's just pray this spiritual exercise wins him permanent parole a bit sooner."

At a champagne and oyster bar, we three mounted stools and ordered brunch.

Expressions relieved, but somber.

"Well, anyway, here's to the future," said Celeste, lifting a glass, straining to sound optimistic. "We're so lucky. I mean, whoever figured we'd get this far? Back there, I was a little worried yesterday, especially in the water. But no more. My mood's changed. We're going to make it now, I can feel it."

Expressions stayed glum.

"Yes," I said. "We've had terrific luck. Except for my leg."

We all nodded, grim-faced.

"You're right, I mean, just look at me," said Celeste. "A few months ago? Didn't have a pot to pee in, pardon my French, now I'm on my way to gazillions."

Solemnity reigned.

"Exactly, darlings," said Lydia, "and this is just the beginning. So here's to us."

"Yes," I said, "to us."

Our orders arrived. Lydia looked with approval on the oysters. "Only thing from water worth eating, except for caviar. So let's not be chintzy, this *is* a celebration—"

And so she ordered four ounces of beluga.

The caviar came, and we finished our meal in silence.

The flight to Boston wasn't much jollier. Although the ladies slept soundly—a possibility, since we were in business class—I dozed in spurts, under two pairs of eyeshades, both ears plugged with those tiny sponges airlines provide as hush kits for muffling engine roar.

Drifting in and out of consciousness, I dreamed, my fitful visions populated by shooters on motorcycles. French policemen and elegant art sharks. Skirt-chasing princes pursuing their prey, across the bizarre landscapes of Picasso-like paintings. Dad, down in his sea on eternal vacation, was winking at me.

And then, Boston.

Passport control. A dash across Logan airport. A local Cape Air hop and, a half-hour's flight later, the tiny airport on Martha's Vineyard, isle of our final refuge.

In a cold gray drizzle, it certainly seemed a long, long way from any-where, Martha's Vineyard.

As cheerful and welcoming as a cemetery.

The hideaway we rented, with a one-year lease, was in Edgar-town on South Water Street, in a ritzy row of starchy white har-borview houses, including several captains' mansions from the town's early whaling days. Although this New England Yankee vil-lage doesn't look at all like old Antibes—Edgartown has been around only a few centuries, not millennia—the two towns do have a few qualities in common: classy seaside setting, aging charm, a reputa-tion for harboring oodles of swank dough-re-me.

Money, in fact, was the subject of our very first conversation in Edgartown, through the open window of the taxi as we pulled up in front of the house.

"Hi? I'm Karen Curdy, your real estate agent?"

Our greeter, waiting for us with the house keys, was one of those young American women for whom every other statement is a tenta-tive question.

"My partner made a big mistake," she wailed, as we emerged from the cab. "Wally quoted you the wrong rent? It's wa-a-ay too low. Stop, please?" She trailed us up the front path, an agitated hiss-ing goose. "It's the wrong rent—"

"Impossible," said Lydia, coolly. "I've known Wally for ages. Wally never makes mistakes."

Lydia went sweeping up the porch steps, without giving the goose even a flash of those violet eyes, which, I could now see, were sparkling with amusement.

"Besides," said Lydia, over her shoulder, "I have a lease. In writ-ing."

Lydia was waving a piece of paper as she whisked through the front door, flaunting a fax she'd asked old flame Wally to have wait-ing for her when we disembarked in Boston.

She went striding into the hall as if she were to this manor born, slowing a moment as she passed a full-length mirror to adjust her invisible crown before sailing on.

"You don't understand," Ms. Curdy keened after her. "This island is premium? The Clintons come here?"

"Don't discourage us," said Lydia, peering into the kitchen, "we've just arrived."

"And Chappaquiddick's just over there—" Ms. Curdy jabbed a trembling finger at the harbor, the infamous isthmus indeed just the other side of the water. "Walter Cronkite sails his boat right in front of you, almost. And lots of famous authors live here, so you have to understand. All this commands quality rents?"

Ms. Curdy proceeded to drop some writers' names I barely recognized, except for Dashiell Hammett, who I knew had died decades before.

Maybe it was true, at least some of what Ms. Curdy claimed, but none of us for a moment thought any of it worth more rent.

In the face of our intransigence, Ms. Curdy surrendered, stomping out the door with a parting shot. "This isn't going to make you people very popular, not around here."

An accurate forecast, it developed. But for entirely unexpected reasons.

60

Our first night in Edgartown.

Winter winds whipped around the house, buffeting our bedroom window, whistling through the cracks and into our bones.

Garlic brought a welcome warmth.

Jet-lagged, melancholy, feelings mixed at being back in the States but still in hiding, Celeste and I lay in each other's arms in bed, her head on my chest.

She: "Didn't look like the marrying kind, did she?"

Me: "Who didn't—"

"Curdy, the real estate hustler."

"What do you mean?"

"I mean, I think I've seen her somewhere before. And if I'm right, then what Lydia said about this place being so starchy and all? How we might have to get married, if we stick around here for awhile? Well, ho-ho-ho, not if they let ol' hurdy Curdy in."

"You know her?"

"Seen her. Or her twin sister. In New York. Wolfie repped her."

"You mean, she's a wh—" I stopped myself, but not in time. I felt Celeste's body stiffen in my arms.

"Go ahead, say it. Call me a whore."

"I didn't mean that, Celeste, I didn't mean you. I mean—"

"But that's *not* what you were thinking." She rolled away from me.

"I'm sorry." And I really was sorry. Boy, was I sorry.

"Skip it," she said, and turned her back to me.

Long silence.

Then, me: "But what do you really think, Celeste, honestly—"

"About?"

". . . about getting married, and all."

And all.

It popped out, just like that. A snap idea beckoned, incredibly. Young wife, kids, summer sailing on Vineyard sound. *Out of it*, as Lydia put it, out of it forever, and in splendid safety.

Celeste turned over and eyed me, cautiously. "What do you mean . . . *'what do I think?'*"

"You know, getting married . . . and so on."

"Jeez, Dan, don't take it so hard. I didn't mean you have to get carried away. Marry me, just to show how sorry you are? Just because you think I used to be a whore?"

"Well, no—"

"All right, maybe I was something *like* that. After all, I did do it. I've got nothing to hide. Maybe not full-time professionally, but certainly part-time for profit. And if that made me a whore, well, if that's how you feel, why bring up marriage? You trying to save me from myself? I don't need saving, thank you very much."

"No, Celeste, c'mon, give me a break. I'm trying to be serious here."

"So who's joking?"

"Look, what I'm actually saying is, I think we're really ready, you know, that's what I mean. I'm like . . . well, in love, okay. You can see that, right? And so, it's only natural, isn't it . . . I want to marry you. Here or almost anywhere, I swear." I was forty years old, almost forty-one, and it was the first time in my life I'd ever proposed. Thought of *us*, instead of mainly me. "And you? How do you feel?"

"Gosh, you *are* serious. Okay, I'm flattered, really I am, Dan, honestly. But if you stop to think about it now . . . it might interfere, you know."

"What might?"

"Being married."

"Interfere with what?"

"My career. My new career."

Mainly me, not us. It took me to age forty to think like an adult, so why should Celeste, all of twenty-two, be any different?

"Don't underestimate me, Mister O. That French movie hasn't been released yet, but when it is, who knows what might happen. Not for Celeste Tranor perhaps, but maybe for Gina Lasagna. I warned you that someday we'd go our separate ways, but I always thought it would be mutual. I just hadn't counted on this."

"On what—"

"On you changing so much."

Nor had I. The footloose fellow I'd fancied myself for twenty years of *la dolce vita* in the sun had at last grown up, and the young woman who'd entered my life—as a beautiful victim, beguiling and bedazzling me—remained a single spirit still, as free as the wind.

I shouldn't have been surprised.

Or shocked.

But to say that I wasn't saddened? Disappointed? Cut down to size? That would be a lie.

"But where will you go?" I asked. "When you do go."

"Hard to say. Anyway, hard to say at least right now. You see, honey, I've always known what I wanted to get away from—that part's been absolutely crystal clear to me all my life—but exactly where I'm headed, that's the part I've never been able to pin down precisely. Still, I've got some time. After all, I'm only twenty-two."

$ $ $

The next morning, we didn't return to the subject.

And, dejected as I was, I decided to let it simmer. To just hope and go with the flow, so to speak, the pace of which picked up right after breakfast, when Lydia's old flame, Wally Converse, accommodating real estate agent and barkeep, materialized on our doorstep.

Lydia introduced Wally as an old friend from her nursing days, although he didn't appear very doctorly. A tall wiry man, about Lydia's age (but considerably more worn), with craggy features and a New Englander's taciturn manner, he wasn't what I thought would ever be her type. (Even if she had displayed rather catholic tastes in men. My overweight father, various royal riffraff, a cardinal.)

After a subdued "hello," the slightest honk of enthusiasm enlivened Wally's foghorn voice. "Got commercial space for you."

Lydia had told him about her art gallery plans.

"Prime," was how he pitched it. "Downtown, right near the harbor. Two-story wood-frame. No bargain rental. But an ocean view. Tons of passing tourists. You'll clean up. In season. You price your stuff right."

And we all rolled off to inspect our new business premises. A lease was signed, on the spot, by Lydia and me—Celeste declined,

263

and refrained from giving further details. I couldn't bear to probe for any, and Lydia's arched eyebrows said she didn't have to.

"I'll just take a commission on anything I sell," said Celeste. "Twenty percent?"

"A deal," said Lydia.

And then we adjourned to Wally's establishment on Main Street, his the only bar in Edgartown that stayed open right through the long bleak winters Vineyard residents so treasure.

Lydia ordered, what else, a round of champagne.

"Don't get to sell much of the stuff," said Wally, pouring the bubbly. "Might even get to like it, with you folks around."

It soon became our custom, the end of most afternoons, to scoot down to Wally's. Lydia's treat, for she always swore it was the champagne that enabled her to keep her model's figure.

Throughout, I kept an eye peeled for any news of our pursuers, watching CNN in Wally's bar and again every evening back at the house.

Each morning over coffee, I scanned the *Times*, always on the lookout for mentions of the former Secretary of the Treasury and his cohorts. The Secretary—like his limousine partner, the ex-Attorney General—had resigned from office, unindicted but under a cloud, I learned through an Internet search of the *Times* archives, but at that point the story—like our trail, I prayed—went cold.

Not a hint of snoops or tails clouded our Vineyard days.

It looked as if Lydia had guessed right. And we were going to make it, free and clear, right in the homeland of, ensconced in the backyard of, under the noses of—who?

For whoever our pursuers were, we still had no idea.

Celeste spent hours every day crooning to tapes of Sinatra and Billy Holiday, when she wasn't watching old videos of Hepburn and Bacall. The singing nuns movie had yet to be released in the States, and the only review Ernesto managed to send us from Europe was in Italian. Gina Lasagna was mentioned twice, we could decipher that much, and Lydia assured her the mentions were highly favorable.

Celeste was pleased. Her hopes seemed on the rise to elsewhere. But to where exactly, I didn't dare ask. She was no longer sharing dreams for her future, or from her past, with the doubting likes of me.

And so our days raced by, as predictably as the tides, and it seemed like no time before our inventory started arriving, the oil paintings and gouaches from Tante Elisabeth, agent for all her artist friends up in the hills behind the Cote d'Azur, all busy splattering away in the styles of Picasso, Miro, Dali, et al.

At the prices we'd be charging, our merchandise looked genuine enough to qualify as real bargains, although we were careful to label—albeit not in the largest of print—the goods' true provenance.

61

We scheduled our gallery opening for Memorial Day weekend.

Right at the start of the season, we weren't expecting much of a crowd. Or any sales. Wally, with a few of the regulars from his bar, dropped by for the preview, to scarf down hors d'oeuvres and free drinks while ogling the art, the cause of more jokes from this irreverent lot of locals than the ooh-ing and ah-ing we'd hoped for.

That is, except for Wally, who followed Lydia around from painting to painting, eager listener to the pitch she'd assiduously assembled from a collection of art books—including *Pricing Modern Art*—all acquired through our local Vineyard bookstores.

Bright and early the morning after the preview, when we opened the doors for real business, the first live customer crossed our gallery threshold.

Bobby Joe Pelmers.

Even at that early point in our Vineyard stay, we knew who he was. Not by sight, but by reputation. For he was, easily, Edgartown's most notorious resident.

For whom prices and labels were of no concern, much to our ultimate regret, it would develop, as well as to his.

"Hi-i-i-i . . ." It was Bobby Joe, laying on a drawl longer than the Pedernales River. He swaggered into our establishment as if the art gallery were the Last Chance Saloon.

"Bobby Joe Pelmers." He shook our hands. "Just bought a helluva place over on Na-a-antucket. So da-a-amn much bigger'n my old cottage here, need a whole new collection to fill the walls."

His "old cottage here" was the largest house on Martha's Vineyard. And the cause of his notoriety.

(Here's Bobby Joe's story. I just read it again recently, in *Pricing Modern Art*, where I'd stuck his obituary clippings. Bobby Joe had made a couple of hundred million the easy way—fairly legal, too. A native of Houston, Texas, abandoned at birth and raised in an orphanage, a high school dropout who finished college at night, Bobby Joe had clawed his way up the corporate ladder to the top of a New England computer company. An all-American hero. After a few years running the company down, stacking the board of directors with candidates for the geriatric ward, Bobby Joe downsized by the thousands, and sold the company bargain-basement cheap to some former business associates in Houston, who rewarded him with a fabulous stake in the new company, which stake they then bought back from him shortly after, making Bobby Joe Pelmers a wealthy man indeed. These shenanigans were quite legitimate, it seemed, except in the eyes of some former employees and stockholders, who were suing Bobby Joe and his buddies at the time of Bobby Joe's death.

A couple of years before our arrival on the Vineyard, Bobby Joe had built his "cottage," fronting the Edgartown inner harbor on the Chappy side, a mammoth four-story confection with thirty-eight windows overlooking the water, all staring right into the starchy white faces of the less large, Greek revival villas arrayed in stately order on the opposite shore.

Which upright stretch included our place.

On the lawn of his behemoth waterfront estate, Bobby Joe had installed an Olympic-size swimming pool, with enough outdoor lighting to illuminate an airport. He moored his sixty-foot cigarette speedster at the end of his own dock, the harbor's longest and widest.

I daresay Gatsby himself couldn't have outdone Bobby Joe. Whenever we looked out to enjoy our harbor view, we couldn't miss his crystal palace.

And so, for all his insolent offenses to local conceptions of good taste, Bobby Joe's membership applications got blackballed at the Chappaquiddick Beach Club, the Edgartown Yacht Club, and the Reading Room private drinking society.

Which meant, for a man of his means, he had nowhere to go but Nantucket.

Which he did, forthwith.

But not before selling his Chappy spread, at an obscene profit, to a rap star from south-central L.A.

The estate soon became a focal point of the annual beach party held on Martha's Vineyard by African-American fraternities and sororities from all across the northeast, highlight of the tourist season, apart from the Clinton visits. Hundreds, maybe thousands of young dudes strut their stuff around that Olympic pool and on the Gatsby dock, straining to Be Like Mike—Tyson, that is, not Jordan, in the view of some residents.)

"This here'll a-a-all look great in my new living room," Bobby Joe assured us, that opening day in our gallery. "Whatcha askin'?"

"Depends," said Lydia, violet eyes beaming as bright as the spotlights on Bobby Joe's pool. "Which pieces would you like?"

"Said a-a-all, mean a-a-all. Lump sum deal."

Lydia, for once, was speechless.

I hurriedly consulted our price list.

Celeste didn't bother. "Half-million." An impromptu price. She held our customer's eye, cool as any Kate Hepburn or Lauren Bacall. "Plus shipping and handling. That still comes to less than we'd have to ask individually. But a fair price, considering."

She never blinked.

Neither did Bobby Joe. He just shook his head in disbelief.

"Don't know how y'all make a living, at that rate. These here are famous. Think I even seen some before, that's what caught my eye. But offer's an offer, and I'm accepting."

He shook our hands again. Filled out a check. Left his new address. And was gone.

We were delirious, running around the gallery sticking little red dots under every piece. Lydia called Tante Elisabeth and ordered a rush on the next order. We were on our way to becoming her artists' bread and butter; maybe their pensions, too.

62

The art gallery trade is, we discovered that summer, a convenient conduit for questionable cash, creative accounting metamorphizing murky moolah into legitimate revenue.

So, after turning over our inventory once more—though at a more sedate piece-by-piece rate—we multiplied our revenue as if by magic, whitewashing the flow of our lucky bucks horde through the gallery's books.

By season's end, we'd become highly respectable citizens. Healthy accounts in all the local banks. Contributors to community charities. Pillars of propriety. And no one, not once, asked if Celeste and I were married. Nor did I dare again raise the subject with her.

The uneventful months of the ensuing fall and early winter now blow around hazily in my memory. The autumnal weather quickly turned subarctic, the days and weeks alike as fallen leaves, then snowflakes.

Until a cold gray day not long after Thanksgiving.

We'd spent the afternoon setting up a Christmas display of antique jewelry in the gallery windows. It was Lydia's idea to use some of her old contacts in the jewelry trade to extend our appeal.

"If customers like our art," was her reasoning, "they'll *love* our jewelry. One's a hook for the other."

This expansion of our inventory, I confess, also greatly increased opportunities for creative accounting, cleansing ever more of our original windfall.

At the end of that cold gray day, we gathered as per usual in Wally Converse's bar on Main Street.

Celeste was reading *Variety*. And I was trying to concentrate on CNN's coverage of a twelve-meter yacht race in the South Pacific.

"Make you want to travel?" said Wally, eyeing the sunshine on the screen.

"No," I said, "not really. Done enough traveling for awhile." And I meant it. The Vineyard had started to grow on me. Maybe like green mold, but there it was.

"Traveling sure tempts me," he replied. "I can't wait to retire and take off."

"Me, too, Mister Converse," said Celeste. "Only I'll be working my way around the globe. Life's cozy here. But after this winter, I think I'll be catching cabin fever. Itchy feet, too."

There had been hints, small signs I started detecting from Celeste as the snow began falling. But she was sensitive enough not to say anything. Just as I took similar care with her. Our mutual consideration a consequence of the growing quiet that simultaneously held us together and drove us apart.

I was expecting she'd probably bolt before winter's end.

End of the affair. The years between us ensuring inevitable closure.

But expecting it didn't make this a more attractive conclusion for me. Just made me miserable. Hearing Celeste now openly discuss departure and, even worse, sharing her intentions with others, I felt my cheeks flush with embarrassment.

A public spat just wasn't my style.

"Jeez," Wally said to me, with a sly grin. "Taking it pretty calm, ain't ya, Danno?"

Wally, a great fan of Oprah and daytime soaps during those winter days behind his bar, seemed to relish the mounting emotional tension between Celeste and me. Like a talk show host, he tried egging me on. "Girl says she'll be walking out on you, Dan, you don't say nothing? Just sit there?"

I was about to answer Wally when an apparition burst in at the door.

It was a man, and he stumbled across the threshold in front of a blast of wind from Main Street, an angry squall of arctic air and disheveled hair.

"Close the door!" said Wally.

But the man ignored him, staggering toward us with a hurtful gaze, searching our faces, as if he were hunting for someone. The wind whipped his trenchcoat around his legs, and he swayed, unsteady, struggling to right himself. He appeared in no need of further liquid refreshment.

His fiery eyes locked on mine.

"Yeah," he snarled, "they said I'd find y'all here."

The voice, blustery as the weather, slurred with alcohol and choked with hatred, was faintly familiar. But I could put no name on it immediately. Or on the face so contorted with rage.

". . . all think I'm dumb, doncha, some goddamn dummy rube."

"Mister Pelmers," said Wally, "just take it easy, sir. No one here's said anything against you."

Bobby Joe Pelmers ignored Wally.

He jabbed a quivering finger at me. ". . . a dummy, uh? Well, this rube made two hundred million, how dumb I am. But y'all here still think I'm a sucker, don't you, sell me this phoney shit—"

He tore some crumpled paper from his trenchcoat and tried to throw it at me. It landed on the bar, a gouache I recognized, one we'd sold him, from the school of Miro.

"Phoney!" he shouted. "Goddamn phoney fake shit, all of it! Like you, you li'l piss-ants. School of? School of? Kind of shit's that? *School of* . . . all my neighbors there on Nantucket laughing their asses off at me. Scumbags, playing me like a fool again. Goddamn rube, so dumb he don't know all this shit you're peddling ain't phoney? Bobby Joe Pelmers's a dummy, oh yeah. Goddamn dumb Texas rube. Show y'all how dumb I am—"

At that, Bobby Joe pulled a gun, and pointed it at me.

We were now, all of us at the bar, frozen in a tableau titled: *Terror.*

Celeste seated next to me.

Lydia behind her.

Wally immovable behind the bar.

I was starting to shake my head, when those clear patrician tones of Lydia's broke the silence.

"Mister Pelmers," she said, with the most amazing warmth, "this is surely a misunderstanding. We'd gladly give . . ."

She was sliding off the barstool, extending her hands toward him in friendship, and Bobby Joe was swinging about to face her, when he wobbled drunkenly, slipping as he moved to catch himself from toppling over, and the gun went off.

A tremendous roar filled the bar, as much of a shock to him as to us.

Then I heard Lydia groan.

And Celeste scream.

Lydia fell to the floor, a gaping bloody hole torn in her side.

Next, Celeste and I were down on our knees beside her, and Wally was calling the police.

Celeste was screaming: "He's gone! He's gone!"

Lydia was breathing in loud, irregular gasps. "Please . . . Celeste," she said, between long pauses. ". . . please, dear . . . lower . . . your voice."

The door was still open, banging against the wall with every gust. Bobby Joe Pelmers had fled.

Wally was coming out from behind the bar, heading for the door, when we heard a second shot, muffled, distant, somewhere down by the harbor.

A police car pulled up abruptly in front, on Main Street, and two policemen hopped out, revolvers in hand.

Wally said: "Get an ambulance!"

And one of the cops shouted, "It's coming!" as they both raced toward the harbor, in the direction of the second shot.

An ambulance arrived right behind the police car. Two paramedics raced in. They unfolded a stretcher and rolled Lydia onto it.

Celeste and I rode to the hospital with her. Celeste in front with the driver, me in back with Lydia and the paramedics, who'd begun to cut away her clothing and apply compresses to her wound front and back. An injection put her out of her pain.

63

The operation lasted until just past midnight.

Celeste and I were waiting in the anteroom to the emergency ward, where Wally joined us.

When they wheeled Lydia out from surgery within an oxygen tent, she looked calm and at ease in her sleep. Tubes ran into her arm and nose. She was whisked straight off to the intensive care unit.

The surgeon, in his green operating gown, mask hanging round his neck, appeared solemn as he approached us.

"Can't tell yet how she'll be," he said, shaking his head. "Done a lot of damage in there, hit some highly vital organs. Tomorrow afternoon, might have a clearer idea."

"Tomorrow," I said, blankly.

"Relative?" he asked me.

"No, but close."

"Then maybe you know where she got those scars on her back."

I shrugged and turned to Celeste.

"Didn't know she had any scars," I said.

"Look like shrapnel wounds," said the doctor. "Fragmentation grenade. I saw that kind last in Vietnam."

"I know she was there," I said. "A nurse."

"Decorated," said Celeste, "but I never heard her say anything about wounded."

"She had a rough time," said Wally, softly. "I was with her over there. At Danang. It was one of ours. Friendly fire. That was early in the war."

At this point the police came in, and soon we were all trying to answer their questions about what had happened.

Why we were all at Wally's bar? How did we know Mr. Pelmers? What motives did we think he had for threatening us? And for shooting Lydia?

They were considerate and polite, the police, and showed no suspicion toward any of us. Which was a great relief, at least to two of us. But they kept repeating their questions, slightly altered, as though the sequence of events couldn't possibly have occurred in the manner of the three versions they were getting all at once.

Neither was it easy sorting things out in my own mind by then.

Nor would it ever be. In fact, I'd often look at *Pricing Modern Art* to refresh my memory. The news clippings I stashed in that volume cover the entire episode in all its gory detail.

Wally wrote a long eyewitness piece for the *Vineyard Gazette*, our local weekly paper, for which he used to cover summer sailing races. He gave his version of the shooting. And his memories of Lydia as a nurse in Vietnam: a moving story that included nothing of the tales of dislocated dukes and princes, the exhausted luxury and the venalities she so enjoyed regaling us with.

The Boston daily papers gave the Edgartown events front-page coverage.

With photos.

Bobby Joe Pelmers got the most attention, naturally, being the only famous person involved, as well as the shooter and eventual suicide.

For it seemed that after Bobby Joe shot Lydia, he stumbled down to the harbor, a short distance away at the foot of Main Street, and then made his way out onto the side deck of the yacht club that had once blackballed him.

That's where he stopped to put a bullet in his head.

His body toppled over into the water, and the incoming tidal current carried him farther up the inner harbor. His corpse became entangled in the timber underpinnings of a pier that runs parallel to the yacht club a few hundred yards away. At the end of the pier stands the Reading Room—a private drinking club that had also rejected Bobby Joe. As one can imagine, the members were less than pleased at the ensuing hullabaloo.

A photo on the front page of the *Vineyard Gazette*, now yellowed with age, shows a patrol boat alongside this pier, police with grappling poles probing in the timbers under the Reading Room for Bobby Joe's corpse.

64

Celeste and I were back at the hospital the next morning.

We waited until midday without getting in to see Lydia. I went out for sandwiches.

Around three in the afternoon, the surgeon from the night before came over to talk to us. He looked slightly more hopeful.

"Strong lady," he said. "Might have her around for awhile after all." He gave us permission to go in and see her, and we rushed right off to her room.

Lydia was no longer in an oxygen tent, but she was lying flat, still with a tangle of tubes in her body. She was conscious, and smiled weakly, winking to greet us. The gleam was gone from her eyes, the violet drained of vitality. Her appearance left us shaken, but we tried to hide it.

"We just heard the good news," said Celeste. "You're gonna be great."

"Splendid," Lydia answered weakly. "Who'd want to get accidentally killed, offering to *return* a half-million dollars." She laughed silently. "Should have offered to cut him in on our partnership." She laughed again, a short scratching sound. "That would have appealed to his better business instincts. I was too slow."

"Lydia," I said, "whatever possessed you to go toward him, reach out like that?"

"Beats me. Nurse's instinct? Too much champagne? Training? Maybe I knew it's almost the end for me anyway, but you two still have years ahead of you. I don't know."

"The doctor," said Celeste, "asked us about your scars. We didn't know what to say."

Lydia smiled faintly again. "What'd Wally say?"

"Danang," I answered.

She nodded weakly. "Yes, long time ago. Before you were born, Celeste. Can I ask you a favor?"

"Of course," we said simultaneously.

"Would you call Ernesto, please? Ask him if he could possibly get a dispensation or whatever they call it . . . to leave Italy and come see me for a short while? That would help enormously."

"We'll call as soon as we leave," I said.

"Lovely," she sighed. "We had such wonderful times, the four of us. Wouldn't it be nice to be together again?"

"We will," Celeste sniffled. "Real soon, too." The tears welled in her eyes.

"Now do me another favor, please," said Lydia. "Get me something to write on."

I took a small electronic organizer from my pocket.

"That's useless," said Lydia. "Never could type anyway. And those buttons are so small. Come here, come close."

I leaned forward, and she spoke with great difficulty. "I want to see Ernesto, but just in case . . . put these numbers down." She whispered the numbers to some bank accounts. And a password, *Old Antibes*. "Now, just give me something to sign." Celeste handed her a napkin and a pen. Lydia signed her name, then wrote our names, Celeste's and mine, and amounts next to each name. "There," said Lydia, "if something happens to me, you fill out the rest for the bank. I have no other offspring. It's for your children, if you get married. For each of you, if you don't. I never did, so I'm no one to preach, not at this late date."

"Don't say that," said Celeste, wiping her eyes. "You've got years."

"Maybe, maybe not. There are years, and there are years. Anyway, the money won't buy time for me. Somebody has to enjoy it, that's what money's for. Maybe not such a bad thing I got shot actually, publicity should do wonders for the gallery's business, don't you think? It's bound to be in all the papers. Just make sure they get the correct address. And you've got to be honest with the press—the jewelry's genuine, but the art is 'from the schools of,' and priced accordingly. They should write that. We don't want anyone going off half-cocked again. How on earth could that poor man have been so deluded?"

A nurse came in and gave us a nod, time to go.

"Do mind the store," said Lydia, as we rose to leave.

65

Two days later, Ernesto Cardinal Tovini arrived on Martha's Vineyard.

Celeste and I met him at the airport. He was dressed in mufti, save for a red tie and his big ring. He was looking very tired, much older than when we last saw him.

We drove him directly from the airport to the hospital. He was very quiet as we rode along those empty country roads, moving his lips as if in prayer, looking out the window, focused on nothing in particular out there.

We told him that the doctor said Lydia's chances appeared good.

"From the doctor's lips," he said, "to the ear of God."

"The doctor," Celeste chirped, "also said Lydia had these incredible scars on her back. From the war, the one in Vietnam."

He nodded. "Yes. But Lydia didn't wish to speak about that. Didn't want people to know. That's why she never went sunbathing, unless we were alone. The war was such a long time ago, she always said she was crazy to go over there. Said if she had to be a nurse, to get it out of her system to mother people, maybe she'd have been better off just staying at home. But she didn't regret her work. Lydia lived a very different life, all her life, not like an ordinary person at all."

"No," I said, "an extraordinary woman. Hard to imagine her—"

But I couldn't continue, I couldn't bring myself to say the unthinkable. I'd reached the point where I felt it would be like losing my own mother all over again.

"You mean, imagine her dying?" said Ernesto. "Perhaps she won't. But if she does, she will be ready."

He grew silent, until we reached the hospital. "I'll want to be alone with her, if you don't mind."

"Certainly," I said, and we walked him to the reception desk, where he introduced himself as Father Tovini. The nurse on duty looked rather dubiously at his red silk tie, but gave him a pass for the intensive care unit.

Celeste and I left the hospital and headed back to the house, intending to return for Ernesto around dinnertime.

As we were rolling into our driveway in Edgartown, a taxi pulled up. Journalists had been pestering the hell out of us since the shooting and suicide, and we groaned when we thought this might be yet another vulture.

A man carrying a briefcase alighted from the cab, and called to us as we walked up the path to the front porch.

"Mr. O'Sullivan? Ms. Tranor?"

We turned.

"Yes?" I said.

"I'm an attorney. Representing someone missing four million, four hundred thousand dollars. May I come in, please? I'd like to speak to you for a few minutes."

And so, at long last, the moment had arrived.

We led him into the living room, and he took a seat in an easy chair facing the couch.

Celeste and I sat on the couch.

Our visitor certainly looked like a lawyer. Horn-rimmed glasses, black wingtips, navy pinstripe, dark blue tie. At least he wasn't the motorcyclist shooter of my nightmares.

"We were wondering when this would happen," said Celeste.

"Yes," I added. "But you're not what I expected."

He shrugged. "Hope I haven't disappointed you." His voice was deep, cultured, confident; he had a Boston accent. If you were ever caught in a legal dispute, he was the sort you hoped would be on your side.

"Sorry I couldn't get to Rome in time," he said, glancing at my leg.

"Me, too."

"Things got a bit rushed there. I must say, you people do get around. Hasn't been easy keeping up with you. In fact, if it hadn't been for all these latest heroics . . ." He reached into his briefcase and extracted the *Boston Globe* from the day before. ". . . it might have been a long time before we had the occasion to meet. I must admit we never thought you'd pop up anywhere in these parts. Ms. Lydia Sands, she's well, I trust?"

"Well as can be expected," I said, "under the circumstances."

"Unfortunate circumstances, for you. But otherwise you're enjoying life on the Vineyard?"

"Yes," said Celeste, doleful, resigned. "It's just peachy."

"Well, then let's not take up too much of your time. My client wants his money back. By Friday. In cash, plus the standard fifty percent. We know you can afford it now, we know that much, and we don't expect you to be irrational about it. We'd prefer a quiet, prompt conclusion to everything. I imagine you would, too."

We nodded.

"Intelligent. I told my client you went to Yale, Mr. O'Sullivan, that you could probably listen to reason. So I hope you don't mind meeting me at the Harvard Club on Friday. In Boston, Commonwealth Avenue. In the afternoon, be there at three. I'll arrive five minutes later. Take a seat in the foyer lounge, with your back to the door."

"Okay," I said, drily.

"Then that's it," he said, rising. "You now have nothing more to worry about. My client gives you his word of honor. And he's always been a man of his word. Goodbye, Ms. Tranor, nice meeting you."

I accompanied him to the door.

"Just one more thing," the lawyer said, as he and I stood on the porch. "My client was wondering, Mr. O'Sullivan, in fact he was more than wondering: We've been very impressed at how you've managed to multiply his money."

I raised my eyebrows.

"We have sources. My client's interests are worldwide. We don't know what your current plans are, Mr. O'Sullivan, or how that young lady inside may fit into your future, but my client's been so impressed with your investment skills, he's authorized me to offer you a postion, anytime, anywhere, managing one of his portfolios. For the Star Ace Corporation. I believe you've heard of it."

I was flabbergasted.

"You do have quite the knack," he said. "Pick it up at Yale?"

I shrugged. "Here and there."

"Looking for a job?"

"I don't think so. Not right now. Got other things on my mind."
Did I ever.

"Well, if you do change your mind, Mr. O'Sullivan, I believe you still remember where you can always contact Mr. Starace."

Starace. The name dropped, like a golden egg out a hen's rump.

"I better be going, my cab is waiting. Thank you for being so reasonable. This may or may not give you any satisfaction, but you're about to save some powerful people a great deal of discomfort. They'll appreciate that. As will Mr. Starace. So you won't have to worry anymore. After Friday, that is."

"Terrific," I said, as he got in his cab. "See you Friday."

Starace.

Mr. F.J. Starace. A man of his word.

And so the spider, Star Ace, wove its web and, having woven, always trapped. Wherever. Whenever. As long as it was mountains of money one was after, the web was inescapable.

Wait until Lydia hears this, I thought. No more shooters.

No more running.

And, by Friday, all the loot that was left would be ours.

Free and clear.

Our kindly benefactor, her dear old friend, the steadfast F. J. Starace. Man of his word, right to the end.

That ought to bring Lydia bouncing back to health, I prayed.

66

It took hours of phoning and faxing to get all that money transferred through the accounts of our far-flung companies, and for a bank in Boston—the name of which I can never mention, for obvious reasons—to assemble the cash as instructed for pickup on Friday.

So, at the appointed hour, there I was in the Harvard Club foyer, seated with my back to the door, two black canvas travel bags at my feet; bags as close in appearance as I could find to the bags the beautiful Celeste had dragged into my Brooklyn apartment on that snowstormy night, which now seemed like a century ago.

"Mister O'Sullivan," said the deep voice behind me. The lawyer placed his hand on my shoulder and leaned forward, as if he were greeting a dear old classmate. "Thank you. You may go now."

"Don't you want to count it?" I asked, incredulous. I had. At the bank. Every last bill.

"Not here, Mister O'Sullivan. And not now. We know where you live. Just leave the bags, and leave the club, please."

I rose, and felt his eyes on my back as I walked out the door onto Commonwealth Avenue.

Two hours later, Celeste picked me up at the Vineyard airport.

"How did it go?" she asked.

"It went," I said. "Four point four. Plus fifty percent. Six point six, total. Weighed a ton."

She leaned over and kissed me, deeply. "But we're still rich, Dan, richer than we ever dreamed." And we both had to laugh. "And we're free! Je-e-e-ezus," she cried, "let's go tell Lydia! Get Ernesto, get some champagne, let's celebrate!"

For the moment, I passed on buying champagne—Lydia certainly wasn't allowed any alcohol—and instead drove straight to the hospital.

The nurse at the desk stood when we entered the lobby.

"Father Tovini is with her now," she said. "He gave her the last rites before she died, about a half-hour ago. We called your house, but there was no answer—"

Then everything stopped.

Our spirits, bird-buoyant in celebration just a moment before, froze, before instantly plummeting, crashing in grief and numbness.

Celeste took my hand, and we walked in silence up to the intensive care unit.

Ernesto was at Lydia's bedside, his head bowed. He looked up as we entered, his eyes filled with tears.

"She was sleeping," he said softly. "It was very quiet . . . very quiet."

Celeste and I each bent to kiss Lydia's forehead.

"When are you going back," Celeste asked Ernesto.

He smiled gently. "Saturday evening, from Boston. I agreed to be back in Rome by Sunday."

"Good," said Celeste, "I'm going with you."

Just like that.

She gave us both a cheerless pinch of a smile. "I'll send you my address," she promised me. "C'mon, Dan, you'll get used to it. You got used to not reading *The New York Times* every day, didn't you? So don't go getting so conventional on me now, and stop looking like that—it's all for the best. Lydia would understand perfectly, Mister O, you know that."

I was stunned.

But not surprised. And yes, Lydia would have indeed understood.

Still, Celeste's sense of place and timing left much to be desired.

Or maybe not.

Maybe she knew exactly what she was doing. For it was no time or place for me to object. I was in no condition.

And upon reflection, I could see her point, although that didn't make it any easier. We'd both had a grand run for our money, and—thanks to the dead woman at whose bedside we stood, this once joyful, scheming, hustling, wounded Lydia Sands, who'd nursed my dying father and lost her life to save mine—Celeste and I were now both even richer. At liberty to live our lives, without fear, exactly as we pleased.

Which didn't at all make Celeste's rapid departure—a departure as abrupt as her arrival in my life—any gentler to absorb.

In the end, the years between us mattered greatly.

Too greatly.

67

During the drive back to the house, Celeste attempted explaining.

"One reason I left Louisiana was that men always wanted everything their own way with me. I thought it could be different in New York. It wasn't, and I'm not letting that happen again. It's a feeling that you've changed, but I haven't. You want to stop, maybe for good. I just want to keep going. It's like I'm just getting started. Remember our deal? How once that happens, we're each completely on our own? No more partners? We're two different people."

"I still feel close to you."

"And I do to you. But it's time now, Dan. Deals have to end sooner or later."

"Where will you go?" I asked.

"Back to Rome first . . . and after that, it depends." She shrugged. "No reason to hide any more. I'll write," she said. "And I'll tell you how everything works out. So you have to write, too. Promise?"

"Sure, but . . ."

"But what? That's how it is. I'm sorry, I'm like, I don't know, so mysterious I guess. But I'll always remember you with love, Dan, always and forever. You've meant loads to me. And if it makes you feel any better, I think you're right."

"About what?"

"About getting married. You probably should."

68

Two days later, I was alone again.

I'd stood at the side of the road as Celeste and Ernesto left for the airport in a taxi, and I'd waved good-bye.

The *Emma K.*, Celeste's morning songs and her afternoon dancing. Our garlicky nights and our art gallery. The chase itself. Even life on the run. All blown away like so much old newspaper left on a beach.

We'd had our time of times. Our beginning, our middle and, at last, an end to it all.

So I went out for a long walk along the shorefront—to clear my head, collect my thoughts—down to the beach, and out past the town lighthouse, the dunes there like great ant hills, without design, the bay sprinkled with the white heads of waves angry in the wind.

By most lights, I was a rich man.

But I could feel no cause for joy then. Fortune had levied some pretty stiff taxes. Wayward though Lydia and Celeste may have been—correction: truly were—even my dim powers of illumination couldn't hide the truth.

The truth. That, however improbable, I'd come to view one woman as surrogate mother. The other, as eventual wife.

And now I'd lost both.

An hypothesis suggested itself. That God—for diversion? for topsy-turvy amusement? for the hell of it?—nurtured a powerful predeliction for mixing and matching vices with vulnerabilities. Greed, guile, gullibility: to name just three of the more appropriate in our case.

My theory, as a lesson drawn, wasn't terribly profound and hardly redemptive. Nor did it do a thing to cheer me. But I had to redirect my anger somewhere and, at that point, divine self-indulgence appeared as good a target as any.

So I railed at the heavens during my walk along Town Beach.

For I hadn't the strength, and certainly not the conditioning—prep school, Yale, my father, the Caribbean sweet life—to look myself in the eye, and aim a fair share of blame where it might, more justly, have belonged.

A lesson late in coming.

Along with a couple of other tardy epiphanies. Such as, being partners-in-crime perhaps wasn't necessarily the firmest foundation for building a healthy relationship.

Or a longer life.

Although, on both counts, I grant that you can usually expect, from certain reliable quarters, to get a sales pitch for quite a contrary view. If nothing else, that much remains a solid bet in this life.

But slouching along the beach, that bleak day, I was still too dumb with sorrow, too shocked by my own stupidity, in my failing to foresee that all those dreams of turning vices into advantage had rested on some rather ridiculous assumptions.

I began to feel as if my head had grown hollow, and the cavity of my chest had become a vacuum.

The sky seemed even colder to me, the sun in retreat, as if chased off by Celeste's departure.

And by Lydia's death.

The light over the sea was shifting.

Looking back at Edgartown, from the point at the end of the beach, down the curve of the shore, I watched the sky grow gray behind racing clouds.

And now the village, so white and snug, acquired a new attraction for me, appearing as good a refuge as anywhere for a while, perhaps even not without a certain special comfort all its own.

Now

$ $ $

69

You know how it is. How we usually remember what we want to remember?

And then just forget what we want to forget.

Me? I'm in the pink, almost fifty now, and still got all my marbles. Also married, at last. Two kids: a boy and a girl.

And still on Martha's Vineyard.

The pleasant memories are always easy. Forever swimming around in the sea of my subconscious, before racing up to the surface, like a school of marlins, with no great effort.

Like the phone call I got late last Saturday afternoon, from Wally Converse.

I hadn't seen Wally for some months. Nothing unusual because, since he retired, he's either off on foreign junkets or at home here hibernating by himself.

Anyone who gets to know Wally Converse, as I have over these years, would say that, despite his name, he's still a hard guy to talk with, no matter what, and impossible if you don't share his late-life enthusiasm for travel. Taciturn Yankee, Wally, even when he was running that bar on Main Street, he got me on the line and, by his lights, he was indeed excited.

An oddly disturbing honk of enthusiasm enlivened his foghorn voice: "Got some champagne, Dan."

And all of a sudden I just couldn't help thinking—hoping—this was about Celeste.

Although Wally didn't say so, just: "Wanna show ya somethin'. Travel video."

I hopped in the car and, through the tail end of a blinding November nor'easter, drove out along the route toward the municipal dump over to Wally's place on Clevelandtown Road.

Wally was, of course, alone. He led me into the kitchen, the only warm room in his house, where he keeps his TV right on the breakfast table, next to the VCR.

Wally opened the refrigerator and brought out a bottle of champagne.

". . . for old times' sake. Wouldn't call you, Danno, this miserable weather, wasn't for old times."

"Heard from her?" I asked.

Wally didn't answer, but he knew who I meant. I'd been hoping she might even be there, that she'd finally come back, sashaying off a plane from somewhere faraway.

Well, whales might've swum through the air in that nor'easter, but it was highly improbable any plane got to land on the Vineyard that afternoon.

Still, my hopes stayed on the boil: Celeste might yet resurface.

Which, in a manner of speaking, she did.

"Strange," said Wally, shaking his head of fine white hair. "Real strange. Know I'm planning a trip to Russia next spring."

A statement really, not a question.

Wally popped the bottle and, with his old bartender's finesse, filled our glasses to the brim without losing a drop.

"Never been to Russia," he said. "You?"

"No," I answered. "So?"

"So, look at this." Wally handed me a video cassette. "Got it through the travel agency."

MOSCOW BY NIGHT, the cassette label read. A SHOW GUIDE TO NIGHTCLUBS & BARS.

I laughed. "Busman's holiday?"

"Something like that. You know me." Wally inserted the cassette in the VCR. "Watch."

Actually, I couldn't watch much of anything. It was all a blur, as Wally hit fast-forward, searching for some exact point on the tape. Clearly, he'd already studied this video, since he knew precisely where to stop and freeze the frame.

"Check that," he croaked.

It was Celeste all right, caught in the glare of spotlights. She was wearing a low-cut evening dress, creamy silk and body-hugging.

She was still beautiful.

290

And not alone.

There was a short, beefy man in a tux right behind her. The way his hands grasped her hips and pulled her rump into his groin upset me a little, but didn't surprise me. I was no longer jealous—been too long, and my marriage is a very happy one; moreover, I'd never heard another word from Celeste after she left—but that picture of her getting pawed over still looked somehow wrong. Not morally. Just simply as an offense to the good taste I preferred to remember her by.

Good taste?

Yes: Because apart from the occasional fit of madness (the singing nuns movie, for example, which I never did see), Celeste wasn't really obvious—certainly not by current standards, and at least not for the fast few months I knew her. Bold, yes. But beneath her svelte surface, she remained, in my memory, the victim-waif; the street-smart yet frightened child-woman, whom I'd once known and cared for.

Yet all I said to Wally now was: "Mmm, maybe . . . Looks like her."

"*Looks?*" Wally grew unusually animated. "That champagne gettin' to you, Danno? Just coupla sips?" Wally jabbed his finger at the TV screen. "It's her, damnit, knew it second I seen her there."

Yes: of course it was Celeste. And I couldn't keep myself from erupting into unrestrained laughter: the lady hadn't changed a bit.

"What's so funny?" said Wally.

"Everything, Wally, *everything*." It all came back, and yes, it was all funny, from this distance. "But why Russia?" I asked.

"Why not?" Wally shrugged. "Never been to Russia. Looks interesting, so figured I'd go. Heard about it on Oprah, a special Oprah did, and Oprah'd never give you a bum tip."

"No, Wally, I mean Celeste. What's she doing in Russia?"

"Business, I guess. Tape says she's got your best nightclub in Moscow. Watch."

Wally reversed the tape and played it back.

The video showed a dressed-to-the-nines crowd waiting in line to pass through a metal detector, after which huge guards frisked all the men before allowing them to proceed to their tables. The soundtrack blasted third-rate rock music from a dance floor deeper within the premises.

The pitch: "Miss Gazillions," intoned a Russian-accented narrator, "is Moscow's leading nightclub. Also the hardest to get into." That, and: "Miss Gazillions has the world's greatest Cajun shrimp!" At which, Celeste's brother Bill appeared on screen, in a chef's hat.

"Remarkably," the voice-over continued, "Miss Gazillions' owners are all American . . ."

And it was at this point the beautiful Celeste made her spotlighted appearance, tuxedoed friend nuzzling her neck for all he was worth. Which, it developed, was a great deal indeed.

". . . including," said the narrator, "the world-famous financier, F. J. Starace." The tuxedoed gentleman smiled at the camera.

Starace.

Over the nightclub din, I could barely hear a word of what Celeste was saying to the interviewer.

"Love it here." "Say hello to Louisiana." "Sure, anyone can get in, you know the right people." and *"Madonna was terrific"* were the most readily discernible of her breathy sound bites. Those, and *"Miss you!"* and *"I owe it all to great friends."*

"That's it," said Wally. "Play it again?"

Wally didn't wait for my answer, but reversed the tape and played it once more, leaning forward the whole while, intent as a bird dog at the hunt, his nose nearly touching the screen.

"So?" he said. "So what do you think?"

I shrugged and laughed. "Hilarious." And I meant it. Because when you got right down to it—and when I got over brief twinges of love long lost—of course it was funny.

Utterly so.

From Louisiana back bayou to New Orleans. Then her New York high life. And on the run across Europe. And now running a Russian nightclub.

Ubiquitous Mr. Starace, the latest partner.

It was all funny. The ever-beautiful Celeste forever racing her motor in the grandest Grand Prix manner, and so just about all I could do was laugh at the great mad spectacle of her life.

"Funny, uh?" Wally grinned. "Gotta admit, even made me feel kinda funny. Anyways, there she is. All I hope is, I hope she's loaded. Gotta be loaded, go screwing around like that in Russia. Jeez, can you believe that stuff?"

"Of course."

"Maybe look her up," said Wally. "When I get there. Think she'll remember?"

How could she forget?

"Well, Danno, let you know, I see her." He sounded hopeful. "Maybe even go a little sooner now, sooner than I planned."

His eyes acquired a yearning, faraway look. It seemed like a good time to leave. Wally followed me to the door.

"Anyways, I run into her? I say hello from you, Danno, she ain't gone by then. You know how Celeste always was, one foot on a plane, ready to run."

"Yeah, right," I said, holding the door, "if she doesn't take off again. Please, do . . . say hello. And give her my love. I mean that, Wally."

Outside, the tail end of the storm had blown over and wispy clouds now raced across the darkening sky. There was slick ice on the road, so I drove back toward town slowly, headed not for home at the other end, but right for the side street, just off the harbor front, where our old art gallery had once stood.

The swank furniture store that replaced it was closed for the season, but that didn't matter. Parked across the road in my car, eyeing the place, all I could picture now was a window full of antique jewelry. And eggshell-white walls covered with paintings and lithographs.

The laughter erupted again, until tears almost ran down my cheeks.

I stayed there for what seemed like an hour, but wasn't more than a few moments. Then I drove back home to my house on Eel Pond, and went straight to the fridge for a bottle of champagne.

Celeste. Brother Bill. F. J. Starace.

And Moscow.

They all deserved another toast.

"What's the champagne for?" my wife asked.

"The hell of it. For us. For everything, honey."

I said no more than that. And while Celeste's undimming bright-lights existence was never one I'd ever planned on for myself, I just had to toast her luck in finding it, and mine for avoiding it.

No, I wasn't about to go into details with my wife about any of this, although I wouldn't have minded telling Celeste how my life turned out. Tell her about my kids and my wife. And about my boat. And that Wally might be coming to see her soon.

And also tell her that—Moscow and Starace, wherever and with whomever—I hope her life really has turned out just as she, and Brother Bill, always hoped.

That she finally has all she deserves. Everything she's dreamed of, prayed for, worked for and—think what you will—but yes, paid a whole heartful hunk of dues for.

And so now, who knows, but maybe Wally will get to tell her for me.